PICTURES OF ANGELS

by
Lucy Dunmore

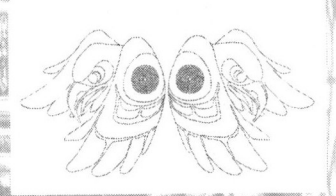

Twin Eagles Publishing
2012

Copyright © 2012 Lucy Dunmore

Lucy Dunmore asserts her moral right to be identified as the only author of this work. Including the right of reproduction in whole or part in any form. The text of this publication may not be reproduced or transmitted in any form by any means, electronic or otherwise be lent, resold, hired out or circulated without the consent of the Author/Publisher in any form of binding or cover other than that which it is published and without a similar condition being imposed on any subsequent purchaser.

Library and Archives Canada Cataloguing in Publication

Dunmore, Lucy, 1944-
Pictures of Angels / Lucy Dunmore.

ISBN 978-1-896238-14-2

1. Title.

PR6104.U56P53 2012   823'.92   C2012-906432-7

Twin Eagles Publishing
Box 2031
Sechelt BC
V0N 3A0
pblakey@telus.net
604 885 7503

www.twineaglespublishing.webs.com

Dedication

For Jim who tossed me an idea and encouraged me to run with it

For Helen and Nick, who had faith in me

For Pat and Alison, for being there and passing on the message

And for Paul, without whom this would not be.

Lucy Dunmore

... has been writing novels since she was 11 years old. She studied the History of Art at London University and has worked as a teacher, administrator and led art and music tours in Europe. Previously unpublished works include *The Province of the Goddess* which came fourth in a Victor Gollanz fantasy novel competition, and *A Sense of Betrayal* which was also warmly praised. *A Poor Choice of Enemies*, the sequel to Pictures of Angels, is presently being written in Spain.

1

"That'll be seven and six, Madam."

I looked into the cabby's pale creased face.

Madam, I thought. I must be showing my age.

He whistled cheerfully as he opened the door for me and carefully unstrapped the luggage from the outside of the cab. Three suitcases, leather, in ascending sizes, plus one small wickerwork hamper. I stepped out into the damp London air. It was far colder and damper than I had been used to these past three months, but not that awful cold that had caused the illness. This winter had been hard, but now the spring was showing even in Chelsea, and young George was scrambling to meet me up the basement steps.

I pulled a ten shilling note from my wallet. If the cabby would take my cases up to my flat, it was worth that. George, my landlady's oldest son and mainstay, cannily grabbed the hamper and the smallest valise. He was short for eleven but adept at earning tips. My flat was at the top of the house. The cabby viewed the stairs and groaned, but he wanted the note. George was already on his way up.

I stood for a while outside what was now, once more, my home.

It had been my great aunt's flat and like her had survived the bombing, but rather better. Before she died she told me "I lived long enough to see that evil bastard, Hitler, out! I can die in peace, which is more than many have done recently." She had been a free spirit, and never married. She had left me the flat, she said, because she saw a reflection of herself in me.

Life, she averred, would be difficult. It had been after the Great War. They wanted you doing men's work for the duration, then back in the kitchen and the bedroom immediately after. Didn't they realize that it didn't work like that?

I loved the old lady. I hadn't always understood her, but standing here, late on a damp afternoon in April, I did now.

I had returned to roost jobless and only a small allowance to tide me over.

As for marriage, I'd given up on that idea.

I was still longing for my wartime companions, and that was just impossible. I missed them terribly, but they, as they said, had moved on.

I'd realized that in March. I'd gone back to the Vercors where I'd worked in ... well, you don't need to know, suffice it to say it was very hush-hush, and I'd been chosen because I was up to the job. I had the language, the background, was careful, although willing to take calculated risks, and a damn good organizer, but on this last trip I'd learned the hard way that although my presence and work had been useful to my comrades' and my grandfather's country from 1942 to 1945, it was surplus to requirements now. I'd been welcomed coolly by new wives and somewhat nervously by their menfolk, my old comrades. Things had changed. Raoul, my very good friend – well, OK, then, my lover, who'd said he'd wait forever – had been gunned down in a reprisal shooting last year

That had been the last straw, really.

A whole year ago and no-one had thought to let me know.

They were sweetly sympathetic, but how could they, they reasoned. They didn't know my address and I was back in Britain, so they guessed I wasn't interested anyway.

Great!

So I'd patted the babies' heads, shook hands sadly, and returned to my Grandfather's house to conclude my convalescence.

Even there I was in the way.

I was twenty seven, single and tall.

In that particular I took after the English side of the family.

I had been told by a cousin that no man would ever look at me, because there were so many pretty younger and shorter girls just waiting to be snapped up (she was nineteen, short, curvy, dark and devastatingly pretty) all willing and desirous of being part of the married state, prostrating themselves before the homecoming heroes. And because they had been cut down in numbers, the men who remained knew they could pick and choose.

I had seen enough marriages to know that when and if, and it was getting more unlikely by the second, I ever did enter that door, the man would have to be very special indeed. With Raoul, it might have just have worked, but I knew in my heart of hearts it wouldn't; I always had. He was a great companion, but a wedding ring does things to people. He'd have wanted a 'little woman' to come home to in the end. I had been hurt by his death, although I had walked away eighteen months ago because I wasn't up to that sort of commitment. I did love him and I missed his presence on the earth. Not knowing he was gone, dammit, dead, I could content myself with the idea that perhaps we might meet up again – like this spring, perhaps we might have made something of a life together, or at least just had a bit of fun; he was a great one for fun. But now even that small comfort had gone. And more to the point, I had never had a chance to really say a proper goodbye to him. That hurt. And made me keep going over the same question – what if?...

He was gone.

Now I had to keep telling myself not to make a martyr of him, and as a result, of myself.

There was life to be lived and work to be sought.

The cabby came down, puffing. "Some staircase you've got there, Madam," he said, but grinned widely as I handed him the note. "Thank you, Madam. May God bless you."

"Thank you, too." I said. I didn't believe in God. It was all random. The war had taught me that.

I went inside.

George was waiting for me just outside the basement door. "Mum got everything you said and the bill's in the basket," he said. "And there's been a man asking for you, Miss."

Well, that made a change.

"What was he like George?" I asked as he followed me up the stairs with the shopping.

"He weren't a toff, Miss. Come on a motorbike. In a black leather coat."

"Did you get his name?"

"No, Miss, but it was a Matchless, and he was short, not as tall as you, Miss, and he said he'd be back for you this evening, round seven."

"That all? Think, George. What else can you remember?" It was a game we both enjoyed.

As we climbed the stairs he combed his memory. "He's got a face that looks like he's been in the sun a lot. I ain't seen him before. His eyes are blue, sparkly, and his hair curly – I saw it under the leather helmet."

"What colour?"

"Dunno, sort of dark with a bit of grey in it. His face was lined. Older than you but not as old as Mr. Stephens," (who was around fifty and lived on the ground floor).

I unlocked the door to my flat. George followed me in and put down the basket. I gave him a sixpence, and got out the bill for the shopping.

"Mum says if you ain't got the money now, it'll do later," he said, pocketing the coin.

I rummaged in my purse and found the cash, rounding it

up to the nearest shilling. "Tell Lily thank you very much," I said. "And thank you, George."

"D'you know who he is?" George asked.

"What else was he wearing?" I asked shifting the heavy suitcases in. "More detail, George, more detail."

"When he came to the door he had those big driving goggles on, and a leather helmet, but he took the goggles off, so I saw his eyes, and a bit of his hair. His nose was sort of ordinary size, a bit turned up, and he smiled a lot and winked at me. You know, sort of cheeky, like 'Do you know the lady on the top floor?'."

"He said that?"

George nodded. "And he had a bit of a singing accent. Didn't sound like me, nor like you, Miss." So not a native Londoner nor someone who was taught to speak properly.

"Teeth?" I asked.

"Yeah, they were his own, because they were a bit brown, but he had all the front ones, and they were even-sized. And he was clean-shaven."

"Well done!" I was impressed. "Did you see his hands? You can't disguise hands."

"Is that why ladies wear gloves, Miss?"

Innocence or cheek? I suspected the latter.

"Possibly. Did he?"

"No, he wore them great big gauntlets that people wear on motorbikes, but he took one off – yes miss, the left one – to ring the bell with. So he's left-handed. And he had a gold signet ring on the little finger."

"Excellent, George! When did you say he'd be back?"

"S'evening, Miss, around seven. Do you know who he is?"

"I've a good idea. Now I've got three quarters of an hour to get things sorted. I don't know what he wants, but I want a bath."

George went to the door. "Right, Miss, I'll be off, then,

and Miss, it's good to have you back." He closed the door behind him and I heard his shoes clattering down the long tiled staircase.

The bell rang exactly on seven. I knew as soon as I saw the shape silhouetted against the street lamp that I'd guessed right.

"Ah, 'tis yourself, Milady!" quipped the stocky figure, bowing deeply so I could take in his dark curls.

"Bobby Gallagher, as I live and breathe!" I was delighted to see him, and quite unconsciously gave him the Gallic salutation, the double *bise*.

"Now you don't want people talking, Milady," said Bobby, happily, stroking his cheek where my lips had touched. "Do you think you dare ask me to come in?"

"Of course. Apologies for the kisses, I've been in France too long," I chuckled.

"Never apologize, Milady. I'm delighted to be in receipt of your greeting. If you'd care to practice, I could come round nightly. I'd do it for nothing but the greeting."

He was ever the same. I ushered him indoors, as swiftly as possible, or he'd be going on all night. "What is it that you want? It's not just to welcome me home," I said as I led him up the stairs.

His tread was, as always, silent. Even his leather coat hardly creaked. I could move quietly, indeed my life and those of others had depended on it, but no-one moved as silently as Bobby Gallagher. He was also adept at blending in with the background, a skill that he had taught me, as far as it could be taught.

"Ah, you're a sour woman, that you are. Here come I to greet you back from your long illness and absence – How are you, by the way? Is this your place? Well, the stairs are Hell, but it's very nice, The little lad down in the basement gave me a good going over with the eyeball."

We entered my living room. Bobby helped himself to

the easy chair in front of the gas fire.

I sat on the sofa. "So how is the Colonel?"

"Leggy? He's just fine. He wants me to bring you over to him."

"Now?"

"Of course. Did you ever know him wait when he could have something immediately?"

"Alright. Do you know what it's about?"

"Not at all. He's keeping me in the dark. Old habits die hard."

"But you're his batman."

"Well, so I am, but he's a canny old bird. Will you be coming?"

"Of course. On the bike?"

"Unless you want me to get you a taxi. He gave me cash enough."

"The bike. I'll get a coat and head scarf."

The Colonel lived in a mansion flat the wrong side of the World's End. There was a lot of bomb damage around that area, but this block looked grand. We parked the Matchless in a garage next to the Colonel's Humber, and went up in the lift. It squeaked and clattered as it took us up the floors, and would have driven me crazy, but the Colonel needed it.

Bobby unlocked the door for us both and announced us loudly. "'Tis only me, Leggy, and I've brought Milady."

He took my coat – my Great Aunt's sable – gloves and head scarf, then ushered me through to the room at the far end, which overlooked the street and had a small balcony, so that the occupant could enjoy the light and grow plants.

The Colonel had the wooden blinds shut tight, thick tapestry curtains around the walls, every wall, except where there were black wooden bookcases stuffed with books and papers, more dark furniture, and patterned fabric on every surface. There was a green desk light on the writing table at which he was sitting, but otherwise only the soft glow and hiss of gas lights from the walls. In the grate, against the cold evening, a small fire gave out minimal heat, most of which was being absorbed by a comatose ginger cat, called Nuts, so-named to replace those he'd lost, I had once been informed.

I breathed in the fug: a mixture of stale pipe tobacco, old tweeds and boiled fish; Nuts didn't come cheap despite the shortages! It wasn't dirty. It just wasn't aired. The Colonel had taken to the wartime blackout precautions like a duck to water, and had never looked back. He liked his fug.

"Alice, my dear, welcome. Let me look at you!" He swiveled in his chair as I entered the room.

The same old Colonel. I'd known him since my early teens, both as a friend of my father's and as a superior officer during my Intelligence days.

"Are you better? Completely?" His voice was full of concern and came out deep and upper crust through his salt-and-pepper moustache stained with nicotine.

"Yes, thank you, sir. And you?"

He had been widowed for a second time during the war, his house being hit by a doodlebug while he was at work. It had knocked him hard, for he was by nature uxorious, but had declared that he appeared to be bad luck to women, so wouldn't be searching for a replacement.

He, too, had been ill. A heart attack had eased him out of his job and into a pension. Theoretically he had to take it easy.

"Oh, I'm doing fine. Bobby looks after me wonderfully, the little spiv." He nodded his head and Bobby, who had entered the room, left it, silently, and closed the door behind him. "Well, Alice, we're both out of uniform now, and I trust friends, so I'm Leggy to you, as I am to my other friends."

"Yes, sir." I shook my head. "It's difficult, sir, but thank you, Leggy."

He chuckled. "I know. Civvy Street comes hard, but

we'll survive. The wise adapt. You never struck me as a foolish person."

He pulled a desk drawer open and took out a bottle of Johnny Walker Black Label and two cut glass tumblers. "You do indulge?"

I nodded.

He poured two very generous measures and handed me one.

"To survival, eh?" He raised his glass.

I clinked it with my own. "I'll drink to that. To a good peace."

The golden liquid burned as it went down. I appreciated the sensation.

He handed me the cigarette box. For someone on rationing he was doing very well. But then he had Bobby to look after him.

I fixed the cigarette in my holder. I hated getting tobacco in my mouth, or getting lipstick on the end of a cigarette. As he held a lighted match for me, Leggy continued.

"I won't beat around the bush. Your father said you were coming back, and had nothing to occupy yourself with, so I've got a proposition to make. You don't have anything pressing at the moment?"

I breathed in the comforting smoke, and shook my head.

Leggy nodded to himself. "Good." He raised his stick to a gong, producing a gentle humming.

Bobby came in, immediately, wearing a dark lounge suit. "You wanted something, Leggy?"

"Tea and sandwiches, and some of the fruit cake." He looked at me, "That'll suit, my dear, won't it?"

I nodded. I hadn't eaten since I'd left the airfield in Northern France early this morning.

Bobby retreated.

Leggy got down to business. "The other day I was

clearing a house and picked up this." He heaved himself out of his chair, picked up his sticks and moved between the sofa and the armchair to the curtained wall. With one deft twitch of his stick he moved the curtains aside. Behind them was a painting. "I told your father I was looking for someone to research it. What do you think?"

I looked at it long and hard. It was weird.

I knew painting, because I'd been surrounded by art since birth. My father is a well-known artist and an even better art historian. His friends are of an artistic bent, Matisse and other world class names amongst them.

This painting was odd, but it was exceptionally well executed. I said as much to the Colonel.

He nodded. He, too, knew quality when he saw it.

But the size and the subject matter...

It dwarfed the room, over six foot tall and half as wide and it loomed, glowered at you. Generally angels don't loom or glower. The mighty figure had wings, but the feathers were almost metallic, and the burning spear and sword looked as though they could do very serious damage. Not an ounce of kindliness there, but just, oh, yes, and amazingly, compellingly powerful. The energy off it almost crackled in the dark room. In the lower right corner was a sigil of compounded letters, and opposite something else in a foreign script. Not Greek, something further East... Hebrew?

"What do you want to know about it?" I asked.

"Everything. Turn it round, and you can see why I asked you."

On the reverse there was a Lot number, and a ticket from my old workplace, Lowther's Auction Rooms. "You still have connections there?" the Colonel asked.

I nodded.

"I can give you a retainer. Do what you can. Now let's put it away. Bobby will be coming in soon." He drew the curtains around it swiftly.

"He doesn't know about this?"

"He distrusts the picture. Thinks it's haunted so I keep it hidden. Wants me to get rid of it, but I want to know more about it first."

He led me over to the sofa. "It doesn't affect you that way?" he asked. "I mean, you're a sensible young woman and weren't brought up Roman Catholic or anything?"

I shook my head and considered the proposition. It would be far more to my taste than a desk job.

"All right, Leggy, I'll give it my best shot, but I need to see it in daylight, and have all the documentation you have on it."

"Good lass, I knew I could rely on you. Come back here tomorrow then, at nine. Bobby will be out so I can open the place up for you. We'll work out details then." He banged gently on the gong again, and Bobby pushed in a trolley piled high with refreshments including another bottle of whisky. Leggy certainly managed to live on a pre-war scale.

2

I dreamed that night of Dark Angels. I've never dreamed of angels of any sort before. There were seven and they were strangely powerful. Disturbing. I put it down to the whisky I had drunk with Bobby and the Colonel before being sent home in a taxi.

Next morning I cycled to Leggy's. The porter took me up and let me in.

The curtains and blinds were drawn back and morning sun flooded in, making the strange dark room look exhausted and musty. Nuts was still in front of the fire and Leggy was finishing his breakfast egg at the dining table.

The picture was out in the light. It looked less menacing, as though the daylight had drained its power.

I took measurements, made a sketch, did a colour description, in case it might be catalogued somewhere, and traced the sigil and the Hebrew text onto sheets of toilet roll with a very light touch; I might not like the painting much, but I didn't want to damage it in any way. Then I turned it over and took the lot number, the sale number. Leggy proposed ten pounds for a week of my time to find out as much as I could. No office job could match that.

"I was looking through the other stuff from the clearance, and found this." He handed me a faded buff envelope which I opened. Inside was an affidavit, yellowish with age, the pale grey letters embossed unevenly into the old paper. Provenance?

I read it. 'To whom it may concern. I confirm that the pictures of Angels were painted by my father shortly before his death and have been in my family ever since.'

I couldn't make out the signature; it was just a scrawl.

I would trace it. The address was there, however, and the date, September 1908. Both would be helpful, although as Leggy had said, there had been two world wars in between then and now.

I noted the details down, tracing the lines of the signature as far as I could.

"Anything else?" I asked.

He said nothing, wiping his lips and moustache with his napkin.

"If this is correct, there were more of these pictures," I said.

"That's what I am hoping for. I only came across this one at the site."

"You really like it? You'd really like to see the rest of them?"

From his raised eyebrows and sardonic expression, I realized I was being naïve to think that one only bought pictures one really liked. But that's what I would do; I wasn't a business person when it came to art. I felt a blush creeping up my face.

Leggy refilled his pipe. "Let's say I find them very interesting. A full set would be worth more than the sum of their parts. I'm in the market, so to speak."

So it was investment he was after.

That made good financial sense.

I helped him stow the picture back behind the curtain, shared the last of his elderly coffee, and let myself out.

It was strange to think of Leggy clearing houses – he was unsteady on his pins for a start, but I could imagine with Bobby and Bobby's friends to help him, he would probably do well enough. Leggy to front the enterprise – he could be very sympathetic and persuasive, as well as having a good eye for quality – and the younger fitter men to do the heavy work. "The wise adapt." That was it. And I could see it being a bit of fun for him. You never knew what you might pick up – like that Angel picture.

Lowther's was in Knightsbridge. I had worked there both before and immediately after my service career. I left when I got sick late in January, but the pneumonia wasn't the reason for leaving, just the catalyst. I had been pining for action too long. I had been a good secretary, but I had lived during the war, and when I returned it was like dying. The job was the same but I wasn't. I'd run a unit. I'd put my life on the line. I'd killed. I'd survived. I couldn't go back to making tea, being a hostess, and a typer of catalogues and letters.

I'd given it my best shot, and Mr. Arnold Lowther had understood. He was a friend as well as a boss. He was also a lover of fine food, and for most people there was precious little of that available in post-war Britain.

I wore my impressing outfit, a belted tweed suit, silk blouse and a string of pearls, and instead of the awful head scarf a small saucy hat. I even wore my nylons and a pair of heeled shoes, black to match my handbag. I looked good, particularly with the lipstick and the real mascara that I had bought in France. I looked expensive, and chic. French haircuts do that, so do the manicures, and before I left I ensured I had both.

Miss Green, the Receptionist, eyed me curiously. "You aren't coming for your job back, are you? He's got a new woman."

"No. I just popped in to say hello. He said to call when I was back and well."

"You'd better go through to your old office, then. Her name's Jackson, Thelma Jackson. She's from oop north!"

Miss Thelma Jackson was wide of face and beam, perhaps ten years my senior. Her Northern accent was only perceptible on the occasional vowel. Miss Green had no call to be snobbish.

While Miss Jackson was informing Mr. Arnold of my presence, I sneaked a look at her shorthand. It was far better than mine, more fluent and correct. And her desk was neatness personified. He would be well served by such a woman.

She waddled back in, her hand-knitted jumper and cardigan stretched around her ample curves. "He'd be delighted to see you, Miss, please go straight in. Would you like some tea?" She was friendly and motherly. I may have been more decorative, but she would have put clients at their ease, reminding them of Nanny. And she had a ready smile. I liked her.

"No, but thank you for asking."

Mr. Arnold was at his door to greet me, tall, well built, and wearing a morning suit, same as ever. We shook hands, and he held out a chair for me in front of his desk. "Well, this is wonderful. You look so well. You looked really peaky last time I saw you."

"I'm very well, thank you, Mr. Arnold." I asked about himself and his family – all very well too.

Business? That was picking up a bit, but slowly rather than quickly. Not a lot of disposable income about, and ... "Er... so was this a social call? Or are you looking for a position?"

I smiled. "Not looking for a job, but I need a favour. To help me do the job I've got."

I brought out a 250 gram tin of foie gras from my handbag and placed it on the desk between us, keeping my hand lightly on it. "I need to go through the archives. I'm on a case." I raised my eyebrows in question, and pushed the tin slowly across to him.

He whistled softly. I could almost see him drooling.

I handed the tin over with the numbers I'd taken from the pictures. "Can I search for them?"

"My dear, for this I'll get Miss Jackson to do the search! It would look better that way, anyway – now that you aren't part of the firm."

Quite right.

And if she were like me, she'd jump at a chance to do something less mundane than usual.

Mr. Arnold's eyes didn't leave the tin. He took it gently in his hand and examined it, breathing swiftly. "Where on earth did you get it?" .

"I went to France to convalesce."

He sighed. He was a law-abiding soul. He wouldn't have liked to have done anything that could be proved to be illegal, but temptation is temptation. I decided to press for more.

"I wondered if I could talk to any of the porters who might know anything about this lot."

"1908? It's well before my time and yours, but you might get something out of the Williamses. They've been here three generations, and the old chap – he's retired now – has a memory like a hawk. One of them might know something." Almost reluctantly he went out to his secretary. When he returned, the first thing that caught his attention was the foie gras. "This really is most generous of you. I do appreciate it."

I handed him my card. "If I'm not there you can leave a message on this number." I scribbled the house number – Lily would take it, or George. "I want to know who sold and who bought these Angel pictures, and how many there were of them. Also, who painted them. I've never seen anything like them before. If they were sold in separate lots, as much information as you can on the buyers."

I descended through the warren of store-rooms and found porter territory. There were a few wolf-whistles, and comments, because that was what porters did when a female dared enter it. Most of the secretaries didn't like challenging the porters with their presence, but I'd never had a problem. I knew some by name, and asked Jacky, the cheeky one, for any member of the Williams family.

"Sid's on his break and Pete's on a job."

I crossed the yard to the lean-to where there was always a brew and a cigarette on the go. The cobbles were at a slight rake, built from the time when horses were used for draught, and when the stables were up the top. They were greasy with dirt and rain. No horses, just the infernal combustion engine. A different dirt. One that didn't improve the roses. I picked my way across carefully, and stood outside the lean-to. This was male property; I was not going to intrude uninvited.

A wiry man of about forty was huffing over an enamel mug of tea. There was a tin of condensed milk on the side and a filthy spoon. "Mr. Sidney Williams?"

"S'right. You used to work here, din't yer?"

"Yes. Alice Chamberlain, Miss." I held out my hand. He took it and gave it a brief shake. "I don't any more," I continued, "But I've had a word with Mr. Arnold, and he says I should talk to you."

"Yeah? What about?"

"Anything you know about this lot, on this sale?" I held out the date and the lot number.

Sid's eyebrows raised.

I pressed on. "He said if you couldn't help me, you'd know someone who could." The face creased into a wide beam. "He said that, did 'e? Mr. Arnold said that? Well, I'll be blowed. He don't mean me, he means the Gaffer. The unofficial record department of Lowther and Sons."

I stood patiently waiting, while he sipped at his steaming brew. It was the colour of polished leather and smelt about as appetizing.

"Tell yer what. You give me that bit of paper and I'll ask the Gaffer if he can remember anything when I go home for lunch. Meet me here around five thirty, and I'll take you to him if he can, and I'm telling you, there's precious little he don't remember from times gone by. It's just the here and now that keeps evading him, poor old sod."

"Thank you, Mr. Williams. I really appreciate that. I'll see you at five thirty. Can I bring anything?"

"No. Gaffer will be delighted just to have a visitor, and you chatting to him for a bit about old times is payment enough for me. Although... tobacco goes down well with him, Old Holborn, oh, and he's partial to ginger nuts."

My next stop was at the Westminster Reference Library Art Section.

I had seen the sigil before, but not on a painting like that. I darkened the tracings now on the little shiny perforated sheets. They were kinder to the pencil than to human anatomy, at least the ones Leggy used were. I looked carefully at the shapes, trying to make some sort of sense out of the sigil and the scrawl. I worked out that the letters in the sigil were or could be FGL, the G being the biggest, the F the smallest. The first letter of the signature could have been anything, a loopy squiggle. But the address was there, and it was relatively close to both the Colonel and to me, being no. 35 The Boltons. A good address, or at least it had been in 1908. It wasn't a bad address now, although a bit far from the West End for anyone with real pretensions to Society. I should have asked Leggy the address of the house he had found the picture in.

I went through the Art Books methodically, checking out signatures – that is sigils and monograms. Originally used in medieval times, they fell into disfavour after the Renaissance, but bloomed once more as a popular form of identification from the Pre-Raphaelites onward, before taking a second nose-dive with the coming of modernism, although my father had his own monogram that he used as a signature. Perhaps their heyday was Arts and Crafts time. The trouble was, the picture looked far too modern and strange for those times.

And yet, there it was. The sigil. The intertwined GLF.
Lawrence Francis Greystoke, R.A.

No. I didn't believe that.

I knew that man's work, and mostly it was sweet and pretty. Nice paintings, not very admired now, by the art world, but still popular with the hoi polloi. Chocolate box pictures. There was no way that he could have produced a work like that dark angel. No way.

I went to the shelf again, to see if there were any books with his works in. I didn't expect any, because although popular at the time he was out of fashion now. I was not disappointed. So I checked in the Benezet, and he was in there, sure enough, with a mention. His best price was in 1930 for a picture of a girl with a kitten outside a cottage door. No mention of angels.

I worked through a selection of reference books and got a little more information which I copied into my notebook. No mention of where he lived, of course, but he was working in the latter half of the nineteenth century, and appeared to have died around the turn of this, the twentieth century. By the time his best price was achieved, he was long dead.

I waited at the rear entrance of Lowther's at five thirty, my green Harrod's bag full of tobacco and biscuits; my coupons and points had built up over my time in France, so the purchase was not a problem.

Sid came out and nodded to me, and we walked together to the bus stop and took the 14, past my stop, and down into Fulham. We got off just past Chelsea Football Ground and turned left, through the side streets to the Kings Road, and then towards the Gasworks. He led me to a tiny terraced house where the Gaffer lived. Sid himself lived next door and his wife kept an eye on her father-in-law; it was she who opened the door for us. Behind the coping, the tiny front path and step were spotless, the brass door furniture shining brightly against the dark green painted door.

Sid kissed the woman, a genuine warm peck to say he was

home, and motioned for me to follow her in. She opened the door to the front parlour, the tidy room which was usually only open on Sundays, or for special people.

I felt the honour the family were according me.

"Here's the young lady to see you, Gaffer. I've set your tea out on the tray." She spoke loudly and slowly as she let me in. "Perhaps you'd like to pour, Miss. He's a bit wobbly at times," she whispered as I passed.

"Yes, thank you so much, Mrs. Williams," I said as I went to greet the Gaffer.

He was an older greyer version of his son. Obviously at one time he had been a stocky sturdy man, but now, well, probably heavy physical work, the war and time had made him into a lean grey person, seated by the immaculate fireplace with its bright coals and gleaming fire irons. His shell might have been well over three-score years and ten, but his eyes were the same bright hazel as his son's, full of life and excitement.

"Miss Chamberlain? Mr. Arnold's secretary as was? He recommended me?" His voice still had a South Wales lilt, unlike the London vowels and sounds of his family.

"Yes, Mr. Williams. I no longer work for Lowther's, but am trying to trace some lots that went ages ago. He said you were the man to help if anyone could." I held out my hand to him. He took it, apologizing for not rising, and indicated the opposite easy chair by the fire.

"Well, I was there ages ago," he chuckled. "The sale you wanted – Wednesday, 23rd September 1908 – that the one? I've got the catalogue here."

He looked appreciatively at my surprised face. "Oh, I kept my copy of all the catalogues. Don't know why really, but I liked to keep tabs on what I did. My Queenie didn't like it, said I was a hoarder, but it's quite often become of use to people, like Mr. Lowther, and of course, there are the memories. I've had some wonderful stuff pass through these hands, wonderful stuff."

He passed me the catalogue, and got out a pouch of tobacco. "Don't mind if I smoke?" he asked. "Sid's wife gives me gyp, but I can't see why." He began rolling a tight little cigarette. I took out the packet of Old Holborn from the Harrod's bag, green with gold writing, made of heavy quality paper. "Would you care to put this with it?" I asked.

His face brightened. "That's very kind..."

I handed across the bag. "And Sid said you were partial to these."

"Ooh, my favourite, thank you again, Miss. They'll see me through to the end of the month. Could I have the bag, too? Sid's wife will enjoy swanking with it." He lit the roll-up, inhaled deeply.

I took out a Gauloise and my cigarette holder. "Do you mind if I smoke? They're French and smell a bit."

He chuckled. "I'd take it as a compliment, Miss. There's an ashtray on the sideboard, or you can do like me, and use the fireplace."

We were comrades.

I fetched the polished brass ashtray and placed it between us and lit up.

Then I picked up the catalogue. It was dog-eared and folded, with a pipe-cleaner hooked over the top. He'd used it to mark the page and lot, bending the cleaner up to highlight it.

There it was.

Lot 207, Oil on board, picture of an archangel, signed by LFG, provenance by his son, William Meredith Greystoke, dimensions 3'6" x 6'6".

"That's it!" I said.

The old man nodded in satisfaction. "Look further, Miss. There were seven of them. Seven angels. Only they weren't like the angels I'd been brought up to recognize."

"No," I said, thoughtfully, "nor me."

"You seen them, then?" the old man's interest was well and truly caught.

"I've seen this one. I have been engaged to trace the others."

"I've seen the lot of them. I handled them all." There was pride in his voice. "I collected them from the vendor, and that was odd in itself. I remember it clear as day." He puffed at the roll-up. "You wouldn't mind pouring the tea, would you? I'll open these biscuits."

While we did our tasks, he continued talking. "I remember it because it was around the time Sid's sister, Gwyneth, was born. She didn't last long, poor little scrap, but she was our first girl. I called her my little angel. So when we were told to get round the Boltons and pick up some pictures of angels, I had a smile on my face." His face softened as he remembered his tiny daughter. Then he came back. "It was an odd call out. Not at all usual."

I handed him a cup of tea; like many people during the war, he had learned to drink it black and sugarless. I did the same, and it was good, as there was not a large amount of leaf in the pot. "Tell me," I said, taking a biscuit.

"Usually, when it's to do with tidying up after a death, you know, getting shot of effects so the money can be shared out among the living, a solicitor or a family member called us out and would be at the place to let us in and often, if it were a family member, they'd come to the auction and see how the stuff went." He took a long pull on the tea cup.

"I remember this call. It was the Friday before the sale, and we took the cart round to the Boltons – a nice neighbourhood, still is. Jack, my immediate boss, had the key to the place. That doesn't happen all that often, only when they want you to take everything, and even then, they tend to have someone keep an eye on you. Here there was no-one to meet us or see us off the premises, nor were there any nosy neighbours looking out at us. It was as though the place was dead.

"Jack said we'd have to go down a side alley, and at the end would be an artist's studio. And there it was. When we got in – nothing but cobwebs and dust, and these seven paintings, all set round in a circle on easels, all facing into the circle, which was a bit queer. Creepy, like. Inside the circle had been swept and polished, quite different from the rest of the room, and there were a couple of rings, one inside the other, painted on the floor with strange signs in them. It gave me the willies. And there was a smell, besides the normal sort of smells you get in old houses, like dust and drains; it was like some sort of smoke." His nose wrinkled at the memory.

"I really didn't like it. I don't think Jack did either. He was a Catholic. I thought he wouldn't mind the smell, being used to incense and all that sort of thing, but he started crossing himself something chronic when he walked inside the circle to take a look at those paintings. He sent Sonny – he was our lad – to bring in the dust sheets and webbing to wrap them and let us two get on with it. He'd normally help, but he didn't that day. He went outside for a smoke. I think he just didn't want to look at them or be in the same room as them. They weren't nice, Miss.

"Well, we got them wrapped and trolleyed them out onto the cart. They were very heavy and you felt like they didn't want to leave the place. And all the time we were there we saw no-one. Not a soul. Not even a bobby on the beat nor a delivery boy, and it was a posh neighbourhood then; not even a servant doing the step. The whole area was dead, and if you knew the Boltons then, you'd know that it was a very lived-in sort of place, probably still is. You'd have expected to see someone, even if it was only a nursemaid and her charges in the gardens in the middle of the area. No-one. We locked up, leaving the easels, as we'd not been authorized to take them, although they would have been worth a bit, and got them carted back to our store rooms." He sighed and shuddered, remembering.

"It was a bright day, and when we unpacked them, the feeling we all had in the studio seemed a lot less. Like the being out in the daylight had got rid of the gloom and dread. We started larking about, taking the mickey out of each other for being scared. I mean, they were only pictures. What harm could a picture do? And they weren't even proper angels. Jack stuck his tongue out at them, which was quite daring for him, as a good catholic, used to being respectful in front of holy pictures and stuff. Then we did the rest of the rounds and went home."

He took another drink. "You couldn't pour me another, could you?"

"Of course," I said, and did his bidding.

"Thank you, Miss, now what do you think happened next?" He put his head on one side, like a cheeky sparrow.

I handed him his tea. "No idea, Mr. Williams," I said. "Did something go wrong?"

"Ah, so you heard about them paintings!"

I frowned. "No," I said. "It was just a guess."

He shook his head. "Not a bad one, then."

He began to roll another cigarette, but kept his eyes on me, eyes as bright as a sparrow's. "Next morning Jack weren't there. He'd fallen off his bike and broken his leg. But, he told me, what made him fall off his bike on his way home from a friend's house that evening was a huge black figure with sort of wings. I told him he'd been drinking, which he swore he hadn't, not that that counted for much, but he said it was like one of them pictures. He said they were cursed!"

The old man looked at me triumphantly, then downed the fresh cup in one. "Course, I didn't believe a thing. I think it's amazing what a religious imagination can make you do and believe, but he was off work for a good six months. Got his fair share off the sick club – not that it's ever enough or begrudged when it's genuine."

"Is there such a thing as coincidence?" I asked. "Or is it just our wish to see similarities and cause and effect?" I didn't like to bring up the matter of little Gwyneth. Besides in those days children didn't always last long. Most families had lost at least one child along the route to adulthood.

"I don't care to think that a picture has that sort of power," he said. Then he lit up, took in a lungful of smoke, and let it out slowly. "Anyway, I watched the pictures go. They were supposed to be by a chap called Greystoke, but I'd seen his work before and a lot more of it since, and it's not his style at all. But there was provenance, a letter, which the boss had, authenticating the works as Greystoke's, as you see in the catalogue."

I nodded. I had the provenance.

He spoke again, between draws on his roll-up. "Surprisingly, there was some fierce bidding for the things. They went to a man and a woman, very bohemian they were, artistic and certainly not regulars; I'd have remembered them if they had been; they were very distinctive, if you get my meaning. They took the lot. I don't think they were both British; she certainly wasn't. They had them shipped out on a motor pantechnicon that afternoon. Don't know where too, but perhaps Mr. Arnold could sneak you a look at the old files if they still exist. I had to wrap them and load them up. They were very heavy again, but I got the feeling they were going home. I think the woman actually said that, something like, 'Come on, my dears, you're coming home at last.' She seemed very happy to have them. I couldn't see what anyone would want them for, to be honest. You wouldn't want them in your house, unless it was to scare guests away. And they were so big."

That was my feeling, too, and I'd only seen the one. "Do you think a set would be more valuable than a single one?"

"Oh yes, sets are always best. Take chairs, or crockery. If you've got pictures by an artist of Spring and Summer, that's fine, but if you've got Autumn and Winter as well, that triples the price. So yes, the whole set would be good. But whether it survived or not, who knows? And tastes have changed." He cocked his head and looked into my face. "What I'm saying is, they could be anywhere, or nowhere."

He was right, of course. "Mr. Williams, you said you'd seen a lot of Greystoke's work. Do you know anything about him?"

"Good Heaven's yes. I took an interest after this. These were possibly the last things he ever painted. I heard he disappeared some time earlier. That's what I meant to tell you. Greystoke was working on these paintings when he disappeared. He didn't die. There was no body found. He just disappeared. It was very fishy." He beamed at me.

I beamed back. "No body, eh? Not ever?"

"I never heard of it. Still, it happens, doesn't it?" He took a final draw on his roll up then tossed the tiny stub into the fire. "The family seemed to do all right out of the situation. Wife, sorry, widow, married her husband's best friend, the oldest son was groomed to take over his stepfather's daughter and fortune."

"Sounds very convenient..." I said.

"Fishy," said Mr. Williams. "Nothing got proved, but there were many people at the house when it happened. Out in Buckinghamshire somewhere. Not in the Boltons house. Mrs. Greystoke was giving a soirée, all the local great and good, you know, were there, and it seems that Mr. Greystoke excused himself after supper as he had to fulfill a deadline with his painting. It was an odd request, but artists are odd people. Everyone saw him go up to his studio, but no-one ever saw him again. They said the paintings that were there were nothing like what he'd done previously..."

I nodded. "These angels?"

"I reckon so, don't you? But who commissioned them? They never got them, nor did they ever come for them, it seems, because that letter reckons they were in the family all the time."

I thought about that. "Anyone could have faked that provenance?" I asked.

"I don't think Mr. Lowther would have let it through if he knew it was faked; he was a canny old chap, Mr. Lowther, but he wasn't openly dishonest, far from it."

"That would be Mr. Arnold Lowther's father?"

"No, Miss. That'd be his grandfather. He'd have known the artist and the family. He knew everyone." His eyes looked over my shoulder, at one with his past.

I sat very still, smoking the last of my cigarette, and was aware that the room was much darker than it had been when I arrived. I glanced at my watch.

The old man caught my movement. "Well, Miss, it's been nice talking to you. I think that's all I can tell you at the moment. I'll rake through my memories and if anything comes up, I'll get Sid to let you know. No doubt you've got a young man waiting to take you out to dinner."

I stood up. "Mr. Williams, thank you so much for your time, and for your help. You have been very helpful indeed." I gathered my things together, shook his hand. It was firm but bony and dry. I took a card from my wallet. "If Mr. Williams needs to get in touch with me," I said. "It's been a pleasure to meet you, sir. Can I get you anything or do anything for you before I go?"

"Just knock on Sid's door, if you would, and let him know you've gone. Then I can have my supper." He was busy stowing the biscuits in the cupboard beside him. "Thank you for these and the tobacco, Miss, and could you let me know how you get on? I'd be most interested?"

3

George met me as I closed the front door. "Your Father called, Miss. He said he would be round tomorrow morning. And that bloke on the Matchless was around earlier. Is he sweet on you?"

"He's sweet on every and any woman, George, but thank you."

"He said will you ring him. He left this number." George handed me a visiting card.

"Thank you, George." I fished for a threepenny bit.

He palmed it into his grey flannel shorts and grinned. "Thank you, Miss!" and disappeared back behind the door to the basement.

In my flat I hung up my clothes to impress for another day, and after a brief wash crawled into my pyjamas. I'd got used to wearing trousers with the *maquisards*, and found men's pyjamas, after I'd sewn the fly-hole up, the most comfortable of garments. Not the sort of thing most young ladies wore at home, but I was not most young ladies. I wasn't even young any more, although I'd not yet reached 'matronly' or 'battleaxe' years. I drank a cup of Oxo while I waited for my potatoes and carrot to boil. I'd not eaten, except for a breakfast of porridge and a ginger nut with the Gaffer, since last night, so I was really hungry. I made up a dried egg omelette. It wasn't a patch on the real egg ones that were available in France, and cooking it in a smidgen of margarine wasn't ideal either, but it was what I'd got used to now, and was quick comfort food. I thought nostalgically of the Colonel's real egg breakfast. The permitted egg ration for a single woman might have been both fair and healthy, but it wasn't enough.

Bobby rang as I was washing up. He wanted to know how I'd got on.

"Leggy says if you need anything, anything at all to do with your work... or anything else, Milady, you're to let me know. It'd be a delight for me, don't you know? I'm a great little fixer, sure enough."

I was only too aware of that and that Bobby worked on favours, given and received. I also knew that he was lonely. Being an expert in that condition I could recognize the signs.

"Thank you, Bobby," I said. There was an awkward silence.

"Milady, I ... I ... er ... I'm in the Anglesey. You don't fancy a small libation? I'd be really delighted if you'd join me."

The Anglesey was my nearest local, north of the Fulham Road, veering into South Kensington, Jerry having put paid to the Queen's Elm, while his was The World's End on the western end of the King's Road, a fair distance away. I wondered what he was doing there. But why not? He could be good fun, and it was either that or washing smalls.

He was sitting in the corner of the snug, nursing a half of Guinness and a Woodbine. He stood and came to greet me as I entered; women (young) were not terribly welcome in pubs unaccompanied which I found irritating. In a French café things were very different, far more civilised.

"What'll you be having?" he asked, and ordered the ginger wine I asked for, and brought it to the table for me.

"Well, this is very nice," I said, sipping the sweet warming drink with pleasure. "Now, what have you invited me here for? It's not for the pleasure of my company."

"Ah, there you'd be wrong... at least in part. It is pure delight to see you looking well again and opposite me. But you're right. It's about Leggy."

"What about Leggy?"

"I think he's going a bit queer."

"How do you mean, queer?" I asked, doubtfully.

Bobby grinned, "Oh, nothing like that. Sure the man was twice married and twice widowed. Straight as a die where that's concerned. No, it's something completely different. And I think that you ought to know."

"You intrigue me, Bobby. Does he know you're here snitching on him?"

"Perish the thought. He thinks I'm doing the washing in the basement."

I chuckled. "So how does his 'queerness' manifest itself?"

"He's been in town, to some weird bookshop. He came home with an armful of books and hasn't got his nose out of them. All occult stuff. You know, magic, ouija boards and stuff. I don't like it. I know he's a Freemason, but that's just an old boys' club, knowing the right people, harmless. But this stuff… " he shuddered, looked seriously worried.

I frowned. "So?" I asked. He should have seen some of the stuff my mother's friends read, my great aunt, too.

"Don't you believe in your immortal soul?" he asked.

"I think there is probably part of us that survives and transcends death, but I don't know. I don't think anyone knows."

"Ah, I should have known you'd not have been brought up in the True Religion. Well, that can't be helped. You believe you do go on, though, afterward. That'll do for me. I'm concerned for Leggy's immortal soul. I think that part of him is getting into serious danger. I think he's going off the rails. He's going where no human being should go."

I looked Bobby coolly in the eye.

There was a touch of madness there – not true madness, but that nervous out-of-control frenzy button was just begging to be pressed.

I sighed slowly, and spoke as calmly as I could. I even

reached out and put my hand over his forearm, gently, though, so it didn't look like a come-on.

"Bobby," I said, "how long have you known him? Leggy's a sensible chap. You, Bobby, you know that well enough. He'd never have held down the jobs he had if he hadn't been sound. He'd never have stayed the sane person he is during the war if he'd not been mentally strong. You do know that, don't you?"

Reluctantly, Bobby nodded his head. "But he's been acting strange lately. I mean, he's been through the war, like we all have, and that'd be enough to change anyone. But he's lost the Memsahib, and then he got the unfit for work. He feels they've put him out to grass. Can you see what it must have done to the chap? The Service was his life, and he's been invalided out. I know we set up this little house-clearing business, but it's not enough for a man like him. And now he's reading all that weird stuff, like he's seeking for something, some excitement, to make up for what he's lost."

I took that on board. I was finding readjustment hard. How much more so for him?

But an odd painting and a few books? Did they constitute a danger?

No, I didn't buy that.

"Bobby, he must have read all sorts of stuff during his lifetime. A few books written by half a dozen self-proclaimed magicians and the like, aren't going to change that soundness. He won't go off the rails. He's one of the most solid people I know."

Bobby sighed. "I hope you're right, Milady. I feel that, but I still have a dread deep inside for him. It's me upbringing. And that bloody picture. I wish I'd never taken him along. We'd have got rid of it, sure we would and there'd be no problem. It's obsessing him."

I was on dodgy ground here. Leggy didn't want Bobby

to know what I was doing, although I had a good idea that Bobby was not fooled by our secrecy.

"What picture?" I asked.

He put down his Guinness and looked at me from lowered eyelids. "What picture, she asks me! Milady, you know exactly what picture. Why did he call you round to see him, you being a painter's daughter and a freethinker? Now what did he want you to find out for him?"

I looked him straight back in the eye. "That's surely between him and me. If he'd wanted to tell you, he would have done." I smiled gently. "Bobby, you and he are so alike. He's as protective of you as you are of him. He doesn't want you to be worried for him, or for me."

"So you can tell me what he wants, what you're to do!"

"Tell you what, I'll do a trade with you."

"Ah, so there is something. What'll you trade, Milady?" He lit another Woodbine and offered me the packet. I pulled out a Gauloise and put it in my holder. They wouldn't last for ever, but I wasn't a Woodbine woman.

"I'll tell you what he's asked me to do, if you tell me where you got the picture, and what else came with it."

"You will?"

"Of course," I said, crossing the fingers of my left hand in my lap beneath the table top. "He wants me to trace its origins, that's all. He likes it because it is strange, out of the ordinary. I'm doing it because he's offered me a week's work on very attractive terms, and like him, and like you, too, I've no doubt, I've discovered that post-war life ain't what it's cracked up to be."

He grinned at my attempt at American slang. "Ah, Milady, you may be able to talk French lingo, but sure as Hell you're a baby when it comes to TransAtlantic and the Good Ole You Ess Uv Eh."

"I've not mixed with a lot of Her Sons," I said primly.

"Ah, but I surely have. Would you like some nylons?

What size would you be taking?"

I was glad he was relaxed again, but needed to get him back on course. "Nine and a half, British, please, dark toned if possible, would be very nice, thank you. Now where did you get that painting?"

"We got it down the Boltons. Number 35A. It was some sort of old artist's studio, down the side of the house. Same again?"

I managed to nod, "That would be lovely, Bobby, thank you," but my mind was racing.

It couldn't be coincidence, could it? I needed more information.

Bobby came back with our drinks and another packet of Woodbines.

"Can you tell me something about the place?" I asked.

Bobby snorted. "Ah, it was a tip, so it was. Some old geezer had lived there all alone. We get called out when there's stuff to be sold off or sorted afterwards. Anyway, they were paying us to take it all away. So we did."

"Try to recall, for me, if you will, Bobby, exactly what you saw, and what you took. Would you do that for me?" I smiled sweetly. "Take as long as you want. I'll be listening." What the Hell, it worked on Raoul, it worked on George, it always worked on my father...

"After Leggy got the call? He and I went out and viewed it at once, on my bike. I left Leggy there while I went off to get the lads and the wagon. It was just the studio they wanted clearing, but there was a lot of stuff. The old chap must have lived in it. We shifted all that, brass bed, bed linen, a wardrobe of stuff, books and sideboard, and a small kitchenette area. All the usual stuff that you'd expect. That's all gone. Rag and bone men, and junk shops mostly..."

"And?"

"There were easels, some canvases, some blank, some painted, mostly not very good – sort of messy, ugly things.

But this painting, all by itself, stared straight at us as we came in. I don't like it, but it is very well painted. Even I can see that. The person who did it knew how to paint. But it gives me the horrors, so it does."

"How did it affect Leggy?" I asked.

"He was stunned by it. Muttered something like, "I've been looking for you all my life," and whistled happily. You know how he does when something goes right? Then he started looking around and picking up books and stuff. He said we could do alright here although the stuff looked a bit elderly to me. Still, a good polish and a bit of joint gluing for the furniture, and a wash for the linen made a difference, and they were paying us to take it all away, which was always good. We cleared it and put it in the warehouse, but Leggy insisted on bringing the painting back home. It was a bug... er, a pain to get in the lift, I can tell you."

"I bet," I grinned. "What about the books? All the papers and stuff that were there?"

Bobby shrugged. "Dunno. Leggy went through them. That's his job. He knows about stuff like that. I took a lot of it to the rag and bone man, like I said. Got a few bob for that. But we sold the easels, all seven of them, and ... here are you all right, Milady?"

Seven easels!

I'd flinched for a moment.

I pulled myself together. "Yes, Bobby, just someone walking over my grave."

Seven easels. "Was there anything strange on the floor, did you notice?"

Now it was his turn to look askance. "Funny you should say that, Milady."

"A circle?" I hazarded, "With funny writing round it?"

"Leggy told you!" he accused, looking hurt.

I shook my head, sipped the ginger wine. "Not a word. Honestly." Bobby looked slightly mollified.

"He told me to stop being a fool!" he said. "It was painted on the floor, just like you said, with signs and strange writing. Not something that you'd show to your parish priest!"

"I don't have a parish priest," I said, with a light smile.

"Sure you do. You just don't accept him, but he's there alright, just waiting for your call."

Bit like God, then, I thought cynically, and just managed to bite my tongue and keep it to myself.

"So what have you found out about this heathen painting?" Bobby asked. He must have realized that I'd got more from him than he had got from me.

"Not a lot," I admitted. "I know who the artist is, and that it is very different from his normal work. I know it was sold by Lowther's to someone in 1908, but that's it at present. I should find out more tomorrow."

"Good. The sooner he gets to the bottom of it all, the sooner we can be shot of it. Will you have another drink?"

"No, Bobby. Thank you, but the washing calls."

Washing done and hung on the airer over the bath, I sat down at my Great Aunt Caroline's desk in the guest bedroom and took out a new large exercise book. I went back through my day, making a summary of it all. I was methodical. It had been drummed into me, and now, because it was no longer war-time, I had the luxury of not having to remember every little detail, but couldn't lose the habit. I wrote and wrote. Around midnight, I finally put the cap on my Parker, and laid it down. I blotted the last page, closed the book, and put it and the notebook from my handbag into the secret drawer of my Great Aunt's bureau. Then I closed the drawer, and the flap, and went to bed.

4

I got back from my swim at the Chelsea Baths at 8.15. It did me good, although I hate the smell of the chlorine, which the showers never get off. George was at the front door to greet me.

"Hello, George, aren't you off to school yet?"

"Just going, Miss. Miss, a lady come with this big envelope, Miss. She said to give it to you personally." It was a large manila envelope with Lowther's printed on the upper left corner.

"Describe, please, George." I said, putting the envelope into my bag, then taking it out again, as I didn't want it next to my damp towel and costume.

"She was short and round, but nice. Like Mrs. Tiggywinkle. And she gave me tuppence."

"Ah," I said. "So if I give you tuppence we'd be equal."

"Yes, Miss, but you'd never be like Mrs. Tiggywinkle. You're too tall, too young and too pretty, Miss."

I gave him a threepenny bit.

Miss Thelma Jackson was a gem.

She'd lifted all the surviving correspondence on the Lots I gave her, and summarized it all on several pieces of paper.

I had the original letter from William Meredith Greystoke requesting that the pictures be sold, the arrangements for access to them to be collected – from the artist studio at the rear of No 35 the Boltons, South Kensington, - key to be collected afterwards. She even included the key, for Heaven's sake, wrapped in a piece of cardboard. I had a proper catalogue, and, at last the name and address of the buyer – a Mr. G. W. Thorburn, of Straddling Hall, Little

Straddling, Suffolk. All seven paintings went to him, for the sum of 350 guineas. A very good result for Lowther's, as well as for Mr. W. M. Greystoke.

I noted this down, as I read through Miss Jackson's summary. As I reached the last page, my jaw dropped.

"We had the cheque made ready for Mr. Greystoke, but he didn't show up to collect it. As you can see by the first letter, he stated he wanted the cheque to be made out to Cash, and he would call in for it – he gave a recognition code – we always insisted on them, but no-one ever came. The cheque is still there, waiting to be honoured. I can't understand it; no-one fails to collect the best part of 350 guineas.

"I think that is as much as I can tell you, Miss Chamberlain, or may I call you Alice? I feel I know you, and would be very glad if you would call me Thelma. I'd really appreciate you getting the archive material back to me as soon as possible, as Mr. Arnold says his 'blind eye' has a limit. And he said to tell you that I like flowers. Yours, etc. etc. Thelma J."

Well, good old Thelma. I knew she was a good egg. I read through the material again. I had the key to the studio – well, possibly – but it had to get back as soon as possible.

The iron-monger peered at the old key. "Long time since I seen one of them."

"Can you match it?" I asked.

"Oh, I should think so. Might take a bit of time, I've got all these old blanks to look through. Tell you what, Madam, if you've got a bit of shopping to do, go and do it. It'll be ready in about half an hour."

"Thank you," I said and left.

There it was again, 'Madam'.

I cycled to Beeton's, the better of the bakers down the King's Road. I was a regular, and knew their quality. I enquired whether there was any cake and struck lucky. They had baked fruit slabs that morning. It took a few points, but Thelma was worth it. They put it in a box with a tie of pretty string. Outside, further down the street, a flower seller had fresh daffodils and narcissi. I got a big bunch of those too, in a sheaf of cheap white paper to protect them on their journey in my bike basket back to the iron-monger's where I picked up and paid for the key, and home. It was a good morning so far.

My father turned up at ten. For an 'artistic type' he was an early riser, horribly punctual, and very much a creature of habit.

I made him French coffee (my suitcases carried more than clothes) and laced it with dark rum that I'd bought in Marseilles before I left the South.

My father is tall and very English. His hair was fading now, but as a young man he looked the archetypal fair-haired, blue-eyed hero who always won the match, led the team to glory, rode a bruising ride. In fact, he was a bit of an indolent creature left to his own devices, and until the war any colour he had had was due to painting outdoors. However, wartime had done him some good. Besides running the local Home Guard Unit he had opened his house to evacuated families and discovered the joys of gardening – kitchen gardening that is. In an odd way, it had probably saved his life, for he looked a lot fitter now than he had eight years ago.

"Mother with you?' I asked.

"No. She's busy sorting out your brother's fiancée and your sister's pregnancy. She might turn up later."

"Ah."

I was a trial to my mother as I had neither a husband in the offing nor a grandchild to offer her – although the latter without the former would have been even more of a trial.

"How was France?" Pa asked.

"It was France. I'm better. I'm glad to be back."

"I'm glad you're back too. Will you come home at the weekend?"

"Not sure. I think I have to thank you. Didn't you put some work my way?"

"Oh, Leggy, you mean? Got some old picture he wanted researched. Be a doddle for a girl like you. Are you doing it?"

I nodded. "Can you tell me all you know about an artist called Greystoke?"

"Greystoke?" My father repeated. "He told me the picture was some sort of angel. Greystoke never painted religious stuff. Did whimsy pictures of sweet children and doggies by cottage doors. Damned good, if you care for that sort of thing. A very painterly artist."

"This painting is very painterly," I said. "Whoever created it was a real craftsman, and there is provenance that says it was painted by Greystoke."

My father shrugged. "Fair enough. Nothing to say that he wasn't allowed to paint an angel. Christmas present for the church – he always painted for money."

"There are another six of them, big ones, taller than you," I said slowly. "And they tend to upset people rather than uplift them."

"You've seen them all? We must re-think his *oeuvre*. There's research to be done here." His eyes glittered. The art historian within was coming up for air.

I shook my head. "Generalising again. I've just seen the one. It wouldn't inspire me to religious ecstasy. Rather the reverse. Leggy wants me to find out about them and if possible locate the rest of them."

My father chuckled and filled his pipe with the heavy black twist he liked to smoke. "You did mention that there had been two world wars since Greystoke's disappearance?"

I fitted a Gauloise into my holder. "You know something, don't you? When did Greystoke die?"

My father puffed himself a cloud. "Got any more of that coffee? No, don't fill it up, just pass the rum."

"What do you know, Pa?" I asked. "How did Greystoke die?"

"When I was a nipper," he began, irritatingly.

I sighed.

"Well, d'you want me to tell you? If so, let me do it my own way." He took a draw on his pipe and eyed me over his horn-rims. I nodded, made a buttoning movement on my mouth, and sat back to enjoy my own *café au rhum* and cigarette.

"There was a lot of talk. Turn of the century. He actually lived not that far from us, for a short while, but of course we didn't know him. He was trade, we were not. Not that he hadn't done very well for himself; he'd been invited to join the R.A. I believe, but that wasn't of any importance to me then. However, our servants knew some of his servants, several times removed, if you see what I mean. I used to spend a lot of time in the kitchen in those days. Must have been about ten. So I got all the gossip first hand. "

I smiled at the thought of Pa earwigging while he shelled peas or helped cook make biscuits.

"Seems that Mr. Greystoke was painting like mad, just before he died, but no-one other than his immediate family, that is his wife and perhaps his youngest son, was allowed to see what he was doing.

"Mrs. Greystoke, she was younger than him, and pretty, and although she had given him three boys, two away at school, was still considered a beauty and at the right side of forty, possibly of thirty five, she was bored out in the country. She took up 'good works'. She liked to be admired, and to be seen to be doing good. No point otherwise, I suppose. So she was on just about every committee, and was held to be a very good hostess. Mr. Greystoke, it seemed was less gregarious, and during the last months of his … er.. what shall I call it? His known existence? Yes, that'll do, well, he was positively reclusive at that point."

I opened my mouth to ask a question, but shut it immediately. Pa was in full flow.

"On the night of his ... er ... demise? Vanishing? Yes, on that particular night, Mrs. Greystoke had arranged a soirée. It was a charity thing, which she did often. You know the drill, get a few friends round, have a meal and some wine, then all throw a fiver in the pot and give it to some deserving cause. Well, it seems that Mr. Greystoke was there for the start of the evening. He welcomed people in, but they all say he looked a little haunted. In retrospect, of course. There were all the local great and good there, including the J.P., the vicar, several well-respected businessmen, including his best friend, Mr. Meredith."

Once more I stopped myself from interrupting. It was hard.

My father continued. "After they'd all eaten, Mr. Greystoke begged to be excused. He had a deadline to keep on some work, he said. It was due to be delivered the following day, and there was a bit of finalizing to arrange. He would get down as soon as he could, but in the mean time, Mr. Meredith was to act as host. Then he started the collection, by putting a tenner, no less, into the pot. The servants told me there were some raised eyebrows at that, because everyone else had to match it. A tenner was a King's ransom in those days."

I didn't beg to differ, for although it may not have ransomed any but a very insignificant king, it would have been pay for an under-servant for a year. It was even now, a fine wage for a week's work for me.

"Well, the party went on. The ladies withdrew to gossip, so I was reliably informed, and Mr. Meredith dispensed a great deal of Mr. Greystoke's best port. Meanwhile, outside the weather turned, and a storm raged. By half past eleven, Mr. Greystoke had not come down from his studio – it was built over the servant's wing on the first floor – and the guests were ready to go, or getting that way. Suddenly there was an almighty crash. The lights all over the house went out, but luckily, the candles were still alight. Everyone agreed the house had been struck by lightning, and they all rushed up to the studio, because that was where they thought it had struck.

"Mrs. Greystoke and Mr. Meredith went in first. They called Mr. Greystoke, but there was no reply. There was also no light; they called for candles and went in again. And came out again, white-faced. He wasn't there. All the windows were locked from the inside. There was no way out. He would have had to pass through the hall if he had wanted to go out. There was absolutely no sign of him.

"The great and the good all went in to have a sniff round. Mr. Meredith comforted Mrs. Greystoke. They sent the servants to search the house, to see if he had crept upstairs and out but everything was secure and all the staff swore on oath that they had not seen him. He had simply vanished."

He saw my face. "Don't you believe me? I thought it a bit odd. Especially as a year later Mrs. Greystoke married Mr. Meredith."

"But how could she do that?" I demanded. "It's seven years to be declared dead, surely?"

"Come on, Alice, the great and the good of the town were there. Everything was in place for him to be declared missing, presumed dead."

"That stinks," I said.

My father smiled. "Oh, youth! Oh innocence! Alice, I saw her once from afar. She was an extremely pretty woman. A woman one would be delighted to be seen with on one's arm ...." He took a sip of his coffee, a draw on his pipe, remembering, I have no doubt, the pretty widow. Then he looked at me over his spectacles once more. "But that's not the end of it. His oldest son also disappeared."

The hairs on the back of my neck began to stand up.

"What?"

My father sighed. "It was in all the papers. I was off to university about that time. Everyone was talking about it. He came up to London ostensibly to sell some paintings and then disappeared. His younger brother, who was a nasty piece of work, let it out that he had run off with the money, and then went and beat up his other brother, the youngest one. Left him for dead. Had to run abroad, for a few years, but that was no problem for him. He had the devil's own luck. Never got caught, always managed to win at cards, you'd find the best-looking woman in the room nuzzling up to him; he had an awful, evil charm."

"'Mad, bad and dangerous to know?'" I suggested.

"Just so. But without Byron's literary gifts. It didn't last, of course. It couldn't. Well, I suppose what goes round comes around."

"What happened to the youngest brother – or were there more?"

"Never heard. Think he was looked after by the local vicar. He was about my age, I'd say, but I didn't know him, not even by sight. By the time I came down from university it had all blown over... Besides, I wasn't that interested any more. I was becoming an artist myself by then." My father turned his blue eyes on me, with a smile, signifying that that was it.

"Thanks," I said.

"You're most welcome, my dear. Now, how about a trip to the RA?"

I looked at my watch.

"I need to meet someone for lunch," I said. "In fact, it would be really helpful if you could do the phone call for me. I don't want her to get into any trouble. But I could meet you there this afternoon, say at two-thirty?"

Thelma met me on her way to the Park – Hyde Park that is – where she usually went for her exercise after lunch in a British restaurant. She accepted the flowers with joy but thought the cake, which I knew she wanted desperately to accept, was extraneous payment.

I forced it upon her. "I'd never get that sort of detail in so short a time," I told her. "You're a real gem. Mr. Arnold is very lucky."

She blushed, took the presents and the returned and resealed manila envelope, and looked, in daylight, several years younger.

"Is your father really Lord Wethersley?" she asked; her Northern bluntness was delightfully refreshing.

"Yes, but you probably know him better as Roger Chamberlain, R.A. He puts the Lord on to impress people or keep them subservient, but he's a pussycat really. He put the Ritz on for you so that Sally Green wouldn't hear my voice and start eavesdropping."

Thelma smiled. "Thank you. She is not the easiest person to get on with, looks down her fairly extensive proboscis at all and sundry."

"But not at a Lord," I assured her.

"Most assuredly not," she agreed. "You didn't mind me dropping the things by this morning? Mr. Arnold said the sooner the better."

"No, I was delighted. So was George. I didn't expect anything like as much so soon. I really appreciate your work. Sorry I wasn't there at the time, I was swimming."

"Oh, I'd love to do that, but I ... well you'll think I'm silly, but I have no-one to go with, and I need that to keep up the impetus."

"Theoretically," I said, "I go every morning, but in reality it will probably be around three times a week, around 7 am at Chelsea Baths. You could come with me, if you want."

"You don't mind?" she was astounded. "Then can I start next Monday? That would be splendid!"

5

I joined my father in the Royal Academy's members' lounge.

It was how I remembered it, the haze of blue cigar and pipe smoke hung lazily over the dark comfortable upholstered furniture. The carpet was a little worse for wear, and they had put up signs marking the fire exits, which was new, but the company was always the same: moneyed and/or artistic. I preferred the artistic, myself. The moneyed were often new, seeking to legitimize themselves with patronage. Nothing wrong with that, but where art was concerned, I preferred my father and his friends to the self-made businessmen (for businessmen read crooks/spivs and the like) who came in to brush against high culture and hope some of it would rub off. That said, it was the money that kept the place running, and I had no right to be snooty about a symbiotic relationship.

Pa was sitting round a table with three of his friends: Emily Shotton-Fell, Padraig Flynn and Josiah Lumley. There was champagne, Veuve Cliquot, in a bucket and a glass was called for. My father was the only one in a suit and tie; the others were all *a la bohemienne* – dressing for the part of artist, in faded glory, velvet jackets, crumpled shirts and cravats for the men, while Emily sported a long velvet dress that may once have been black or midnight blue, and made for someone in the dress reform movement half a century ago, her hennaed hair twisted into an awkward but becoming chignon, kept in place by a selection of decorative pins. They each hugged me to them – there is a camaraderie among artists that I really like – and welcomed me back into their fold.

Padraig, whom I'd known since childhood gave me a

smacking kiss on the cheek. He dwarfed me in his bear hug, then ushered me into his seat, pulling another across from a nearby table. "You're looking a lot better Milady," he said, and poured me a glass of bright golden bubbles. I wondered where and how they had access to this, but was too polite to ask. One didn't.

I raised my glass to the company. "Chin chin!" It was good to be back.

"Old Roger tells us you are hunting angels," he said.

Bright faces beamed at me. They all wanted to be in on the hunt.

"Does he? Very nice champagne, dear friends. Thank you very much."

"Who wants them?" asked Josiah Lumley. He was small and round. If he hadn't worn the regulation velvet jacket and spotted cravat, you would have taken him for a greengrocer.

"Do I know him?"

"I'm not at liberty to say," I replied. "Client confidentiality and all that."

"The war's over," Padraig laughed. "You can trust us. We might be able to help you."

"I'd be most grateful for any help any of you can give, but I honestly can't reveal my client. You must understand that. If it got out, then the element of surprise when he comes to sell will be lost."

I sipped the bubbles. Nice.

"So can any of you give me any leads?" I took out my Gauloises and handed them around, fitting one into my holder. "I've discovered they were painted by Lawrence Greystoke."

As I'd expected the packet returned to me almost empty. Even my father, who swears they're made of donkey dung, took one. There was a general lighting up, and a call for another bottle of The Widow.

"Lawrence Greystoke went a bit peculiar towards the

end," said Josiah. "He was reading all sorts of strange stuff. They were an odd family. Plodding along very nicely thank you; he'd made a name for himself, become a member here, and things were beginning to be a bit easier for him, yet he moved out to the country, instead of staying in London where the money was, and then all of a sudden, he's gone. And his wife's married his best friend, and his kids are suddenly very wealthy, oldest son marries the best friend's daughter, takes over the business, next one is suddenly a man about town with money to burn. Then it all starts going off. Oldest son's wife dies in childbirth, nothing odd about that, it happens all the time, but the twins survive. Their grandparents bring them up, oldest son hangs on to the business but begins to go off the rails. Then the grandparents die. In a freak accident."

"How do you know all this, Josiah?" I asked, astounded.

"Went to school with the twins for a short while. What a strange couple of lads they were!"

"Are they still alive?" I dared to ask.

"Lord bless you, yes. You must have heard of them. Percy and Archie Meredith."

I frowned and flicked through my inner card indexes. The names rang a bell, but …

"She's far too young to have heard of them, Josiah," said Padraig. "They're well before her time."

"And I have tried to shelter her from such people," said my father. "Although trying to shelter her is perhaps counter-productive. She is very resourceful at finding trouble."

"Tell me about the twins," I said to the company in general.

Josiah took the floor by common consent.

"They inherited the lot. Old Meredith's business and houses, old Greystoke's estate, through their paternal grandmother; they'd never be short of a bob or two, and they also inherited through various other relatives once or twice removed. Like the Great Aunt who brought them up for a while after Grandfather died, and the uncle – Greystoke's second son. Golden boys, if you like, when it came to money and riches coming to them. Became property developers like their grandfather after the Great War, which they cannily managed to miss. Lived in their Great Aunt's houses for a while, both of them – there was one in Kensington, and another in the country and they entertained in both. No wives. Seemed to be content with each other's company, and were always in demand in Town. Young, wealthy, up-and-coming men, don't you see. Great party-givers, although some of the stuff was very much over the top. I mean, I can get drunk with the best of them…"

"And you do, Josiah, you do," said my father, topping up glasses.

"But I don't like drugs. I don't like the stuff that people used in the twenties and thirties. I don't like what it does to people. White powders. They take your soul away. Steal it from your body. Oh, the twins always had access to plenty of that sort of stuff. And gambling. I was never one for that either. I saw amazing sums passing ownership at their tables…"

"Thank you, Pa," I said, fondling my father's hand.

He blushed.

I'd never have thought he would blush in front of his cronies, but he did.

"Did they traffic in drugs?" asked Padraig.

A general consensus round the table suggested that there was no hard evidence, but it was possible, more than that, extremely likely. They had contacts for all sorts of things.

"They ran with the Bright Young Things, but they used people," said Josiah. "And they treated people like things. Especially during the Depression. They'd make a lot of money from a business but never plough it back. Once they realized there was not a lot of profit to be made, they would cut and run. World-wide, I heard. And they're still doing it, and yet still accepted into high society because they bring in what the people want.

"Presently they're taking the profit out of building development. They always did, but Mr. Hitler was a godsend to them, as was Kaiser Bill before him. Homes fit for heroes to live in is what they're into now. They did it before, and they're at it again. And I don't mean pre-fabs. Proper homes, built with bricks and mortar, only perhaps the homes will be a little less than perfect, just as our heroes mostly have feet of clay. There's a lot of money to be made in building right now, and a lot of landowners feeling a bit of a pinch. The war was a great leveler, not only of buildings."

Yes, I thought. My mother was always saying she couldn't get the right caliber of staff, but I doubted she would countenance cutting back and doing some of the washing, for instance, or more housework than a little light dusting, flower arranging and plumping of cushions, checking the table-settings before a dinner party. She'd order the menu, but would she cook the food or scrub the pans afterwards? I think not. But my generation would, and did, although on a much more restricted scale. Even my Father, who was certainly not short of a bob or two, had been forced by wartime to make cutbacks.

"Keep your eye on the gossip columns," suggested Padraig to me. "And the business pages. They're not going to go into early retirement. Now, what about these paintings? The old man died while he was painting them, and the oldest son disappeared or died while he was trying to sell them. Don't you think there was something dodgy about them?"

"Have you seen any?" asked Josiah. "Tell us about them."

"I've seen one." I described it.

Emily Shotton-Fell, the only woman in the group, had

remained silent but now she listened avidly, biting her bottom lip. "I've seen that. Sure I have. Before the War, though." She glared at Padraig. "This War, not the Great War, before you ask."

She smoothed her faded velvet dress over her knees as a prelude to taking centre stage, then looked around at us, ensuring herself of our full attention.

"I was down in Suffolk. Must have been 1936 or 1937. Yes, about ten years or so ago. I was painting a series of portraits for ... now who was it, ... Lady Finching. Yes, that was she. We were invited to a séance. Well, not exactly a séance. Something rather more like a dramatic exposition. I suppose you'd call it that. I don't like emotive words like 'wicked ritual', but that was closer to the truth."

"You took part in a satanist's meeting?" Padraig asked, awed. "Oh, Emily, what were you doing there? Why haven't you told me this before? What was it like? Why did you go?"

Emily polished her pince-nez on the edge of her fringed shawl. "Shut up, Padraig. I went because I was invited, but I didn't know to what I was invited. I thought it was just an evening party, and as Lady Finching was feeding me, keeping me, and paying me to paint pictures, I felt unable to refuse."

"Where did this take place?" I asked. I wasn't the only one to want to know.

She had the floor and she knew it.

She took a draw on her stained ivory cigarette holder. "I was living at Lady Finching's place; that's near Framlingham... Now where was the séance? It wasn't that far away, physically, but ... it was an eerie place, set out of the way along a track, an old hall. Moated. Crumbling a bit, but holding its own. They didn't have any electric or gas as far as I could see. I don't know if you've been to Finching Hall. It's wonderful, Everything totally new, totally Style

Internationale, every, every convenience. I mean, I was lodged over the garages, but it was a proper studio, with an attached bed-sitting room, with hot and cold, and my own bath. And it was centrally heated. It was wonderful…'

"Emily," I said gently, "I'm sure it was lovely, but…"

"Yes, dear, the other place. Well it was a bit like 'the other place', although I didn't think so at the time. It was simply a large house set far out in the country. It had a moat, but it was a strange house, a mixture of styles. I only got a quick view, and I never went back. Never wanted to…" she shuddered. "What amazed me was the number of cars there. I mean, cars aren't that frequent even now in Suffolk. It's very rural."

"What sort of cars?" I asked.

"Oh, don't ask me, darling, I've no idea what cars are called. Besides, it was dark. Yes, it was Hallowe'en come to think of it. But they were big cars. They would have cost a bit to run, I can tell you. Big old-fashioned coach-built ones. They didn't belong to the local rustics. Cars like those had chauffeurs. Must have been at least twelve outside. At least twelve. Each could have held about six people, plus a chauffeur, of course. I didn't notice any chauffeurs though, apart from our own, and he didn't come in with us. I don't know where he went."

Padraig asked "What happened then when you got there?"

"Well at first I thought it was a party. We were all great on parties then. Everyone was dressed in Black and Silver – or as near to it as we could be, even our group, and there were Lady Finching's two young daughters with us – they were only about twelve and thirteen, definitely not yet out, so black was totally unsuitable for them. I think they wore dark blue, yes, a sort of indigo, with silver stitching – they looked beautiful… Lady Finching had been most insistent that we didn't wear bright colours; it would be just a bit of fun, as it was Halloween. I wore this. It looked a lot better then, and so did I, but, well, we survive."

"You look as lovely as you always did," my father assured her gallantly. "And I prefer women with a bit of age and character. Can't be doing with the young fillies nowadays."

"Thanks, Pa."

"You don't count, Alice. You were 30 years old when you were born," he chuckled.

"What happened then, Emily?" Josiah asked.

"Well, we went in, but there was no actual host to greet us, just a large hall all candle-lit, with a huge fire and circulating waiters who brought us tankards of hot drink, even the girls had it, and it was a sort of very alcoholic spicy red punch. Very nice but exceedingly strong, and I had come out with a very empty stomach. Then we were all summoned through to the Long Gallery. We were led by 'a wrinkled old retainer'," she said; you could hear the quotation marks in her voice.

I heard my father mutter under his breath, "Ah, Scrote!" as was his wont, but Emily ignored that.

"He was carrying a flaming torch. It lit the place up most atmospherically – for the candles and oil lamps had all been snuffed. Only the flaming torch, and you could smell the resin of the pine branches, and the really quite eerie dancing shadows – imagine the stuffed heads of stags with their huge antlers that hung along the high corridor.

"When we got to the end of the corridor, the man hefted what looked like a mace, and struck the door on it three times.

"I was shocked. I thought we were coming to a party.

"The three bangs echoed through the silence and hung on the air. It wasn't my idea of a Hallowe'en party. I was expecting punch, of course, possibly a ouija board and apple-bobbing, and I was hoping for some spicy food or pumpkin pie and a bit of country dancing, that sort of thing. This was altogether darker."

Josiah poured her some more Widow, and topped up my glass.

"Suddenly the door opened and a huge figure dressed all in black, like a monk, demanded who we were and what we wanted. He was carrying a sword, a big one, double-handed, double-edged. Talk about threatening! I wanted to go home, I can tell you. But the old retainer said we were pilgrims coming in search of the Truth. I didn't like that. I didn't like someone speaking for me and I didn't like the way things were shaping out.

"I looked at Lady Finching, and she at me. She put her finger to her lips, and then whispered that it was alright. I had to trust her. She had her arms round both her daughters, but they seemed calm enough. I mouthed to her, "I want to go home." She mouthed back, "We can't." Then she whispered across, "It's only a bit of fun. Don't take it seriously." I ask you!

"The inner figure closed the door. I was ready to run, in fact I made for the rear of the group, but there were now two figures, short and round, dressed in some sort of black medieval garb barring my path, each bearing an axe."

I caught my father's eye. I was waiting for his 'Ah, the brothers Balls! They always come in pairs,' comment, but my father wasn't smiling now. He had put himself in Emily's place and was deadly serious.

Emily continued. "Well, the knocking business started up again, and again we were refused entry. Then after the third knock we were allowed in, but at sword-point, and threatened that if we told anyone about this, then we should be damned. Oh!" Her hand flew to her mouth. "Oh dear! I didn't mean to tell you." She raised the glass to her lips. "Um, that rather causes a complication, doesn't it?"

We were silent for a moment, then Padraig spoke. "Only if you think it does, Emily," he purred, his voice smooth as honey. "I mean, did you make the oath willingly, or was it coerced out of you?"

"They had a sword to my throat. Of course I swore." Emily was indignant. "I crossed my fingers behind my back, though. I was very angry as well as very scared."

"Then it was coercion," said Padraig, confidently, "and doesn't count in the great scheme of things. I have that from my spiritual adviser."

My father stared at him. I could see the words forming. Spiritual adviser? You?

Padraig nodded and smiled.

"You did?" she asked. "You're sure it's alright? I mean I really didn't want to swear anything of the sort. I didn't want to be there. But oath-breaking is a ... well, you know."

"The Lord in Heaven knows how you felt and understands and is merciful," Padraig assured her, going for broke in the pastoral role. "He will punish those who caused your torment."

"Come on Padraig, that's a bit too far," Josiah muttered.

"Well I hope He does," Emily said with some force. "They deserve it. It was horrible. It will be a relief to unburden myself at last. If you don't mind." Her fingers plucked at the fringing on the Aesthetic shawl again. I found myself wondering how old she was, but couldn't say. Anything between late thirties and early fifties, although I have no doubt she would have not agreed to the latter assumption.

"Please, go ahead," said my father, standing up to survey the room. "Actually, I suggest we migrate to a more private area... There are some newly vacated chairs and a table over there."

He was right. We were in the open here, and everyone or anyone could overhear or interrupt. If Emily broke down, and she did look agitated, she would be on view to all and sundry. To the far side of the fire was a little nook, whence we repaired, to ensconce ourselves in some leather winged chairs round another table. Padraig touched a passing waiter's arm and indicated the empty wine bucket.

The man nodded. "And something to eat, something suitable. Whatever you have available." The man nodded again.

Emily began. "I suppose I was privileged. Lady Finching certainly told me I was afterwards. I didn't feel it at the time. The long gallery was unforgettable, but one thing it wasn't, was welcoming. It was all in darkness, and there was a stink of something unpleasant. Not church incense, but it was making clouds of smoke. There were candles set in pairs to mark out a pathway to the far end of the hall. There were people in dark robes on either side, a Stuart ceiling above, and rows of dark ancestor portraits lining the path. But it was as if all of that didn't exist. It was the circle of light and action at the far end, with the parody of an altar that demanded my whole attention. That was where I saw the paintings. There were actually more than one."

"How many?" demanded Josiah and Padraig together.

"I don't remember. They were all along the back wall, either side of the altar. Hold on... Let me think." She closed her eyes, held her forehead with her hand theatrically, and then spoke as if describing an inner picture. "There was one immediately behind the altar. It was a sort of angel, as big as a man." She opened her eyes and turned to Padraig, smiling. "Not as big as you, Padraig, but closer to Roger's build. And as lean."

My father preened. He had a very good figure and he knew it. That others, especially women with artistic eyes, admired it was an extra bonus.

Emily missed it all; she was still focusing within. "I think there were three on either side of the centre. Yes, I'm sure there were. But I didn't get a chance to get a good look, at that time. We were led to the – well, I suppose you'd call him the High Priest. He was dressed most strangely, like an Egyptian, an ancient one, and he had a crook and flail, both of which he used on us. I really didn't like that!"

"He whipped you?" Josiah gasped, shocked. "He hit you! That's assault!"

Emily nodded. "Not hard, the whip, but it was still a violation. Across the face, too, and then he knocked us on the head with the crook. That was not gentle! I understood it was to beat our impurities from us and open us to the higher worlds. It felt like physical violence. Then we were led round to a row of seats on the right hand wall, inside the circle part of the room, presumably to shut up and enjoy the show. That's what I thought, anyway."

"And did you?" my father asked.

"Shut up? Yes. Enjoy the show? Not at all. I was very cold and the incense – I use the term loosely - I'm sure there was a large proportion of dung in it – was making me choke and my eyes stream. I wanted to be anywhere but there, but I knew I'd not be allowed to leave. There was that guard with the big sword by the door anyway, and the two chaps with choppers; I think that was the only way out. I'd never have made it. I had to simply grin and bear it. Lady Finching was looking distinctly strange, I noticed. Somewhat wild of eye."

"So what did they do?" Padraig asked. "Did they sacrifice a virgin?"

Josiah frowned at him. "Bit indelicate, old man," he admonished.

Emily ignored them. "There was a lot of ... invoking. I think that is the word. All in some sort of gobbledy-gook language. Could have meant anything or nothing. And there was a lot of walking round the circle, waving censers, sprinkling water around, more waving of censers, and swords and wands and then even more chanting. It went on for ages. The clouds on incense smoke started to get to me really badly, and I had all I could do to keep myself from having a coughing fit. Well, I managed to control myself and

I started to drift off. It was quite mesmeric.

"Then it all changed. The people who were already in the room on the sides of the path, were led into the circle proper. I couldn't tell who they were, because they were all dressed in black robes with deep hoods, with white leading cords around their necks. I could hazard a guess at gender or age by the way they stood and walked but I couldn't do more than that. I recognized no-one. They were led, one by one, to the High Priest, who did the same to them as he did to us, then they were sprinkled with water, censed, and shown a candle, before being taken to kneel before each of the seven paintings in turn."

"All seven of them?" I asked. I could see the scene in my mind's eye.

"Oh yes," Emily said. "They knelt before each one, and each person took off a knife from their belts, and cut themselves." She looked at us with wide eyes. "I've never seen anyone cut themselves on purpose before. Some of them had a really difficult time, because their knives were not sharp. Others bled at once and copiously into a dish before each painting."

She looked round us again, wildly now. The telling was beginning to get to her. "I can tell you I felt really sick. I'm not good with blood at the best of times, and this was really not for me. At my end of the line, there was a person with bandages, but few used them. There were about fifteen people there, going through these motions, and the noise was incredible. It really was all gobbledy-gook to me, some sort of ululating sound. They all did it as soon as they got the blood flowing. It was horrible.

"I did the only thing I could think of: I closed my eyes and thought of a summer's day in a rose garden and tried to focus on that. I didn't want to look any more. I'm not a particularly religious person, but this, blood offerings to paintings, this was not right. I even started saying the

Lord's Prayer, which is not something I do terribly often. I got halfway through, when I felt someone standing in front of me."

"Cigarette?" I offered.

She nodded, took the Gauloise and lit up. "The High Priest had come up to our little party. We were offered the opportunity to ask for favours from the forces of the archangels.

"They must have known very few of us would do it. They must have. Yet Lady Finching got up, and took me by the arm. 'Come on, Emily,' she said, 'you could do with a bit of good luck, and I always take all the luck I can get.'

"She dragged me into the circle. I was horrified. Here was my employer, a friend, even, a woman I trusted and depended on, dragging me into something I felt was really diabolic. Yes, I mean that. And I don't use that sort of term lightly. It was diabolic. When I accepted her commission, I hadn't signed up for this sort of thing, yet how could I get out of it?

"The High Priest did the extra cleansing on her, and handed her a little scalpel as she obviously hadn't got a ritual blade. Horrified, I watched her as she cut into her fourth finger, and kneel down before the first picture. I didn't believe this was going on. She seemed to be a perfectly rational woman most of the time, yet here she was doing something so alien to me... then she crossed herself, only not the usual way, started that awful unnatural singing sound, stood up, and moved to the second picture. I looked on spell-bound. Literally.

"The High Priest stood behind me and guided me very firmly over to the first picture. I was rigid with fear, and he was strong. He put his hands on my shoulders and pushed me down. 'This is Bartzabel,' he said, or something like that. He forced the scalpel into my hand, 'Make your sacrifice,' he said, 'and he will teach you anything you want to know.

Make your sacrifice, Lady, and learn.' I remember that all right. It was as though he were talking inside my head. I just cowered there, terrified, refusing to take the scalpel. The picture was in front of me. I was looking up at this very beautifully painted but extremely unnerving being, whose black feather wings seemed to be moving.

"The High Priest swung the incense a little closer until I was in a stinking cloud. I couldn't escape. I was transfixed by the picture. It was moving. The wings stretched, and the face – it was a cruel heartless face – turned down to sneer at me. Then it smiled; I suppose you could call it a smile, but there was no warmth in it. And it moved toward me, stepping down out of the frame. I screamed, I think, and I felt someone grab my hand and slash across it with the scalpel fast across my palm. I screamed again at the pain and the shock, and saw the blood surge out like a deep red ribbon that became red spray."

Emily took a sip at her champagne. I noticed that her brow was covered with beads of sweat, but she kept herself in check. "Well, as I said, me and blood, we are not good bedfellows. I screamed again. And the High Priest hit me; he grabbed at my hand and held it over a bowl. I was pouring blood all over the place. I tried to make to run for the bandages, but now I was being held upright before the first picture. And the figure from the picture came out and caught the blood in a chalice, and drank it. I did see it. I know I did. And it laughed. I know I saw it and I heard it, yet I was aware that it could not happen, not in the world that I know. I knew I was having hallucinations, it could have been due to the drink, or more probably to the incense, or both, but they were so real. I watched my blood dripping all over the place. It was a fair sized wound."

She held out her left hand palm upwards and showed a fine scar stretching from her wrist to just below her middle finger. "And I did what you would have expected. I blacked out."

"Bloody Hell!" Padraig exploded. "Why the Devil didn't you tell me earlier, Emily. I'd have taken great joy in sorting the scoundrels out."

"Then what happened?" Josiah asked softly, and nodded a thank you to the waiter who silently placed a plate of smoked salmon sandwiches (brown bread, fresh butter – again it would be extremely bad form to ask for the source) and replaced the now empty bottle with a small popping flourish.

Emily looked confused. "I really don't know. I found myself back in the car being taken home. Lady Finching was seriously annoyed with me, but her two daughters were as shocked as I was. May and June were hugging me. They were very lovely girls. My hand had been sewn up neatly and I was told not to use it. I could stay on to finish the paintings but as soon as they were completed, I was to go. I couldn't wait, to be honest. But we managed to part on civilized terms, and she paid me a very nice bonus. Mind, I deserved it. The portraits I did of them all were very good." She eyed the sandwiches hungrily. "May I?"

Emily's story had a deep affect upon the rest of us, but what was really joyful, was the way she tucked in. "I feel so much better," she said after the sandwiches had grounded her. "Thank you all so much for listening. It was so queer, I've never dared to share it, but it's been preying on my mind for the past ten years. It's so good to bring it out into the open where I can see it for what it was, and evil episode that no longer has any hold on me. It's in the past and I have survived and lived on. Thank you."

"No-one had the right to subject you to that sort of ordeal," Padraig growled. "I wish you had spoken to me. Do you want me to see Lady Finching? I'd like to give her a piece of my mind."

"No point," Emily said, dabbing her mouth with a

serviette. "She's in a home for the permanently bewildered. Her daughters have both married over the Atlantic. I think they are in the film industry."

"Was there a Lord Finching?" Josiah asked.

"There is a Lord Finching," my father said drily. "He's rather eccentric, and spends large periods of his time up in Scotland in a pseudo-medieval castle where he dresses like Rob Roy."

Padraig guffawed. "Bloody Hell," he said again, "I take it you've had personal experience of this, Roger!"

"Indeed. But not for some years. He's as batty as they come. When he's not Rob Roy, he's Merlin the Magician. Floats about in a pointed hat with stars on it, and a cloak and long robe. The girls are better off spreading the gene pool over the Water, even if they do loose a few duff ones on the world unwittingly."

I knew my father could be cynical, but this was harsh stuff.

Josiah chuckled. "You believe in exporting your problems, then, Roger!"

My father shrugged. "Seems as good a solution as any with this family. Did you meet Lord Finching, Emily?"

"Just the once. Shortly before Halloween. I never saw him afterwards, but he seemed quite a pleasant man with his family. A bit distant to me, but both Lady Finching and the girls were very happy to have him there. He didn't stay very long. I got the impression he was abroad on government work."

We demolished the final sandwiches and the last of the Widow, then Emily and I went to wash and brush up while the men sorted out the bill.

Emily washed her face and reapplied powder and lipstick. She retwined her hennaed hair into its usual twist and stabbed it into place with a battery of exotic hairpins.

Beside her I put on extra mascara, dipping the brush

in water and shaking it before scraping it on the black dye block and applying it to my eyelashes. "Emily, I'm going to ask you to do something for me, but you're at complete liberty to say no," I said, tucking the little brush away and closing the box.

"Very well, Alice, fire away." She was her usual self now, I was glad to see.

"Would you come to the Library with me and see if you could find the house where all this happened on a map for me?" I asked.

"When? Now?"

"That would be very nice. Just over to the Westminster Reference. It would take around half an hour of your time."

Emily beamed a toothy brilliant scarlet smile. "What are we waiting for?"

I said goodbye to Pa at the tube. I promised to go and stay at the weekend. It was a long time since I'd seen the family. I asked if I needed special clothing – my mother loved putting on a bit of a show and expected us all to join in – I don't know how she managed it even through the darkest days of the war, but she always did.

"I'll get your mother to ring, Alice. She'll be able to tell you what you'll need. And thanks for the day. It was fun. I hope I've been of help."

"Tremendously," I said, "See you Friday night, or possibly Saturday morning."

"I'll look forward to it, my dear. Go and stop Emily getting accosted, for Heaven's sake."

I leaned forward and gave him a kiss on the cheek. "Fat chance of that with Padraig glowering at any myopic punter," I chuckled.

I promise, I didn't prime her. I simply laid out a selection of the new Ordnance Survey maps of the Framlingham area, three in all. She read them like a professional. And her gloved finger came down swiftly. "There it is. See, it says moat, too."

Straddling Hall. Nearest village, half a mile away, Little Straddling. "You're sure?"

"As sure as I'll ever be. Is that all you want? Good. I'm formally handing those pictures over to you. I don't want to see them ever again." She looked up at Padraig and smiled. "You can buy me that drink now, Mr Flynn, and take me to see your etchings."

6

I went to the specialist shop in Longacre and bought a copy of the relevant map. It had been a very good day, and it was not yet five o'clock. I went into a public phone box and dialed Leggy's number.

"Armitage Clearers and Removals," Leggy's upmarket voice informed me. I should be impressed with that tone. "How may we help you?"

"Alice here. I'm hiring a car tomorrow. I've got a lead, but it may be nothing."

"What do you need transporting, Madam?" Leggy asked suavely.

"No, Leggy, I'm just telling you I'm hiring a car. This is just a recce, but I've got leads. If anything comes of them, I'll let you know, I promise. I don't want to waste your time."

"I can pick up your package tomorrow morning, Madam, and promise you it'll arrive before noon. Would that suffice?" Leggy persisted.

"No, Leggy. I'll do this my way. This is for information only"

"Very well then. You must do as you think best. Thank you for your call Madam, I'm sorry we can't help you in this instance, but do remember us. Goodbye." The line clicked dead on me.

Leggy obviously had his own reasons for not wanting Bobby to know what I was doing.

I caught a bus, getting off a stop early to book a little Austin for the following day.

I spent a long time that evening thinking over what I had learned so far, and planning the next day's route with my maps (AA and OS). Then I wrote to the Rector of St Michael and All Angels in Amersham which was where the Greystoke family had been based. I doubted it would be the same incumbent, but he might be able to give me a lead or two; most vicars were keen keepers of the parish records, so I asked if might visit this Saturday afternoon to discuss some matters of local history. I nipped out and posted it immediately.

At 9 pm my mother phoned to tell me there was to be a formal dinner on Saturday evening, and I'd need a decent dress. "Something French, I think," she said.

"All my dresses are French, Maman," I reminded her.

"I don't mean something provincial," she said reverting into her mother tongue. "Nor do I mean something that you would have made out of nothing."

"Important people coming?" I asked, switching to French automatically. "Care to name any?"

"Some, but it's Guy's show and your father's listening. I want it to be a surprise. Besides, he doesn't know that I've earmarked his pre-War *Chateau Haut-Brion*, but it will be worth it, I promise."

"I shall dress for the wine, Maman," I assured her.

It was raining the following morning and the wireless announcer promised it would continue for the next couple of days.

Great. Still, we'd had three days without it, so I had no reason to complain.

I dressed accordingly, with a shopping bag of spare items, and set out under my umbrella for the garage. The little black car was waiting for me. I signed forms and handed over a cheque, then settled into the driver's seat. It was good to be back in a car, and even driving through the first bit of the rush hour was a pleasure.

Living west of London, I'd hardly ever been east of the City. I had experienced the Blitz, in small part, of course

I had, and seen the news-reels at the cinema, but I hadn't realized just how extensive was the bomb damage suffered by the eastern side of London. Great tracts of land were razed, not to mention the docks.

There would certainly be money to be made in reconstruction if you could get the planning permission and the materials.

Rain apart, the journey was uneventful. I hit traffic through the towns, particularly busy Ipswich where it was Market Day and there were animals and farm vehicles everywhere but finally I was through off to Framlingham and Little Straddling. It was certainly rural.

I did an exploratory cruise round the area, to find my bearings then drew to a halt at a quarter past eleven outside the Rose Tea Room in the centre of Framlingham. Despite the rain, it was surprisingly busy with lady shoppers in tweed suits and galoshes taking a revivifying break, their umbrellas and rubberized rain capes hanging on hooks by the door, like a sad collection of bats.

I smiled at the room, said "Good morning," and settled myself down at the one small table that was free, accepting the returned greetings and nods. I ordered a pot of tea, and asked the waitress for suggestions.

"Slab cake's good," she said. "And there's mock apricot slice."

"Take the chocolate sponge," whispered a voice from my right. A rosy-faced woman, also alone, nodded at me. "It's famous here."

"Do you have any chocolate sponge?" I asked, looking hopeful.

"Of course, Madam, I'm sure we can find you some, Madam," she said, looking daggers at my advisor.

"You won't be disappointed," the woman assured me as the waitress flounced off. "Would you care to join me? It's so nice to have a chat with your elevenses."

"I'd be delighted." I shifted across, put my shopping bag on the spare chair, and ensconced myself. "Sally Carson, Miss," I said, proffering my hand.

"Beryl Crowe, Mrs." said my new friend. We complained to each other about the weather until my order arrived.

I poured my tea and surreptitiously sniffed the cake. "Thank you, Mrs. Crowe, for suggesting this," I said as I took my first tentative forkful. It was very good indeed. "Definitely worth the visit."

"You're most welcome. And call me Beryl, do, everyone does."

"Then call me Sally," I invited, through chocolate sponge.

"What are you doing here?" Beryl asked. "I mean, it's not exactly on the beaten track, and you don't appear to be local. I'm not being rude, just nosy," she smiled encouragingly. You couldn't have taken offence.

"Sort of sentimental journey, really," I said, vaguely. "I was driving back to town from Bungay – I've been staying with an old friend there – and on the way saw this sign to Framlingham. I wondered whether Lady Finching still lived here. I knew her daughters when they were young – family friends, you know how you lose touch. I thought it would be nice to look them up again."

Beryl frowned. "You have been out of circulation," she said. "Lady Finching's been gone these six years and Finching Hall has been sold. Some people called Meredith have it now. Very nice, they are. Doing a lot for the area, which is more than one could say for the Finchings, begging your pardon."

"Oh, I didn't like them that much, to tell the truth," I said quickly. "I liked the house though."

Beryl smiled. "It's amazing, isn't it? Not necessarily easy to live in, but very modern. And the Merediths have made it even more so. They've done a lot of extra building, and that's meant work locally, which we really need. Do you know, they've got a heated swimming pool? How about that?"

"Very nice indeed," I agreed. "The Merediths? Not Archie or Percy? I haven't seen them in years. Saw them all the time before the war, but you know how things go base over apex."

"Oh, you know them too? That's nice. They've been here since around 1941, I think. Got it for a song, I heard, but what's a song for some is a lot closer to a complete choral work for another. No-one round here could have afforded it, not to buy it nor even to keep it up, so Messrs. Meredith were delighted to take it off Lord Finching's hands. It wasn't as though he ever stayed there much, anyway. He had it built for his wife, and after she went doolally and his daughters decided they wanted to be film stars, he must have lost heart. I imagine there were debts entailed, because Lady Finching and her daughters were hardly frugal types. His Lordship's better off without them and it, so I've heard."

"What about Straddling Hall?" I asked. "I was taken there once, with the girls, years ago."

She gave me a queer look, sucked in her teeth. "I wouldn't go mentioning that around here, if I were you, Sally. It's got an odd reputation. Not that it's there any more. It got struck by lightning, back in '39. Went up like a blaze of glory, and good job too. There were some very odd goings-on there. The two Mr Merediths bought the place and the land up recently, I heard. Want to build on it. Personally, I wouldn't like to live there, but people from London, who've lost their homes, they'd be grateful, never mind the atmosphere down there."

"Atmosphere?" I asked.

She nodded sagely. "I don't know what it was like when you went there, Sally, but there were all sorts of stories about that house, and not a hundred years ago, either. When it was struck by lightning, it was the best thing that happened to it. Got rid of the Thorburns. They were a very odd family. He was English, but she was German, and very hard to like. And the daughter! Well, you wouldn't have been proud of her, although she's a good-looking woman. We were all glad when they decided to leave. Did you know them at all?"

"No. I just got taken there once. We girls were told to wait in the car, but we got out and ran around the moat, having races." I wondered where I got the lies from.

"Moat's pretty filthy now, I've heard. Only people who go there are Mr. Meredith and the builders."

"Then I'll give it a miss, Beryl," I said.

"Looks like you've had a wasted journey," she said, ruefully.

"Not at all. I've met you and been introduced to the best chocolate cake I've had for ages, and thanks to you, been saved a lot of extra time-wasting. It's been good."

We finished our elevenses and paid. "Can I give you a lift anywhere?"

I looped back after dropping her at her cottage on the Saxtead Road. I wanted to see what the damage was at Straddling Hall.

When I had set out this morning, this had been my great hope, and I was loath to return to town without having had a sniff around. I had also intended to have a look at Finching Hall, but that was less pressing now, although when I saw a sign to it, I followed the road, and came to a pair of Art Deco metal gates set into the wall to the right of the lane, and a sign "Finching Hall" in Style Odeon script. I parked up a little way beyond, walked back and used my field glasses. It was indeed a very fine large modern house, as out of place in the damp Suffolk countryside as the gates were in the hedgerow, but I saw lights in the lower rooms. I wondered who was in residence, but decided not to call, regained my car, and drove to Little Straddling.

The village ran to an old church that was in serious need of renovation, a general store-cum-post office, and a pub around a damp cricket pitch/village green.

I parked up a small road behind the church, turning the car so that I wouldn't have to back out, then pulled on a pair of thick socks and stout brogues over my stockings, preparatory to country walking. Next came a heavy duty riding mac and a beret, both of which I put on, stuffing my hair off my face into the hat. Last of all I got my OS map of the area. According to the map, if I continued along this road, it would become a track that led to the moated manor house.

After couple of run-down houses on either side the road petered out into a path between allotments and then over a stile into a field that had been ploughed but wasn't showing any sign of life. I walked along the muddy edge, beside bushes of hawthorn, sloe and hazel. The wind blew raindrops from them onto me, but the rain itself was just about easing off. In the high elms that guarded the end of the field, a rookery was in full nesting throat. I crossed another stile and kept walking.

I wondered how the paintings would have arrived nearly forty years ago.

The Gaffer had mentioned a motor pantechnicon, a rare and expensive vehicle in those days. Who had seen them? Who had done the moving? Who was the woman?

Mrs. Thorburn? Who was she and how did she fit in? I'd need to see the parish register, perhaps talk to the vicar, or better still, a local historian. But not let on about the pictures.

I began to concoct a plausible tale as I strode out towards Straddling. At last there were signs of spring even though the day was grey and watery, and it lifted my spirit – yellow primroses peeked out beneath the hedgerows among, the first bright green shoots of cow parsley. White blackthorn blossomed occasionally, and the hawthorns had little green jagged leaves. One thing it didn't feel was threatening. I was glad of that.

I turned a sharp corner, and found my way barred by a hurdle crossing the road, the paved lane and main entrance to Straddling Hall. A notice 'No Entry by Order of Meredith & Meredith' swung in the wind. Beyond was the gated road of Straddling Hall; a short driveway leading to a moated manor house, and beyond the moated area, a clumsy group of timber and brick farm buildings.

It had been at some point a working farm, but there was no sign of that now. The fields and yards were un-cared for and sprouting weeds, and there was a distinct absence of animals, fowl or machinery.

Not threatening at all, more unloved, un-cared for. A wasteland. I ducked under the hurdle and walked towards the ruin. It had been burned, but not as thoroughly as I had imagined.

I suppose I had wanted it to be a gothic horror, hunched evilly within its moat, but in reality it was just a pathetic run down shell, the upper storeys protected by a collection of tarpaulins over one range where the fire had done its damage.

I followed the path of tyre tracks that led past the sad building, to and from it to the farm sheds. They were deep but there was no sign of the vehicle that had made them, probably a tractor or something with large wheels and deep tyres.

I went boldly over to the sheds and looked beyond where the fields were scoured of topsoil. So the building project was on its way. It was a large area. There would have been room for a small hamlet here.

I tried to imagine it. It was difficult. The naked earth, although laid out into some sort of plan, didn't mean a great deal to me, although it seemed very regimented.

As no-one called out to me to get out of the place, I turned my attention to the lock of the site office. I knew it was a site office because it had a sign to tell me. It also was the only shed with a window. The lock was old and weak.

Within half a minute I was inside.

On the walls were pinned plans and drawings, some of which made more sense to me than the site itself. On the desk a grubby note pad and an indelible pencil took pride of place over a works schedule. There was a copy of standard building regulations, well thumbed and scribbled over, and a filthy ashtray.

I opened the desk drawer and saw, among the stubs of pencils, old rubbers, paper clips and pins, a bunch of keys on a string, marked "House". I stared at them in disbelief. I took them, slid out of the shed and made my way to the moat.

7

There was a drawbridge, and it was down, so I strode out upon it, up to the main gate. Thankfully, there was no portcullis, no boiling oil or other stinking ordure to greet me, for this was a gentleman's house, and had been modified over the centuries. I passed beneath the vaulted gatehouse, saw the iron gate hanging above me in its slot, and hoped that the chains that held it were good. Once through I was within a cobbled courtyard, surrounded by four distinctly different wings, medieval (the gatehouse wing), Tudor, Georgian and Victorian. It had had a chequered history, obviously.

The grand entrance was in the Georgian wing, directly opposite the gatehouse, a range of basement (vermiculated rustication), piano nobile and attic set either side of a Classical pedimented porch which would have sheltered the arriving visitors. I guessed the long gallery would have been in the Tudor wing, to my left. The cars that Emily described would have parked in the courtyard. About twelve big old ones, she said. There would have been plenty of room for them, and the chauffeurs would no doubt have gone for refreshments in the servants' areas, which would have been, I guessed, either side of the gatehouse.

I climbed the seven steps to the front door. I had the keys.

I knew what I was about to do was illegal, but I wasn't going to steal anything, was I? I was only going to look.

I couldn't have taken a picture, even if I found one. They were far too cumbersome.

I took a look at the lock, and tried what seemed to be a likely key. There was no joy. It didn't even fit. I tried several others, and then one turned in my hand.

I felt a guilty pang of triumph.
I knew I had no right to be here.
But who would know?

I pushed the door open. It was stiff, but moved.
I went into the echoing gloom and shuddered. The air tasted stale, musty, the windows hadn't been cleaned for years. The entrance hall took up the two storeys, in the Palladian manner. It was crumbling, a real case of decaying grandeur, but there was enough here to see that at one point it had been impressive, although not top of the First Division.

I took it all in, black and white tiled floor, faux-marble columns made of wood and cleverly painted, more faux marble on the door surrounds and window frames. All wood, interspersed with ancient damask wall coverings and curtains. This should, by rights have gone up and disappeared completely if there was any sort of fire nearby. I was impressed that it had lasted so long anyway, in an age that heated and lit its houses with naked and unprotected flames. I was also surprised that squatters or vandals hadn't had them away. Perhaps the reputation of the place had kept them at bay.

So where did the fire take place?

I made my way into the first room to my left. It was bereft of furniture, very depressing. The next room was the same, everything bar the fittings had gone. Ditto the third. It seemed to be a dead end, then I saw a door in the wall, for servants' access. It wasn't locked. I went through. I was in a servants' staircase, small and tight compared to the grand ones that circled the walls of the entrance hall. I went up it, on the premise that long galleries were usually on an upper floor, and came to a landing. To my left was a tall door with linen-fold carving. To my right was one of chestnut.

I chose the Tudor option.

Again, it was locked. Again it took me several tries to find the right key. The door finally creaked open, and I went through.

I knew at once that I was in the very room that Emily described the day before. It smelt right. I felt a choking in my chest.

I could see where the ancestor portraits had been. I could see a huge hole in the roof, covered with grey tarpaulin. I was at the business end of the room, I knew that.

But there were no paintings.

A wonderful strap-work ceiling had taken the brunt of the lightning strike, but there was soot and fire damage all the way through this room, particularly at this end, where a large area of the floor had become a blackened-edged hole.

I pictured Emily all those years ago, bleeding and fainting, and it seemed to me that the strike had hit the very spot she would have stood on. I shuddered once more. The house had a very definite atmosphere.

I told myself off for being a fanciful woman. Too much imagination is not a good thing. I checked mine.

Sidled round the hole, keeping to the firmest looking parts of the floors and walls, until I was out of the severely burned area.

At the far end, the door was also locked.

This time I unlocked it on the first attempt and discovered the long corridor, with stag's heads which continued with rooms off both sides round two ranges of the house; when I got past the medieval wing, the stags and roebuck gave way to bigger game from Africa and India; the Victorians had obviously liked the idea. They would!

I continued right round the house until I reached the Georgian rooms on the right of the portico. I continued through the chestnut door, and through more empty rooms. It was clear that anything of any value had gone from here.

I reached the top of the central staircase, and started down. I should have liked to have done the lower floors, explored the whole house, but glancing at my watch I knew

I didn't have time.

Lunch time was almost over.

I made for the big entrance door.

I was turning round, having just locked it behind me when I heard it.

"Hey, you! Who do you think you are, and what the Hell are you doing here?"

A man's voice, strong and angry. And from his accent, he wasn't one of the humble poor.

I faced him, chin up, and gave him the once-over.

He was a big man, with an elderly black and white spaniel on a tight leash, an air-gun in his other hand and a pipe gripped tightly between his teeth. He didn't look friendly. He was stomping towards me fast.

I pocketed the keys, stuffed a handkerchief over them to stop them jingling as I moved, then drew out my OS map. I was glad of that. I was on the steps now, and fluttered the map open.

With far more confidence than I felt, I walked forcefully towards him, holding out my hand, speaking in my fruitiest voice and gushed. "Good afternoon. How do you do? Lady Sarah Carson, née Markham. I was trying to look in. Seems like some disaster struck, doesn't it? Look, I've been away for a while, but I used to come here when I was a small girl, friend of the family, don't you know? I hadn't realized they had all gone. Terrible shame, an old house like this."

By now I'd shaken his hand – he'd actually removed the dog's leash to the gun-hand, which made me feel a lot better – but I didn't give over.

I made for the gatehouse and strode out purposefully, gushing forth all the while in a parody of a member of my own class. It wasn't much, but the best I think of at the time. I hoped he hadn't seen me come through the door, but I think he was as shocked at seeing me as I was at seeing him.

His jaw gaped.

I seized the advantage. "I'm on a walking holiday, don't you see? Damn bad weather for it, but then, it's early in the year." I waved the map in his face. "My uncle, the Colonel, had some business in the area, and left me to roam around, so I thought I'd come and see my old friends. They're not here, are they?"

I glanced at my watch. "Goodness, is that the time? I mustn't keep you. The Colonel will be expecting me." I was under the gatehouse now, out on the drive. The chap was still gawping. I turned and shook his hand firmly, once again. "Well, it's been nice talking to you, Mr er... what was your name?"

He found his tongue. "Crowe. Joshua Crowe," His voice was slow now, and flat.

"Well, Mr. Crowe, I think it's goodbye. You don't know where the Thorburns went, do you? I'd really like to get in touch with Miss Thorburn again."

Mr. Crowe's face set into an even harder mask. "Miss Thorburn? Her!" he spat. "You better ask Mr. Meredith about that one. Mr. Percy Meredith. Lives down at Finchings. He, that is. Personally, I'd keep well away from her. And this place, too. It's unsafe, which is why the signs are up. This place should be out of bounds to all while there's building going on. We don't want people hurt, now, do we?" He looked hard at me. "Now, if you're going back to the village ..."

I peered at my OS map myopically. "Er... Is there a way to Little Straddling across the fields?" I asked. "I seem to remember there was a footpath?" I ducked under the hurdle, and took a pathway through the hedge just outside the gate.

I thanked him and waved goodbye, and skipped off down the path.

Yes, I did.

I wanted to look a real upper class dimwit, just in case I was remembered.

I didn't know who or what Mr. Crowe was, but I was taking no chances.

My friend Beryl's husband? I hoped not. A brother perhaps? Could she have mentioned me over lunch? But I'd said I wasn't coming here. Plus, if he were her brother, he would have very likely spoken with the same local burr, even if he'd had a better education. This chap didn't. He spoke with an accent that said privilege, money in the family. Beryl was totally local.

I put my hand into my pocket for a handkerchief, and found the keys.

Damn! They would be sure to be missed. I should have put them back, but it was too late for that now.

By the time I came out by my car my socks, stockings and my coat were soaking from rain from the plants that grew alongside the path. I looked a mess, but right in character.

I stripped off my disguise, put on my driving shoes and climbed behind the wheel. I headed out of the village. The best place for local history would be in the locality, but I felt I had rattled enough round here. I drove to Ipswich via back lanes, wondering about the links that were building.

Everywhere there seemed to be Merediths and Thorburns. There must be a link between what was happening at Straddling and Finching when Emily was there ten years or so ago, and what was happening to the two houses now, but I needed more background. I also could do with some confirmation on whether what Emily experienced was a frequent occurrence, although from what Beryl had said, I thought it likely.

Not being particularly religiously inclined, occultism held relatively little fascination for me. There was more than enough happening on the physical plane for me to have to go diving into the astral for a bit of light relief. Oh, I believed Emily actually had taken part in some sort of ritual, but how did people get mixed up in that sort of stuff?

Was Leggy getting drawn in as Bobby feared?

I had no idea. From what Emily had told us, it looked like a group that knew about the effect of drugs that would tempt the easily-led and then bind them to them, thus a black group. Where would they have got their followers?

That was easy enough.

My mother's friends, society ladies with no purpose in their lives or too much time on their hands sought things that are just a bit different. Seances were always a popular form of entertainment, my mother said, when we didn't have the wireless, and my Great Aunt Caroline had been interested in such things in the twenties and early thirties.

Finding bored people, inadequate people, inquisitive people, that was easy. Just offer them the promise of secret knowledge, a way of making your life more exciting, the possibility of joining an elite group... and spiritual power – that was the keyword, and every inadequate in the area would be homing in.

Of course, it would have to be kept elite. Which meant you would have to have money to join, and more still to continue.

The poor would be excluded – what could they bring to the project? I figured it was a money-making project. There were those expensive cars in the courtyard, the dramatic and theatrical set up, which would have cost a bit. Your average hard-working family person wouldn't have had the time, let alone the money to have belonged, but quirky singletons, those with a donnish turn of mind, or a taste for theatricals and the bizarre, and a bit of disposable income, even those looking for more than Mother Church in any of her dresses could offer; they would make the time, find the money. Spiritual power, elitism – the biggest draw of all and the most difficult to quantify. It had to be a power-web for those in charge.

And there were the pictures.

What were they doing with them?

Offering blood sacrifice!

I didn't like that at all.

That smacked of Old Testament pacts with Yahweh.

Yahweh! The Old God. The God who was superseded by the Bright new Son of God, Christ.

The old god becomes the devil of the new order. I'd read that somewhere, and it had struck me, even as a teenager, that that was right.

I thought about the pictures. Angels and demons. One and the same. Yet different, oh so different. Never mind about the odd name he was given, Emily's painted angel was a demon. That was how she experienced him.

I shivered. They were invoking and making pacts with demons.

No. I didn't believe that. I couldn't believe that, not in the 20th century. That was all medieval stuff.

But I knew, deep down, it wasn't.

That was precisely what had been going on.

And the pictures were the key.

I wondered if Leggy had already known all this and was at this very moment quietly researching how to call up his own demon.

Perhaps Bobby was right to be nervous.

The librarian in charge of the reference section of Ipswich public library was also the local historian, and an enthusiast. "I've made a study of country houses. So many are going to seed, what with death duties and the cost of upkeep. My predecessor, a Mr. Petts, he started it off, and I kept it going. What houses were you interested in?"

She got me two box-files labeled, Straddling Hall and Finchings and installed me with them at the far end of the room. Other readers steaming gently in their wet clothes ignored me. A few had nodded off over their reading. It was that sort of room, stuffy, not particularly well-lit, and redolent with the sort of breathing that is a result of too heavy a lunch, or perhaps too liquid.

I went carefully through the contents of the Straddling box – a typed up 'short history', an architectural history and study, an inventory and household book of 1834, and another inventory of 1910. That one I went through thoroughly, but it was soporific work, until my eyes kicked my brain into touch. There, in front of me: "Seven pictures of archangels by the late Lawrence Greystoke R.A., dimensions in plain gold frames: 6'6" by 3'6". I punched the air. "Eureka!"

"Hush!" from three readers who hadn't nodded off.

I was wide awake now. I kept that document out, and delved through the other papers – cuttings from newspapers, a drawing in ink, and some old photographs. Right at the bottom of the heap was a small pamphlet entitled "Famous paintings in Suffolk" From the style of the artwork on the cover, I would have said it had been created in the Thirties. I opened it with trepidation. I wanted there to be pictures. And of course there were.

Black and white photographic images.

There was a Hogarth in a big house near Bury St. Edmunds, a couple of Turners with a family Woodbridge, some Pre-Raphaelites in a private collection in Ipswich, a collection of Constable drawings in the Museum, and, "The Straddling Angels".

Yes, here they were! Someone had thought them worth recording. I blessed him – it was probably the librarian's predecessor – for he had documented all seven of them.

I flicked back to the front of the pamphlet. Issued by the Ipswich Local History group, photographs by Hereward Petts, price three shillings and sixpence. He was a very fine photographer, for the detail, even on this scale, was very sharp.

I continued to go through the items on the hall. I wanted anything on the time Emily was there, but I found nothing.

However, I did see a cutting from the local paper about the Hall fire. There was an artist's impression, which was probably over-enthusiastic, since it happened at night, but, the text said the fire brigade was called at once by the people on site, who had already made inroads with water from the moat, so that the damage, bad though it was, was curtailed. Mr. and Mrs. Thorburn had decided to remove to London until they had a chance to assess things.

I frowned.

The war had started by then.

If I were living in quiet rural Suffolk, at this time I wouldn't rush down to London as the safest place on earth.

I shook my head.

I was thinking with hindsight, of course.

I had been nineteen that year. It was 1939. We all expected the war to be over by Christmas. No-one expected the Blitz.

I tidied away all the papers, and started to browse through the other box.

Finchings in the form it is today, was built after the previous house was razed in the 1920s and the land sold to Lord Finching shortly afterwards.

Oddly, another fire, but in this case, arson was suspected, though never proved.

The Finching family had a bit of a local reputation for wizardry, certainly for eccentricity. Lord Finching sold the house and grounds to Messrs. A and P Meredith in 1941, after Lady Finching agreed to live in a nursing home for health reasons. Lord Finching resides in Inverness-shire; his two daughters now live in California.

And a newspaper cutting: Tycoon twins plans for Suffolk Houses, more recent, June 1946. "We'll take two houses and build two thousand" –"Houses for heroes in our own Suffolk countryside."

I read the article then tidied up.

The Librarian looked at the pamphlet, and nodded. "I'm sure we've still got a few copies in the archives," she said, and disappeared for a minute, returning with a toothy smile and a slightly less used copy. "Actually, it's the last one."

I handed over the money. At least now I'd have some idea what I was looking for.

I took the car back around six thirty, then walked the short half mile home. The rain had stopped although the air was still damp, and street lights reflected in puddles. I was glad to be back in my own area, gladder still that, when I closed the front door, I wasn't accosted by George.

Mr. Stephens was playing his music again, but my flat was quiet.

I unlocked my living room door and put on a kettle, then went to change my clothes. More washing, but not a problem as socks and stockings didn't need ironing, and as for underwear... Tantange, whom I must remember to call by her real name, Angelique, would sniff at my slovenliness, but then she had a permanent Gallic sniff. She and my mother had signed up for the Red Cross when they were supposed to be studying in Paris in World War One. Angelique was Maman's personal maid and best friend. When Maman fell for Pa (and vice versa) in 1916, Angelique fell for the chap in the next bed, who became Pa's chauffeur and made an honest woman of her as soon as hostilities ceased. She had continued as Maman's maid, but was in fact a much loved family member, and when we were children was our honorary Aunt, just as her husband (now deceased) was Uncle Martin. Thinking of her, I remembered to hang out my Dress to give it a good air. I wasn't about to get it cleaned for the occasion, as there wasn't time for the awful smell of dry-cleaning to disappear before Saturday. Besides, it was far too good to be handed over to the local dry cleaners.

I put on my pyjamas and a dressing gown, and went back into the living room, lit the gas-fire and tuned in my Great

Aunt's elderly radio. She had never being one for throwing things out if they could still work. I found a programme playing lively music, not that old dreary stuff that Mr. Stephens listened to, and turned it up high. Then I made tea and chopped up a mixture of old vegetables into some Oxo stock and put them on to simmer thickened up with red lentils and some rice. I'd pretend there was meat in it. A little wine wouldn't have gone amiss. There had always been wine in France. I missed that. In cooking as much as in drinking. Here in Britain it was unheard of, except in little specialized i.e. wealthy, pockets. My French side wasn't that impressed.

While the food was cooking I brought Hereward Petts's pamphlet out. I had a copy of the originals. I'd need a good magnifying glass to go through the pictures properly, and an angle-poise. The names of Finching, Meredith and Thorburn kept going through my head. I'd still not asked Leggy who called them out to collect the painting in the first place. I went to my phone now.

I got Bobby. "Leggy's soaking in the bath, Milady. Do you want me to get him out? He's been doing drumming up business with his friends today, he tells me, and the socializing's done him in, poor old chap. I can get him to ring you back, or perhaps I could help you?"

I asked my question. Bobby asked me to hold for a moment. "It was a solicitor, according to the book – I just checked. He didn't give a name, but said it was part of the estate of a Mr. Thorburn. I think he owned the house but had recently died. Is that all?"

"He only wanted the studio cleared?"

"Yes. I told you before. Just the studio. He gave Leggy the cash for the job while I was getting the boys together. I never saw the man."

"That's perfect," I said. So here we are again. "Thank you, Bobby."

"You're welcome. Oh, by the way, I have your nylons here. Shall I bring them across to you? Ten pairs, a couple of quid."

"You're an angel, but I'll call in for them tomorrow. I'm busy tonight. Look after Leggy, eh? Tell him from me he shouldn't be overdoing it."

"Sure I will. He'll like that. See you tomorrow, Milady. Have a roistering evening! I'm jealous of your escort. You can tell him that, too. Bye now."

I'd just hooked the phone off when it rang again. A gentle rather wavering voice asked for me, and introduced himself as the Reverend Simmons, St Michael and All Angels. I thanked him for calling back so promptly, but he assured me it was no trouble. "I can see you around three in the afternoon, on Saturday," he said. "Could you give me any idea what it is about?"

I told him I was researching on the life and paintings of Lawrence Greystoke, and any background he could give me on that – through parish records, for instance, would be very useful.

"Ah, then you will be most welcome. You'll take tea with me?"

"I'd like that very much, thank you, Reverend Simmons."

I took the complete address of the Vicarage from him, although as he said, you can't miss the church; it's at the centre of the town. I knew the little town and could visualize the church, a pretty 15th century one, with a tower and a surrounding churchyard bounded by the old yews.

I thought I should recognize the adjacent house, but I obviously hadn't taken as much notice as I had vainly thought. It was, after all, a little market town, like many others. My family lived up on the chalk beyond the confines of such places. We owned some of them. Several villages, in fact and a cluster of farms. And, I hasten to add, we were not bad landlords. We ploughed back. Or so my father told me. It was part of the deal for him. And we almost always shopped locally – except for Mother's clothes, which latterly she and Angelique had created of reclaimed or cheap material, but always from French patterns. For the pair of them, when it came to fashion, only France would do. Before the war they had nailed their colours to Madame Coco Chanel. But Madame Coco had blotted her copybook by siding with the enemy and had taken herself off to Switzerland latterly, and Maman and Angelique had declared themselves ready to change allegiance when we last spoke about fashion. I currently had the Dior atelier as front runner – he'd just brought out his New Look.

I was eating my second bowl of Oxo soup when the phone rang.

It was my brother Guy. He who was getting married to the Sylvia Nesmith-Brown at Caxton Hall with a blessing at her family's local church, St. Mary's, Marsham in June. He was a twerp, and a snob to boot, and never rang me from one year's end to the next, given the choice.

I turned the radio down. "Hello, Guy," I said (pronouncing it the French way, like Mother did, not the English way as he did). "How are you doing, old man? Is there something wrong?"

"No, Alice, of course not. Why should there be?"

"Well, I don't usually get a call. You must want something."

There was a silence.

Then "Ah! One of your jokes. Not funny. Still, what I was ringing for was … well, Mummy said you'd be down this weekend. Is that right?"

"Oh yes, best bib and tucker. I shall be wearing my one really good dress."

"Good, good," he said.

Another silence.

"Look, Alice, I'm bringing someone high-powered down. I've got something lined up. Don't let me down, will you? It could do us all a lot of good."

"Care to elaborate?" I asked, spooning in another mouthful. "An inkling would be good."

"No, it's better as a surprise. Sylvia and her family think it's a really good idea, and so do I. I think you'll like it too. It's time we made our own fortunes, don't you know?"

"I'm paying my way," I said drily.

"Oh you're not working in that Auction Rooms again, are you? I'm so embarrassed by a sister working for pin-money. The parents could give you an allowance until you've met the right man."

I bit my tongue, or I would have blown him away with a tirade of Franco-English curses. "Hey, the last little contretemps we had with Fritz appears to have put paid to my marital prospects, Guy," I told him. "Besides I like living on my own and making my own decisions. I won't ask the Aged P's to keep me in perpetuity."

"Then do charity work. You do see my position, don't you? When Pa kicks the bucket I'll be a Lord. Can't have my sister in trade. Get into some nice charity work, Alice. You'll meet a good sort of person there, on committees, and get back into society again…"

I cut him short. "Guy, I will behave as properly as I can on Saturday night. Not for your sake, but for the Aged Ps'. I have not asked you to live my life nor have I told you how to live yours. I hope you and Sylvia are very happy and will stay that way, but that's the best I can offer. I am myself. I make my own decisions, and no-one tells me what to do. Understood? Now go and tell your fiancée that you've spoken to me, as she told you to. Nighty-night, Guy."

He was a clot. His brother, my favourite, Gilles (pronounced the French way in the family, the English way at school) was worth a million of Guy, but like Raoul, was no more. He'd perished early on, flying missions over the North Sea. I missed him tremendously at first, but c'est la guerre. Guy had managed to avoid going overseas, having spent most of the war in the bunker under Whitehall, in strategic planning. I think he was a glorified office boy, but it had kept him safe. He was the first-born, the heir, and fully intended to take over the title that father used so lightly, and wring every ounce of power from it.

My meal had lost its heat and its savour. I put it aside for the pig-bin tomorrow morning, and went back to the radio, but it was someone talking about God. I turned it off, wondering vaguely who and what Guy was up to, and ran the bath.

8

Friday morning I got out my bike again. It was just a boring old sit-up-and-beg ladies' frame with a colourful skirt-guard on the back wheel and a wicker basket on the front. I gave it a clean, oiled it, pumped up its tyres, tested the brakes, did all the things to make it feel good, then took it out for a spin.

It was grey, but not wet. Well, not yet. So I went down Drayton Gardens, towards Gloucester Road and then down the back doubles until I came to the Boltons.

I was delighted with it, for I'd not seen it before.

It was a beautiful place to live. An oval of grand houses, built sometime in the middle of the last century, situated round a green garden space in the centre, with a church. The London planes were just coming into leaf, and daffodils and polyanthus beginning to peek out brightly in the front gardens. I cycled the circuit twice, for the sheer visual joy of the place. Then I went to number 35.

It was a tall house, three storeys and an attic, in a mixture of styles.

The original plan must have been Italianate, but later a jobbing builder had come and added Gothic bits, including a porch, a pointed roof-line, and probably at the same time, because it was in the same brick, a studio at the back. However, the whole place could have used a lick of paint; the windows were grubby, with their blackout curtains down and the front garden weedy and overgrown. It looked 'shut'.

A postman came whistling down the road, delivering a sheaf of letters to 34, and then shoving a small wad of envelopes into the letter-box of 35. He caught my eye as he came back down the small garden path. "Nice day for a ride.

You lookin' for somethin' partic'lar?"

"Old school-friend used to live there," I said. "Thought I'd look her up. She must have moved."

"Yeah, people do. No-one's there now. Old bloke died a few weeks ago. His daughter's only just come back from America to take the place over, so the word is. You know 'em well?"

"Only at school," I said.

"She's done well for 'erself, though." The postman pulled out a half-smoked roll-up from behind his ear and lit it with a Swan Vesta. He drew on the squashed yellow-tipped stub meditatively. "She's got 'erself engaged to some big building contractor. Was in all the papers. Dunno where she's living now. Thought she'd be in here, by now. Someone must call in from time to time, cos the letters still go through the box and they're addressed to 'er or the old man." He gazed up at the house thoughtfully. "Bet there's some nice stuff in there, though. Saw some stuff coming out a week or so ago, but not a lot. Must be a load more left in there that she'd want to change, wealthy woman like her." He shouldered his sack and went on with his delivery.

I got back on my bike. I had some nylons to collect. Then I'd check the electoral register at the Town Hall, and then I had to pack.

I always enjoyed the train out to Buckinghamshire, and today was no exception. At the station I took a taxi home, out into the chalk hills.

I got scolded for not ringing for a car, but as a first homecoming, after several months away – I'd last been here at Christmas and we were already past Easter – it was good. My mother agreed that I did look better for my stay with her family in Provence.

"Did you see your friends? Any chance of…?" she asked as she followed me into my old bedroom.

"No, Maman. I cannot make you a mother-in-law or a

grandmother in the foreseeable future. But I'll get over it, and so will you."

I gave her a huge hug and her present, a box of sweets, but what sweets! I had paid dear for them, and they were beautifully presented. Not having a particularly sweet tooth myself, it hadn't been a problem keeping them wrapped and intact.

My little mother – she was 5'2" ("and a half!" she always insisted, but that was with shoes on) – crooned with delight. "You shouldn't have, Alice, but I'm so glad you did. How I have missed *calissons* and *nougat*. And you've brought me both, and both sorts of nougat, and some fruits d'Apt."

Yes, all the local specialties. It was worth every sou to see her delight. "You can open them," I told her. "They're yours."

"Oh, but they are so beautiful as they are. I shall feast with the eyes first."

"Don't hand them round tomorrow," I warned nastily. "If these people are that high-powered, they can buy their own."

"Oh, these are strictly *en famille*. And even just for your father, you and me. And Angelique and the Macs, course. I don't want to waste them on Guy. I don't know how he does it on rationing, but he's putting on weight." She sighed. "It's always rather a shock when your children start to look middle-aged."

"And his fiancée?" I asked. "Do you have much to do with her?"

Maman sniffed. "Enough. I can't honestly say that I warm to her, somehow, but she is Guy's choice. I'm grateful that he's found someone at last. I'm having a difficult time catering for this do he's arranged for tomorrow. I mean, you want to do the boy proud, but food is so scarce these days. And Basil and Madeleine are coming down too. You'll be able to see little Enid, won't that be nice!"

I chuckled. It would be, but better still to see my little sister. "Will you share the sweets with Maddy?" I asked. "After all she's making you a grandmother for the second time."

Maman nodded. "She deserves a share, but she's only going to get one to start with. She's been suffering terribly with this pregnancy, and can't keep anything down. It usually stops after three months, but not with poor Maddy. I do worry for her. Basil's very good to her, though, and she has the best medical attention. She wasn't like this with little Enid. They'll be down tomorrow morning. How long are you staying, dear?"

"I've got to be back in town on Sunday night."

"Good. I'll let Mrs. Mac know you'll be staying for lunch then. And she'll get a parcel ready for you to take back. I don't know, we fought a war for better conditions and we're still having to use ration books. Good job we live on the land."

"Off the land," I corrected, without thinking.

My mother sniffed – she and Angelique shared this ability. "As pedantic as ever, Alice. Now, let's see the Dress. Angelique will do your hair if you wish, and help you get ready tomorrow. She said to send you her love, but she's busy today sorting out the fitting of a wedding dress down at Wethersley. A rush job!"

I didn't ask for whom. "I'd like that," I said. "What's it all in aid of? Do you know who are coming?"

"It's a secret. I think perhaps Guy may have got things right this time. I do hope so."

That was all I got out of her. Apart from approval on the Dress. One she and Father had bought me before the war, from Chanel.

I took tea with my parents, and the tray down to the kitchen to talk to the friends of my childhood, Mrs. McMurdy the Cook/Housekeeper, and Mr. McMurdy, the Butler who did lots of other things. There were others, too, but these were the mainstay, my alternative parents so to speak, and I got an extra biscuit and cup of tea while we briefly chatted ourselves up to date and I shared out presents – a bottle of good claret for Mr. Mac, and some perfume – she liked *Femme* – for Mrs. Mac, and a string of garlic which I do believe pleased them both more. They would use some, sprout some and plant some, they said, totally delighted. Onions had been very scarce this year.

I asked them what was happening tomorrow night. They knew that there would be twelve at table, and it would be formal, "We're bringing in extra staff," Mr. McMurdy told me, but who the mystery guests were, they hadn't been told.

"Mr. Guy said it would be a secret, and we'd all do very well out of it," Mrs. Mac said, rolling out pastry. Her faint Scottish accent told me she didn't believe a single word.

"He told me that," I said. "I'd like a hint. I know Guy's get-rich-quick schemes. They always backfire."

"Ah," said Mr. Mac, "then we must pray that working in a finance house in London and having a new fiancée has strengthened his mind and his business acumen a little – you never heard me say that, Miss Alice."

"What was that?" I asked brightly. "Could swear I didn't hear something. No matter."

I spent the last of the afternoon wandering through my past. I visited the flower beds, the walled kitchen garden that had kept us all going throughout the war; both looked bare for the time of year although there were signs of recent visits and some new growth – the winter had been unusually severe and even the walled garden was somewhat exposed. By now we would normally have had a lot more spring promise, but I'd have said from the soil and the lack of growth that it was February, not April. Likewise the poultry yard and rabbit hutches. There were no small fluffy chicks around; there was nothing much for the hens to scratch, and greens to feed rabbits were in as short a supply as greens to feed humans. It had been a hard winter and a slow spring.

I went down off the chalk into the valley and the beechwood beyond, through the cathedral grey trunks, and the lack of undergrowth beneath. Shafts of late sunlight poured between white clouds and pale blue sky above, through the pattern of twigs and branches. I longed for the fresh green of new leaf; perhaps in a week or two? No matter, I was glad to be back. I walked through the wood, came out the other side, into the fields beyond. Further on still was Home Farm at the edge of the village of Wethersley, whence my father's appellation, and the water meadows round the little river that meandered through the clay valley, the tower of St George's church, and a cluster of tiled roofs or thatched cottages that housed its congregation. I was very aware of how lucky I was to have been born into all this. I loved France, but this was the place I would willingly die for. This was my place.

I walked and walked, turning over the week's events in my mind, wondering how it would all end. Then suddenly I was aware of the chill in the air, now that the sun had gone below the flanking hill, leaving the sky aflame. I turned on my heel and headed uphill.

I took supper with my parents. We ate a suet roly-poly stuffed with shredded bacon and leeks, Golden syrup and pepper. Mrs. Mac always managed to make it light, and offered really good gravy with it, and today some of last year's runner beans that had been salted down.. My mother's sweet tooth and my father's taste for good rib-sticking stuff were both satisfied. We drank water with it. My parents tended to be social drinkers. Tomorrow they'd push the boat out, but tonight was good plain fare.

"How's the sleuthing coming?" my father asked.

"Sleuthing?" Maman looked at her husband. "Our daughter isn't getting involved with the police, surely?"

I shook my head. "I'm doing a bit of work for Leggy. He sends his best wishes by the way. I'm trying to find some paintings for him."

"Oh, that's all right then. That won't be dangerous. I did worry so much about you, you know..."

"I know, and I appreciate your care, but you shouldn't, you know." I forked in the final piece of bacon roll with relish.

"No, I know, but when you are a mother, you'll understand."

My father gave me a look over his glasses that said it all.

"I shall be going to see someone in connection with this little job tomorrow afternoon," I said. "Could I borrow the car? Or a push bike would do just as well. If you are short of petrol."

"Of course you can borrow the car," my father said.

"We might need it, for Madeleine..." my mother put in.

"If Madeleine needs to be taken to town for any reason, Basil can take her. He's her husband, and got her this way, after all. It's his responsibility!"

My father didn't believe in women being poorly, especially when they were pregnant, because Maman had never had a moment's trouble. It was part of the grand scheme of things, and if a woman couldn't pull herself through, well, it was a damn bad show. The fact that women died in childbed was completely lost on him. His woman hadn't and if she could pull through, tiny as she was, then why couldn't everyone else? They were just malingerers, even his youngest daughter.

It was my mother's turn to give me a look from under her Coco fringe.

"So I'll borrow the car from a quarter to three until around six," I said.

"Oh, do get back before that. Angelique will need a bit

of time to do your hair."

"Why can't Alice do her own hair? She looks very pretty tonight, and she didn't have Angelique fussing over her."

"It's a quite different situation, Roger," said Maman, stroking his hand. "You will wear your dinner suit and white tie. Yes, the whole thing. I've had it cleaned, and the shirt is starched. You will look splendid. You always do. Very impressive. You have such a fine height and profile. It is a very important occasion."

"Then why won't you tell me who's coming? Do you know? Am I to be dressed up like a penguin for strangers?"

"It is a dinner for Guy to introduce us his business colleagues. It is very important to him. Of course, Sylvia and her family will be along as well."

My father groaned. "Sylvia's family! We don't need to be introduced to them. We already know them. Unfortunately."

I allowed myself to chuckle.

Mother's mouth went down at the corners. "You will be polite, the pair of you," she said. "And you will both be in your best clothes."

My father's nose wrinkled. "Oh now, Chérie, not for Bulgy Algy. I don't have to dress up like a penguin for Bulgy Algy." He looked plaintive, then began to chuckle.

"What's so funny, chéri?" snapped Maman suspiciously. "And you must not call him that. It's not nice!"

My father twinkled. "But it is exact. He looks like a walrus! And has the same table manners. I can accept the girl, if she truly is Guy's choice, although she's no great catch, but the family?" He looked at Maman like a whipped hound. "Do I really have to?"

"Of course, my dear. You will look so much more handsome and cultured in comparison. I've invited them because Guy asked me. He wants to suggest a business deal. It might be advantageous to us all. You know how much our finances have suffered the last few years." She dared with us to disagree.

We couldn't.

"Maman," I said slowly. "Who have you brought in to make up the numbers?"

"I don't know what you mean, Alice." Her chin went up, and her face was a mask.

"Oh yes, you do. Mrs. Mac says there will be twelve at table. Which totally inept eligible male have I been partnered with?" my voice was dangerously low. I didn't know Sylvia's family, but there was a son, Nigel, of whom I'd heard poor reports: village gossip is cruel.

"Basil is bringing a friend along from the Foreign Office." My mother glared at me. "Well Nigel's not available at the moment, so I asked Maddy. She said Basil has this young man working for him, who's a good sort, so I invited him. And I'm warning you, Alice, to be nice."

I groaned.

"Well, you could have brought your own partner. Beggars can't be choosers."

"You wouldn't approve of my friends," I sighed theatrically. "I'm sorry I'm such a trial, Maman. I don't mean to be."

Madeleine's party arrived at half past eleven the following morning. Basil was with her, of course, and Enid and her nursemaid, and the unfortunate chap destined to be my partner for the weekend. I wasn't impressed on principle but he had his own teeth and hair, and the right number of fingers. Hopefully the toes matched. However, it was lovely to see my little sister again and my niece, who was now a noisy two-year-old, into everything. My mother soon took her with the nursemaid up to the old nursery, while Basil and his protégé, Jeremy Arkwright, disappeared with my father to the games room.

Madeleine looked tired, a shadow of her usual self, while the bump sat uneasily under her smock. "Never have babies, Al," she said, heaving herself into the settee and kicking off her shoes. "Enid wasn't too bad, but this one's the very devil. I can't wait for it to show its face so I can smack it."

"That bad, eh? A drink?"

"Is Bas out of the way? If so, I'll have a brandy and soda. It settles my stomach. Not that you'd notice. He thinks all I should worry about is the bloody bump, and keeps forcing me to drink milk. I hate milk! Er, you might pour me a half glass in case he comes back, but what I really need is something to make me feel good."

I fetched her drink, a good slug of Pa's brandy but with lots of soda.

She purred. "You look a lot better than when I last saw you. How's Raoul?"

"Dead," I said. "It's a bugger, but more of a bugger for him."

I poured the last of the milk from the coffee tray into a tumbler for her. "Not a good year so far for the Chamberlain girls."

"It'll pass," she said, patting my hand.

"I know. It doesn't hurt now. And you will have a new baby to care for."

"That'll be three."

"Twins?" Not in our family.

"No, Bas is the biggest kid of the lot. He looks so terribly manly, and he's even in line for a posting abroad, yet he's such a child."

"My little sister all grown-up! The diplomat's wife."

"My big sister, the ... what are you up to now?"

"I'm working for Leggy – in a private capacity – trying to locate some missing pictures. Pa calls me the Sleuth!"

She chortled. "Does Guy know? He'd be seriously peeved!"

I shook my head.

She was serious again, "Pictures? Leggy? I trust he's paying you for it."

"Oh yes. But to be honest, I was at a loose end anyway. I'm off to meet a contact this very afternoon."

"Ah, that's a shame. I wanted you to get to know Jeremy a bit."

"The chap you have so generously dealt me? I need that like a hole in the head, Maddy!"

"C'mon, Al, this isn't about you being landed with a sad fish – there's a deal involved."

"Oh yeah? Don't patronize me just because you are Mrs Diplomat!"

"Shut up and listen for a moment, will you? Thank you. Here's the deal. One, he's personable, and needs an entry into society. Two, you have the intro, but don't have a partner. No, no, stop getting all hot under the collar. You have nothing to fear from Jeremy, who is an absolute gentleman – although his birth is not – and everything to fear from the sort of partners Maman will fix you up with."

I had to admit she had a point.

I smiled, and she continued. "He's a good egg, Alice, although in his cups can be a bit waspish. He's brilliant fun, when he's on his own, and more to the point, he can dance. Like an angel, but this is strictly between you and me. As you know, Bas has two left feet when it comes to the ballroom."

I chuckled. That was the only negative in her marriage. She was prepared to turn a blind eye to it, but we were a family who danced from day one, even staid Guy could trip the light fantastic if he needed to do so.

Maddy continued. "Basil has a lot of time for the man, and wants to ensure that when we get posted abroad – and that is on the cards – Jeremy will accompany us. But he needs a bit of polishing. He's good on the theory, but drawing room practice is what he needs. Bas trusts him implicitly, and says he's far sounder on the work front than anyone else in the office. So, will you be nice to our protégé and give him a bit of polish?"

"Maman has already told me I have to be." I assured her.

She gurgled. "And you always obeyed her! Oh yes."

"For this weekend, I will be polite and nice. That's all I can offer." I smiled at her, "And I am truly grateful that you've brought me this paragon of virtue to ensure that lesser mortals stay at more than arm's length. As Maman says, one must have standards!"

I heard my father's voice rising from the games room in the basement. The men were coming to join us.

I took the empty brandy glass from Maddy, and handed her the milk, which she sipped daintily, looking the picture of innocence when they walked in.

"Ah, helped yourselves, I see," said my father, at the drinks table, "Well, gentlemen, what will you have?"

9

I knocked on the Vicarage door as the church clock was striking three. The door was opened by a tall man wrapped in a belted mackintosh and a trilby hat, followed by the Reverend Simmons himself.

"Ah, Miss Chamberlain," he greeted, holding out an aged lined veined hand to me, "do come in. This is my foster-grandson, Sam, and he's just leaving. Off you go, Sam, and I'll see you again this evening. Shoo, shoo!" He pushed the man out onto the path, before he could do more than tip his hat at me, then took my arm and brought me into his sitting room.

It was a Georgian room, and the proportions were serene. He had a bright fire in the hearth, but the smell of woodsmoke was overpowered by the scent of the blue hyacinths that he had growing in a bowl on an elegant mahogany table in the window. The whole room was full of light and serenity, as much due to the restrained colour and furnishings as to Reverend Simmons' beaming smile and gentle attitude.

He was old, past seventy, I'd say, slightly stooped, with an aureole of white hair, a cross between a tonsure and a dandelion clock, and the most lively and kindly blue eyes I had seen for many a long day.

"I didn't want you to send your family away for my sake," I said, shaking his hand and sitting down in an armchair by the fire, opposite him.

"Nor did you make me do it. Sam was just leaving. He's a reporter. It seems there is a story on offer for him. Now in what way can I help you?"

I told him that I was searching for Mr. Greystoke's lost Angel pictures, so anything at all upon the Greystoke family or the Meredith family would be of interest to me. If I could have a look in the parish registers, that would be useful, too. "Although," I said, "I don't know whether I will find anything that could lead me to the other pictures. It's just background at the moment."

The Rev. Simmons looked straight at me.

Into the eyes. I felt he was reading my soul. It was very uncomfortable.

Finally, he sighed. "It was all so long ago," he said. "I don't suppose it will matter now. I don't like to speak ill of the dead, so I'll do my best not to, Miss Chamberlain. I knew the Greystoke family very well. I was a young curate here when the 'disappearance' took place. What do you want to know?"

He told me that he came here directly after his university degree – "My family is local anyway, so when this place came up I was delighted to take it – it was a large congregation in those days, and as a curate I was needed to spell the incumbent, but also, with my education, I took on teaching the Classics to various boys of good family in the area, one of whom was Lawrence Greystoke's youngest son, Arthur. He was a nice young lad, very bright. His mother, Mrs Greystoke, asked me. They had moved down here from London, shortly before I took on my position, so we were all new together. She was a very active lady, and wanted the best for her sons. She wanted Arthur to go to university like his brothers, which meant he needed the Classics, and she paid me for my trouble, although I would have done it for nothing. Arthur was a lovely child, bright as a button with a sort of purity about him. You find that in children sometimes, and when you do, you nurture it."

He paused for a while, eyes unfocussed, remembering. I let him be.

The peaceful smile that had played on his lips disappeared. "Mr. Greystoke was an artist, and when I first met him a regular member of the congregation. Mrs. Greystoke always came along, and was very much a charity lady. She and Mr. Meredith were always getting involved in good works. Mr. Meredith was Mr. Greystoke's best friend, so it was said. Popular rumour would have it that he was the reason for the Greystokes arrival in the area. You can make up your own mind on that, Miss Chamberlain."

A log dropped out of the fire, and he bent and replaced it using the fire-tongs, then turned to me once more. "Mr. Meredith, then…" he took a deep breath, and after some reflection, began. "He was a self-made man – was involved in many businesses, particularly the railway and in building – he had a brickworks, I seem to remember. A finger in every pie sort of chap. He had one daughter, a sickly young woman, Florence, called after her mother, who had died some time before I turned up at the church, and he was reputed to be interested in the para-normal. There were stories going about, but I won't repeat them, as it's mostly servants' gossip, and believe me, no-one can gossip like Buckinghamshire servants!

"No, his name was linked with some 'accidents' – nothing was ever proved, you understand. It was all hushed up, whatever it was, sometimes with an extra unavoidable mishap that proved to be fatal. It was no wonder that he was anxious to be seen to be doing good."

He smiled at me. "Forgive me, that was uncharitable." I nodded my forgiveness, "Or possibly just observant," I said, and let him continue. "This is just so you know the background," he said.

"Now at some time just before the turn of the century, I think it was in the late spring of 1899, Mr. Greystoke began talking of angels. Arthur told me, but of course, I knew already because he'd been talking to the Vicar. My boss was a great one at socializing, and went everywhere. It seems that Mr. Greystoke and Mr. Meredith had been reading about angels – and Mr. Greystoke wanted to contact them. Their energies, you understand. Well, my boss, he was always one for the main chance. 'Why don't you do me a series for the church?' he suggested. 'Seven, one for each day of the week. You'll contact the forces right enough, simply by putting the work in. And of course, every time you came into church you'd reconnect with them.' Mr. Greystoke seemed to like the idea. He actually produced us seven sketches. But then, as you know, he didn't stay around to finish the final paintings."

I opened my mouth, closed it again, and then said, "You don't happen to have the sketches still?"

"Of course we do. Did you ever hear of the church throwing anything away? Come across with me, and I'll show you."

Days of the week? I supposed there were angels for them, but I never knew them. My mother might know, or Bobby – they both had Catholicism drummed into them. All I knew were the gods and planets: Sun, Moon, Tiw/Mars, Woden/Mercury, Thor/Jove, Freya/Venus, Saturn.

We were striding across to the church, up the damp path through a graveyard bright with daffodils. "Why not the traditional archangels?" I asked.

"Who knows who they are? Even then people had only heard of Gabriel, Raphael and Michael. Perhaps Mr. Greystoke wanted a bigger arena to play in. My old boss was a crafty cove, too. The Church is St Michael and all Angels. He wouldn't accept three when he could get seven."

I chuckled. "Very canny," I said.

"Oh yes. And the days are linked to the pagan gods, of course. Our old vicar was a great one at trying to show people that Christianity was foreshadowed by paganism, you know, like the Old Testament implying what happened in the New Testament before it happened. It was quite the thing then."

He took me through the body of the church and unlocked the vestry. There he undid the locked chest in the corner, opened a flap and pulled out a drawer. "We'll take them back with us," he said, tucking a large shagreen folder under his arm. "Do you want to look at the register while you're here?"

I discovered that Mr. Greystoke moved into the area with his wife and three sons when his last son, Arthur was three. His friend, Mr. Meredith, newly widowed, and left with a twelve year old daughter, at that time, had a large house at the edge of the town. Mr. Greystoke moved into a slightly smaller house close by. I was poring over the registers when another familiar name cropped up.

"What do you know about the Thorburns?" I asked.

Reverend Simmons, who had been packing items away, looked up with a frown. "Thorburns? Old Manny Thorburn was Mr. Meredith's business partner at one time. Had a son, George. Bit of a strange chap, so I heard. Married a foreign woman but that was long after. A German. The old man wanted nothing to do with her. Said she was the very devil and meant it. Not a nice thing to say about your prospective daughter-in-law. Mind, he didn't last much longer after that. Not that there was anything unusual in his death. If he had the chance to over-indulge or under-indulge himself, he would always choose the former option. But the two youngsters, George and his German wife, they upped and left. Bought a place in East Anglia. They were great friends with the Greystoke's oldest boy, and Meredith's daughter Florence, for a while at least."

"The eldest Greystoke boy," I said, "Didn't he marry Florence?"

"That's right. It's down there in the register. William Meredith Anderson (that was his mother's name) Greystoke and Florence Emily Meredith. And if you look the following year, you'll find them mentioned again. Births and deaths

– Florence Emily dies in childbirth. The twins survive. Archibald and Percival."

"So the Meredith twins never took their father's name?"

"I think that was part of the deal, when William inherited the business, the house, Florence and the Meredith fortune. He seemed happy enough to lose the Greystoke on his sons. Besides, his mother was a Meredith too. She didn't marry him here, because there would have been an outcry. Although the inquest put Mr. Greystoke down as 'missing, presumed dead' there would have had to be a seven year wait, and Mr. Meredith was not getting any younger. No, they went over to America, got it annulled and themselves married there. It wasn't totally approved of locally of course, but you can't please everyone all the time. And when they re-established themselves as local philanthropists, well, money has a way of smoothing things out.

"The two oldest sons were away at school, and Arthur came and stayed with us at the Vicarage. After his father's death he was more at home here than at the Big House."

"Why was that?" I asked.

"I think you'd have to ask him that."

"You know where he is? He's still alive?"

"Oh yes. I'd have to ask his permission to let you get in touch with him, but he's the chap to help you with the paintings."

We went back to the Vicarage and I opened the shagreen folder. Inside were seven squared up drawings, beautifully executed in ink and pale colour washes, of angels. They were obviously allied to the planets, with, as Reverend Simmons pointed out, all the proper symbolism.

"But the one I saw – I have a sketch of it here," I opened my bag and passed across my sketch of Leggy's painting "has what looks like Hebrew writing on it. So do these others, which I haven't seen apart from in these prints." I handed the pamphlet across. He ignored those for the present.

"Indeed?" Reverend Simmons took out his reading spectacles and perched them on his nose. "That's it there?" he asked, pointing to the page opposite my drawing.

I nodded.

He looked at it and then nodded. "That's interesting."

"What does it say?" I asked. "Can you read it?"

"Oh yes. It's the God-name and angelic name of the sphere of Mars, Tuesday. The sphere of Geburah."

"What's that?" I asked.

"It's Cabbala, which is what I suspect is at the bottom of these pictures."

"What's a Cabbala?" I asked. I'd heard of cabals, secret groups, powers behind the throne type of thing, but had never heard the word cabbala before.

"My dear Miss Chamberlain, it would take me far too long to explain. Suffice it to say that it is part Jewish Mysticism, part of the Western Mystery Tradition, and is studied by those who are interested in the Mysteries. The Bible, both Old and New Testaments are full of it, so it has a very long provenance. You may know that at the turn of the century there was a lot of interest in Ceremonial Magic?"

I shook my head.

"Ah, well, take it from me there was, and it's continued to this day. Under wraps of course. I think that these paintings may have something to do with it, too. But don't ask me what, as I have only ever worked within the confines of the Church of England."

"Yet you can read Hebrew letters?" I said.

"Oh, I love the Mysteries. But I'm an armchair occultist. Tackling the devil within is my sphere of action, not raising him."

"Do you mind if I draw copies of these pictures?" I asked.

"Not at all. We could compare them with those you have in that pamphlet. I think that would be most edifying."

He moved across the room to a desk lit by a directional lamp. We spent a joyous half hour comparing and contrasting.

"Well," he said at last. "I honestly never thought he had done the pictures, but I believe he must have. Mr. Greystoke, sir, I have wronged you."

"The differences are mostly in detail," I said. He nodded. "Give me a copy of the Hebrew on those paintings. I'll translate it for you. Oh, Miss Chamberlain, this is so exciting. Might I possibly have a view of the one you have seen? It would be such a privilege."

"I'll do my best to arrange it, sir," I said, and meant it. As an older person, he appeared very spry. I didn't think the journey to Leggy's would seriously tax him.

By the time I was back in the car, I knew that oldest son, William had scooped the board of goodies, second son, Henry had become a man-about-town, living off his inheritance, his gambling skills and his friends, that Archibald and Percival were brought up by their grandparents, after Florence's death, and William didn't remarry. Arthur stayed with Mr. and Mrs. Meredith, but wasn't happy. He was almost always to be found at the Vicarage, and Reverend Simmons took on the job of teaching him, rather than sending him away to school.

The Merediths were happy with this arrangement, as it got him out of their way and saved considerably on school fees. They were seen to be doing both well and good, being noted for lavish spending on goodly works. And then suddenly, they were caught up in an accident. The car they were driving blew up. Luckily, no-one else was hurt, as the road was empty and Mr. Meredith eschewed the services of a chauffeur. A local shepherd found them, past help, up on the downs. The inquest recorded 'accidental death'. This was 1908. Arthur said he wanted the paintings sold. Henry said they shouldn't be, but William was more than willing. And then it got muddy.

William took them down to London. They were sold, but William was never seen again.

Henry reckoned William ran off with the cash and the paintings – I told Reverend Simmons if Henry had done his homework, he would have found out that he was wrong there – and vented his anger on Arthur. Henry was a hot-headed poisonous individual it seemed to me, and when he'd finished nearly killing his brother, headed for France where he lived for some time, building a reputation as a gambler and a seducer of women. Arthur took some time to recover from his beating and during that time was cared for at the Vicarage. It came as no surprise when he decided to take holy orders, and went out to work in New Zealand.

10

I drove back to Wethersley with plenty to think about, and was only really brought back to the real world by seeing a Bentley and a Humber Super Snipe in the carriage circle in front of the house. The sun was already low.

I parked the Citroen in the garage and set off at a gallop, to make my apologies to Angelique before it was too late. She looked up from pinning a paper dress pattern onto a piece of fabric that I recognized as a curtain. I got the glorious hug, the double *bise* and a nod at the apology. Then she sniffed, said she would be with me in a quarter of an hour and replaced the pins between her tightened lips and got back to her work.

I was ready for her, showered, in my slip and stockings, hair towel dried, when she appeared in my room, without so much as a knock. She was a short lady, very meridionale, dark-haired and -eyed, with, when she chose to honour you with it, a bewitching smile. I basked in it. Her hair was cut like my mothers, in a Coco Chanel bob with a heavy fringe, not because it was fashionable, but because it hid lines and brought one's eyes (they both had wonderful eyes) into play. Like my mother she wore simple easy clothes in neutral colours, and her jewellery was equally simple – but good! Gold and pearl disc ear-rings, an elegant gold watch, both presents from my parents for her continued care of us all as well as for her friendship, and a long string of pearls wound several times round her neck in a very dégagé manner to relieve the plainness of her outfit. Her shoes were simple courts with a medium heel, and her stockings toned beautifully.

We got down to business: I gave her a sheaf of newsprint

that contained everything I could find on the New Look. Her smile broadened, then she eyed my Dress and, amazingly, failed to sniff. She took me in with a sweeping gaze, and sat me in front of the dressing table and began her transformation.

I know I moan about her sometimes but she is first class at making a silk purse out of a sow's ear.

We spoke in French: she still had the Provençale way of rolling her 'r's, I was pleased to note. My own French was accented with the harsher sounds of the Vercors. She sniffed at that, and told me I sounded like a peasant *montagnard*, then smiled and added, but you will look like a fine lady when I have finished with you, and not at all English. English style, she opined, was very acceptable for men, but the women here had no idea how to make themselves alluring, although perhaps the war had helped; Utility had at least made people aware of design.

"See that unfortunate creature your brother has allied himself to," she whispered, carefully working the comb through my hair. "No sense of style. What does he see in her? Does she have lots of money? Is she the only daughter of an elderly millionaire? And she laughs like a horse."

I didn't reply. I had only come across her at a distance, never been introduced to her. She was much younger than me, a different generation.

She shrugged. "Well, I suppose she must have something."

"Eagerness?" I suggested. "The grapevine says she likes to stick her bottom in the air at gymkhanas."

Angelique gave a bark of laughter, tugged at my hair and said "Surely your brother could attract something better than that. I know he's not the most go-ahead young man, but he's milord's son, your mother's son; he has nothing to be ashamed of."

"I wouldn't be attracted to him," I said glumly.

"He's a pompous wretch, with about as much brain as a caterpillar!"

"You two never did get on. But he's got a good job, he'll inherit the estate, and the title. He could try a bit harder and do a lot better. How your mother can countenance it?"

"She wants grandchildren," I said darkly. "What's Maman wearing tonight?"

"The ivory silk, of course. Your father so loves her in it."

By the time I had been tweaked and polished and allowed, after twirls and final checkings, to leave my room, in my little black dress, I looked, indeed, and felt, a very fine lady. Angelique could give you poise and confidence that you never knew you had.

I heard the first gong as I was going down the stairs, and there was the sound of braying laughter from below. As usual, we all gathered in the hall, and I peeped over the balustrade to see whether I was last.

I wasn't.

My sister wasn't there either.

The hall was warm, lit by candles and softly shaded electric lights as well as a fine wood fire. The staff had worked hard, I could see, and in the light of the flames copper dishes gleamed and reflected, and wooden surfaces shone. But this was all outdone by the people therein.

The men wore regulation dark dinner suits with white shirts and ties. My father always looked well in a suit, having the height to carry it off. Basil, Maddy's husband, was shorter and slightly stockier since marriage had come his way, but he didn't disgrace the suit either. My partner for the duration, Mr. Arkwright, was made for the thing, and the thing made for him, by a very competent tailor, if I was any judge of such matters. He outshone my brother by several suns in formal dress. Guy had drawn the unlucky straw when it came to shoulders and hips – they were less than impressive. While his waist was more than. I'm sure he'd put on a bit round the middle since New Year, which was when I last saw him. I wondered how, with rationing.

I shot another look at Mr. Arkwright. He really was a bit of alright. I didn't want to like him. I really didn't.

He was talking to the most elegantly dressed woman in the room and she was loving it, twinkling, touching his arm, flirting like mad. Well, Maman was French, it was what she did best, I thought, spitting out vinegar. But she did look stunning, classical, and for fifty something – no, I'm not allowed to mention her years, she having reached the 'interesting' stage – she knocked the rest of the women into a cocked hat. They were all colourfully dressed. As Angelique said, *le style anglais* suits men, but the women had no idea.

I hid behind a pillar gathering my breath. And sneaked yet another look at Mr. Jeremy Arkwright. I thought about Maddy's deal.

I could get him into society.

Dammit, he didn't need me.

He was charming my mother, for Heaven's sake; all the old biddies with young daughters would welcome him with open arms. He'd make wonderful grandchildren. Of course, money might be a problem if he didn't have any, but if you looked that good in a penguin suit and could dance, at this time when men were in short supply, he'd be home and dried.

I snorted a laugh. Well, for this evening at least I'd have a partner who didn't look like something dreamed up by Dr Frankenstein, or who had appeared as a result of too much in-breeding.

I began to make my way down the steps.

As I did so I caught sight of a tallish man, talking very loudly to my brother Guy and my father.

He stopped me in my tracks.

He had to be the important person that my brother had dragged us all here for. He was definitely dominating that conversation.

My heart leapt into my mouth then sank again.

Oh, God, no!

What the hell was he doing here?

I'd never seen him before in the whole of 27 years, yet this was the second time in three days.

My father had on his mask face. From his stance I knew that he was simmering with controlled anger, although you had to know him well to see it. He wouldn't make a scene, but I knew that look. I'd been on the receiving end of it several times, all justified, too, I might add.

What was Joshua Crowe doing here?

More to the point, would he recognize me?

And if he did, how would I explain myself?

Who had I said I was? Good old Sarah Carson, née Markham, wasn't it?

Joshua Crowe sported a finely tailored dinner suit, definitely Savile Row, and the top end at that, a pristine starched shirt with large diamond studs on the shirt front. I would not have thought the man I had blethered at was the possessor of such things, or such style, which only goes to show how wrong snap judgements can be.

Draped on his arm was his Scarlet Woman. The epithet sprang to mind immediately because of her wonderfully fitting velvet dress with its sprinkling of rhinestones around the deep neckline.

These were our guests of honour?

But what exactly were they?

Squire at most, I would have said, but he didn't even appear to have that much breeding when I last saw him.

And a parvenue?

I felt distinctly uneasy as I descended the last few steps.

My mother came to greet me. "Darling, you look

absolutely beautiful. Now just let's show our guests what class really is," she hissed in French, then ushered me across to Joshua Crowe and the blonde on his arm.

I stood tall, chin up, prepared to deny absolutely everything.

My mother touched Joshua Crowe's arm, "Mr. Meredith, may I introduce my oldest daughter? Alice, this is Mr. Percival Meredith, of property and construction fame, and his fiancée, Miss Elisabeth Thorburn. Mr. Meredith, Miss Thorburn, my daughter, Alice Chamberlain."

I hope I didn't gape.

I was shocked to the core, but I managed to shake hands and say "Charmed," to them.

"What do you do, Miss Chamberlain?" Miss Thorburn asked.

That 'What?' rather than 'How?' spoke volumes.

My sister would have asked 'How?' Ladies, real ladies, didn't do, they just were.

"Actually I'm still recovering from convalescence. I had a rather bad bout of pneumonia early in the year, which laid me very low. But I'm up and running now. As to how I shall spend my time, who knows? I have no plans at the moment."

I saw the thought cross Mr. Meredith's face – another spoilt waste of space. That was fine by me.

I shook hands with them, assured them I was delighted to make their acquaintance, and asked "Are you friends of my brother, Guy?" I used the French pronunciation.

"Ghee? Ah, you mean Guy!" Mr. Meredith drawled, superciliously. "Well, more business associates. I've a proposal to make to your father and to his prospective father-in-law. Just the possibility of some mutual self-help, but I won't bother you with such talk, m'dear. Ladies don't care for it, do they? This little lady certainly don't, what!"

Miss Thorburn simpered on his arm, eyeing him perhaps

a little too tenderly. I got a closer look at her and realized I would have done myself no favours by saying I went to school with her. I would have been in the kindergarten when she was being sent to be finished. But there was more behind her green eyes than her actions suggested. She may have been bottle blonde – yes, I was my mother's daughter, and had an artist's eye – but she was not stupid.

Mr. Arkwright came up and took my arm. "Alice, I've been looking for you all over. You'll have a drink? Please excuse us, Mr. Meredith, Miss Thorburn, I've not spoken to Alice all afternoon." So we were on first name terms. I was fine with that, but I saw what Maddy meant by needing a bit of drawing room experience.

I allowed him to glide me away from them. "Thank you, but I could have got away myself," I hissed.

He poured me a whisky and soda. "They're dangerous people. I don't like them being here."

I raised my eyebrows. "Indeed! Don't you think I know that? Look at my father's face. If he knows, my mother knows, you know, and I don't even know you, surely my brother must know. Where's Maddy, by the way?"

"She'll be down shortly. Look, there she is now." We both moved over to the stairs to greet her.

She looked stunning. Then she always did, but tonight she had on a dull black satin Chinese pyjama suit, the coat of which was finished in glorious brocade, all dragons and pagodas. It disguised her bump nicely, and I noted Angelique's hand in the make-up and hair. She was duly introduced and with Jeremy and myself did the rounds of our future sister and her parents, the Nesmith-Browns.

Bulgy Algy, Sylvia's father, was just that. A large man whose suits just managed to contain him. He was polishing off large glasses of my father's gin, hardly tempered with tonic, and seemed to be very content with life. His wife had a perpetual look of faint disgust on her face, her thin mouth down-turned. She drank parsimoniously of a small sweet sherry, and wore brightly coloured draped floral satin round her stocky well-corseted figure, a little flowery hat with a tiny veil that covered the steel-grey perm, and answered to the name of Anthea.

Sylvia bounded from her seat, grasped my hands and kissed me on both cheeks, a Gallicism she must have learned from us. "Alice," she gushed, "I've been longing to meet you. I've heard so much about you!" She was a large fair-haired girl in blue moiré silk with a loose bright red mouth.

"Lovely to meet you at last, Sylvia," I said but she wasn't listening. She was eyeing up my escort.

She simpered at Jeremy, "Who's your friend, Alice?"

"Mr. Jeremy Arkwright is staying with us for a weekend," said my sister. "He's partnering Alice this evening."

Sylvia's eyebrows rose. "Lucky Alice!"

Not what was expected of my brother's fiancée, but she had been hitting the sherry less abstemiously than her mother.

Guy was back talking with Mr. Meredith and drawing my father in, while my mother did the decent thing with Miss Thorburn.

"Your father's best wine is going to be wasted on this lot," Jeremy observed drily. I'd been thinking much the same but I wasn't going to let him know.

"What exactly do you do, Jeremy?" I asked.

"Bit like yourself, from what I've heard," he said. "I'm based with Basil, but I do anything that comes along." He offered me a cigarette from a very stylish gold cigarette case – a Pasha, divine Turkish tobacco, but it wouldn't fit into my holder.

I took one. I'd smoke it nude. I wasn't letting that get away.

My sister came over with her hand out. "That's half a crown you owe me. I knew she'd take it," she said.

"Only when she's smoked it," he said. "She may yet pull back."

"Not a chance," I said. "Give me a light, please. Maddy, you should not bet on certainties. It's not sporting."

I accepted the light from Jeremy after he had slipped a half crown to my sister.

"I'm sorry, I shouldn't have accepted Maddy's bet. It was tawdry of me."

I didn't think he meant that.

But he flashed me a lightning smile before asking "Can I get you anything – to compensate?"

"Another drink. This evening is going to be a long one."

11

It was.

But the food was excellent, given the restrictions of rationing, and the wine perfect.

We started with a light vegetable soup – Mrs. Mac could turn anything into a delightful soup – which was followed by the main part of the meal, a joint of beef, locally reared and hung by a butcher who knew his trade, was as good as anything I have had in fine restaurants before the war; how it had been acquired and at what cost, I dreaded to think. The whole household must have been living on air for weeks to collect the coupons and points for this joint. There were roasted potatoes, parsnips and Yorkshire puddings feather light, and spring greens; the gravy boat swam with an elixir I hadn't tasted for years, and there was good mustard and horseradish sauce that made your nose run and your eyes water. And to follow… oh, a tiny cheese savoury, then new forced rhubarb from the garden, made into the tiniest of crumbles, and custard.

My father always managed to keep a good cellar, so the company was cheerful and relaxed. Although this was a formal dinner – and Guy must have been aware of how far my parents had pushed out the boat for him – we were a noisy group, once the wine began to hit. Even Sylvia's mother lost her sour look when she saw the joint and all its tracklements. After she and her husband had worked their way through two helpings of everything of the main course, she declared herself unable to do justice to the cheese, (my mother served cheeses before dessert in the French manner as no-one wanted to engage in dancing or close conversation with someone who smelled of Stilton) but subsequently found she could discern a little place for Mrs. Mac's dessert! If her daughter had the same propensities (and from this evening's showing I thought she had), Guy would be under pressure to earn far more than he was doing at the moment.

When all was accomplished, as my father would say, or as Mrs. Mac commented later, 'when they'd eaten you out of house and home,' Mr. Meredith looked around at the company and said "I take it the ladies will now withdraw," He patted Miss Thorburn's bottom (she was already on her feet). "Up you get, sweetie, and leave us gents to our business talk. I'm sure you've got lots to gossip about over your tea."

I felt my own hackles rise and glanced at Pa, and then Maman. No-one was going to tell them how to behave in their own home.

"The ladies of my house only withdraw if they so wish, Mr. Meredith," said Pa. "We don't have gender divide here. Of course, ladies, if you wish to freshen up or take tea in the drawing room, you may do so, but you are equally welcome to stay with us over the port and cigars. Or a brandy, or other *digestif* if you wish. The choice is, as always, yours."

I caught his eye. I was staying. It was an order. Not that I intended to do otherwise.

My sister said she would take tea, and Sylvia, her mother and 'Sweetie' Thorburn followed her obediently out.

My mother stayed put too. "I want to hear what you are proposing, Guy. And I should like a *fine champagne*."

Jeremy stood up, "I'll join the ladies, if you don't mind. This appears to be family business. Excuse me, ladies, gentlemen."

He moved elegantly. I wondered just how good he was on the dance floor.

Basil got to his feet. "I'll go keep the girls company, as well," he said. "My wife needs keeping an eye on in her condition," and trotted out behind Jeremy.

Mr. Mac brought in the glasses and the port, and a bottle of cognac for my mother, then offered a box of cigars. I declined, but fixed a Gauloise into my holder and lit up. I was enjoying this.

Mr. Meredith frowned at the smoke, but I smiled sweetly back. He could say nothing; he was in my father's house, and father was going to be of use to him – so he thought.

"Now, Guy. Your turn to speak," Pa invited.

Guy made a fuss of lighting his cigar. "Well, yes. I think so. Only I'd rather do it without Maman and Alice here."

Mother raised her eyebrows. "Oh, your own mother and your little sister are so intimidating are they, my son? I promise you that Alice and I will sit as quiet as a couple of little mice. It's just that we do enjoy a smoke and a *digestif.* Isn't that so, Alice?"

"*B'en sûr*, Maman!" I agreed, puffing at my cigarette.

He was a long-winded pompous boy, and I could have punched him. His idea was, and of course it was his idea, nothing to do with anyone else around the table, that he, Father and Bulgy Algy got together with Mr. Meredith and made their corporate fortunes.

How was this to be done?

Well, father had some spare land – including and surrounding Wethersley village – and Bulgy Algy had some in Marsham, the adjoining village, and Mr. Meredith had a great deal of expertise in obtaining planning permission and building houses. And he, Guy, had banking knowledge and ability. People always need homes, but particularly now what with the bombing and the sudden rise in birthrate that followed the end of hostilities; we could build a small town and do well by doing good.

I watched Algy and Mr. Meredith nodding their approval. Pa's face was guarded. Even Maman was silent, a tactic that I knew well.

Guy took the rope that was metaphorically handed him

and slipped his head through the noose. "It's not as though the present Wethersley was a particularly pretty village, after all, but it is in commuting distance of London. As well as all the local towns. We could do very well here, bring a bit of life into the area, fresh blood and all that."

My father's face hardly changed, as he said pleasantly "Whatever makes you think I would want to build a town on my back door, Guy? I like the village. I like its people, I like the area around it, and I like living here. How about you, Algy? Do you want to build over Marsham?"

Bulgy Algy bulged a bit more. "Actually, Roger, I think it's a damn good idea. Look at what we'd gain. We'd have income and to spare once the houses were up, and the whole area would be more lively. Think of it as an investment for our grand-children."

My mother nodded her head.

She was keen on investment for grand-children. Actually she was keen on generating extra income anyway. Left to her own devices she could joyfully dispose of large tracts of it. I wondered whether she knew of this beforehand. She swore she didn't, but I wouldn't put it past her. She wouldn't even think of it as lying; it would be business.

"What areas were you actually thinking of?" Father asked, having given the matter some thought – i.e. let my mother get her way. "Not that I'm in favour. I'm just curious."

Mr. Meredith moved his glass. "I have a proposal roughly drawn up," he said.

Had Guy and Bulgy Algy already given him the go-ahead?

"My company, you've heard of us, Lord Wethersley? Good, good. We would suggest building an estate of say a thousand dwellings, to start with, on the land between Wethersley village and Marsham. This way we'd keep the two villages more or less intact, but run them together to form a new urban area – let's call it Wethersley Marsham as a working title. The local district council appear to be very interested; I'm sure planning permission would be forthcoming quite easily for the right proposal, so we'd put in amenities, a new school, a health centre, or vastly improve those already there, attract the right sort of person, families with good jobs in town – as we know, the access here is good, once the railways get themselves sorted out properly. No riff-raff, just good solid decent family people. I don't think you'd need to fear that you'd get the hoi polloi in, as we'd build pleasant convenient houses, detached or semi-detached in pretty residential streets. We are in negotiations with a brick builder as I speak. Let me assure you, it would not be hastily thrown-up prefabs, along serried rows, perish the thought!"

I remembered the block-like building plan I'd seen on the wall in the Site Office at Straddling Hall; that certainly wasn't the Garden Suburb effect that Mr. Meredith was trying to sell to my father.

"We're offering you a chance to get in at the bottom of the ladder, Father," said Guy, pettishly. "A chance to make a fortune."

Pa looked at Guy over his glasses benignly. "What you are saying is true, Guy, I'll give you that. But you need my input to make your friends a fortune. I hold a large area of land. I know Algy, that your stake will probably be as large as mine, but I'm not sure that I want to give up Wethersley's farmland. The meal you have all just enjoyed was its gift to us. I'd hate to have to tell my farmer friends that they have to get rid of their animals, their homes and their livelihoods and find jobs elsewhere."

"But there'd be jobs here for them, good regular work, none of this backbreaking sons-of-the-soil stuff," Guy assured him, inadvisedly.

Pa turned to my mother. "What do you think, my dear? What would your father do if Jean-Paul suggested this?"

Both she and I collapsed into giggles. He would have taken his whip to his son and we all knew it.

Guy pushed out his lower lip and chin, as he always had done when people told him no, but the others didn't notice because my father was speaking again.

"Mr. Meredith, Percy," Pa said. "Do you have any idea what you are asking me to do? This land's been in the family since ... oh, I don't know, the Conqueror? At least since the Dissolution of the Monasteries," he continued, waving his hand vaguely in the air. "Since time immemorial..."

Pure lies.

My great-great-grandfather, an industrialist who had an eye for the gee-gees had won it and the title of the 17th Lord Wethersley in the reign of Queen Victoria, after a bet on a horse-race. It was in a very poor state, and Lord Wethersley the 16th was glad to be rid of it, with a handful of sovereigns to spare, while my ancestor had put in what capital he had (derived from clever speculation and the railways) and pulled the place around.

"And yet," Pa went on, "I'm not totally against the idea."

Mr. Meredith, Bulgy Algy and Guy all let out the breath they had been holding in a concerted hiss of relief.

"How can I persuade you, Lord Wethersley?" asked Mr. Meredith.

"Well, do you have any developments already made, so that I can see them up and running? That would be a good idea."

"There is one not a million miles away from here," Mr. Meredith said. "I'd be delighted to take you there tomorrow, if you would like it. All of you."

"Church first," said Mother, piously, as though she were a regular attendee!

Almost on cue, a peal of laughter blasted to us from the drawing room.

Pa nodded, and began standing up. "Certainly, we'd be delighted to visit your development, and hear your plans, but I think we should join the others now."

"Did you know about this?" I whispered to my mother, in French, as we led the way. She looked fleetingly over her shoulder to check that the men were taking their time and spoke softly.

"Both Roger and I had some suspicions, but we didn't have anything concrete. Guy's been nosing around Wethersley and Marsham far too often lately, even for a man whose fiancée lives in the area. But we honestly didn't know who he was bringing and Roger is very unhappy at having that man in the house. I don't know what he's got against him."

I had a good idea. "But he's stringing him along?"

"He wants to find out how deep Guy is in with this plan. Basil warned him of it this morning."

How did Basil know about it, I wondered. I got an uncomfortable feeling around the back of my neck as we entered the drawing room.

Basil and Madeleine were over by the radiogram. "We thought we'd have some music," my sister said, and without a moment's delay Louis Armstrong's unmistakable trumpet was braying through the air.

So we rolled up the carpet and danced, which was a family habit. Apart from Bulgy Algy and his wife, who had foundered side by side upon a large chesterfield, allowing the digestive processes to make inroads on the generous meal they had recently put away.

My parents had a good collection of records, and you could dance to all of them. They weren't for listening to, like the classics, but were mostly popular, jazzy and upbeat. They were very keen on the Hot Club of France. Basil went to collect his case of 78s that he had chosen especially for the evening, and they were brilliant: loud, brash American bands, which demanded violent movement. I hadn't heard music like this for ages, or felt well enough to do it justice.

Basil nodded at Jeremy. "Ask her, she jitterbugs too!" he said. "She's Maddy's sister. Of course she does."

Maddy was right.

He was a great dancer, so fluid and full of rhythm, and confident. There is nothing worse than 'being led' by someone who doesn't know where he's going; that holds true in life as on the dance floor. We both gave ourselves over to the music, but with a little more decorum than the dance demanded – some of the less inhibited moves were not to be contemplated at a first acquaintance – well certainly not in front of the company we were in. But having said that, it wasn't until the record came to an end and the others were giving us a standing ovation that I thought of the incongruity of us jitterbugging in full evening clothes in my parents' drawing room.

The dancing continued.

Not as strenuous as the jitterbug, but very pleasurable. By the end of the evening I had danced with every gentleman present except Bulgy Algy who spent the post-prandial time digesting. My partner for the evening was in serious demand, both by my mother and my sister-in-law-to-be, and I was pretty certain that Maddy would have pushed me aside had she not been so very pregnant. Sylvia positively hogged him. I expected my brother to get jealous, but he smiled benevolently when I suggested we dance and shook his head. Of all the Chamberlains, he was the least extrovert. He preferred the slower dances to the upbeat rhythms that Maddy kept putting on the turntable. He looked at his fiancée and said softly, "She's enjoying herself, isn't she? I'm glad. She deserves a bit of fun."

I followed his glance. Sylvia was definitely flirting with every partner she had, which included every male in the room except her father.

That, when out with her fiancé, was not on in my book. One had rules. We might be becoming family, but one still had standards.

"How well do you know this Jeremy chap?" Guy asked as the music stopped. "Only I'd hate to see Sylvia get hurt. She's such a trusting little thing."

I bit back a catty remark about her size and behaviour. "Just this evening, Guy. If you want the low-down you best ask Maddy. He's a friend of Basil's so of course he's alright!" I added as I caught sight of Jeremy fetching Sylvia a glass of lemonade, being very attentive indeed. I slipped out to powder my nose.

What sort of partner was that?

When I returned Pa was putting on his end-of-evening record.

Jeremy returned to me, and we stepped out into a slow waltz. He held me close. "Forgive my inattention, Alice," he whispered. "I was on duty."

Well, that explained everything.

"Come dancing with me back in town?" he asked. "I know some great little dives in Soho."

"I bet you do!"

And he guffawed.

Stifled it almost immediately, but that set me off, and any possible romance was kicked out of play.

We stopped dancing and gave in to giggles, and were bumped into by Sylvia's parents who had eased themselves vertical and mobile.

"Sorry," I said, as we sought our way off the floor.

"Watch the company," Jeremy said, lighting my Pasha. I did.

Pa and Maman still had it.

So did Basil and Maddy. They all danced like lovers.

Mr. Meredith and Miss Thorburn? Did they dance a slow

waltz like an engaged couple?

No.

She held herself proud and slightly apart. Or was I imagining it?

She was in control.

My brother and Sylvia? Surely she was leading him. In quite a different way from Miss Thorburn. She was all over him, and as he turned in the dance I was certain I glimpsed panic on his face.

I sucked in my breath. "Oops!"

Beside me Jeremy nodded. "Oops indeed." he said quietly.

Yes, I thought; you are on duty, aren't you? I wondered what he'd be like off duty.

Mr. Meredith's development appeared quite different from Straddling.

We walked around it after church, and I smelt the aroma of Sunday roasts on the Spring air. It was the right day to see the place. The houses were set on a low hill outside Amersham, and I could see the tower of St Michael and All Angels from the ridge. The roads that curved up and down the slope, arranged to appear as if they had 'evolved', sported houses of different styles and shapes, but all 'cottagey' and as such, small. Very garden suburb, very bijou. Terraces had charming roof-lines, set at angles to each other, and no block contained more than eight houses, artfully designed to appear to be one longer larger traditional building. Semis leaned against each other, bay windows on two storeys and oriels above the wide porches. They were all small scale, but very pretty. Only the end houses, the detached ones, which set within their own surrounding gardens would have had any room that could compare with the size of my own sitting room in Chelsea.

"We built this just before the war. They're all either sold, on mortgages, naturally, or let. It's a very popular estate, is Greystokes," Mr. Meredith said proudly.

Greystokes!

Was this where their grandfather disappeared?

I caught my father's eye, and he inclined his head once. I sucked in my breath.

"Who lives here? What sort of people?" Basil asked. "These larger houses are beyond the reach of the urban poor, surely? And the average country person couldn't aspire to them." Mr. Meredith ignored Basil's question.

"They are now worth a thousand pounds or more each," Mr. Meredith averred, "depending upon location of course. That's according to local estate agents, independent ones. The semis would bring an income of around eight hundred, and the terraces five. I don't need to tell you gentlemen, they don't cost anywhere near that to build and finish. We set up our own mortgage company too, with young Guy's help; that's the beauty of the scheme. People are desperate for decent housing these days. Gentlemen, there is a sincerely large profit margin involved here. I can furnish you with details, be glad to. And the houses are very popular. This whole area is very up and coming. Wethersley-Marsham would be a certain money-spinner. You simply cannot lose. And you'd be doing people a favour."

I wandered away. I was more interested in looking than listening to Mr. Meredith's sales pitch.

I made my way down to a crescent of terraced housing, where some children were playing on home-made go-carts along the road. I looked hard at the building. Red brick with yellow London brick detailing, which had already started mellowing. But as I looked, I saw a crack, over the doorway of the end house. I didn't like that at all. The wall was pulling away from itself already. It was perhaps nine years old. It wasn't bomb damage; there was no evidence of any bomb damage here; I'd ask my father or, failing that,

Reverend Simmons.

    As I walked back to the group, I looked more carefully at the semis we had been whisked past and saw further signs of cracking.

12

Bobby let me in with a bow, then called out to Leggy that I had arrived. "You'll be taking morning coffee with us?" he asked.

"Love to. Shall I go through?"

"Of course."

Leggy was sitting in his armchair, with Nuts on his lap.

"Don't get up," I said. "You both look so comfortable." I came and shook his hand and stroked Nuts, who purred contentedly. I handed my report to Leggy.

It was long.

I'd typed it up the previous night, making copies for myself, and finalized it this morning when I had got back from my swim with Thelma. That had been fun, and we'd had a stand-up breakfast of a buttered roll and Bovril at the snack counter. She was a good swimmer, and looked a lot less lumpy in the water; we'd both do each other some good. The trouble with office work generally was the inactivity of it. The only part of you that got exercised was your fingers.

"My, you have been busy, Alice," Leggy said, taking the thick folder. "Do you mind if I just skim through? I'll give it my full attention when you've gone."

"Fine," I said. "What do you know about Jeremy Arkwright?"

"Should I know anything about him?"

"Possibly. About thirty, tall, dark, personable. Works with my brother-in-law, Basil, at the F.O. I've been told, but a bit cagey when push comes to shove."

Bobby came into the room with a tray set with a Royal Worcester coffee set, and a plate of Glengarry shortbread biscuits. "Who are we maligning today, milady?" he asked, ever one for a bit of gossip.

"Chap called Jeremy Arkwright. I met him this weekend. My brother-in-law brought him down as a make-weight at table."

"Works at the F.O.?" Leggy mused. "Fancy him, do you?"

I ignored that. "I need to know more, and Basil won't tell me." Besides, I suspected he fancied my sister. "He likes jazz, likes dancing."

"Don't we all," said Bobby. "Visits Soho, does he? What's he like? To look at I mean." Bobby knew everyone in the clubs, he always told me.

I wasn't one to disagree. Whenever I'd gone dancing with him, everyone seemed to know him. It was a revelation.

"About 5'11", dark hair, blue eyes, bit of a Brylcreem boy, but an open face, bony rather than fat. Clean-shaven, regular features, nothing outstanding. Hands smooth and manicured, so doesn't appear to work manually, wears gold signet ring on his right third finger, well-spoken, but a hint of an accent from time to time – Northern, but not Tyneside. Well-turned out – his evening suit was made for him, not hired, I'd swear to it, but otherwise he wore a tweed jacket, misty green and blue mix, grey flannels and brogues, with Argyll socks. White shirt, blue tie with green stripes, nothing I'd recognize as old school. Drives an old red Morgan."

"Jem! That Jeremy Arkwright!" Bobby expostulated. "That swine! He pinched my girl!"

"Looks like it might be happening again," Leggy told him archly.

Bobby snorted. "Milady and I are just good friends, are we not?" he said.

"Quite," I replied. "But did he really pinch your girl? That was reprehensible."

"Not really. All's fair in love and war, and well, actually she was getting a bit of a pain. Wanted to get married. I told

136

her I already was, to Leggy."

"I sincerely hope you didn't!" Leggy countered at once. "I've been happily married twice, and there are certain aspects of that felicitous state that, incomprehensible as it may be to you, Bobby, as I care for you dearly, I would not wish to share with you."

Bobby chuckled. "Sure, it was just a joke, sir. But you know what I mean. You'd not like me to bring another female into the equation here. Where would we put her?" He poured coffee for us all.

"Where indeed?" mused Leggy.

"So, apart from him stealing your girlfriend, Bobby, what can you tell me about this chap?" I asked.

"He's a ducker and weaver. You said he's in the F.O., but he's into a lot more things than that. I'll ask around for you, so I will." He handed me a coffee and the biscuit plate. "Anything else I can help with?"

"Building regulations?" I suggested.

Leggy's head shot up. "What do you want to know about them for?"

I told them about Guy's plans, and my trip to Greystokes.

"Did the housing look sub-standard?" Leggy asked, when Bobby had taken the tray out. I had no idea how much he had told his batman.

"It looked nice," I said. "But there were cracks in the brickwork. There must have been complaints. But you're right. It doesn't concern this project."

"Not directly. Now what's all this about the seven pictures? You've got a copy of them in this pamphlet and drawings of pictures of angels as days of the week. Does this make sense? How like my picture are these Greystoke sketches?"

"The pictures were beautiful. Mine can't do them justice," I told him. "A suite of pictures would make sense.

137

The church is dedicated to St Michael and all angels. The vicar thinks your angel would be dedicated to Mars and Tuesday." I went over to the curtain, behind which it stood, but when I pulled the curtain aside, it was no longer there.

"It's in my bedroom, behind the wardrobe," Leggy said quickly. "I feel happier with it there and Bobby thinks I've got rid of it."

I felt a cold shiver. I dislike subterfuge where friends are concerned, but I already knew that was going on in a minor way. Then I realized I didn't like the idea of Leggy sleeping in the same room as the picture.

I pulled myself together, hoping he hadn't noticed. I had to clarify my own position.

"If you've got rid of it, I'm superfluous," I said. "He thinks you've sold it? You've told him that? He'll want to see the profit."

"I've told him it's being cleaned, that it's with a friend who's a restorer, and who would also be inclined to search for the other six paintings. He's very interested. So you are not superfluous, and we need to find them, Alice. The sooner the better."

We came to an arrangement very quickly.

Bobby dropped me home on the bike. "I'm still worried about him," he said, as he left. "He's got the picture in his bedroom – thinks I don't know, silly old fool – and he's reading all sorts of weird stuff. We've got to sort this thing soon. I'll find out more about this Jeremy creature for you. You find out what Leggy wants. The other six paintings, isn't it?"

He looked at me for confirmation. "You don't have to say anything, Milady, but of course I know. I don't like it, but I'm involved. He's my employer and I care for the old buffer." He dropped a kiss on my cheek. "You take care of yourself, hear? And I'll try to take care of him. And if you need anything, anything at all, let me know."

He dropped the bike into gear and was off.

It was half past eleven, and shouting my name as he hurried down the road at me, came Padraig Flynn.

"Ah, saints be praised," he said. "I was hoping you'd be in. Can I come up? It's about your work."

I nodded. Gave him a hug. "Of course, Padraig. Was Emily OK after I left you?"

"Yes. She's fine. You've got some fierce stairs here, Milady."

I let him into the living room, put on the kettle and went to hang up my coat.

He tossed his trilby on the table and went to the window. "Nice view across the gardens," he said. "Spring really is on the way at last. Milk and two sugars if you've got it, but otherwise black and as it comes."

"You've been talking with Emily and Josiah," I said, busying myself with cups.

"Indeed. And a few others. See, despite our care in keeping our voices down and sitting in the corner at the Academy, there were some Big Ears there. They approached us that evening."

I groaned. I knew artists – like theatre people, the biggest gossips going. "I thought you were meant to be showing Emily your etchings," I said.

He chuckled. "I did that too. She was very impressed. But that wasn't the point. I've been deputed to give you some information. We all think it could be quite important."

I handed him a cup of tea, opened the biscuit barrel, and we sat opposite one another at the table by the window. I had my note pad and pen nearby, to look official. He liked that.

"First of all, Josiah wants to tell you about the Meredith twins. He went to school with them, like he said. I think he was a year or two younger, but he was in the same house. And they were already a legend. They had told everyone that their father owned magic pictures of angels, which could make people disappear, but would, if you asked the right way, give you everything you could possibly want. Other boys laughed at them at first, and then they started flexing their psychic muscles. If a boy upset them (and it seems it was easy to upset them), they'd say they would tell the angels, and something untoward, usually quite nasty would happen to him. At their previous school he said one child upset them and shortly after broke his leg. It never properly mended. Another died of diphtheria, soon after they'd 'told the angels,' and a master was dismissed without a fair hearing on their say so, again shortly after he'd chastised them. Other things happened, and people soon learned not to get on the wrong side of them."

"They sound a couple of charmers. It was mind games, nothing more. Nasty little mind games played by a pair of bullies," I said.

Padraig nodded. "At first. But they became a lot more daring. No-one ever saw the pictures, by the way. No-one was invited to their home – after their grandparents and father died, they became wards of court and were looked after by a Great Aunt who was not exactly the ideal carer for two very strange youngsters – so no-one actually saw the pictures. No, they told their cronies they were going to kill their aunt and take her money. And by the end of term the old lady had died, leaving all she owned to them, her only living relatives, in trust of course, but they could wait. They then came and lived with one of the masters at the school. They left him alone, so it seemed, but they abused a very privileged position."

"I see," I said. "So everyone in the school virtually knew about these pictures. But no-one ever saw them. I'm not sure they would have been in possession of them. Someone would have noticed them somewhere along the line. They are big."

"I know, I know, Milady. And I do know someone who has seen them, and a lot more recently."

"You do? Tell me."

"Do you know Rufus Grassington? He's a restorer rather than a fine artist."

I had heard of him. Mr. Arnold said he was a very sound restorer and not over-priced, which was praise indeed. He also said he was a 'bit of a character'.

"He cleaned and restored all seven of them!"

I gaped. "Why didn't you tell me this at the beginning, Padraig? Where did he do it? Who was he working for? And when?"

Padraig grinned. "He wouldn't tell me. Just said he'd done them. He wants to meet you."

"Did he mention these pictures after you told him about me?" I asked.

"Heaven forfend. Do you think I'd trust him if he did? We were in the pub, and Josiah and Emily were talking about angel paintings – just general, no specifics, and up comes Rufus and says, 'I've worked on some angel pictures, about six years ago. Strange things, but beautifully painted.' So we asked him where and for whom, and he shook his head. I said I had someone researching them, and he said he'd speak to that person. I should imagine a bottle of spirits would do the trick."

I smiled. "I'd like to have a word with Mr. Grassington. Just to check they were these pictures." I opened my bag and took out Mr. Petts' pamphlet which Leggy agreed I should retain for the moment. I passed it across to Padraig. "Look at the last four pages."

He hunched forward, putting on a pair of gold half-glasses at the same time as opening the pages.

He took a long intake of breath and began nodding. I wondered if he were going to burst, for he didn't exhale for some thirty seconds.

"Jesus, Mary and Joseph!" he breathed at last. "Where did you get these?" He flipped the pamphlet shut and read the title page.

I held my hand out. "It's the last one, Padraig. I need it back, please."

"Of course you do. Now we could show it to Emily, but she's back in Gloucester this week, or I can take you to Rufus's studio, or failing that, his favourite watering hole."

We found Rufus in the French Pub, where he was chatting familiarly to a 'model' who was tanking up before her next punter. He bought her a treble brandy, patted her bottom and said, " 'Scuse me, doll-face, work rears it's ugly head."

"Tell me about it!" She raised her black-rimmed eyes to the clock over the bar, checked her small wristwatch then downed the brandy in one. "Ciao, heart-face! Back to the old grind!" she said, planting a smacking kiss on his forehead, and was gone in a flurry of long black hair and leopard-skin.

"Sorry to have spooked the quarry," Padraig apologized, filling her space at the bar, and the spaces of at least two others.

"She was on her way, anyway," Rufus told him, holding out a pint glass. "Make a change for her to turn up early for a John."

Rufus was a striking individual, having based his look on Titian's portrait of Ariosto in the National Gallery. His face was adorned with a well-trimmed but luxuriant black beard, carefully cultivated, and grown to equal his straight black hair; it was all beautifully kept, but very long by today's standards, ending as it all did, just above his shoulders He had fine black arched brows over dark eyes, pale skin and a sensuous pink mouth beneath the moustache. Naturally, his jacket was velvet, of the same soft blue as Ariosto's silken doublet, and even sported some form of quilting that must have been done by a loving seamstress, as it was all hand sewn. He leaned on the bar, showing his best profile.

I enjoyed the show.

What a ham!

Padraig introduced me.

He took my hand, bent over it and kissed my glove. "*Enchanté*, Milady," he breathed, looking up at me under thick black lashes. "How can I be of service?"

I handed the pamphlet to him, with the Angel pictures open. "Do you recognize these?"

Padraig was getting drinks in, Rufus elbowed to a table by the door.

"I worked on these," he said. "But they were in a bit of a state. Some of them had fire damage, some had been hacked at with sharp implements, and there was water damage too. Why?"

"Where were they?"

"Who wants to know?" The dark eyes were shrewd.

I stared back. Opened my bag and let the Johnny Walker Black Label bottle, purchased with some difficulty, peek out.

"My client," I said. "He's a man of impeccable references, someone who served his country during the war at the highest level, who is very conscious of the need for discretion. As am I."

Rufus's eyebrows raised. He chewed his lower lip reflectively. "Understood. Nice whisky by the way. Class."

I closed my bag, took the red wine that Padraig had brought for me, and tossed it back in one. It was the only way to deal with it. Padraig, who had seen me pull that trick before, dropped his face and smiled.

Rufus stared at me with open admiration.

I filled my cigarette holder and lit up a Gauloise, and watched him. I knew all I had to be was silent, and he'd crack. He wanted the bottle, he wanted to be seen with me. He didn't give a damn about his client's confidentiality – that was in the past, and if I read him right, what was past, was past.

He drew on a Woodbine, sipped his beer, didn't take his eyes off me.

I played inscrutable. I could wait.

Padraig looked from one of us to the other and back again, as he worked through his pint.

Finally, Rufus wiped the foam from his moustache and stood up. "You wouldn't care for a turn round the block, Milady? London is so pleasant at this time of year."

I inclined my head and rose.

Padraig started to rise but I shook my head. "Just a turn round the block, Padraig. I'll be back in five minutes. Enjoy your drink."

Rufus opened the door and we went out into the cold air of London.

Rufus began speaking very softly as soon as we were on the pavement. "October 1940 I got a phone call asking if I was still restoring pictures. I said 'yes'. Then I was asked if I would be willing to work on a small private collection. I said I'd need to see it, before I could make a decision, but I was keen. There wasn't a lot of work around in those days and I was expecting to get called up. The voice said it would send a car for me the following day. Fair enough, I said, and gave him my address."

He took out another Woodbine and lit it from the stub of the first one, taking a long draw of the tobacco, and breathed out. "Next day, a car turns up at 11.30, and the chauffeur gets out, and says, 'Is this all you're taking, sir?' I had my coat and hat, and my paintbox. 'What else should I take?' I asked. He sniffed, and said, 'No matter. Forget I said that, sir.' So I did.

"I got in the car and off we set. I asked the chauffeur

where we were going. 'You'll see,' he said, and that was all I got out of him. We took the Great North Road, and just kept going, at a gentle pace. He told me there was a thermos and some sandwiches in a hamper on the seat beside me and to tuck in. Actually we shared them in a lay-by. I thought of running away and hitching a lift home, but there wasn't much passing traffic and it was foggy. I'd have as soon been run over as given a lift. Besides, in some strange way, I was enjoying being kidnapped. It was a bit of an adventure, and I was looking forward to meeting the owner of the voice.

"Just before it got dark, he headed off into the hinterland, and we stopped at a large country house which appeared out of nowhere. It was currently being used as a school, and we were fed simply by the staff there and given a room each. I asked where the paintings were, and was greeted with incomprehension. I began to get uneasy. Everything was very 'damped down', like they'd all taken on board the Government's 'careless talk costs lives'. No-one spoke to anyone else, but I was given everything I needed, pyjamas, a dressing gown, towels, even a toothbrush – by the housekeeper, and managed, by dint of reading over her shoulder as she checked items off on a ledger, to find out what the place was.

"We went to bed early – everyone did – and got up at cock-crow. We had breakfast, were given a packed lunch and, somehow, I don't know how they managed it, a full tank of petrol. Then we were off on the road again, in the rain. The chauffeur knew his route, but I couldn't make head or tail of it. For a large part of the day we were driving through mist. We spent that night in a house up a lane in an equally desolate area. Exactly the same, and yet another night the same. Then, on the afternoon of the fourth day I met my patron, in his own castle overlooking Loch Ness."

He took a final tug on his Woodbine then threw it into the gutter, where it hissed in a puddle before sinking. "It's all true. You understand why I don't want it spread around. I mean, I was kidnapped. What would that do for my reputation?"

I smiled gently. "Your secret's safe with me," I assured him. "So what happened then?" I asked. I had already guessed who the patron was.

"Lord Finching – mad as a hatter, but a really likeable old devil – showed me the pictures and made me an offer I couldn't refuse. So I restored them. That's all."

"Tell me about it?"

Rufus frowned for a moment then nodded. "Why not? Course, when I had them, they weren't exactly pristine. All of them had a bit of fire damage, although one of them was a real mess. A couple had some sort of dark red pigment splashed all over them, and at least three had been attacked with an edged instrument, like an axe, and showed evidence of being soaked through at some point. There was a lot of work. It took me the best part of six months."

I was impressed. "And Lord Finching kept you all that time?"

"Yes. Although it was the coldest winter I've ever experienced. Even worse than this one. Have you ever been snowed into a castle for a month? Luckily I had organized my studio before the weather broke and we seemed to have an unending supply of whisky. Food was frugal, simple, but kept us alive. And at the end of my work, which pleased Lord Finching very much, I was given what I was promised, and the train fare home."

"So what did you tell people when you got back?" I asked.

He tossed his hair and gave me a very sexy wink. "Told them I was on government business." He put his forefinger across his lips. "Hush-hush. Should have used that excuse years ago. It certainly pulled the ladies for me."

If he only knew how hush-hush work really was!

"So do you think Lord Finching still has the angels?" I asked.

He shook his head. "I shouldn't think so. He had this thing about people coming to destroy them, which is what appeared to have been done to them already, and talked about separating them for their own good. How much I could believe of this, I don't know. He said there would be people who would take a picture each, to keep them safe. It seems that there were other people out there who wanted to either destroy them or use them."

"Use them?"

"Oh yes," Rufus said. "You have to know how to do it, but they are very powerful."

I didn't comment. "Do you know who the people who would keep the pictures safe were?"

Rufus looked quizzical. "Why should I answer that?"

"Because I asked. Do you honestly think people are out to get these pictures and destroy them?"

Rufus stood still for a moment, causing a blockage among the office-workers on their lunch break. He rubbed his head. "Don't know that I do believe that," he replied at last. "What I do believe is that those places I stopped at on the way to Lord Finching's are possibly involved. I'll write down the names for you when we get back to the pub, as far as I can remember. If you get them all together again, the angels, I'd like to see them. Can you arrange that for me?"

He flashed a smile. Playing me along, I thought.

I smiled back. "I'll do my very best, and I appreciate your frankness, Mr. Grassington."

His face dropped. "Oh, you call me by my surname. I thought we were friends."

"We've been talking business," I said. "But thank you for your time, Rufus. Your secrets are safe with me. I promise." I put my finger across my lips. "Hush-hush!"

He gave a gurgling laugh. "Come on, I'll buy you a

drink."

I left the French pub with a list of leads and without a bottle of Johnnie Walker. Padraig hailed me a cab, and returned to the pub.

Back home I got out my maps out. I looked up the places on my list and realized I'd need more information; Rufus's memories were not exactly crystal clear – more artistic than scientific. I smoked a cigarette and drank a milky cup of Camp coffee. When I was done, I picked up my bike and headed off to the local reference library with a collection of notebooks and pencils. I stayed until the light went and it was throwing out time. It was a good afternoon's work. I felt, as I cycled home, that I'd done a good work-out, exhausted, but satisfied. The chip van was open. I bought rock and chips to celebrate.

13

George waylaid me at the door. "I'll put your bike away, Miss. There's been a couple of gents asking for you. He handed me a large used brown envelope with my name on, and forcibly removed my bike from my hands. "You get upstairs and have them chips. I'll come an' report after I've finished with the bike."

I allowed myself to be bullied, and climbed the silent stairs; Mr Stephens must be out.

I opened the door, put the kettle on and set out two plates on the table, got out the salt and vinegar, and a heel end of bread. It was still on ration, but would be too stale for tomorrow. Then I investigated the inside of the envelope.

Two calling cards, with scribbled pencil messages on them.

One said: Would like to meet you. Think we may be able to be of mutual assistance.

The other said: Dance with me? Ring to confirm.

George came in, wiping his hands on the back of his shorts and looking hopeful. "Have you had your tea, George?" I asked.

"Yeah, but…"

"You could manage a few chips and a bit of fish?" I suggested. "I've set you a place. Wash your hands and sit down. Then you can tell me about these."

"Thank you, Miss. You sure you got enough?"

"I think we'll manage," I said, pouring us both cups of tea and sawing the bread into two.

George settled into the chair opposite me, beaming. He tossed salt wantonly across his plate of food then poured the malt vinegar carefully over the chips using the cut-glass stopper to regulate the flow.

"First one came around an hour ago. He was a bit of a toff, Miss. Drove up in a red Morgan. Asked me to give you this one" he pointed to Jeremy's elegantly turned out card. "I got threepence from him, but I had to look pathetic. Nice car though. I wouldn't mind a spin in that."

"And the other?"

"He come later. Just before you turned up, in fact. If you'd come down the road the other way you would have met him. He was tall, and wore a trilby and a belted raincoat. Said you met him on his grandfather's doorstep on Saturday, and he thought he might have something useful for you. I think he'd been in the war. He had a scar on his face, from his left eye down his cheek. He asked me where the nearest pub was, and I told him the Anglesey. He give me sixpence if I would make sure you nip round and meet him there this evening." George stuffed a chip into his mouth and chewed while I thought about it. Then he swallowed, took a swig of tea and mopped his mouth with his hand. "Miss, I - er, I promised him you would."

"You mean you took his bribe," I said grinning. He nodded. We were both at the mopping up stage, bread folded around the remaining crispy end bits of chips being the mop, and when he next spoke, both our plates were spotless.

"You don't want me to give it back, now, Miss? Look, I've saved you washing up."

"No, I don't want you to give it back, George. What did you think of him?"

"He was all right. Not a toff, and he had a bit of a funny accent. I don't know it, but he wasn't from round here. I think he was OK." George frowned slightly, then nodded.

"OK, I'll nip round to the pub."

George's face split into a wide smile. "Ta, Miss."

"Have you finished?"

"Yes, thank you Miss. Shall I go?"

"That would be very nice, George."

"If you talk to the first chap, do you think I could go for a spin in his car?" he asked as he closed the door.

"I think that's going a bit too far," I chuckled.

George sounded aggrieved. "Miss, you told me yourself, you can only ask. I'd like the answer to be yes, but I'll always accept a no." His voice echoed along with his boots as he ran back down the stairs.

I poured myself another cup of tea, tidied up, then rang the Anglesey Arms, and asked if there was a Mr. Sam Simmons in the bar. They put me through.

"Mr. Simmons?" I asked. "Give me three good reasons why I should come for a drink with you."

"Miss Chamberlain? Thank you for ringing. One, the Rev says you're sound, and I trust his judgement. Two, our interests coincide. I'm trying to get to the bottom of the Greystoke mysteries. And three, I'd really like to buy you a drink. You had a lovely smile when I saw you on Saturday. I could go on?"

"I'm here because George promised I would be," I said. "I don't believe in bribing minors."

"The little fellow only wanted to be helpful." Mr. Simmons had a very distinct Antipodean accent. It was quite attractive. So was his crooked smile. "You should nurture enterprise. What'll you have? They don't do tea here, do they?"

"Oddly enough, no. A ginger wine would be very acceptable. Thank you, Mr. Simmons."

He led me to the same table I had shared with Bobby a few evenings ago. I drew off my gloves and filled my cigarette holder. He returned with the drinks and immediately offered me a light. Then he sniffed appreciatively. "French? Where do you get those from?"

"I brought them back from France with me. Do help yourself, if you'd like one. Eventually I may have to learn to love Woodbines or Weights, but not yet."

"I hope you won't have to. I'll leave you your dark tobacco. You don't mind if I smoke my pipe?"

"Not at all. Cheers."

I sipped the ginger wine: hot, sweet, warming. It would settle the meal nicely. "Now, how can I help you?"

He looked up at me while stuffing a dark pipe with an aromatic tobacco. "Let me introduce myself. Then you can choose whether you want to or not." He turned adjusted the flame on his lighter and puffed on the stem of the pipe until the tobacco caught.

I waited.

"My name's Sam Simmons, as you know. My father is the Rev's foster son. They are very close. His name is Arthur…"

I made the leap. "He is the youngest of Lawrence Greystoke's sons?" I hazarded.

"Hole in one! He is the only one of the three left. He lives in New Zealand with my mother. I was brought up there, but I served with the Anzacs. When I was demobbed I decided to come over here and keep and eye on the Rev. If it hadn't been for him, my Dad would have been killed by his brother, I have no doubt whatsoever of that. I owe him a great deal – my father's life and my very existence. So I came back to live with the old fellow and got a job on the local paper."

He took the pipe out of his mouth and looked me in the eyes. "Miss Chamberlain, I'm interested in those so-called angel pictures. They scared the hell out of my Dad when he was a kid. He watched his Dad painting them, and he told me it was like watching a man go mad. And then he disappeared."

I nodded. Yes, they must have had a terrifying effect upon a small child, particularly when his beloved parent simply vanished. I said as much.

"Miss Chamberlain, I don't believe he just disappeared. Nor do I believe that my uncle William just disappeared eight or nine years later. I want to find those pictures because I think they are at the bottom of it all. I think you might be able to help me."

I nodded. "I think I probably could. What does Reverend Simmons think of you doing this?"

"He says whatever I want to do is fine by him. He knew about the pictures that were in the church, and he knew there were big ones, because my father told him about them, but never saw them himself, as he may have told you. When he saw your pictures, those you showed him, he said he understood why my father was frightened. He was just a nipper when they were being painted, and they would have been very large and very menacing – I've had this from both Dad and the Rev." He took a draw on the pipe and sent up a blue scented cloud. "You don't happen to have that pamphlet on you?"

"No."

"Why are you interested in the pictures, Miss Chamberlain?"

I found myself telling him, briefly and without divulging any names.

"You know that my cousins are after the pictures?" he asked when I had finished.

I shook my head. "I get the feeling you don't want them to get hold of them?"

I waited. Raised my eyebrows willing him to tell me more.

"They're unsavoury people, Miss Chamberlain," he said with a sigh, adding "On all levels – physical, emotional, intellectual and spiritual."

I stared in amazement. "Blimey, guv'nor. That's rich. You got proof?"

He chuckled at my cheeky cockney sparrow imitation.

"Some. I don't like what they do, or what they stand for."

Echoes of Josiah, and my father. "I might be able to help you, then. My father was propositioned by Percy Meredith to develop some land he owns, this weekend – in some sort of consortium."

It was Mr. Simmons turn to be surprised.

I seized the initiative, "And when I visited Greystokes, yesterday, I saw some bad cracks in the buildings."

"Yes. There's a lot of that sort of thing in Meredith and Meredith work. It usually comes out after the new build guarantee runs out, strangely enough. You went to Greystokes. Why?"

"To see how things might look when our fortunes are made," I said drily. "Of course, he only showed us the most prestigious bit, but I wandered off. It helps being a woman. Mr. Meredith has a very low opinion of women's mental and/or business faculties."

Mr. Simmons nodded. "Neither of them do. I wouldn't touch either with a barge pole."

"Don't worry; I don't think my father will."

"Good. The only people who would make any real money would be my cousins in the long run."

"If that's so, why do people keep on trusting them?" I mused.

He drew at his pipe and let out another cloud of smoke with a sigh. "The Merediths usually have some hold over their partners. I can't prove this but I've heard hints to this effect on the grapevine, so I will say 'allegedly'. Or their less well-heeled partners are blinded by greed and the possibilities of huge influxes of cash, again 'allegedly'."

I took that on board. And wondered.

My father?

My mother?

I couldn't see them letting the Merediths apply the screws on them. They didn't appear to have any skeletons in any cupboards, but did they? I'd think about that later.

My brother Guy?

He wanted to bring them in. I didn't think he was bright enough to have anything to hide but the possibility of excessive amounts of cash without working for it – well, that would always attract him.

And Bulgy Algy Nesmith-Brown? What did I know about him and his?

Only gossip – they'd taken Marsham Meads when it had ceased to be a war-time sanatorium, and had had a lot of work done on it, as well they might have had to. Algy and his son Nigel worked in town – I never found out at what – I think they kept a place on there too - but Sylvia and her mother were often found at Marsham, both being horsewomen, although Anthea was far more sedate than her daughter.

Could the Merediths have anything on them? And if so, what?

Algy seemed pretty keen on the development of Wethersley Marsham.

Sam allowed me a time for silent reflection.

I pulled out another cigarette, fitted it into the holder and accepted the light.

"Do you want to see the pictures?" I asked at last. "Only the copies, of course. And I can also show you the house where the one I have seen was discovered."

It was around nine-thirty when we turned into the Boltons.

I hadn't given the address, but Sam Simmons started when he saw the road nameplate. "This is Kensington, yes?"

"More or less," I said. I wasn't that sure where the borough boundaries started and ended in this huge agglomeration of villages and localities that called itself London. I knew I lived in Chelsea, and this was the 'other' side of the Fulham

Road, and that was about it. "Is it important?"

"Possibly," he replied.

We walked on in silence. If he wanted to be stand-offish, that was fine. I wasn't going to press him.

Again, although there were bright lights coming through chinks in heavy lined curtains, or, in the case of upper rooms, through the single thickness of cheaper window coverings, in some of the houses, no-one else was abroad, and despite the little oblongs or slits of brightness, and the pale glow from street lights amid branches just putting forth the start of leaves around the oval roadway, it all felt desolate. It also felt like there'd be rain soon.

Hidden behind a tall London plane and its overgrown front garden, No. 35 appeared to be in total darkness. I slipped my hands into my coat pockets, shrugged deeper within its warmth and walked towards the house, but said nothing.

"Hold on," Sam said, checking the house numbers.

He looked up at the lowering mansion that was number 35. "My grandmother lived here," he said at last, taking another pull at his pipe. "When she was a child. My father told me he was taken here to see his grandparents, both before and after his dad died. He said it was a strange place. Didn't say how, but told me his Grandfather had a studio out the back. My grandmother was the daughter of a fairly well-known portrait artist at the time."

He looked at me quizzically. "Was this where you were bringing me?"

I said softly. "The studio is still there. This is where the angel picture I know about was collected from."

He whistled softly again, "Then the house is still in the family?"

"Uh-uh. I checked this out this afternoon. The person who last lived in it – and that is up until the end of March – was one G. W. Thorburn. At the moment I am pretty certain that it is uninhabited, although it might be the property of a certain Miss Thorburn who is engaged to marry one of your Mr. Merediths."

"Thorburn? That sounds familiar." He tapped his pipe out, tucked it into his pocket, and walked purposely along the front path, then turned down the side passage.

"What are you doing, Sam?" I hissed, following him.

"I want a look inside. This was my family's house. It should be mine."

He was at the end of the passage, and round the corner by the door now and his face was set into a determined scowl. "Look, Alice, you don't have to come in. Officially what I am about to do is illegal, but I feel I have a moral obligation and right. So why don't you go home? You've been really helpful, but I don't want you to get into any trouble." He was bending down with a tiny torch focused on the lock, rooting in his pocket.

"Might this be of any use to you?" I asked, holding out the key. "It's a copy of the one your uncle William left with Lowther's the auctioneers. I don't think the lock's been changed. It's worth a try, anyway."

He stood up, and looked down at me with a new appreciation.

"And I'm coming in," I told him quietly but firmly. "No-one leaves me out of the action."

The lock gave easily, although it squeaked and clicked.

I didn't like that.

And the door grated against something on the floor as we pushed it gently open.

Sam's torch was flickering across the floor when I put my hand over the bulb. "Do you want us to be found?" I hissed.

"There's no-one here, Alice! The place is empty." His voice echoed. He tried to pull the torch from my hand.

"Sam, do me a favour, please," I said in a voice that my

maquisards knew never to disobey. "Turn off the torch. Close your eyes and count to twenty, then go inside. You don't need your torch yet, and you don't need to flash it around like a searchlight. Just in case. It's standard practice."

"And you don't need to come here like you know everything," he snapped. "What have you ever done? I've been in the war, Madam, and survived, while you stayed at home. Just because you had the key, there's no need to tell me how to go into my own house." His voice was loud and angry now. I wondered whether the Reverend Simmons had seen this side of his adoptive grandson.

I was pretty angry myself. No-one treated me like that.

I had thought we were friends.

I stepped back outside, took the key from the lock and pocketed it. "Suit yourself," I said. "I'm going home. You can do what you like."

I was walking huffily round the corner of the studio to the side passage when a motorbike drew up outside.

I'd know that sound anywhere.

A Matchless.

A very familiar Matchless.

I heard it being lifted up onto its stand, and the familiar whistle of an old friend as he walked to the front door. He knocked three times.

I flattened myself against the door in the side alley that was the servants' entrance and hoped Bobby wasn't making a delivery of something illegal. From inside I heard the sound of someone coming downstairs, quite heavily, as though there were no carpets.

I heard the door open, and Bobby's voice. "Ah, Milady, you're looking as lovely as ever. Will you be letting a poor traveler bearing gifts into your life again?"

There was a snort of laughter, and a soft reply, then the sound of the front door shutting, and of people going upstairs. I heard only the heavy-footed female feet. Bobby, as ever, was light on his feet, but his blarney and charm echoed through the dark empty spaces.

I was shocked.

No, that wasn't the word.

I was disturbed.

I didn't know who the female was, but he'd called her Milady, and that was my name.

I was piqued about that, but then, on reflection I realised it was also a generic. Like 'Guv'nor' or 'Squire' for men whose names you didn't know - if you were working class.

But I was more shocked by the fact that Bobby Gallagher was on the premises.

No matter how annoyed I was with Sam, I had to warn him that he was not alone, that the house was very much occupied.

I nipped back round the corner – he'd left the door wide open! – and went into the studio. It wasn't what I expected.

It was in the process of being painted white.

How did I know? Apart from the smell? And the ladders and paint pots and sheets around the place?

Sam was kneeling in the middle of the magic circle with the central electric light on, drawing the sigils into a little notebook!

I began to wonder how he had survived the war. It explained the scar on his face.

"Sam!" I hissed. "There are people in the house. Dowse the light! Let's go." He looked up at me. "I've got to get these for the Rev. You go ahead."

"Sam, there are two people in the house, one of whom I know, and the other of whom I might know. I can't let you stay here to get caught as a housebreaker."

I found the light switch and flicked it, and not before time, for above me, from the house, I heard gales of laughter, and heavy footsteps making their way to the door above the steps which led from the house over the passage to the garden, to the door and stairs above me in the studio.

Sam also heard. "Right, coming," he said, and we dashed through the doorway, closing it and locking it as the indoor entrance above was breached.

Neither of us moved.

We heard the clatter of two people coming down the stairs, and a voice, Bobby's voice, say "I'm sure I saw the light on, Milady. I'd swear before the Holy Virgin and all the saints."

There was a low laugh, one that I had heard recently. "Nonsense, Bobby. You just wanted to get me down here in the Temple and have your wicked way with me." Then bubbling laughter again.

But no sound from Bobby.

"Well, you can, you know. Have you ever had a woman over the altar?"

I touched Sam's arm, and pointed to the way out. He nodded in the gloom, and we crept.

As we gained the pavement the rain decided its time had come. No warning drizzle, just a battery of large heavy drops that soaked right through your clothing to your skin.

Bobby would have a wet bum before he got home.

Sam set the double brandy on the table before me, then sat down opposite me with his own. "OK, Alice? I apologise. I shouldn't have been such a bally ass. You were right, all the way along the line, and you got me out of there, as well as getting me in, for which I thank you most sincerely. Can't we be friends?"

We were sitting in the Goat in Boots, not one of my favourite pubs, but it was dry. We weren't. The Heavens had opened on us. We steamed gently in the smoky fug.

I sighed.

He wasn't a bad chap. And he had apologized, but the snipe about me doing nothing in the war had really annoyed me. He had taken me at face value. A woman. Not a soldier like him. Hell, I had trained soldiers albeit informal ones, *maquisards*, as a woman, no mean feat, I can tell you, and I had survived too. Thanks to my wits as well as to my courage. I would never have acted as stupidly as he did. Yet I couldn't tell him this; it was still all hush-hush.

Besides, I doubt he would have believed me. He was a man, and would of course generalise and take me at face value; I was a posh bird and no-one expected posh birds to do anything useful – probably the most remotely useful thing I had ever done during the whole duration of the war, while he was sleeping out in no-man's-land, was to roll a few bandages, in his mind. It rankled, oh how it rankled. Girls and women had kept the country going and now they were treated like this. I had thought the antipodeans had a more equal way of looking at things. Obviously not this one.

But I swallowed the gall. I didn't want to make waves, or create enemies. On this trail, I was sure, there would be enemies enough.

I stuck out my little finger for him to link with. "I'd rather be friends than enemies."

He crooked his little finger in mine and we shook, like children, then clinked glasses and drank.

"So, who were the people? You haven't said a word since we left."

"The guy on the motorbike is a ..." I didn't know how I would describe Bobby. A friend? Yes, but... possibly more, possibly less, more than an acquaintance, though, and almost, I had thought, a colleague, or at least a fellow-traveller. "He's someone I know, reasonably well. He works for an old friend of my father's. I didn't expect to see him there. In fact, he was the last person I expected to find in that particular place."

"And the woman? She was giving him the come-on, alright, wasn't she?"

"Ah," I said, taking another sip of liquid warmth. "She

had every right to be there. It is probably her house."

I took in his knitted brow. "You have a problem with this?"

"But she's ... er ... correct me if I am wrong, but is she not engaged to be married to a Mr Percy Meredith?"

I nodded.

"Oops!"

I shook my head. "Nothing could be more innocent," I said.

"What? She propositioned him! I heard her. So did you. Don't deny it."

"Don't jump to conclusions, Sam. He is a spiv. He gets things, he fixes things for people. I heard him say he came bearing gifts. He does a good line in nylons, and I imagine he can get most things, for a price, that the rest of us cannot."

"So she pays in kind?"

"You are very prurient, Sam," I said tartly.

"I'm a journalist, Alice."

"Point taken. And you may well be right." I could see it being a mutually agreeable arrangement, in principle, but not in the specific way that was offered tonight.

Could she have been teasing Bobby? I didn't know the answer to that.

The landlord struck the bell by the bar for last orders. Sam raised his eyebrow in question.

I shook my head. "It's been a long day. Are you going back to the Rev tonight?"

"I'm staying in town. He knows. Can I walk you home?"

14

I slept late the following morning, and was awakened by the doorbell. My friends knew to give me time to let them in, so I wasn't surprised when I saw a short round shape silhouetted through the stained glass door panels. My sister had come to call.

I was still dozy when I ushered her, breathless, into the sitting room. She edged herself down into the armchair in front of the gas fire. I lit it with a spill then used the same one to light the gas-ring under the kettle.

"What's up?" I asked.

She was still wheezing. "Why do you live so damned far up in the air?" she managed.

I shrugged my dressing gown closer round me. "It suits me. Except when I've got suitcases or a lot of shopping."

"I'm carrying a pair of suitcases and a Harrod's hamper around all the time," she grumbled, patting her stomach.

I handed her the biscuit barrel. "I thought you and Basil shopped at Fortnum's."

"Oh, spare me! Home and Colonial." I chuckled. "Tea? Milk and two sugars?"

"Yes, please. What do you think of Jeremy?"

I busied myself with making tea. "Did Maman send you?"

"Ever cynical! No. She didn't. Bas did."

"Bas! What business is it of his?"

"He's your brother-in-law," said Maddy. "In case you forgot."

I sighed. "He's a devious devil as well. What's he want of me? Not that I'm promising anything." I kept my voice light, but my back to her. She was too good at reading faces.

"Why, Alice, he wants you to be happy." She trilled. She actually trilled. "Surely you want that, too?"

"Come on, Maddy, he wants a lot more than that," I said.

I handed her a tea in a floral bone china cup and saucer that had survived the flat's previous owner. "He wouldn't have sent you to climb all my stairs if it hadn't been more than a vague desire for my long-term and continuing happiness."

"Ooh, you are getting vinegary."

Yes, and with reason too. I put my mind back to answer her question. "What do I think of Jeremy? He's personable, a good dancer, quite pleasing to look at but perhaps he tries a little too hard with the ladies."

My sister frowned. "I don't understand."

"Don't you? He likes the ladies. As you know!"

"I don't know what you mean!" her chin came up. She looked daggers at me.

"I think you have a faint inkling what I mean," I told her. "He stole a friend of mine's girlfriend from him. I have that on good authority. I also can give you chapter and verse on sweet nothings, if you want. So, although he is a good dancer – a very good dancer – and can be charming, I would not trust him further than I could throw him. What department does he work for?"

"Good Heavens, Al, I don't know. I think he's sort of 'floating'. Why does it matter?"

"It doesn't. But it would help me pin-point a few things."

She raised her beautifully tailored eyebrows while nibbling a biscuit. "Look, we're having some people to dinner tomorrow. Bas wants him there, and we need you to make up the numbers."

"Charming!"

"Oh, come on, Al, you'll get a free dinner and you look

so damn good together."

"Yes, don't we? I thought. But I hid the thought from my face and reached for a biscuit. "Well, he put himself out for me, so I suppose it's only fair that I do the same for him. Who'll be there?"

"Pretty much the same bunch as were at Wethersley – Percy and Elisabeth, Guy and Sylvia, us, you and Jeremy…"

"Hold on a minute," I exclaimed. "What are you up to? And who is Elisabeth?"

"Percy's fiancée, Miss Thorburn. Surely you knew her name?"

"Oh, you mean 'Sweetie'? I'd forgotten. So what's going on?"

"Er… I think Bas ought to tell you himself." She sipped her tea. "Nice tea, Al. You haven't got a cigarette?"

I tossed my last packet of Gauloises at her and watched her select one, light it from a spill that she stuck into the gas fire. "OK, when can he tell me? And what has Jeremy got to do with all this?" I took back the packet, and found my holder. "And does Guy have any idea of what you are up to?"

"Bas will meet us for lunch," she said. "Just you and me. No Jeremy. But he is involved. It's all a bit hush-hush. And no. Guy has no idea at all what he is getting into. Whether Sylvia does, that's debatable."

"Hell!" I exclaimed. "It doesn't have anything to do with dodgy practices by any chance? In building, in finance, in just about everything?"

My little sister's face was a picture of innocence. "How would I know, Al? I'm just a simple housewife."

We met Basil in St James's Park, on the bridge. We had brought sandwiches and a flask, and eventually found a bench on one of the grassy knolls of Green Park, which was completely isolated.

165

By the time Basil had stopped talking I was perfectly willing to stooge as Jeremy's partner. In an odd sort of way it linked with what I was doing for Leggy. But of course there was no evidence. No evidence of any sort. That's what we would have to provide.

My sister was put in a taxi to take her home. I walked back to the Foreign Office with Basil then went on to Whitehall where I got an 11 bus. "World's End, please," I said, without thinking, and paid the fare. The instinct had been right. I needed to talk to Leggy.

And possibly Bobby.

Leggy was in. Bobby was out. Very convenient.

"What do you know about the Meredith twins?" I asked shooing Nuts off the chair and sitting down.

"Aah!"

"You went to school with them, didn't you?"

I watched him, his mouth opening and closing like a beached fish, trying to decide whether or not to talk.

"Leggy, for Heaven's sake, why do you want these pictures? What do you want them for?"

"Whisky?" he suggested. "Bobby's managed to track down some Glenlivet."

"Don't change the subject, Leggy. Yes, I'd love a whisky. But I'd rather have the truth."

"Aah, truth. That's a big word."

"Only five letters, Leggy; please stop prevaricating. Am I right?"

He sighed, leaned over to the glass cabinet and got out two heavy squat squat tumblers. "Of course you are, Alice. Look, I've read all that you've done, and I'm impressed. It's time I leveled with you. I would have done sooner, if I'd thought about it, but, well, it's not easy to admit to people that you've been a little twerp. I was only about ten at the time, but I was still a little twerp, a complete and utter twerp." He set the tumblers on the table beside him then felt down beside his chair for the bottle.

"As you said, I went to school with the little devils, and got suckered in by them. I had a lot of time to think in Sick Bay. I swore I'd get them, get even with them, and get the bloody pictures. Swore I'd never get suckered again."

He held up a bottle full of pale amber liquid, opened it and sniffed appreciatively. "And I never have. Not like that. And as I grew older I forgot all about it. I was having too much of a good time getting on with my life."

He poured two fingers in each glass and handed me one. "Alice, I forgot all about both the Merediths and the pictures. Can you imagine how I felt when the damn thing was standing there in front of me? I knew it so well. It was like a bloody avenging angel, taunting me. I had to get my own back!"

"Yes…" I said. "Where did you first come across them? I mean, as far as I can make out they didn't have possession of the things. They were sold in 1908 to a Mr. Thorburn who lived in Suffolk."

Leggy smiled. "I went to school in Suffolk. So did the Merediths." He settled back in his chair now, prior to spinning the yarn. I did likewise, cradling the tumbler in my hands.

"They told me that they had these magic pictures, pictures that give them what they wanted, always, pictures that granted wishes. I asked them where they were. They said they were in a safe place, but if I was nice to them, they'd take me there. Only I'd have to be very good and do exactly what they said. There was always a price, they said. I agreed."

He sucked in the spirit and rolled it round his mouth appreciatively, and gave a wan smile. "I became their bloody slave, virtually. They had all my pocket money, all my tuck, I did all sorts of favours, but I really wanted to see those pictures. I was willing to pay the price."

I smiled.

His face had changed. I could see, beneath the years, the tobacco-stained moustache, the eager boy, who desperately needed to look upon magic pictures.

He took another deep draw of whisky then continued. "It was one winter Saturday. We had free time. Officially they were taking me home with them for tea with their Aunt. She didn't live far away, and we were allowed to go alone. Instead, we went to this big house. It was moated, and very old looking. Impressive. It was also empty, closed up. But they had the keys. Archie let us in. All the furniture was under covers, and it smelled a bit damp, and there was only the light coming from outside, through blinds. Percy had a candle, and we lit it. It was very eerie."

"I bet. Where were the pictures?"

I sipped at my Scotch. It burned, but it was a good burn.

"On the top floor, in the long gallery. There was a sort of temple set up there. In the candle-light it was very spooky, all the old ancestors peering down at you and cobwebs. I was really scared. It was already getting dark outside, and inside the house was really gloomy. At the far end there were these seven huge ... well... things was the best way to describe them. They were human-sized, so to me, a short ten-year-old they were enormous, with wings and strange severe faces. Some had weapons, there was one with a spear, and creatures alongside them, and they were set in a semi-circle, watching you as you came down the gallery."

He looked at me. "I was younger than them, as I say, and quite a small child, but I had a very big imagination, and it was working overtime and more. I really didn't want to go any further. They each grabbed my by an arm, and laughed, and dragged me forward. We were right up close to these huge figures. Then they told me who they were. And what they did. Then they forced me right up close to each one, and asked the angel to curse me if I wasn't up to scratch."

He took another sip of his whisky and eyed me over the glass. "It sounds so stupid now, but at the time I was absolutely terrified. Each face was boring into mine, and they seemed to come alive. I don't remember any of the angel names, or what they were supposed to do, but I do remember the twins telling me that I would be cursed. I hadn't come up to scratch. I had failed. I twisted away from them and ran for my life. Ran down the stairs, ran out into the rain, and kept running, until I found the way back to school. I knew a back way in. We all knew the back path, it was traditional among us lads. You had to cross a plank bridge over a stream. It was raining, as I said, and bloody cold, and muddy. I ran that way.

"All the time I was hearing their voices, telling me the angels were cursing me, and I caught my foot. The plank splintered and I slithered and twisted my leg, falling through, and the bone broke with a snap. I screamed and screamed, but no-one came. Not even the twins. It was cold, and I was stuck; I couldn't move, I was caught in the broken bridge, with the little stream licking my boots and rain falling heavily. All I could think of was these angels and their curse. I was certain that was what it was, and I just knew I was going to die. So why struggle?" He looked at me over his glasses. "There was no need to struggle, the angels whispered, give in, die!"

"But you didn't. You're still here, Leggy," I told him.

"Indeed! Of course I struggled. I was fighting for my life, and I knew it. I managed to pull myself out of the bridge's clutches and heave myself onto terra firma. I don't use the term dry land, because by now it was soaking. I had my school uniform on, and the coat was pretty serviceable, but it wasn't waterproof, and my leg was hurting so much I couldn't stop crying. I couldn't walk. I couldn't even crawl. It was almost dark and I kept seeing the angels' faces. I kept hearing Percy's and Archie's voices telling me that I was cursed, and it seemed true. Oh, yes, that evening I really knew I was going to die."

"So what happened, Leggy?" I asked gently.

He poured himself another whisky and offered me the bottle. I shook my head. He stoppered the bottle, put it back beside his chair. "It was the Games Master, my House Master, who found me. He missed me at bedtime. The Meredith's had said I had run ahead on the way back from their Aunt's. He had asked them why, and they said they didn't know. They had assumed I had got back before them.

"It was two in the morning when he found me, I learned later. I felt he was the Good Shepherd. He left me the lantern and a small bar of chocolate and promised he would be back with a stretcher. I had been going in and out of consciousness for some time, but from then on I managed to stay awake. I wasn't going to die. I knew then. But nor was I going to tell anyone about the Angels. As far as anyone else knew I had been to tea with Percy and Archie and their Aunt, and had run on ahead. No-one was going to know about me flunking out with the angels!"

"So you let them get away with it?"

"What do you mean? I stayed in Sick Bay for three months, and hardly saw anyone. I had nightmares, of course, but what child doesn't? When I'd recovered enough to walk around and go back to lessons properly, Percy and Archie were at public school. I was glad. I figured it was my own fault, but I was still scared of those angels. But then I too moved school and then it was the war – the Great War – and everything changed. As I said, I had too much going on to worry about them any more."

"Leggy," I asked, "Why didn't you tell me all this at the beginning?"

"I couldn't. I didn't know the name of the place – we went overland, across fields and through woods – and I never wanted to find it."

"Straddling Hall," I said.

"Precisely. You've done very well, Alice."

"Do you have any idea where the rest of the pictures are now?"

"I might. I've got some leads, as yet unproven. Why are you after the pictures? It's not to use them, is it?"

"I want to see them reunited. But mostly, I want to get back at the Merediths. I think, that is to say, I have heard, that they are looking for them."

"Okay."

"You've heard too?"

"Indirectly. They got split up after the fire at Straddling Hall. I've spoken to the artist who restored them."

"He restored all of them? Then they're all together? Where?"

"Were. He thought they were separated as soon as he'd finished the job. The person who had them was worried lest we were invaded. He thought Hitler might have use for them all together."

Leggy grunted. "If he'd heard of them, he might have."

"From other sources, I get the impression that he might well have heard of them."

"Now how would he have heard about them?" Leggy mused. "We had files on the bastards and they always came out squeaky clean."

"Perhaps you didn't delve deep enough," I said. "My brother-in-law has dug a little deeper."

"Ah, the chappie from the Foreign Office. Good. Oh, by the way, I asked around for your beau, Jeremy. He is thought to be the coming man, by powers that be."

"But not by Bobby?"

"Personal is not the same as important."

"How was Bobby last night?" I asked.

"I never ask what Bobby does on his time off, Alice. It's

not my business."

"But?"

"But he came in with the hump. Must have been turned down. Drank three glasses of whisky – and I mean glasses, not pub-measures – and went to bed cursing. Why do you ask?" He reached for his own bottle.

"I thought I saw him, well his bike, really. I wondered what he was up to."

"No good, I should imagine." It was said with kindness rather than malice.

He waved the bottle at me. I nodded now.

"Leggy," I said, accepting his refill, "Do you have anything else at all that is relevant to these pictures? Any papers? Documents? That might shed light on the stuff?"

"It's important?"

"I think it's very important. And it might also be personal." I told him about my weekend, and the proposal for Wethersley Marsham. "My brother Guy is convinced this scheme is going to make all our fortunes. I don't want to be filthy rich but equally, I don't want to be a pauper. From what you and others have told me of the Merediths, their friendship is not conducive to a healthy life financially." Leggy sucked another half-glass of whisky, took a long pull on his pipe. "I've got all the books and papers from the place. They're in the garage. If I give you the keys, you could pack them into the Humber and take them to your place. It is safe there?"

"I have a safe place," I assured him.

He dug into his waistcoat pocket, and pulled out his bunch of keys. "There you go, then. Bring them back as soon as you can. The stuff is in boxes on the right of the car."

At last, I felt, things are beginning to move.

I hooted outside my door, and George appeared like a nosy

mole from the basement. "I've got a job for you, George," I said. He nodded, swallowing a mouthful of whatever he was in the process of eating for his tea.

We got the boxes up to my flat – there were four of them – and stowed in my Aunt's study. I locked the door behind me, and then came down the stairs behind George, dropping him threepence. "If anyone asks you whether you did this, or saw this, you did not, George," I said.

He nodded. "I've been eating me tea, Miss. I never saw you drive up with no car, never saw no boxes, cross me heart."

"Good boy. And if anyone asks you, find out his or her name, and let me know, and the purse-strings might well be loosened further."

"Cross me heart, Miss. I'll not let you down."

"Thank you, George. Enjoy your tea. I hope it's not cold now."

"'S only paste samwidges, they don't get cold, Miss."

I drove the car back, garaged it and returned to Leggy's flat.

I rang the bell. If Bobby were there I would have to explain why I had Leggy's keys.

Bobby let me in. "Hello, Milady. Welcome to our humble abode. Leggy said I might expect you. Have you found anything else out about these heathen pictures?"

"How much has he told you?" I asked.

"No more than I knew last time we spoke." He tapped his nose. "Milady, there are other people looking for them. We need to get Leggy to put that painting in a safe place." He opened the rickety lift door for me.

"But I thought it was in a safe place."

"Here? You're joking!"

"Who knows where it is?" I asked, my face close to his.

He bit his lip, but said nothing.

Oh gods!

"Who do you fear knows it's here?" I demanded. "Bobby, I need to know."

He shook his head. "You don't need to know, Milady. You really don't."

"I think you and I need to talk with Leggy, Bobby. We've got to all put our cards on the table this time."

They were neither of them keen to, but I insisted. I needed to know where and how I stood, whether indeed I was prepared to go on with this job.

Leggy filled a pipe, and puffed at it. "I'm not prepared to give up on the paintings. I know they existed. I've seen them all very briefly. I don't now think they were powerful in themselves, but they have been used by unscrupulous people to gain power over others. The results are fed back into the paintings, giving them perceived 'power' – see how when I was set up I would believe anything. And the boys who heard about my 'accident' were only too willing to set the cause with the malefic angels. It becomes a self-fulfilling prophesy. I want to see those angels together again, to look at them with an adult's eye, and see what the Hell terrified a child into breaking his own leg. It's personal. And it is important, too. I know of people who have suffered because of them. Suffered considerably. And I need to know if they are still being used, and by whom."

He smiled at Bobby. "You see, Bobby, old chum, I may be reading all this witchy-woo-woo stuff, but I'm as sane as I ever was. I'm not out to join some strange cult. I want to see the pictures, and then I want to turn them on the Meredith Twins. From what I've been hearing lately, it's time."

"How will you do that, Leggy?" asked Bobby. "Seems from what I've heard – no names, no pack-drill – these chaps are also looking for the paintings at the moment. From what I heard, too, they knew where they were – with the Thorburns at Straddling, right until the time of the Fire. There was some sort of unholy group that met there. It had been since around the start of the Great War, on and off, my sources tell me."

I nodded. That made sense.

"The paintings were damaged," I said. "They were taken somewhere safe, and restored. I spoke to the restorer. They were all together in the winter of 1940 and 1941. And after that they were separated. For safety's sake, I was told. I had thought that it was so the things didn't get bombed, at first, but I think that perhaps things might have been deeper implications. If you believe in something, and can make others believe in it, you can control them. These paintings, as used by the Merediths, seem to be a means of control. I don't know about the Thorburns. I only know that at least some of the people whom I can link with these paintings seem to either disappear or go doolally, and people who come into contact with them seem to have little accidents."

I noticed Bobby looking uneasy, saw him cross himself, surreptitiously.

"Apart from the Meredith twins. Now why are they different?"

"They're a pair of unprincipled bastards?" suggested Bobby. "Begging your pardon, Milady."

"Have we proof?" I asked.

"I'm sure we will have it – or someone will," Leggy said, adding, "quite soon, actually."

He knew something. I knew he knew. He knew because he had done some enquiries about Jeremy.

So there were a lot of people in on this.

Too many, possibly.

I said, "Do you want me to continue searching for these paintings? I'm happy to do so, but again, no guarantees."

Leggy looked at Bobby, who nodded.

"I think so. I think that would be helpful, and I'm happy to pay a small retainer and expenses."

Bobby continued to nod, although I'm sure it wasn't his money that was coming my way.

"I think," he said, "we should get a new safe place for the picture, Leggy. I don't like it in your bedroom. Oh, Leggy, sure you didn't think I wouldn't notice? All the furniture's been shunted around and rucked up the carpet. Of course I noticed. Thing is, though, if the Merediths get even a sniff of it being here, they're going to be after it. One is better than none, isn't it? They'll be round for it. And you won't give it back, and they'll get nasty, and although we could stand back to back and see them off in the old days, we can't do that in peace-time. So I'd be much happier if you could find an alternative safe place. Very soon."

"So would I," I said. "But for the safety of the painting as much as for your safety. It's big and heavy, but it could still get damaged stuck behind your wardrobe."

Leggy snorted. "Ah, the artist's daughter speaks. I don't suppose you've got any ideas of a good safe place?"

I shrugged. "Best place to hide a painting is with a lot of other paintings. I could have a word with my father. His studio's crowded, but he could find space for a few more. Just a suggestion," I added.

"I like it. I trust Roger. Are you happy with that, Bobby?"

"Sure. I trust him too, but I never thought clearing that old place would have caused so many problems. I mean, we should have simply sold the damn thing, or burnt it."

"Oh, you can't burn an angel," Leggy reproached him. "Not a good Catholic boy like yourself, Bobby!"

"Ah, you may be right, but for the wrong reasons," Bobby answered Jesuitically. "So we'll be looking to get rid of him, will we? Could you ring your father now, Milady, while I make us some tea?"

I handed the keys back to Leggy after I dialed the exchange and waited.

"Of course I've got a storage space for an old friend," Pa said when I had eventually got through.

I handed the receiver to Leggy to organize the collection and transfer, thinking there might be a bonus for Pa possessing the picture, if he needed leverage over the Merediths.

Bobby brought in tea and slices of fruit cake and poured. "Did he say yes?" he asked.

"All set. He'll send someone down to collect it tomorrow morning. We need to wrap it up to keep it safe."

"I'll sort that out as soon as we've had this," Bobby said. "I'll be no end of pleased to see the back of that thing."

Before I left I got the contact number of the solicitor who had invited Leggy to clear the studio. I rang to make an appointment for the following morning. Then at last I was on the back of the Matchless whizzing home.

Bobby had perked up considerably. As he dropped me outside my front door he told me he felt the air had cleared. He didn't know what to make of the paintings, but those involved with them had some odd habits. Certainly not Christian! He'd personally be glad to see them – the paintings and their possessors – in Hell.

He blew a kiss as he roared off.

I remembered Miss Thorburn's voice propositioning him into unholy sexuality, and chuckled.

Was she having him on?

I don't know.

All I knew was that I would be facing her over dinner tomorrow night.

I wondered if her fiancé knew her predilections for rough trade – for let's be honest, that was what Bobby was. Something to file away for later.

I climbed the stairs and let myself into the flat. I was glad to be back. A lot had happened. I needed to organize my thoughts before I did anything else. I had cleared the dining table – it was bigger than the desk – and got my paperwork out when the phone rang. I was tempted to leave it, but was glad that I picked it up. It was Jeremy.

"I hear we are dining at your sister's tomorrow," he said. "Can I call for you?"

"That would be nice. She wants us there at seven, I think."

"Are you up to dancing tonight? We could go to a club and eat."

"I'm very busy tonight, Jeremy," I said. "No, truly, I am. Not washing my hair, although I may do later, but I've quite a lot on."

"I think we need to talk about tomorrow," he said. "I could come over for an hour or so, around nine."

I looked at my watch.

It was five thirty, and I wanted to get some reading and thinking done, but I found myself saying, "That would be lovely, Jeremy. You know the address?"

He rang off, saying he looked forward to seeing me again. Only courtesy, but it felt nice.

I went back to thinking, writing up and juggling with ideas and pieces of paper for a bit, then cleared a space and opened the first of the boxes.

Heavens!

It wasn't papers, it was full of old leather-bound ledgers. Inside, written in green ink, in a fine copperplate hand, were the details and proceedings of the *Templum Sanctum Angelorum,* the Minutes and records of a magical lodge that was run, on and off, by Mr. G. W. Thorburn.

Gold dust!

I flicked through the books – there were twenty – and found the one with the earliest date, January 1910.

The writing was beautiful, and described the establishment of a Magical Lodge at Straddling Hall and those present: Mr. Thorburn, *Magister Templi*, Mrs. Thorburn, *High Priestess,* Mr. Greystoke, *Ceremonarius*, Miss Jensen, *Seer*, Mr. Duffy, *Guardian*, Mr. Lloyd, *Officer of the South*, Mrs. Lloyd, *Officer of the North*, Mrs. Maltravers, *Messenger*.

I had no idea that things were so formal in magical work.

Mr. Greystoke?

But that could only have been Henry.

I thought he escaped abroad after beating up Arthur.

Or was it William, who was supposed to have disappeared?

Or even his father, ditto? Greystoke wasn't that common a name.

It had to be either Henry or William.

He, Mr. Thorburn, was a close friend of William. Could he have helped William disappear? But why would he want to? William, I mean?

Where would he go? He already had everything going for him; there was no need to leave. He could have stayed and done exactly as he wished, life had handed him so much on a plate.

Yet he came to London to sell these paintings, which were bought through auction by one of his close friends.

That didn't make sense.

Why not sell them to Mr. Thorburn direct and cut out the middle man?

And why disappear?

To keep them out of his brother, Henry's, hands?

Why?

Or if Mr. Greystoke on the list were Henry, what was he doing in this place?

I had understood he was abroad for a lot of this time. Perhaps I'd been misinformed.

I sighed.

Already these boxes were opening up more questions than they were answering.

I noted the question then continued reading.

It was fascinating. I had come to realise this sort of thing went on, obviously, but not the details. After a while I stopped sitting at the table, and took the book and curled up in an armchair by the gas-fire.

Skimming through the books, I learned how a lodge was 'built' on the outer and inner levels. I learned how 'Power' was raised, using the elements of Earth Air Fire and Water. I learned Lodge Etiquette – which intrigued me. It was all slowly and systematically done, with the Thorburns – our Miss Thorburn's parents, I imagine – acting as teachers and priest and priestess.

I was intrigued, interested. I'd not heard of priestesses in modern times – Christianity had knocked them for six – but here was one, alive and well in East Anglia in the earlier part of this century.

I stopped around a quarter to nine, my head buzzing, and realized I had to tidy away, tidy the living room a little, and tidy myself.

Dead on the dot, the bell rang.

I put the hairbrush down, and went downstairs.

15

He was wearing a belted raincoat and a dark trilby. Eat your heart out Sam Spade, I thought and wondered whether he had a blue-nosed automatic in his pocket. He shook hands with me, and followed me upstairs. He was another light stepper. Not as quiet as Bobby, but good.

I ushered him into the living room. He didn't seem to have felt the stairs at all. Fit, then.

I took his coat and hat and hung them on a hook on the door beside my own. "Please sit down," I pointed to the chairs by the fire. "I was about to make some tea. Would you like some?"

He smiled and brought a half bottle of Teacher's from his inside pocket. "I thought you might like this," he said. "I had tea at tea time."

Highland Cream, eh? Not a bad choice at all. I had to remember I had swimming in the morning. I got two heavy tumblers and set them in front of him, but put the kettle on anyway. I was thirsty, and I'd already had Scotch this afternoon.

"Do you mind if I smoke?" He poured the drinks – generously – then, as I put an ashtray in front of him, pulled out a cigarette case, silver this time, and offered it to me. I took a Turkish cigarette. He lit it for me, then handed me the glass, and lit his own, with a very stylish lighter.

He was stylish.

Understatedly so.

I caught him watching me appraisingly too.

"So, Jeremy, what is it that can't wait?"

"I heard you lunched with B. Has he filled you in?"

"Not completely. What is your interest in the Merediths?

Basil was a bit reticent."

He drew on his cigarette. "Damn. I thought he'd covered it all."

He took in my raised eyebrows as he exhaled. "OK. I'll give you all I've got. We are both interested in these blighters. He because of stuff that has gone on abroad – there have been complaints from nations where they have worked before – a hospital falling down here, a college building being less than perfect there, a government building showing building faults somewhere else. All on Meredith and Meredith construction sites. They won the contracts through our government, but used less than perfect materials, which they had specified must come from their own manufacturers. That's B's interest."

I nodded. That made perfect sense and matched in with what I was getting to know. "And yours?"

He smiled. "Mine's closer to home. My roots aren't in the privileged classes as you may have guessed. My mother taught dancing, my father worked at the local brickworks. It's closed now. Originally, when my father started there, before the Great War, it was a good respectable firm, quality materials, kept to deadlines, you know?"

I nodded. "And then?"

"About twelve, fifteen years ago things changed. The Merediths came on the scene. And it was very good for the firm. Lots of big orders at a time when work was hard to come by. To cut a long story short, they started to produce sub-standard bricks, as a policy, which might be acceptable in wartime, when you needed to build something quickly and had neither the access or the man-power to get at the basic raw materials, but not before, nor now, particularly when we need to export quality goods to survive. But when the Meredith orders came in, the company provided sub-standard materials, but got receipts for the best quality. "

I nodded. Drew on my cigarette. "That makes sense,"

I said.

"My father knew this. He also knew that the difference in payment was split between the buyer – M and M, and the seller – his boss, but before he could lay the evidence out to the police he met with an 'accident'. In one of the kilns."

His voice was cold and hard. "My father was a gentle soul, moral, ethical. He was also extremely careful about safety procedures. He would never have got into that situation. The inquest said it was accidental death. I don't believe a word of it. But I wasn't there to object. I was on government work. I didn't hear about it until about three months later, when everything was all over."

"I'm sorry," I said. "I had no idea. And your mother, how did she take it?"

He shook his head. "Badly. I got all this from my sister. She and her husband are looking after Mam now. She's not an easy house-mate. They say she might get better, but I think she's given up."

"I'm sorry," I said again, for want of anything more useful.

"Thank you." He drained the glass and poured another, for each of us. "I didn't come here to bore you with my family's problems, though. We'll survive, or not... in spite of the Meredith boys."

"Quite right! Basil mentioned cultivating them. Does that mean ploughing a trench and digging them in?"

He smiled. "I would like to do that, to be honest, but not yet. No. It seems your brother Guy has been charmed by them, so we, too, play along. That is to say, if you're willing. B said you were, but I know he's very persuasive."

"I'm willing," I said quietly. "But I must insist on one thing. No attachments. Let people think what they will, but we are both free individuals. Professionalism is important."

He let out a long sigh. "Thank you. I couldn't put it

better. We're playing a part, but it's only a part?"

I held out a hand. "I'll shake on that," I said. "Just friends."

He took my hand and pumped it. "Just friends – and equals. Business partners."

I took a draw of the whisky. "Right, now we've got that out of the way, what else do we have to do?"

"Gain their confidence, infiltrate their circle and see what can be found out. We want to find all their contacts. There are big names supporting them. We want to find out who and why."

I nodded. "Righty-ho. And we let Guy get his fingers burned if necessary. But I won't have my father ruined."

"Oh, he knows all about it. He's as keen to get them as we are. I think he holds them responsible for something nasty, something personal, but he wouldn't say what and it would have been churlish of me to enquire, having only just met the man."

So that's what they had been talking about over snooker. You live and learn.

I wasn't sure whether to bring him in on the paintings.

The kettle whistled on the gas-ring. I got up and made a pot of tea. "Will you change your mind and join me?"

"Actually, yes, if I may. Will you join me, get me into society?"

"Oh, I'm sure you could do it perfectly well without me," I said. "Personable young men with all four limbs, two eyes, hair and full set of teeth can go anywhere these days: they are positively lionized. Whereas spinsters over twenty-five are not nearly as popular with hostesses, particularly those with younger daughters to marry off."

"Are you saying no? I can take no for an answer."

"Not at all. I told Basil I was happy to join you. It will be very pleasant not to have friends trying to set me up with 'spare' men. They're almost always disasters."

"I have had the experience of being a make-weight," he

said, gravely. "Present company excepted, the girls have all been dire."

I handed him a cup. "Milk and sugar?"

"No, they were either pudding or vinegar."

I chuckled. "I'm no pudding, but I can be vinegary," I warned.

"But you dance beautifully. Milk, please, no sugar."

I said, "Do you know Bobby Gallagher?"

He took his tea. "Thanks. Bobby Gallagher? Should I? In what context?"

"He says you stole his girl."

His eyebrows raised. "Oh, that Bobby Gallagher! Little spiv. Great chap. No, I didn't steal his girl. She was fed up with him, and wanted me to make him jealous. Bit of fun. I've not seen him after we had a fracas at the Dumbwaiter. We both got slung out. He split my lip and I floored him. She loved it. I put her in my car and drove her home. To her home. Then I went home. To mine. That's about it. Why do you ask?"

"I'm working for his boss."

"Working for Leggy!" I could hear admiration in his voice. "But I thought he was out of the service now."

"This is private. But it concerns the Merediths." I was still unsure about telling everything.

"You want to clear it with him?" he asked. "I've heard all the stories about Leggy. He's very respected. I don't want to step on his toes. Look, I'll wait outside, if you want, while you ring him."

I sipped my tea. It was the decent thing for both of us to do. I nodded, and picked up the phone. Jeremy stood up and went to the door. While I dialed, he went out, closing it behind him.

Bobby answered.

I asked for Leggy, and eventually got him, explained the situation.

Jeremy came in when I called him. "OK," I said. "Make yourself comfortable. I've got clearance."

He left me at 11.30 with an empty whisky bottle and a full ashtray. I watched the little red car speed off from my bedroom window. Well, at least I would have an escort for the immediate future. Maman would start getting ideas, of course, but I was used to that.

I swam with Thelma in the morning, breakfasting together in a café afterwards. We arranged for Friday. Back home I dressed formally, to see Mr. Thorburn's solicitor.

I found him in an upstairs office in Gloucester Road. It was a small concern, and his secretary was a drab woman seemingly snowed under with files and papers.

She got off her typing chair with a sigh and led me into the great man's inner sanctum. "Miss Chamberlain, Mr. Woods," she said, her voice that complaining nasal of the perpetually put-upon.

He was a heavy man, balding, with his remaining hair swept backward into a polished dark semicircle. His jowls wobbled as he spoke, but his eyes were sharp. He rose, shook my hand, and handed me into a seat while the secretary shut the door behind her. He looked at the clock and noted the time on his blotter. "How may I be of assistance, Miss Chamberlain?"

"I wonder if you could tell me anything about the last will and testament of Mr. G. W. Thorburn."

"What makes you think I am the person to ask?"

"You employed a friend's firm to clear his studio after he died. I take it you are his executor. If so, you would be precisely the person to ask."

"Are you a friend of Miss Thorburn?" he asked.

"An acquaintance," I said.

"She sent you?"

"Not at all. Should she have?"

He steepled his fingers and inspected the nails. "She was not around when her father died," he said. "They were not estranged, but they were not close. Did you know Mr. Thorburn at all?"

I shook my head. "Not personally. Only by reputation. He was considered a specialist in his field and an honourable man. I would have very much liked to have met him. Our interests would have gone along many of the same lines."

"Ah," he said. "You are interested in his life's work?"

"Very much so. I wanted to know if there were things left of an... esoteric nature, do you see?"

"Mmm. Well, I don't think I can help you much in that way. He gave most of his ... er... specialist equipment away as soon as he realized he was not going to get better. He only kept a few things – the picture, of course, which he really didn't want his daughter getting hold of – and the papers. He instructed me to get rid of them for him in the most expedient way possible. I called in a local clearing firm. I imagine they've got rid of the stuff in the usual way – rag and bone men, local auctions, or even the bonfire, that sort of thing. They did a good job. I checked."

"What about the rest of the house?" I asked.

"Oh, he had already willed that over to his daughter, with the studio, to save on death duties, years ago. I advise all my clients to do that, there's no point throwing money away."

"He left no other bequests? To friends? Family?"

"Miss Chamberlain, he'd been sick for some time; he used that time to make his peace with his friends and say his goodbyes. It had all been done. He was a very orderly gentleman."

"Thank you, Mr. Wood," I said. "I appreciate your frankness and your time." I stood up to go, holding my hand out.

He took it, but didn't shake, "Er... You really are interested in his work, Miss Chamberlain?"

"Oh yes. Very much so." I found myself repeating the same phrase, and disliked myself for it. But it worked. After some consideration he made a decision.

"I wouldn't normally do this but ... perhaps you might like to ring this number? Say you've spoken to me, and your interests." He drew the cap off a fine Parker fountain pen with a gold nib and wrote a number in a small perfect black copper-plate script on a sheet of headed notepaper, blotted it, then handed to me. "It's been a pleasure to meet you, Miss Chamberlain. Good luck in your quest." He rose, shook my hand and ushered me to the door.

As I slipped the paper into my handbag, I was jubilant. I recognized the number. It was the first on the list that Rufus had given me.

Now I had the link between Thorburn and Finching confirmed.

And an introduction.

Life was good.

I noted the clock above the door. Seven minutes. Whatever his miserable secretary decided to charge me, it was worth it.

I put through a trunk call to the number at home. Eventually I reached the local operator; she told me in a precise Highland accent that there was no answer from that number, that tonight might be a better time to try. I thanked her, and hung up.

Tonight it would be difficult to make a private phone call.

I thought about writing – I knew that the number belonged to Lord Finching, and hence had the address – but I didn't actually want to commit myself to paper. It had to be by phone. An ex-Directory number would be best.

I went through my wardrobe. If I was going to start going out into society, I would need some new clothes. I had one other decent frock – neither as expensive nor as politically dubious as the Chanel – that would more than pass muster tonight.

I wondered how Basil had managed to get it all sorted at such short notice – or had it all been planned some time ago? I wouldn't put it past him. Or Maddy. She looked like butter wouldn't melt in her mouth, but she was and always had been a cunning little minx. But with rationing, entertaining at home was a luxury for the very rich indeed.

I needed time to think, and time to unwind.

I took myself to Harrods and booked an afternoon appointment with the beauticians, then spent the intervening time studying what fabrics and clothes they had available, catching up with fashion and things of style and elegance while letting my brain mull over all that I had learned over the past ten days.

I treated myself to a new lipstick, and a real orchid corsage that picked up the colour to lift the severe lines of this evening's dress. I liked the idea of living jewellery, even if the flower was a parasite.

Jeremy turned up on the dot in a taxi. He opened the door for me.

"No little red sports car?"

"Never turn up in the Morgan when you have a lady who has pulled out all the stops," he said. "You look absolutely stunning." He gave the cabbie the address, and we were off.

I told him about my visit to Mr. Woods.

He whistled softly. "So he didn't want his daughter getting hold of the information or the picture? Well I never!"

"I would have thought that Thorburn would have given those to his friends in the time leading up to his death," I said. "He got rid of lots of stuff, but kept the records and the picture."

"Perhaps they meant a great deal to him. Or that he hadn't decided upon whom to bestow them," Jeremy suggested.

"Who knows?" I shrugged. "Perhaps he died sooner than he expected. Thing is, we have the things."

"You are quite sure that the number Woods gave you is that of Lord Finching?"

"Boleskine 666, yes," I said.

"Very well; we ring him before we get to B's." He tapped and opened the glass partition between us and the driver. "Change of plan. Can you drop us off just beyond these lights and wait. We may be about ..." he looked at me questioningly.

"Ten minutes, possibly a quarter of an hour," I supplied.

The cabbie looked round. "Sure, Guv. I'll keep the meter running."

"Of course you will," said Jeremy. "Quite right too." The car slewed to a halt outside the Hyde Park Hotel, and we bundled out.

Jeremy was greeted by name by the clerk at reception. "Could you put through a call for me?" he asked, handing over the number.

"No problem at all, sir. Cabin number three, sir. You're well, sir?"

"Excellently so, Joseph, thank you. And yourself?"

"Mustn't grumble, sir, thank you for asking."

We went to the third phone booth and waited. To give Joseph his due, he got through much quicker than I had done this morning. I saw him wave from the desk, and the phone began to ring.

I lifted the receiver. "Putting you through now, sir."

A click, and then a Highland burr on the line. "Boleskine 666. Good evening to you."

"Good evening," I said. "My name is Alice Chamberlain, and I have been given your number by Mr. Woods, executor to the late Mr. G. W. Thorburn. He thinks you may be able to help me, as I am very interested in Mr. Thorburn's life and work."

"Ah, you'll be wanting the Master, and he's not here at the moment," said an elderly male voice, which reeked of Highland mist .

"Could you give me a contact number, please, sir?" I asked.

"Och, I possibly could. But I'd prefer you to give me a contact number, so that I can ring him and then get back to you. He's a very secretive man, you understand, and a very busy man."

"I understand," I said. I gave him my own number, which was ex-Directory.

"I would be very grateful if you would deal with this as a matter of urgency, but I will not be there this evening."

"I shall not be contacting the Master this evening, Miss ... er ... what was the name again?"

"Alice Chamberlain. Thank you for your time and trouble, sir. Good evening to you."

I heard his farewell then put the receiver down. "It's in his court," I said to Jeremy. "Best I could do."

He nodded, opening the door for me. "You can do no more than that."

He dropped the clerk, Joseph, a ten shilling note for the call. No wonder he was given royalty treatment. Our taxi door was open, and we were away. The cabbie showed us his skill, swinging a full semicircle and diving round into Sloane Street, despite traffic coming at us from all directions, to catch up time. He seemed to be enjoying himself.

16

Basil and Madeleine lived in one of the elegant town houses in Pont Street. Madeleine had done extremely well for herself when she married Basil, and he didn't underestimate his own luck. A good ten years older than her, although he didn't look it, when she was a sweet young woman of 18, he was nudging his third decade.

Basil had just been promoted, and it had been suggested to him that to climb the diplomatic ladder, he would need a wife.

A wife who would be an asset.

He had taken that on board and scouted the latest bunch of lambs to the slaughter.

No competition.

Maddy was such a darling to behold and still is; far more Maman's build and just as stylish, she has Pa's fair English colouring.

He was smitten, and when she saw the life that she could lead, once the bloody war was over, so was she. The deal came with a fine house in London, the opportunity to be a hostess of the first order, and the promise of travel. She loved Basil, and their child, but she would be able to survive without him. Whether he could without her was another matter.

Jeremy paid off the taxi and followed me into the house. Basil kept a small staff, but came to greet us himself, and as I kissed him on both cheeks, I smelt an expensive gentleman's cologne. "Come in, my dears. We need a council of war before the others come!"

Just the four of us, then.

Maddy tossed me a packet of Gauloises, while Basil

dispensed whisky. "The aim is to simply let them feel at ease with us," he said. "We are out to get into their circle, that's all. We all know about the magical stories, the pictures and the interesting substances and things that went on before the war, but we are after facts – and evidence. The construction and development businesses are one of the things they seem to use both to make money and to launder money. They play on people's cupidity, and seem to have levers over quite a few of their friends."

Maddy sat on the sofa beside her husband. "Guy was approached because he works in finance and is acquisitive. But he was introduced by his prospective father-in-law," she said. "He is very keen on the development of Wethersley Marsham."

"We are pretty certain the Merediths have something over the Nesmith-Browns," Basil continued. "Look at their antecedents. They were minor squirearchy in Cambridgeshire, and had not a lot going for them. Usual problems, the ancestors hadn't been provident and they themselves were unsuited to working, allied to a taste for champagne with brown ale income. Enter the Merediths in their life in the mid-thirties. Suddenly, money was no problem. They sold up the Cambridgeshire property, took a place in town, traveling extensively in and around Europe until the War which they mostly spent in the South East.

"They recently took the place at Marsham. In Cambridgeshire, the house was knocked down and the area redeveloped by the Merediths into a dormitory village for the university. The Nesmith-Browns, wherever they go, become part of society, not top-hole, but acceptable, both locally and nationally, and both he and she extol the virtues of M and M. They have been very useful allies. Jeremy and I are compiling a list of people whom they have introduced and about their little financial schemes here and abroad. I've no doubt it's a favourite working ploy."

I nodded. I knew that.

Basil continued. "However, it does seem that there might be some mileage to be gained on the magical front. You all know the stories of the angel pictures. I have it on good authority that the Merediths are looking for them. They are keen to have possession of them once more. They had access to them in years gone by, but it seems that the legal owner, Thorburn, who worked as a bona fide ritual magician, if such a thing can be, saw their effect and decided to keep them safe. We are reliably informed that his daughter Miss Elisabeth Thorburn, engaged to Mr. Percy Meredith, is about to open a new temple in London. She is actively searching for new acolytes."

Basil looked directly at me, and at Jeremy. "I trust you have no objections to infiltrating?"

"None at all," Jeremy said, glancing at me.

I shook my head. "No problem, Basil. A question though. Does Guy know about this?"

"Not that I am aware of. His interest in the Wethersley Marsham project is solely to increase his financial and social standing."

There was a ring at the front door. "All clear? Then let's meet the guests."

It was a civilized dinner – the food, as promised, was good. We spent a lot of our time being friendly and encouraging, so much so that Guy commented on how much sunnier I was now I had a beau.

"She can be very waspish, Jeremy," he said, swilling down the last of his Beaujolais. "Take my advice, and if the stinging tongue starts, nip it in the bud."

"I wouldn't dream of it, Guy. Alice is her own person. Besides, to change her you'd have to use magic."

"Don't believe in that sort of stuff," Guy averred.

"You don't?" That was Sweetie. Although she had invited me to call her Elisabeth, I still thought of her as

Sweetie, particularly as Percy (yes, I had permission to call him that, too) always referred to her as such. "Percy, darling, tell the young man. Magic works." Her voice was husky, seductive, her demeanour the same.

"Magic makes the world go round, Sweetie, as you and I know only too well." Percy winked at her, wiped his mouth on his napkin and held up his glass and drank deeply.

"Never!" expostulated Guy, pompous as ever. "That's just bilge-water. Stuff for babies, all fairies and witches. No-one actually does magic any more, except conjurors at the Music Hall – if they ever did. It's all down to luck, who you know and being in the right place at the right time."

"Oh, indeed," Sweetie agreed, bestowing a 'come-hither' smile on him. "But magic gets you the luck, the contacts and the time and place. That's why ordinary people have it so hard. With magic, you can get anything you want. It's all available for you, and once you know how to use it, you can have a really wonderful life." She sounded persuasive, but also ever-so-slightly squiffy.

I leaned forward. "You obviously know these practices, Elisabeth," I said. "You've traveled the world, have a comfortable life, and a nice fiancé. Could you teach me how to use magic?" I put on a winning smile.

"Me too," said Jeremy. "I'd really like to learn. I was good at wishing for things as a kid. They almost always turned up."

Percy looked at him appraisingly. "Young man, that is a very fine start, but there's a long hard haul before you become a true Magus. Years of study and service."

"I've got all the time in the world," said Jeremy, going for broke in front of his boss.

"So have I," I added. "I'm at a bit of an impasse at present, to be honest. Guy, don't you think it would be a good thing for me, to take up a course of magical study? I would be very discreet. You know you don't want me working for a living, and I've got to do something, or I'll go mad of boredom."

"Discretion is very important," mused Elisabeth thoughtfully. "Discretion, discipline and dedication."

"Oh, that's Alice to a tee," said my sister tartly. "When she goes at something, she really gives it all she's got, and she certainly knows how to be secretive, I can vouch for that."

"And I can vouch for Jeremy," added Basil with a chuckle. "He's extremely discreet and very hardworking. But he could use a bit of home-made luck."

"Thank you, sir, I'm not quite on my uppers yet!" Jeremy quipped.

Percy looked us up and down, frowning. He chewed, trying to free a morsel of meat from his interstices, while he considered us. Finally the meat must have dislodged, for he gulped, and looked at Elisabeth. "What do you think, Sweetie? Shall we give them a go?"

"Nothing ventured, nothing gained. Why not?" she said, stretching her neck upwards, then drawing it back to peer at her empty glass.

Basil's butler immediately refilled it.

That's magic, her triumphant gaze said. Even Guy looked impressed. Then the butler spoiled it by filling everyone else's glasses.

"How about you both come to our next meeting?" Elisabeth suggested, dabbing her lips with her napkin.

"I'd like that very much indeed," I said. "Thank you."

"So should I," Jeremy added. "Will you let us know when and where, and what we need to bring?"

"Of course," said Percy. "Sweetie will contact you both with details shortly." He looked at my brother questioningly. "You not interested, Guy? Couldn't tempt you a little?"

"Er… Rather too much on at the moment, thanks, Percy." His voice was a little shaky.

Fear!

I'd got him scared.

Yes!

He glared at me. I smiled back sweetly.

He flushed with annoyance, but whether it was because I'd got an invite from his friends or that he didn't trust the idea of magic, I wasn't sure. Or it could simply have been the result of the wine and the food; he was becoming a good trencherman.

Sylvia kissed his cheek, "Oh Guy, darling, don't be such a wet blanket. It's just a bit of fun, and if it works, so much the better. And it will make your sister happy. I might go along. You'd let me, wouldn't you, Uncle Percy?"

Percy turned his face to Sylvia and shook his head. "Not without your father's written permission, Sylvie, dear. You are not yet twenty-one."

So they had a no-minor rule! Well, what did that mean?

"But I'll be married before I'm twenty-one," Sylvia complained, "and then you'll have to ask Guy's permission, and he'll be an old fuddy-duddy and refuse to give it, won't you, darling?" She reached out and caught the flesh of his cheek in her hand and gave it a shake. "Who's a wittle fuddy-duddy, den? But we love him, don't we, diddums?" she said, then dropped a kiss on his forehead, then looked at Percy defiantly. "But I will join. I'll ask uncle Archie. He will let me come," she said with a toss of her head. "Uncle Archie always gives me what I want."

A challenge then? Guy's face darkened even. I felt myself, despite everything, feeling sorry for my brother.

"Dessert?" Maddy suggested brightly. "We have *riz a la crème au rhum.* Or rice pud."

This time I did withdraw with the ladies. We went to the living room where there was a well-stoked coal fire and a hostess trolley with a choice of tea or coffee and liqueurs. It was a cosy room, with comfortable traditional furniture, heavy velvet curtains and some of Basil's family pictures. Rich Persian carpets covered the floor, and brass and copper gleamed in the light of the fire and the standard and table lamps. In short it was rich without being flashy, intimate without being decadent, traditional without being stuck-in-the mud. I liked this room very much, and joined Maddy at the trolley.

"*Digestifs*, anyone? Before the tea or coffee?" she asked.

"Or the men?" I suggested.

"Mine's a small Benedictine, Alice, and no wise-cracks, thank you!"

I poured my sister a thimble of the liqueur. "Anyone else?"

"Have you got cherry brandy?" asked Sylvia. "I love cherry brandy."

"Grand Marnier, if you've got it," said Sweetie. "If not anything else with oranges in it."

I dispensed their drinks and poured myself a Remy Martin. "Does it worry you if we smoke?" I asked Maddy.

"Not at all." She handed ashtrays around. "Last Saturday was the first time I managed to feel myself again, and it's stayed with me, so do as you will. It's so good not to be sick all the time." She looked at the two engaged ladies. "Do not take pregnancy lightly. It seems such a simple option, but it's damned uncomfortable, the birth is hell and the result lasts with you for years."

I chuckled. They had probably not seen this side of Maddy, and needed to not be shocked. "I heard that if you find out what causes it and stop…" I suggested.

Maddy threw a cushion at me, Sweetie chuckled and Sylvia looked puzzled.

"You mean it doesn't just happen?"

Oh God!

Three pairs of eyes gazed at her in disbelief.

"Er, you really don't know?" said Maddy gently.

The girl frowned. "Know what? I mean you get married, and then you have children, more or less, depending on what is meant to be. That's right, isn't it?"

Sweetie groaned softly.

Maddy's jaw dropped, and she looked at me for help.

"Er... Not exactly," I said. "There is a bit more to it than that."

I fished around in my memory – who had told me?

Well, there were stories at school, of course, all wrong, dubious, scare-mongering, and downright horrible, and Maman had never really mentioned it. I got told about periods on my thirteenth birthday, and what to do about them, which I thought was pretty unpleasant as a birthday present, but not the whys and wherefores, nor the actual mechanics of conception. That came through the war. They made sure we knew exactly what caused what, and were duly prepared. And warned off, but of course, when you're warned off something enough, what are you going to do? But I was very choosy and very very careful. If I'd succumbed to pregnancy or a nasty little disease, there would have been Hell to pay, literally.

Poor Sylvia, I thought. But she wouldn't have been alone, strange as it may seem. Her 'coming out', such as it was, had hardly prepared her for womanhood.

"I should have a word with your Mother, if I were you," said Elisabeth. "It's her duty."

Sylvia looked puzzled. "But that's what Mother told me," she said. "You're surely not telling me she's wrong?"

Maddy groaned.

Elisabeth and I looked at her. "You're the one, Maddy. You're the only one who's married," I told her.

"I knew you'd say that. I just knew."

Elisabeth backed me up, quick as a flash. "And you will be family, too."

"It'll be good practice for when Enid's older," I said. "And any other children that might just happen."

"OK, don't rub it in. I'm the only one with the credentials," Maddy agreed. "Never let it be said I shirked my duty." She poured herself another Benedictine and tossed it back in one then looked at her future sister-in-law. "Sylvia, come and see me one afternoon, and I will reveal all. No, not literally. But I will try to explain how life on earth works."

"The ins and outs, so to speak?" I suggested.

Elisabeth grinned. "The ups and downs of connubial bliss?"

Maddy chuckled. "Oh, shut up, the pair of you. The things I do for my bloody brother." She cocked her head and moved back to the trolley. "Right, girls, tea or coffee? I can hear the men coming to join us."

We said goodbye to each other on the porch shortly after eleven.

Guy shook my hand, and pulled me close to him for a kiss. "Take care, Alice," he whispered. "Dabbling in magic is a dangerous game."

I hugged him close, and said softly, "You know me, Guy, always up for dangerous games, and I never dabble. But I will take care. I have a very wide streak of skepticism running through my character."

"You'll do, then. Safe journey home."

"You, too," I said. He was driving Sylvia back to her parents' house, some thirty miles away. I hoped there were no police around. He'd had a skin-full.

Jeremy and I handed our cards to Elisabeth before we saw them into their cab. "I'll be in touch," she called out of the window, "shortly. Promise."

We waved them all on their way. "Come in for an extra night-cap," Basil invited. "We need to share our information."

Maddy burst out laughing. "Believe me, you don't!" she

told her husband. "And I need to get to bed, I'm dying on my feet. I can fill you in, and Jeremy and Alice can do the same. Say 'goodnight' Basil."

"Goodnight, Basil," he mimicked, his arm around her. "See how henpecked I am. She's so tiny, but so forceful."

"Goodnight, Basil," I said, hugging them both and dropping a kiss on each.

"Goodnight, both of you," said Jeremy, shaking their hands. "And thank you."

We walked towards Sloane Street in companionable silence.

"Penny for them?" Jeremy said as we reached the crossroads.

"Mmm. I think I need to read all the stuff Leggy gave me."

"And that was?"

"Thorburn Senior's magical diaries, records, etc. I made a start on them yesterday, but ... tomorrow will do." I sighed. "Do you think they really believed we were keen? I thought we were a bit exaggerated, myself."

"They'd had enough to drink for our youthful over-enthusiasm to be taken for just that, and I think they really want us in. I mean, they've got Guy, so with you in their circle they can put more pressure on your father. What did you ladies talk about while Percy and Guy were going on about redeveloping the countryside for profit?"

"As my sister said, you do not want to know. She has been elected to tell Sylvia about the birds and the bees."

The laughter came slowly, gently, bubbling up until it became a great guffaw.

"It's not that funny!" I said.

"It is when you know Sylvia's background. Trust me on this."

"What? What are you saying?" I demanded. "Are you saying she's having us on? How would you know?" I turned to face him, troubled. This was classified information he had. "What exactly do you know? My brother's going to marry her! She didn't appear to know anything about anything. Naïve wasn't in it."

Jeremy's face quietened. "I'm not saying she isn't naïve. I'm just saying she hasn't put two and two together."

"I don't think I like the implications," I snapped.

"Hey, don't come all high and mighty with me. You're the one who's making judgements. What does it matter in the long run, anyway? They'll get married, because she wants it and he wants it, it'll be good or bad or tolerable, they'll have a few kids and then they'll die. That's what life's about, isn't it?"

"God, you're more cynical than I am!" I said, angrily.

"Unfortunately, yes. I probably am."

We were squaring up to each other under the streetlight. I could feel the temper boiling up in me.

He shook his head, took a step back then sighed. Stepped forward and put his hands very gently on my shoulders. "I don't want to fight you, Alice," he said at last. "If you can, please forget I ever laughed, ever said what I did. Maddy will be excellent at her task. Let's call an end to it. I'm sorry I asked."

"Yes," I said slowly. I let the anger subside. If we were to work together, and it was work work, nothing more, we had to stay compatible. "Yes. You're right. In the long run, who gives a toss? Sorry I blew up. It's a character flaw. I admit it."

He smiled and shook his head. "Then it's forgotten."

"Thank you. Look, I've got someone you might like to meet. I'll contact him tomorrow."

17

I was ironing when the phone rang. I gave my name. No number.

"Ah," said the Scottish voice. "Miss Chamberlain. The Master will call on you in half an hour. He is in your vicinity. You will be in?"

"Yes," I said. "But you don't have my address."

"That is of little consequence, the Master knows where you live."

The phone clicked dead.

I felt the hairs on my neck stand on end.

I didn't like that. The reason the number was ex-Directory was for security. My Great Aunt had insisted on that, she being a single woman living alone. I had naturally simply taken over her number, and gave it out rarely. There was no way my address could be known.

Unsettling. Very.

I finished the ironing, hung my clothes away and tidied up a little. Put on the kettle. I could be polite.

The door bell rang. I went downstairs.

On the step was a tall well-built man, around my father's age.

Nothing odd in that.

He wore a knee-length black cloak over his dark town suit and shoes, and a flat black Spanish sombrero. He leant casually upon a tall black cane with a silver head.

I smiled. "Welcome, Lord Finching. Your factor said you'd be around. Do come up!"

That caught him. He looked visibly disconcerted. "How do you know my name?" I ushered him inside.

I smiled. "I've got the kettle on, my Lord. I apologise for

the stairs, but I'm sure you're familiar with them."

"Ah," he said. "So your Aunt mentioned me, then?" he preened, as we climbed upwards.

I opened the door to my living room. "May I take your cloak, your hat?"

He did look a bit of a Charlie in them in my flat, a real duck out of water. I could understand people saying he was mad as a hatter. Perhaps he was. I'd have to find out. I hung the garments on a peg, sat him down and got out the biscuit barrel.

"You normally live in Scotland, my Lord," I said. "Are you down here on business, or pleasure?" He was looking about the room, smiling. "You haven't changed much. I thought I recognized the name when Mac mentioned it, but once I had the phone number, I was certain. Your great-aunt was a fine woman. She wasn't prejudiced in any way about anything. I liked her a lot, and miss her greatly."

I didn't want him getting maudlin. "Tea or coffee, sir? With or without milk or sugar?"

He came out of his reverie. "Er, tea, please with both if you have it. You are very like her, Miss Chamberlain. Stick to the point. Yes. Very like her..." He was wandering again.

I let him float, made him tea in the remains of my Aunt's best bone china tea set, and sat down opposite him, across the fire place, putting the tray on a small table between us.

The refreshment appeared to revive him. "I've been to see the memsahib," he said. "Bad business, that. She wasn't a well woman to start with, up and down all the time, you know, but ... well, she's better off where she is now. Seemed quite lucid today. Sometimes I wonder whether she really is mad now. She seems so ... well ... ordinary. But they tell me that at other times she's vicious, raving, and really quite terrifying. Yes... Blandings is the safest place for her. They look after her there... At least she says they do, and it costs enough... Not that I mind. As long as she's looked after, kept comfortable." He put his cup and saucer on the table. "It was those bloody paintings. They have a terrible effect on people. And the drugs, of course, but I didn't know about them, not until it was too late..."

Hell, I thought, and noted the name Blandings down for later. "What paintings, sir? What drugs?" I asked gently.

"I've told you before, Caroline," he said, using my Great Aunt's name.

Oh, Heavens!

"But I've forgotten," I said, gently. "Bear with me. I've got so many things going on inside my head, I can't remember them all."

His eyes glazed over. "Know what you mean, Caroline. Too damn much going on. Never used to be like that. Not when we were young, eh?"

"The paintings," I prompted.

"Yes, the bloody paintings. The bloody angels. I told Thorburn. 'They're misusing them,' I said. 'They're coming to Straddling when you're not there and misusing the place.' It was such a lovely temple when we first went, wasn't it, Caro? We were there to learn more about ourselves, the nature of the universe, the nature of the mind. And we were doing well, weren't we? The paintings weren't evil then. They were powerful, but not evil. They were plus and minus. Neither white nor black. We could use the power.

"Only when those two spawns of Satan turned up, all sweetness and light, the paintings began to change. But I didn't see it. You did, Caro, because you decided to get out. I remember you saying you felt things had changed, you'd gone as far as you felt you could with the group. You were the only one who had any idea what was going on. We didn't, none of us. We let those two young men – something magic about twins, isn't there? – take over. We let them bring in substances, techniques, attitudes which were dubious. Bloody dubious. Oh, they got results alright. They also brought in pleasure.

"Thorburn didn't notice. He was too busy writing books in London, and starting a new group off down there. He never lived at Straddling after his wife left. It was left to me and the Memsahib to keep an eye on the place, and I was out of the country for months on end for the government…"

He took out a fine monogrammed handkerchief and blew his nose noisily, replaced it in his top pocket. "I thought she'd have a good life. She had the beautiful house she always wanted, the two girls, plenty of staff. How was I to know she was getting deeper and deeper under the power of those bloody twins?"

He looked up at me. I didn't know whether he was seeing me or my great aunt. It didn't matter.

Again he blew his nose loudly, and dabbed his eyes. "I couldn't do anything other than what I did! I had to work, I couldn't be there all the time for her, but oh, how I regret it. I didn't even know she was sick. Well, they call it sick. She's just gone a long way away, not the person I married, not at all. The girls told me. They were frightened. And then there was the accident. I had to get them away. And luckily there was someone they could go to. They could do well in America. It was a big place. They can put the past behind them, start afresh. They'll survive."

I nodded, handed him the plate of biscuits. "I'm sure you did your best, sir," I said softly.

He blew his nose again, replaced the handkerchief, and took a biscuit. The act of eating, swallowing, seemed to bring him back.

His eyes focused on me, querying. "Where was I, Miss Chamberlain, I seem to have gone away for a bit. I do now and then, but it's nothing to worry about. How can I help you? You wanted to know about Thorburn, I hear?"

"I'm interested in his work, sir. Particularly with the

angels."

"Yes. He did work with angels. You understand all about that?"

"Some," I said. "I got the impression from Mr. Wood that you could help fill me in on bits that were missing."

He bit into his ginger nut and looked squarely at me. "Wood's a good egg. Your aunt was a good egg. That's good enough for me. Fire away, young lady. I'm at your disposal."

"Do you mind if I make notes?" I asked, hoping it wouldn't interrupt the flow. "So that I don't miss anything?

"Not at all, so long as it's just for your own use. Don't show them around. No journalists. Certainly not the Meredith boys, damn their eyes. Thorburn was safeguarding those pictures. They must not come into their hands again. I cannot stress this strongly enough. If you want proof, go and see the memsahib."

I took out my pencil and notebook. My shorthand was rusty, but, as I explained to him, it was so idiosyncratic that only I could read it back.

"Your personal code, then? I like that."

I didn't mention I'd transcribe it as soon as he had left.

"George Thorburn was part of Mr. Meredith Senior's magical lodge," he said, settling back in the chair. "What? So I can surprise you? Good. Well, it's all a very long time ago. End of last century. Big revival in Arts Magical, Golden Dawn and all that. Yes, Mr. Meredith Senior, Greystoke's best friend, was a practicing magician. So was Mrs. Greystoke. Very keen, she was, according to Thorburn. His father worked with them, too, and it would seem, that later, so did both of Greystoke's sons."

"The oldest two," I said, interested. "He had three. The youngest was not interested at all."

"Didn't know that. Sensible chap. Thought he only had two. Not to worry. Greystoke himself was not so much a practicing as an armchair magician. He liked the study, not the actual work, if you know what I mean. For him, the study, old documents, texts, that sort of stuff, rooting through the Bible, classical mythology and traipsing round the British Museum, all that, and drawing conclusions, that was what he liked. He was basically a Christian. Got no problem with that, me, except that there are as many sorts of Christians as there are stars in the sky. Do you mind if I smoke?"

I shook my head, fetched him an ashtray, and fitted a Gauloise into my holder. He lit it for me, and pulled out a long slender cigar of Dutch origin. He might be in and out of the real world but he knew good tobacco.

"I heard that Greystoke disappeared the night the paintings were finished, and that they were possibly intended for the church," I said, taking a long draw on the cigarette.

"You heard correctly on both counts," he confirmed. "Thorburn Senior – George's father – was a churchwarden and it was common knowledge that that paintings were being done. It seemed that once they were allied with the disappearance of the artist the church decided to distance itself. Not that they would have had much chance of having them, the widow kept them and took them with her when she married her new husband."

"Hmm," I said.

"Yes," said his Lordship, catching my thoughts. "I always thought that smelt a bit, but then I was always a simple man. No-one ever saw Greystoke after that evening, and the pictures stayed in the family until William put them on sale after his father's death."

"Half a mo', sir," I said. "If he knew how to use them, why should he do that?"

"He couldn't give them away. He knew that people wanted them – they were and still are well known in certain circles, I assure you, Miss Chamberlain. The Merediths aren't the only ones looking for them, oh dear me no! He thought by putting them through a legitimate auction house they would be bought by an art lover. In fact, his old friend Thorburn with his bride-to-be bought them, to stop anyone else with less than honest intentions getting them."

"But he could have signed them over privately," I said, not understanding.

"Yes. But he didn't. And there were reasons for that. One, Thorburn didn't have the cash – he wasn't a wealthy man. But he had contacts. The sale had to be legitimized, don't you see? There needed to be papers, receipts, etc."

"That I understand. But I've seen the cheque. William never collected it. He, too, seemed to have disappeared."

"Ah. Just like his father. Makes you wonder, doesn't it?" he said cocking his head on one side.

"It makes me worry, to be honest," I said. "Did he actually disappear?"

Lord Finching shrugged. "Who knows? There were ways and means of doing it in those days – but to leave a substantial cheque behind? That seems a bit odd." He took a long draw on his cigar, while he considered. "Perhaps he did flee the country, then come back later, under an assumed name, with a changed face – you can change a lot with hair and whiskers and a bit of weight."

"Exactly." I agreed.

That seemed to cheer him. "So, now we've got the pictures safely in the hands of Mr. Thorburn and his lady. And they were not black magicians. Not at all. There is no such thing as black magic, I should tell you right now, Miss Chamberlain. Magic is neutral, the power is there for you to use, like electricity. You can use it in any way you wish. There are ways that are considered 'black', that is to say harmful, both to the user and to those he or she seeks to harm: cursing for example. And then there are ways that are considered 'white', or positive, such as healing. But really, you can do something harmful to the grand plan of things when you work what you really think is white magic. And good can come out of a curse – I've seen that happen time and again."

He sighed. "I consider myself Grey. All good magicians do. And they eventually come to realize that you don't need it. Or they should. Thorburn was an excellent magician. He will be sadly missed."

"He used the pictures in ritual work?" I asked.

"Oh yes. They were aids to concentration. All magic is concentration of the mind. The angels were to help us focus on what we were aiming for. Angels, traditionally, as you may understand, have no free will. They are designed to do certain things, and only their particular thing. If you can contact them or that particular energy and interact with it, then it will work for you, within you: it's all about fooling the mind. Oh yes, the mind can be fooled to do one's will."

I frowned, but I thought I understood.

Lord Finching continued. "These angels were designed to teach us more about ourselves. Each one has both positive and negative attributes which can be contacted."

That I did understand. "But I thought these were supposed to be the days of the week," I said.

"Well? Think of the planets, the old pagan gods and goddesses that rule the days of the week. Everything is interconnected, Miss Chamberlain. That is the basis of the whole thing."

"Yes," I said softly. It made sense. "So where did Mr. Thorburn work?"

"Magically? At his place in Straddling originally, his wife's family bought it years earlier for a song from some old down-on-his-luck aristo. It was always happening."

Yes, I thought, just like my family. And his.

"He and she set up there quite early on. I met him after the Great War. At a party, actually. Good party, fancy dress, bands playing, lots to drink and beautiful women wearing those silly little frocks that showed a great deal of what their mothers had hidden. Golden days, eh? God, those girls were goers. Flappers? Everything was flapping, I tell you. Those clothes left nothing to the imagination. Rolled down hose, peekaboo clothes, whoo! If you sat in the right place, you could glimpse heaven through lace camiknickers. After the Great War, just about anything went." He was off again..."

"You sound as though you enjoyed yourself," I smiled. "But what about in London? You said he had a group in London later."

"Oh, yes! But when I met Thorburn and joined his group it was at Straddling. Enjoying yourself is one thing, and it palls after a while. Knowing yourself is something else. That is what magic is all about, Miss Chamberlain. Don't let anyone tell you otherwise – they're doing it wrong."

"I'll remember that, sir," I said. "Mr. Thorburn and the pictures?"

"I was getting to that. We worked up at Straddling, one weekend in four, don't you know? Full moons or as near to them as we could. I'd met the Memsahib by then, love at first sight, and when the opportunity arose, I bought the nearby estate which had gone fallow and let the Merediths build me Finchings. Wonderful place it was, in the early days. Let the Memsahib have what she wanted, because that's the only way to deal with women. And she made a superb job of the place. You been there at all? No, well, I think you would have loved it. Not now, though.

"The Meredith twins have got it now. They ruined the Memsahib with drugs and stuff, and got her to sell it to them. No, seriously. They got her hooked on that white stuff, and let her run up a debt of ... well, she owed more than either of us could manage, so she suggested – oh yes, she was lucid then, but I think they had suggested it, and quite forcibly too – that we sell to them. They'd give us a fair price. Ha! Of course they didn't. But they had leverage. They had pictures of her, stories, evidence! And then there was the accident. That was horrible. And somehow they'd learned about that. Me, I was glad to put her into the sanatorium. She'd be cared for, and I could get on with my life. When the government service died out I went back to Scotland where I was brought up. It's a lot healthier up there."

"You mentioned the pictures at Straddling," I reminded him. You used to work magically there once every four weeks. When was this?"

"We started in the early twenties but it was going before then. Continued on and off until the fire – just after war broke out, I suppose. Second World War that was. But Thorburn didn't live there then. He was working with his group in London, strangely enough. Had got in with Dion Fortune and her bunch by then. They did some powerful stuff, by all accounts and at least he kept his home. Hers was struck by the Luftwaffe. Never mind. Where was I?"

"You were telling me about the group at Straddling," I said.

"Ah, yes. Right. Well, I didn't go all the time, none of us did – we went as and when we could. Your great aunt went there for a while. Wonderful woman…"

I had to stop him going on about her. "Lord Finching, did you see the pictures there every time?"

"Of course. They were part of the temple. We'd invoke them at the start, but briefly only. Then we'd get on with the job in hand." He frowned. "Look, I shouldn't really be telling you all this…"

"But it might help me put the Merediths away for a very long time," I whispered.

His face was suddenly alert. "You're after the bounders?"

"Exactly so, sir," I said.

He sighed, and a smile flickered across his features. "Caro would be so proud of you. They used to come and use the place between times. Dark Moon. Not necessarily a good time for magical work. I was out in India at that point, while the family stayed here. Then I was up and down to Scotland. The Memsahib was obviously bored. She went along. She enjoyed ritual. Like some people enjoy church, I suppose. Said it made her feel better. A good ritual should do that. Make you feel good, good and tired, like after a ride in the wind on a spirited horse, that sort of thing. I couldn't deny her her pleasure. I didn't know they used drugs in the wine. Or afterwards. I didn't think…" He held his head in his hands, in genuine distress.

"We very rarely do, sir, where our own are concerned. So the seven pictures were there all through the thirties. What about the forties?"

"Ah, I took them out. After the fire. Thorburn asked me to. And I took them straight up to Scotland. Some of them were in a damaged state, and I had them restored. Nice chap, Rufus. Fancies himself as a renaissance man, dresses like a Titian painting. Good company for a recluse like me, well-read and interested in everything. I liked him. But I didn't trust him. Oh, I trusted him as an artist, as a craftsman, but as a person… No. Not at all. He wanted to know where the paintings were going. I wouldn't tell him. I think he was seduced by the stories. They had to be kept away from the Dark Side. They still have to. Now Thorburn's gone, I know that one of them is on the loose. The others I know about. I sent them to their places of safety. I have to keep them out of the hands of the Dark Side, and that is the Merediths, but as I said, I think there are others after them too. And I don't mean you, Miss Chamberlain."

"Then who?" I asked.

"A splinter group from the lodge. It was infiltrated by some sort of religious, possibly Christian, organization in the late thirties. We were very naïve and unworldly, more's the shame. It was they, I believe, who started the fire. Oh, locals say it was the devil, but then they would. This bunch is still around. Rufus rang me and said he'd been questioned lately. He mentioned you, interestingly enough, but it wasn't you he was referring to. I thought perhaps he was still trying to find out for himself where they were. I'll not tell him. He's too venal. He was always keen on the angel Hanael, sacred to Venus, and there are two sides to that coin – pure love and darkest lust."

I thought about Rufus. That certainly wasn't a naïve appraisal.

"So you don't know who they are? The others who are after them? Not personally? As in a name or two?"

He took a draught of tea. "They call themselves Soldiers of the Dawn. We call them the SODs. I think they are High Church, possibly Catholic. As for recruitment, standing in society is not important, only one's commitment to the cause. Their emblem is a sword in a mailed glove against a rising sun. Does that ring any bells with you, Miss Chamberlain?"

"Not exactly," I lied. I'd seen in before, but I couldn't remember where. "What's their interest in the paintings?"

"They want them destroyed."

"Ah!" I drained my cup. "More tea?" I refilled the pot and poured. "Sir, can I level with you?"

"I've leveled with you, haven't I? I have a good feeling about you. When Mac phoned me, I knew who you were – the phone number – checked in Who's Who, and worked out your horoscope. You are a good egg. Besides, you're Caro's niece, or great niece, or whatever, and she'd spoken highly of you. I respect her views. Also, Wood said you seemed good, and I've come across others who rate you as a moral and discreet person. When you told me you were after the Merediths, I felt a little surge of joy, like Spring-time coming again after a long cruel winter. So, yes, Miss Chamberlain, I'd be delighted if you'd level with me. And I too can be discreet."

"Very well, then. I'm part of an informal team, no names given,-"

"Nor expected," he agreed.

"We are trying to locate the pictures, but also locate anything at all upon the Merediths. Anything you would be prepared to swear an oath that could give us leverage would be greatly appreciated. We would also like to get the pictures together, and disempower them."

That was a *blague* and I knew it.

How did you disempower something?

To my surprise, it worked.

He nodded sagely. "I think that's a wonderful idea. So simple. So very simple. It would work!" He drank his tea thirstily. "Why the Deuce didn't we think of that?" He turned to me.

"Very well, Miss Chamberlain, I'll give you addresses and passwords. Get the things together somewhere safe, and do it. I'll go through my papers and see what we can come up with against the Merediths. There's got to be something we can do. Especially after what they are doing at Straddling."

"You mean the new development?"

"That's what they call it. It'll fall down in less than twenty years, but they'll be long gone. This is how they work. They get a hold over someone, someone with property, then get him to sign it over for whatever they want – they can be very persuasive. I know. They give them everything – whatever they want, it's there – and then slowly they start to take it away. Then they twist. If you want more of this, then you will give us more of that. That's how they got Finchings. That's how they got that place in Cambridgeshire, Little Waddling, was it? Used to belong to that frightful old bore Algy Nesmith-Brown. He was one of us in the thirties. The Memsahib was great friends with his wife. He got suckered before I did, but the method was the same." He looked at me questioningly. "Have I said something you didn't know?"

I said slowly "My brother is engaged to marry Sylvia Nesmith-Brown. Percy Meredith wants to develop land owned by her father and my father. Algy and my brother are very keen."

"But your father's got his head screwed on, eh? Ask yourself what they have over your brother! Might they have forwarded him money for some reason or another or allowed him to gamble a little further than was wise? Might they have something on him that he doesn't want sounded abroad? They'll be calling for settlement, and offering an arrangement by which they can all benefit and the debt be cancelled. Only they won't cancel it."

I whistled softly. Of course, that had to be it. And Bulgy Algy and his memsahib and the divine Sylvia were already in the game, of course.

I handed him my pencil and paper. "Names and addresses? I'll commit them to memory then destroy them."

He smiled. "Just like Caro. Very businesslike." He puffed on his cigar and filled up four pages with large swirly writing. "I've put the passwords underneath. Tell them I've given you permission. No, hold on, better still…"

He reached into his shirt collar and fiddled with something, then pulled out a gold chain with a seal ring hanging from it. He slid the ring onto my hand. The stone was smooth, a dark orange-brown carnelian, with a tiny figure engraved into it, a man's torso, a pair of snake legs, a rooster's head, bearing a zigzag thunderbolt in each hand. Tiny work, beautifully carved. A very ancient jewel.

"It's Abraxas," he said. "Show the people when you go for the pictures. They'll know you have my permission. I'll have him back when you've finished with him. He's an old friend."

"Yes, sir, of course." I was gaping again. There was such power in the ring. It zinged on my hand. "You are sure you don't mind me having it? It's very old."

"Old, oh yes. I trust you to use it impeccably."
He took the pencil again and wrote in my book. "There. My address, and where my wife is ensconced. You might like to talk to her. When she's lucid, she might be able to help you, but you couldn't use her evidence in court under the current situation. I'd like her to know what you are doing. It won't get out from there. It's virtually a prison."

I nodded. I found it incredibly sad. His wife gone, the girls gone.

"I'll go and see her. And when you come down again, sir, please feel free to call in."

"Thank you, I will. I've enjoyed meeting you, Miss Chamberlain." He clicked his fingers. "Tell you what, if you don't mind me using your phone, I'll telegram those people, let them know you're coming. Then they can't be suspicious." He looked at me questioningly.

"Please go ahead, sir," I said. "I've got some things to do, so I'll leave you to it." Although he had given me passwords, I didn't want to appear nosy.

I picked up the book and went to memorise the names and addresses in my office. I copied them in my own code onto a sheet of paper which I put in the secret compartment of my Great Aunt's desk, then did some more desultory tidying and went to the loo. I was washing my hands when I heard the living room door rattle. He'd obviously finished.

"All in order," he said, with a smile. "They will expect you within the next fifteen days. I said I didn't know what you had on, and the distances are not small."

He pulled a half hunter from his waistcoat pocket and inspected it at length. "Nearly noon. I'd best be gone. Things to do, places to go, people to meet, don't you know?"

He replaced the watch, swung his cloak over his shoulders, set his sombrero at a rakish angle and picked up his cane. "It's been a pleasure to meet you, Miss Chamberlain. Don't bother to come down. I'll see myself out."

18

"What was Zorro's Dad doing here?" Jeremy asked, hanging his raincoat on a hook; he had arrived as Lord Finching went out.

"Helping us greatly," I said. I gave him a run-down of our meeting.

"Excellent. What about that meeting you were going to set up?"

"Give me five minutes. I've not managed to get through yet."

I put through a call to Sam's number, and left a message with *The Mercury* to get him to ring me. I had just put the phone down when it rang again, and I was put through to the Reverend Simmons.

"Miss Chamberlain, I've done quite a bit of work on those angels. When do you think I might see one?"

Heavens, he was perky.

Shortly I should think. I'll check with the person who has it first and ring you back."

"I'll look forward to your call," he said.

"Is Sam there?" I asked.

"Not at the moment, but I'm expecting him for lunch. Can I get him to ring you?"

"Yes, please. I've got a contact for him who might be useful."

"Then I'll tell him to ring as soon as he gets in."

We said our goodbyes and I cut the connection then asked the operator to get me my father's number.

"Alice," he said, "Guy was here last night. He was burbling about you becoming a black magician. I told him he was stinking drunk, and was diplomatically out when he came down to breakfast. Could you tell me what's going on?"

"Guy was drunk," I assured him. "Look, I'll come down and explain. With Jeremy if you don't mind. We need to meet some people, and... you do have the picture?"

"Of course. It's in my studio. Hidden among a pile of others. Mind, it's very different from my work, I mean, it's on board and it's huge."

"Have you had a look at it?"

"Of course. Not terribly pleasant, but I've put it face to the wall, why?"

"I've got someone who needs to see it."

"Young Jeremy? Of course." Young Jeremy, eh? My father obviously approved.

"And the Reverend Simmons and his grandson."

"Hellfire, Alice, I thought this was supposed to be hush-hush."

"Ah, but I need provenance."

"Then I'll get in touch with Emily. When are you coming down?"

"Probably this afternoon. I'll fetch the Rev from there. Can I use the car?"

My father sighed theatrically. "Oh yes, we are your disposal, Milady! Garage, hotel, storage facility, picker-uppers of unconsidered trifles. I'll tell your Mother you'll both be down. She'll be delighted. You know how she loves company."

I chuckled and said goodbye, putting down the phone.

Jeremy had been checking the addresses. "Not exactly in a compact area, are they?" he said with my AA Road map of Britain book on his lap.

"They're not meant to be, but I didn't realize he could call on so widespread a group of people," I said. "I hadn't thought that magic was that popular."

"Or scattered, eh? Me neither. Do you want to collect

them alone? I could come with you if you wanted."

"You can get time off, just like that?"

"If I talk to B nicely and don't ask too often. No, actually, I've got some leave owing," he admitted. "If you needed me, I could get it."

"Thanks." I meant it. Someone to help with shifting the things would be helpful. And it would lend me more credence. I was impressed that he'd use his valuable leave this way, too. "I'd like that very much. But only if it's no trouble. This is private work, not official."

I rang Rev. Simmons and told him I'd be down this afternoon and could take him to see the angel. "Wonderful, around 5 five o'clock please. It's Mothers' Union afternoon. Ah, here's Sam."

"Alice, how nice. The Rev says you've got something for me."

"I've got something and someone, Sam. Can he meet you this afternoon?"

"I can be here when you pick up the Rev. Be lovely to see you again Alice."

"Likewise, Sam. See you around five at the Rev's."

I cradled the phone. "Could you get some of that leave this afternoon and drive me to Wethersley?" I asked. "We'll be back this evening, but you want to see the picture, don't you?"

My father's studio was separate from the house, a barn conversion with a wall of glass to the North for even light, at the end of the stable block. I drew the car with Reverend Simmons, Sam and Jeremy inside to a halt in front of it. Pa was there already, and I knew he had the painting out, set up on a low easel for viewing. He'd been working on it with a rag dipped in acetone when we had arrived earlier, cleaning off dirt in a small patch. For a painting that had been restored less than a decade ago, it was surprisingly filthy.

More introductions, and then the 'treat'.

It was an education to observe the various reactions.
My own had been instinctive and aesthetic.

My father said his was purely aesthetic but I knew better; he quite liked the picture, he said, and the craftsman knew his job, but there was the historical context too. A thorough reappraisal of the *oeuvre* of Lawrence Greystoke, R.A, was called for in the light of this new 'evidence'.

Jeremy had frowned, shuddered and muttered about not being the sort of thing he'd like hanging on his wall, thank you very much, but seemed impressed by the size and the weight of the painting – he had had to help my father lift it onto the easel.

Now it was Reverend Simmons's turn, and of course Sam's, who was in a way related to the picture.

The Rev's eyes shone. He positively beamed at the angel, raising a hand in greeting and bowing his head. "It's Kamael, Archangel of Geburah," he said. "The planet he aligns with is Mars, and Tuesday. It isn't surprising he gives you a bit of a jolt. Master of War, but also of Surgeons, the Cutter Away of Dead Wood." He sighed happily. "I can see why a child might think him frightening. He's awesome."

He looked at my father, who was smiling, rag in hand. "You are giving him a clean, my lord? I think he would like that very much. I've a feeling he has been misused. Very much misused."

Sam stood alone, silhouetted in the doorway, and viewed from afar, his face a grey stone mask.

Finally he said, "There are seven of these? No wonder my father was terrified. Imagine the mind of the man who created such a thing. It's pure evil. Pure malevolence, peering out from there."

My father frowned. "We all see different things, Mr. Simmons. We see what we want to see, what we expect to see. I, for example, have no emotional ties to this work, and I see like a painter. What I see is the skill of a fellow craftsman, and he was skilful, your Grandfather. I only know him as a minor decorative painter, but this work makes us all view him in a very new light."

"Yes," said Sam stonily. "And not a very nice one. No surprise the man disappeared. The evil must have consumed him."

Jeremy, standing behind Sam, caught my eye. The glance said "Oops!"

Reverend Simmons took Sam's arm. "No, Sam, your grandfather wasn't at all evil, I assure you. Misguided, possibly, but generally a good person. I don't say this lightly. And I think Lord Wethersley is right. We should be looking at his skill, reviewing the good within his work, not focusing on the emotive factors." He looked at my father again. "Lord Wethersley, could I ask you to clean that painting, as you have done that small patch? I'm sure it will bring up a lot more of the beauty, and release any lingering negativity. We all feel much more positive in clean clothes and bright tidy rooms than in old messy rags and a filthy hovel."

"Exactly my sentiment, Reverend Simmons," my father agreed. "It was what I intended, all along. I checked with its owner, and he is in accord."

"The owner?" Sam's head snapped up. "Who is he?"

"I'm not at liberty to say." My father's voice was calm, but had that tone he used on us as children which meant you didn't answer back. "Suffice it to say that the painting is here for its safety and restoration. If you've seen enough, we could go indoors and have some refreshment. My wife is so looking forward to meeting you all."

He herded us out, fastened the shutters and locked the door. I led the way to the house.

My mother was waiting in the sitting room with the tea trolley laden with plates of tiny sandwiches and jam tarts, a treat indeed. The fire was blazing in the grate, and the atmosphere warmed at once. We were all ready for a cosy break.

I helped my mother dispense the tea. She and the Reverend were chatting about flowers almost immediately. Jeremy sat next to Sam in the window seat, with a small mountain of food between them. They were talking in low voices about the Merediths. I left them too it.

I sat next to my father and stirred sugar into my black tea. "Thank you for that, Pa," I said.

"For what, Alice?"

"Getting us out of there when you did. I hadn't realized what Sam's reaction would be."

"Well, it's understandable. He's been brought up on it. Of course he's going to see it in a very personal way."

"Yes and no. I met Lord Finching this morning. Did you know he knew Great Aunt Caroline?"

"Everyone knew Great Aunt Caroline, Alice. Was he mad as a hatter? Was he dressed as Merlin?"

I chuckled. "No, like the chap on the bottle of Sandeman's Port. Jeremy saw him, called him Zorro's Dad. But I liked him. He seemed a gentle chap. Quite sad. He's still in love with his wife, you know. Says that the Merediths did that to her."

"What, turned her doolally? How'd they do that?"

"Drugs and the pictures," I said.

"He said that?" My father sat up. "He really told you that?"

"He implied it. Off the record."

"Damn! I thought we had them for the moment."

"We? Since when has it been 'we', Pa?"

"It's always been we, Alice. We are family. And I'm not having my family buggered about with by the likes of the Merediths. Think about it. They're after Guy, and he's stupid enough to be taken. The boy's virtually got the word 'Mug' tattooed on his forehead. You've told me about you and Jeremy acting as decoys in the coven or whatever they call it, and there's Maddy involved through Basil's work. Of course I'm involved. Besides, your mother told me I've got to keep an eye on you all."

I groaned. "And I suppose when I was working in France she had *Grand-père* keeping an eye on me, and silly Lucien? We're all grown up people Dad. Even Guy, who's never been a child."

My father chuckled now. "I can still show a little concern, though. Your Mother's enjoying the Rev's company. Nice man. What are those two young men talking about like that? They look like they're planning a bank robbery. Go and give them some more tea and find out, there's a good girl."

I drove our guests home some time later. Reverend Simmons thanked me, and promised to be in touch.

Sam shook my hand. "Lovely to see you again, Alice. Thank you for introducing me to your beau. We'll keep in touch about the pictures and the Merediths. I think we can be of use to each other. It was good of you to think of introducing us."

"Think nothing of it," I said. Was he getting pompous again? Or was I getting too touchy? "I'll see you around, Sam."

"Yes, Alice. I hope you'll both be happy together."

I bit my lip. "Thank you." I climbed back in the car and drove off. What had Jeremy been telling him?

"Nothing, Alice, I swear!" Jeremy held his hands up, palm out. "If he said I had told him then, he's lying."

"Honest?"

"Scout's honour!" Jeremy did the scout salute. "He sees what he wants to sees. I think he is a great jumper to conclusions."

That was true enough. "Goes with the job, I suppose, but it'll get him into bother if he's not careful," I mused. I had liked Sam when I first met him, but he seemed to see things in glorious black or white, rather than myriad shades of grey.

"I'll keep in touch with him," Jeremy said. "If he thinks we're a couple he may be inclined to be freer with his information for your sake. He holds you in high regard – he was amazed that you got him out of the Boltons place – but it goes against everything he holds dear to be beholden to a woman. He wouldn't work well with you in charge, Alice."

"Blimey, guv! You got him bang to rights," I said.

"Elementary, my dear Watson!"

"Hey, I'm not a second fiddle. Remember that."

"Couldn't fail to do so, Alice. So, mission accomplished. Back to town?" He gave me an open smile. "Fancy going dancing?"

"Why not?"

George's eyes popped when I climbed out of the little red car. "Cor, Miss, you lucky thing," he said.

"What are you doing out at this time of night, George?" I asked.

"I just come out to buy the supper. Goin' up the chip shop."

"Want a lift?" Jeremy asked. "I could murder some chips."

"So could I," I agreed.

"Hop in both, then. You, young man, will have to sit in the back, OK?" He opened the back seat.

"Top 'ole, mister!" George clambered in. "Wait till I tell my mates!"

While we waited in the queue George said, "There was a bloke who come looking for you, Miss. An' a lady. She was nobby, 'ad an animal round 'er neck, with its legs all hanging down 'er front. Not a fox, bigger than that. She left you a letter, Miss. Give me tuppence, she did, for bein' nice. Says she'll see you at the weekend. But the bloke, 'e didn't leave no message. 'E wanted to go up and wait for you. Bloomin' cheek, I thought. I never seen 'im before."

"Give, George," I said.

"In a mo', Miss." He stretched up to the counter of the van. "Fish and chips twice and a wally and a couple of onions, Mister," he said. Then he turned back to me. "He was a big bloke. Taller than you, Mister," nodding at Jeremy, "and big. Like an O on legs. I thought he might be a sailor – full set of whiskers, but he didn't talk like a sailor. Talked with a singing accent, but posh with it. Dark whiskers, couldn't see 'is hair beneath 'is 'at – it was a berry. And he had a long mac on, not very clean. Thought it'd be cleaner with the way he talked. It wasn't any particular colour, like dishwater, or old washing water. Only underneath it, he had a smart suit. Black, with a white shirt, black tie, and really nice polished black shoes." He looked up at us. "How'm I doin'?"

"Very impressive," said Jeremy, and meant it.

George winked at me. Jeremy gave our order across the counter – Fish and chips twice, and two wallies – then looked down at the boy. "You don't miss much, do you son?"

"Hey, I've hardly started, mister," George said. "Hands, big, long fingers, thick, too. A signet ring with a big sparkly blue stone on, gold band. Funny, though, there was bits of dirt under one or two of the nails, like it wouldn't come off. And when he leaned down to talk to me, his coat came open at the neck. He had a sort of thing – you know, like a lady would wear a brooch, and a bloke would wear something stuck in his lapel? One of those. Like some of the old soldiers wear, to say they belong. It wasn't exactly a badge, but it had a hand holding a sword. I thought of King Arthur – but it weren't a lady's hand, it was a knight's hand. And there were something like half a sun with rays sticking out of it behind it."

I whistled softly. "Thank you, George, thank you very much indeed."

"Did alright, did I?"

"You deserve your supper bought for you for that," Jeremy told him, handing over a ten shilling note and taking charge of the hot newspaper parcels. He handed one to George. "You keep your money, son, this is on us."

"Cor, thanks, mister. You're a toff!"

"Actually, I'm not, but I can play the part," Jeremy said with a grin.

"Did he leave any message?" I asked.

"No. Odd that. Most of 'em are only too happy to, but he said if he couldn't wait inside the flat he would make … er… alternative arrangements. I think that was it. He sounded a bit put out!"

We got back in the car. "Is it to do with them boxes, Miss?"

"Eh, you're a quick one," Jeremy said.

"Only you could keep 'em in the bike shed. They won't think of that. I can always bring 'em up if you need them, an' I won't look, promise, cross my heart."

We were eating our supper some time later, with the boxes stowed in their new hiding place.

"You've got a hell of a kid there," said Jeremy. "He's great."

"Trained him myself," I said, with more than a touch of pride, "but most of it's natural talent. He's bright as a button. Wants to be a spy or a racing driver when he grows up. Isn't sure which."

"I guess they both require you to be a risk-taker and have instant reactions."

"And to take care – no good being just a risk-taker. You've got to be able to evaluate them at once, and he's got that ability. And observation. He's really good at noticing."

"So, the SODs know about you," Jeremy said. "How did that happen?"

"I didn't know about them until this morning. Never heard of them. Although I have seen the symbol somewhere. Can't remember where, though." I frowned, trying to remember, but it wouldn't come. "What's in a name – Soldiers of the Dawn. Could have been Servants of Darkness!"

I sighed as I reviewed Lord Finching's visit. "I suppose one of them could have trailed Lord Finching. I never looked out for him, or peered up and down the street. It never occurred to me. I was too busy putting stuff away and making myself presentable." I should have looked. I was getting slack.

Jeremy read my thoughts. "No, he should have looked out. He knew people were after the things. He told you about the SODs, for Heaven's sake. If that was the case, it was his look out. I've a damn good mind to go and tell him so."

"Shouldn't bother," I said drily. "He's probably halfway to Scotland by now. Said he had things to do, people to meet, places to go, and was suddenly off. Then you came in."

"And I didn't notice anyone in the street, either. Well, there were a couple of women with kids, little kids, and shopping, and a window-cleaner on a bike with his ladder, but that was about it. No-one anything like young George's description."

"It wouldn't have to be, of course."

"Quite so. Do you recognize the description?"

"Could be anyone. Well, not anyone, but ..."

"What about your other caller?"

"Heavens!" I'd forgotten her.

I pulled the folded note out of my bag, where I had slipped it while we sorted the boxes out. "It's from Sweetie, and I quote," I said. "If you are still of the same mind as you were when we last met, come to tea on Friday, 4 p.m. There are things we need to discuss. Light in Extension, Elisabeth – with lots of flourishes. RSVP."

I held it out to him. "I hope you've got one, too. I take it that it's about the Dark Arts. I'm not superstitious by any means, but I'd prefer not going alone, even though it's only in the Boltons."

He looked at me in astonishment. "I don't believe it. No, I don't. I'm sure I misheard. Must have done."

"What?"

"Er, was that an admission of not being completely fearless, Alice?"

I chuckled. "Might be," I agreed. I was getting used to having him around, and someone to give me credence and support would be a bonus, particularly if Archie Meredith happened to drop in. Mr. Crowe might just recognize Alice Chamberlain as the Mad Lady Sarah Carson née Markham, he had disturbed at Straddling Hall, but was certainly less likely to if she were part of a couple.

"Let's go dancing," I said brightly. "I want to forget all this stuff for a while."

George rushed out as we were getting in the car. "Miss, Mister, I got something for you," he said, and thrust a Woolworth's exercise book into my hand. "I done drawings, and wrote it all up."

"Hey, that's really helpful, George!" I said. "Thank you, thank you very much."

We started off at the Lyceum, but left shortly after. It was too sedate. We ended up in a little dive bar in Soho where the jazz was hot, the atmosphere smoky, and the dancing close. I'd been to places like this during the war with my dead brother and his friends, in London, and with Raoul in Lyon. I hoped I wasn't a Jonah. I was enjoying myself with Jeremy. I think it was reciprocated. Dammit, I'm sure it was! But we were working together and letting the world believe what it chose to. That was the thing. We were doing a job. I told myself to focus on that.

We turned out into Greek Street and rain at 2 p.m., heads still full of Cab Calloway numbers. A splendid evening, even if Cab himself had been absent. We sidled along the pavement, hand in hand, to the car, Flat-Foot Floogie-ing through the puddles, giggling.

We weren't alone. Clubs were turning out here and there. There were plenty of people, some squiffy or worse, along the way, now that there was no blackout. I felt very happy about that. People needed somewhere to go and blow off steam; musicians and entertainers needed to make a living. I was glad to be here, that life was getting back to normal, despite rationing.

Jeremy dropped me off politely, with a handshake, a kiss on the cheek and a promise to keep in touch. I waved him on his way and took my shoes off when I closed the front door – force of habit when returning late. It had been a good day. I was looking forward to my bed. I pressed the timer switch and the hall lights came on. The tiled stairs were icy beneath my feet as I climbed them. I suppose the best thing that could be said about them was that they kept one fit.

19

My living room door hung open.
I knew I had locked it. My stomach lurched. I patted the door and listened, flattening myself against the jamb.
There was no sound.
I went in. Used my head scarf to turn on the light. And looked at the mess.
It was heart-breaking.
I went to the other rooms, and upstairs to the maid's rooms which, since I had no maid, were full of my great aunt's stuff that I had no use for and I normally kept locked.
Whoever had been here had been very angry indeed.
Every lock had been broken, every drawer ransacked, every box spilled out.
My Great Aunt's desk had been opened and emptied onto the floor, the guest bed stripped and the covers thrown about, and in my room, all my clothes and belongings thrown everywhere, and the jewel-box smashed and emptied.
Great!
It didn't contain a lot, being mostly costume jewelry or relatively inexpensive keepsakes, including a pretty bracelet from Raoul. That hurt.
It occurred to me that I ought to get a safe installed here. Another case of locking the stable door after the horse has bolted.
I began to laugh, but it was really to stop me from crying. I was disgusted by the wholesale destruction of the nuts and bolts of my life.
Who would do such a thing?
I went back to the desk, and by dint of lying on my

stomach and fiddling with a head-scarf over my hands, managed to ascertain that the secret drawer had held.

A blessing there.

I began to tremble.

When had this happened? And what if I had been in the house? This was vandalism and I don't think my chances would have been very good. I realized I had had a lucky escape, in a way, but it didn't make me feel any better.

This wasn't an opportunistic burglary. It was a warning.

I went back into the living room, where crockery and glass were smashed, cushions ripped, and furniture thrown about. The telephone had been tossed amid the chaos, but the cable had not been cut.

Another small blessing, for which I was duly grateful.

I picked it up and dialed the police to report a break-in, and then because I needed someone to talk to, rang Jeremy. He hadn't yet returned, but his sleepy flat-mate woke up with a jolt when I told him what had happened. He said he'd get him to ring me back as soon as he came in and asked if there was anything he could do. I thanked him, but said that was more than enough, and apologized for waking him.

Then I went to the loo and was sick.

I gargled with some mouthwash, to take away the taste and the smell, and redid my make up. I had to wait now.

I managed to find my slippers. My feet were freezing, and having got rid of most of my inner warmth, so was the rest of me. I couldn't stay in the ravished flat. It felt all wrong. I slipped down the stairs, wearing my great aunt's sable coat and furry slippers and awaited the arrival of the local constabulary.

The little red car skidded to a halt and Jeremy swept up the pavement to gather me up in his arms. I leaned into him, still shaking.

"Are you alright, Alice?" he asked, hugging me to him.

I nodded. "Yes, just shocked. I never expected this," I said softly. I was glad to have him to lean against, and he was very warm.

"What have they taken?" he asked.

I told him briefly about the mess and breakages, "But as far as I can make out, the only things they've actually taken are some old bits of jewelry. Nothing of any real financial value, but part of my past - irreplaceable." I took a deep breath, stepped away from him and flashed him a smile, "But... They didn't find my notes. I'm sure that's what they were looking for. So they broke the flat up, the living room's just a bomb-site. It's horrible!"

"You're insured?"

I nodded. "Go up and have a look before the police come."

"You'll be all right, here? On your own?"

I looked at him with raised eyebrows. "What do you think!"

"No answer to that! I'll be down again in a tick."

I lit a cigarette and leaned back against the column of the porch, and looked at my watch. It was three fifteen; I'd been back here twenty-five minutes.

I was wide awake now and couldn't see myself going to sleep at all.

And I was very very angry. I smoked very fast indeed.

Jeremy joined me on the step as two officers came round the corner.

We took them upstairs, and I gave my statement. They were nice men, one nearing retirement, the other a young chap with poor skin. They looked around, and said someone would be round in the morning, to do whatever they did.

"Have you got somewhere to stay, Miss?" asked the older one. "I wouldn't like to see you staying here with it like this."

"Bit difficult at this time of night, Sarge," said the younger one, and was stopped immediately by a frown.

"I can find somewhere," I said. "In which case, Lily, the woman in the basement has my key. She's a trusted family friend, she and her family. They would let your men in if I'm not here. I wouldn't try to waken them now. Nor Mr Stephens on the ground floor. I doubt he would have heard anything with his radio on so loud."

"Thank you, Miss. I'll leave you to lock up. And if you'd be so kind as to come down to the Station to sign your statement some time tomorrow. I'm sorry you have been so inconvenienced."

"Thank you, Sergeant, Constable. Thank you for coming so swiftly. I'll just take some overnight things, then go. Will you wait for me, Jeremy?"

We let the police see themselves out then carefully got all my working papers, the aforesaid overnight bag and I changed into a set of warm comfortable clothing, trousers, thick socks and boots, a warm shirt and jumper and a short jacket. I tucked a head scarf carefully into my handbag, alongside a fresh handkerchief, and came out from the bathroom.

"Where to, Milady?" Jeremy asked.

"Why are you calling me that?"

"You're the boss. You've got an idea? I'm your man!"

"How do you feel about picking up one of those pictures? The blighters shan't have them!"

I was impressed. He went into his flat as the gentleman I knew, and came out like a mechanic carrying his greasy overalls in one arm. His boots were scuffed, the cord trousers worn thin at the knees, and the jumper had one elbow darned. He wore a collar and tie, but they were both elderly, and his hair, which had been slicked back and stylish was now hanging loosely forward. "Where to, luv? I ain't got all day." His voice had slouched downward into a lazy London accent to match his casual appearance.

"Blimey, Guvnor, I 'ad you down for a toff!" I said.

We went down to the garage behind his apartment block and picked up a medium-sized delivery van with Stacey's Plumbers in curly letters along each side, and across the two back doors.

"Where did you get this?" I asked.

"John's off sick. He said his Dad will never miss it. We just have to keep the tank full and we can have it for the next couple of days. So where'll it be?"

I climbed aboard. It felt comfortingly familiar, being in the cab of a van again. The smell wasn't the same of course. John smoked Player's Navy Cut. But it was close enough.

"The closest one. Near Wantage. We can drop the picture at Wethersley afterwards. Did you get a message from Sweetie?"

"Eh? Oh, Elisabeth? Yes, but I haven't replied yet." He lit a cigarette. In character he was now smoking Woodbines. He offered me the packet. I shook my head. He winked.

"So you're my bit of rough?" I asked.

"I'm putty in yer 'ands, luv, just say the word." A cheeky grin and another wink.

Well, there was a thought!

At four forty-five we were on the Great West Road, aiming for Reading. It was dark, and there was little traffic. The van was noisy but it went. We rumbled on past the big factories, Firestone and Gillette among them, all wonderful elegant buildings on this wide road out of the capital, carefully keeping to the speed limit; there was no point in courting problems. Or wasting fuel, it was precious stuff.

"Companionable silence or were you nodding off?" the driver asked as we entered Reading.

"Just resting my eyes," I said, more thickly than I intended. "Any chance of a roadside caff?"

"Unlikely. I'll keep an eye open, though. I could murder a mug of tea."

We passed sedately through the town, and out the other side, and, as we cleared through the village of Pangbourne the church clock struck six. The darkness was less intense, and although we were going north-westwards, the sky ahead of us was brightening cheerfully. There were signs of life now, lights in some windows, the occasional cyclist on his way to work, and in Goring, a bit further on, a well-lit newsagent's with paper-boys chattering before they did their rounds, and a milk cart.

"A bottle of milk?" Jeremy suggested.

"Rather have something warm," I replied.

"Should be something in Wantage. There must be people awake there, hungry people. There's got to be a somewhere open."

I wasn't so sanguine. "These are country people," I said. "They don't eat out for breakfast. At least not at half past six in the morning."

I finally voiced the question that had been occupying me all morning. "Who do you think broke into my flat?"

"Could be Lord Finching?"

"But why?"

"Perhaps he changed his mind about letting you have the pictures."

"If that was so, I don't think he would have wrecked the place. He had a genuine regard for my Great Aunt, and he didn't appear to be a violent man."

"Point taken. It was someone who knew you had something on the pictures then. And before you say it, I have an alibi. The best."

I smiled. "I never suspected you. Nor even that you put someone up to it. You didn't have time. Unless you set it up while I was powdering my nose."

"I was doing something similar myself at that time, if I remember rightly, but thank you for accepting my alibi."

I reflected aloud on the past week. "Who knows I am

working on gathering the pictures? My parents. I discount them. Basil and Maddy?"

"I discount them. I don't think the pictures are important to them. Who else?"

"The Rev. Simmons. And Sam. Leggy and Bobby. Emily, Padraig and Joseph."

"And?"

"Oh God, Thelma, Mr. Arnold Lowther, my old boss, the Williamses ... Lord Finching himself... Too many. Far too many."

"As you say. But you didn't think the pictures were actively evil. Or produced active evil. Or did you?"

I shook my head.

"Tell me about these people. Can you see any of them breaking into your flat and causing that sort of chaos. Whoever it was wanted something you had, and didn't find it. You've got to be careful, Alice."

He didn't have to remind me.

I worked through the list, thinking aloud while he drove on, silently.

No-one immediately sprang to mind, although there were some people I had reservations about – Sam for instance, but that was because of his attitudes. I didn't think he would smash my flat up. He simply didn't seem that sort. But he did know where I lived...

The Rev would have been horrified to be considered on the list. I discounted him at once.

Leggy I'd known for years. He'd employed me. All he had to do was ask for any information and I was honour-bound to give it to him. He was paying for it.

Bobby? Bobby might have had reasons of his own, but he would have tried wheedling information out of me first. He could be vicious in a fight, but he wasn't by nature a destroyer. And I flattered myself that he actually quite cared for me. He wouldn't have smashed my things. If he had broken into my flat, he would not have left such a mess. I doubt that I would have even known he'd even been there.

Then Emily, Padraig and Joseph?

Couldn't see it, myself.

Although they were all London-based, they were artists, respectable 'unrespectable' members of the Establishment. Emily was a spinster, living in Chiswick, and Padraig unmarried, lived in Bloomsbury, while Joseph had a wife and family at Blackheath. None of them had any reason...

So Thelma? She only knew I was looking for the pictures, but she seemed a quiet party, not given to gossip. Besides, I liked her. I didn't want her to have snitched on me.

Mr. Arnold Lowther? Now he did have connections all over the place. He could have mentioned it, in passing, to the wrong person. He might have shared the foie gras with an old friend, who just happened to be ... interested in the pictures as well.

My God! He could have mentioned it to one of the Merediths. Or someone else.

The Williamses? It was just possible I was mentioned at the pub, or at work, and it spread.

Jeremy was right. Too many people did know.

And of course, there was the one chap I had overlooked.

Rufus Grassington. He wanted the pictures. He implied that himself. So did Lord Finching. Rufus saw himself a Renaissance man, and dressed accordingly. But Ariosto, the poet, I told myself, not Macchiavelli's Prince.

I didn't know about Rufus. I could imagine him furious at being thwarted. But perhaps I was imagining too much.

And then of course, there were the Soldiers of the Dawn... Of whom I knew damn all!

Suddenly there was traffic everywhere, trucks and lorries and horse-drawn carts, all loaded with produce and the sounds and smells of farm animals, and 'the country' in general. We joined the throng, and headed with it into Wantage's main square.

We managed to park and stumbled across the cobbles to the mobile tea-wagon, stationed aptly beneath the statue of King Alfred. We each made welcome inroads into a chipped enamel mug of dark stewed tea with a chunk of crisp-coated-but-just-this-side-of-burnt lardy cake. The tea came scalding hot, almost mahogany, with a dash of condensed milk, the cake with a scattering of plump currants embedded in its layers of sweet fatty dough beneath its wonderful crunchy crust. After a night without sleep, it was heaven. The sort of food that would get you back on your feet and see you through a day of outdoor activity with plenty of beer, which was what a lot of market days were about, as far as the locals were concerned.

We wandered round until eight o'clock, watching the activities of animals, fowls and humans about their various business – it didn't always coincide, and there were always laughs to be had – and stretched our legs, took comfort stops, and had a smoke before getting back into the van and heading off along the back road that ran along the foot of the downs.

I counted the turnings.

I knew it was before the White Horse, and brought us to a crossroad that was a track to the left, but a metalled lane to the right, hidden between some elms.

"Just round here," I said. "I'm sure it's here."

We drew up almost at once outside a pair of cottages built in the last century of flint, with brick quoins, window and door trims, and steep-pitched slate roofs. As I opened the van door I was hit by the scent of an early flowering currant, its deep pink drooping flowers full out. I checked the sign on the green-painted front gate: Blowing Stone Cottage. Inside the front garden was a huge stone, set upright, honeycombed with holes. Somewhere nearby a dog began to bark.

I walked up the path between late flowering purple and yellow crocus and tiny blue scilla, and knocked on the door.

I hoped we weren't too early. Half past eight is a bit of a cheeky time to come calling, but I trusted the people within kept country hours.

A small woman in a faded wrap-around overall and Wellingtons came round the side of the cottage.

"Yes?" she said. She had that soft slight drawl that said she was local.

"I'm Alice Chamberlain. Lord Finching might have mentioned me. He said you had something for me if I gave you the password, which is Artemis."

Oh, God it sounded so pathetic!

I felt a complete twerp.

To hide my embarrassment, I fiddled with the Abraxas ring, which I had put, like its previous wearer, on a gold chain round my neck, and held it out to her.

The woman looked at me steadily, with deep brown eyes, her lips pursed then at the ring, which was about her eye level. I towered over her, and waited. She looked up at me again, and I stood still watching her. Her hair was still in curlers under a head scarf, and she had a countrywoman's skin, soft pinky-red and crinkled. Her eyes said young, but the rest of her was the far side of fifty.

Finally she spoke. "You got help, then? I can't see you and me shifting her."

"I have help," I managed to say, and waved to Jeremy, who was leaning by the van with a cigarette on. He pinched it out, stuck it behind his ear, and slouched across.

The woman looked at him unimpressed. "Best we go round the back, then," she said tartly.

The picture was in an outhouse, wrapped in sacking.

"Tell you the truth, Miss Chamberlain, I'm glad the Master rang. Since th'old Master died a few weeks ago, I've been getting fretful about the Lady here. She oughtn't be in a barn. Should be looked after somehow, at least indoors proper. And working again. Or just being looked at, cos she's beautiful. Man who painted her knew what he was doing, and no mistake."

We unwrapped the sacking, to check the condition of the picture; 'the Lady' was an angel, in blue and orange, set against an evening seascape, the full moon reflecting a path to herself on the waves. Monday's angel.

So now I had Monday and Tuesday.

Only the rest of the week to find.

"I'll take her to a place she can be looked after," I promised. There was work to be done here. The damp was getting into the wood, and the paint was coming away in places. So much for Rufus's work. But then sitting wrapped in damp sacking in a country outhouse was not the ideal place for a work of art.

"I'll get you an old sheet," said the woman. "Was going to turn it into dusters and dishcloths, but I've got plenty of them. Give the Lady a new overcoat to travel in." She bustled off into the house, and came back shortly after clutching a sheet that had been turned side to middle at least twice in its long career, but was of good linen.

We wrapped the picture and begged some twine to fasten it, then, Jeremy at the front, me at the back, we humped it out of its old home, round the house, down the path. It was heavy – it was all board after all – and I was glad to have Jeremy to help. I could have managed, but I could have caused more damage had I tried to carry it off alone, or with its current guardian.

We shimmied it into the back of the van. It fitted well, flat on the floor. We wedged it round with some packing materials that John kept in there, and thanked the woman, shaking hands.

"Keep her safe, and you're welcome to her. Use her ill, and you'll know it," she said, closing the garden gate. "Give my best to the Master, when you see him. Cheerio!" She had disappeared behind the house before we had got into the cab.

"That was too easy," Jeremy said. "I'm not complaining. Where to now?"

"My parent's house."

I had the map book out, and was already reading the way back. "We need to skip Wantage; it'll be heaving."

20

My father was impressed, and extremely excited at the thought of another angel.

My mother was glad to see us, no matter how scruffy we looked. By the time we had got the picture unpacked in the studio, she had arranged a poached egg on toast for us both. "You look like you've been through a hedge backwards, the pair of you," she said. "Don't you ever sleep, Alice? If you want to keep your skin in good condition, you need your sleep. It's not war-time now. You don't have to exhaust yourself and lose your looks."

"I was about to go to bed, but my flat was broken into, Maman," I said, between mouthfuls.

Damn. I had not intended to tell her.

That did it.

She went off into French, and I switched off.

Jeremy gave me a worried look.

"It's OK," I told him gently, "she's just an excitable foreigner. No English phlegm."

"What did they take?" Pa asked.

"My jewels. That's what burglars do, isn't it?"

"They took your jewels, Alice?" screeched my mother. "How can you be so calm? *Ma chérie*, you are too English with your bloody cold."

I looked up at Maman. "*Calme-toi*, Maman. They smashed up a lot of Great Aunt's stuff. The jewels, such as they were, were not worth much. The mess they made is horrible, and I am really not looking forward to sorting it out, but they didn't get what they came for."

My father raised an eyebrow. "You mean it has something to do with these pictures?"

"Almost certainly."

"Does Leggy know?"

"Not yet. Only the police and the burglar him or herself."

"Good, you at least called the police," my mother said, slightly mollified.

"How did they get in? How did they get into the house? It's not as though you live on street level."

I sighed. I'd been through all this myself. I shook my head. "The front door? We don't bolt it. I don't know. Perhaps the police can tell me later."

"Does this mean anything to you?" the sergeant asked, holding out an envelope, and tipping the contents onto his table.

I was red-eyed in Chelsea Police Station. Jeremy had dropped me there before going home himself.

I bit my lip.

It was a small lapel badge, in gold, or at least in yellow metal, of a mailed fist holding a sword against a rising sun.

"Well?" he asked.

"I've never seen it before," I said. "It doesn't belong to me. I don't know how it got there. Where was it?"

"But you do recognize it?" the sergeant persisted.

"I know it's a badge of some sort," I said. "I don't know anything of the organization it represents. But I have heard of it. That's all I can tell you."

"And what is the organization, Miss?"

"I've heard it called the Soldiers of the Dawn. I don't know what it does. I thought it had religious leanings, but that's all."

"Really? And you have no links with this organization?"

"None at all. I'm not a religious person, sergeant."

"But they have links with you, obviously. This was on

your mantel. You are sure it's not yours, Miss?"

"Not mine," I said. "I shouldn't think an organization called Soldiers of the Dawn would allow women in."

He looked thoughtful and nodded. "Probably not. But you were meant to discover it, I'd say."

Yes, I thought, and be duly scared.

And I'd missed it. So had Jeremy – unless he'd put it there… I really didn't want to go down that alley, but I'd have to.

I scrutinized the little badge and shook my head. "No idea why," I said. "Can't think why they wanted to smash the place up. I really can't. And how did they get in? I don't know. I'm always very punctilious about locking my flat."

I sighed. I was feeling very tired now. I yawned. "I guess I'll have to go home and sort it out."

"I'll get someone give you a lift, Miss," he said gently. "If you remember anything, anything at all, then I'll be pleased to listen."

The place was a tip, but Lily, bless her, had cleared the worst of it. "Those fingerprint men make such a mess," she said, rubbing at my Great Aunt's desk with a duster. "I never heard a thing, Miss Alice. Mind, there was a huge thunderstorm last night."

"Was there?"

She chuckled. "Where were you and what were you doing? It was horrendous! I had all the kids in bed with me, they were that scared."

"Want a cup of tea?" I asked, about to put the kettle on as a matter of habit.

Lily raised her eyebrows. "You think so?" She pointed to a row of cardboard boxes filled with parcels wrapped in fabric and old newspapers. "I don't think there are any cups left. Nor no plates either. And no glasses. It's wicked what they did. And they ripped all the cushions. It was spite, pure spite."

"At least they didn't set fire to the curtains," I said, shuddering at the thought.

She turned to me, cocking her head to one side. "Who you been upsetting, Miss Alice?"

I shook my head. "No-one that I'm aware of, Lily. I hadn't expected something like this."

"'Tain't good. I'll send George up for the rest of the boxes later."

I was about to thank her when my doorbell pealed.

"You expecting anyone?"

I shook my head. We both picked up a couple of boxes and made our way down the stairs. Halfway down the bell rang again.

"Impatient bugger," muttered Lily, "Don't they know where you live?"

I put the boxes down at the foot of the stairs and opened the door.

It was my sister, Maddy, breathless and concerned. "Maman rang. What do you need? We'll go and buy it. I've got the car and a cheque book." She looked me up and down. "Alice, are you alright? You look like you've been up all night."

"Ah," I said. "It shows. Sorry. Come on up and sort out what I need, I'm floating a bit. And I need to RSVP Sweetie."

"Eh? You're talking scribble, Alice," Maddy said, following me up the stairs. We took it slowly, ostensibly for her, but I was glad not to hurry. I felt as though I was not quite within the confines of my body. It wasn't unpleasant, simply a bit disorienting.

I took in her face when she entered the flat. Lily had brought the rooms back into stunning order, but Maddy's expression was of shock and horror.

"Who?" she asked.

I shrugged. "Whoever." I plonked down into an armchair. "I need new crockery, some new cushions, a mirror, glasses, a vase or two, and eventually some more furniture. OK, sis, let's go. But first this." I scribbled a note of acceptance on my calling card, and slipped it into a tiny envelope. "Can we drop it in? It's out of the way, but it needs to be done."

"She lives here?" Maddy sniffed – I swear she'd caught it from Maman and Angelique. "Funny, I always thought of her as a more in-town person."
"Ouch! This was her father's house. I think she's taken it over since coming back from the States."
"She was there for a large part of the War, wasn't she? Wonder what she did."
"Avoided Hitler's bombs," I said drily. "I'll find out this Friday for you, if you like."
"My sister the occultist sleuth!"
"My sister the nosy parker." I was tired; it was the best I could manage.

We hurtled round the Army & Navy Stores in Westminster and were back with our purchases an hour later. The next problem was getting them upstairs. I wouldn't let Maddy carry them and I had gone past my second and third wind, and now only wanted to sleep. I left them in the hallway, to bring up later, kissed my lovely sister goodbye, and staggered up the stairs for some long overdue sleep.

I was dreaming of strange angels closing in on me when the telephone ringing shattered it, leaving me breathlessly awake with a bad taste in my mouth. I staggered upright. It was dark outside, and I had no idea what the time was. I crossed the landing to the living room and the phone. It stopped ringing before I got to it.

I groaned, put on the kettle, and realized I'd have to go downstairs to get my new crockery.

I shrugged on a dressing gown over my pyjamas, toed on

my slippers and started the long downward trek. The parcels were still there. I picked up the crockery. It was heavy, but the sleep had done its work. I carried that up, then came down for the glassware.

George was already waiting for me. "Oy, Miss, I could have done that," he said reproachfully, "You only had to ask."

I pointed to a couple of relatively light but awkwardly shaped parcels. "You take those two, and I'll take these then, George. I'd be most grateful."

He showed no sign of going, and clearly wanted to help unwrap everything, being naturally inquisitive. "Who do you think done it, Miss?"

"Don't know, George. You didn't hear anything odd last night?"

"Only a blinking great storm. It didn't half go some. You couldn't hear the radio, even."

"What time was this?" I asked.

"You never heard it?" he sounded astonished. "How could you miss it, Miss, it was like the Blitz!"

"I was probably dancing to a very loud band," I said. "About ten, ten thirty?"

"No, later. 'Bout half past eleven. For about half an hour."

"And you were listening to the radio?"

"Trying to, Miss," he grinned. "None of us could sleep. An' all we could get was interference and these weird foreign channels. Did you know, Miss, there's one called Nice, and it's not nice at all. Can't make out anything it says and the music's rubbish."

I grinned. My Grandfather agreed with him. "Going to help me unpack then?"

We soon had the flat looking habitable again. The new crockery was to my taste, simple white Utility ware, but elegantly balanced, rather than my Great Aunt's more florid choice. We had tea and toast together to christen it, and I handed George a sixpence for his help. "And can you tell me what your Mum would like as a present? I know she won't accept money, but she's been very helpful and I want to give her something."

George nodded. He had no compunction in accepting anything that was going, but he understood his mother's code too. "She likes chocolates, only she ends up giving them to us kids. But nylons – she's always going on about laddering them. She don't like going out in old lady stockings, Miss, my Mum, and she'd rather have cold legs than wear socks."

I'd noticed, of course, but never put it together. She was a tall woman, nearly as tall as me. "What size shoe does she take, George?" I asked.

"Er, five and a half, I think. She says she's a five and a half. But really she's more comfortable in a six. Only she don't like asking for six, says it makes her feet sound like fish-boxes. Can I make a bit more toast, Miss?"

"Of course you can, George." I went to my bedroom and found Bobby's nylons. Four pairs should last Lily a bit. I took them through and handed them to George. "Do you think she'd like these? I seem to have bought a few too many."

"Blimey, Miss, four pairs too many? You made of money?" He was turning the toast over.

"No, but I was offered a deal, so I took it."

"Quite right, Miss. She'd love 'em. I'll tell her you sent them to say thank you, shall I?"

"Please." I sawed myself a piece of bread, and stuck it on the toasting fork.

"Your friend, Miss, the one in the car…?"

"Yes?"

"Will he be coming round today? Only it was really great last night driving around…"

"I don't know," I said. "He's probably asleep."

"It was good we got your stuff into the bike shed, wasn't it? Do you think that bloke came back, him with the funny badge on?"

"I really don't know," I said at last. "It's possible."

I spread the toast with marge and Marmite, and poured us both some more tea. I remembered I wanted to phone Leggy, indeed I needed to see him. I reached for the phone and dialed his number. Bobby answered.

"Hello Bobby, is Leggy in?"

"We're just thinking of having supper, Milady. ... Er, just a moment... Leggy says why don't you come on over, as we haven't seen you for some time. Call a cab and come on over. It'd be great to see you again."

It wasn't what I wanted, and I wasn't fishing for a free meal, but I knew Bobby's cooking. "Give me about half an hour," I said, putting the phone down.

No sooner had I done so, than the doorbell rang.

"That's your friend with the car, Miss," said George, stuffing a final mouthful of toast in, and dusting himself free of crumbs. "I'll be off, then. Leave you two alone," and he gave me a wink as he picked up the stockings.

I followed him down, and opened the door myself.

It was indeed Jeremy, in his more usual guise. "I wondered how you were, Alice," he said, looking me up and down. I suddenly remembered I was in my night wear, not exactly seduction quality, either; harvest festival, rather, all safely gathered in.

"Come in, I'm fine, despite my appearance. Did you get some sleep?"

He nodded. "An hour or two."

"Did you RSVP to Sweetie?" I asked as we walked upwards.

"Yes, I delivered it just now. B said Maddy had taken you shopping. How did it go?"

"As fast as I could manage. George helped me set it up.

The place is a lot better than when you last saw it."

I opened the door, which still needed a new lock, and swanked. It did look more me. I had actually been forced to make my own mark on the flat, and I'd enjoyed it.

"It's lighter," he said appreciatively. "More modern. Classy." He looked back at the door. "I'll change the locks for you tomorrow if you like. Any chance of a cup of tea?"

"For someone who will change my locks, there is always a cup of tea," I told him. "However, I'm due at Leggy's any moment now. If you can spare the time, it would be good to introduce you – but be warned, Bobby will be there."

I poured some more boiling water into the teapot and swirled it around a few times. It would be fine.

"I can handle that," he said. "Don't know about Bobby, though. Do you want me there?"

I hadn't thought about it when I had suggested he came, but I realized I did. Leggy had inadvertently recommended him. He wasn't on Leggy's pay-roll, but I was pulling him off official work. He should get some recognition. And I got the impression that he was keen to meet Leggy.

"Yes, Jeremy, I think it would be useful. I think you'd get on well together."

I dialed Leggy's number. Bobby answered. "Bobby, a colleague who's been helping me has just turned up. I think Leggy would like to meet him. Would that be OK with you both?"

"I'll check, Milady. On the food front it'll be fine. I've got a pot full of Irish stew and plenty of soda bread. People always turn up when that's on the menu, for some reason." I heard him talking to Leggy. "Of course it's all right. See you soon, bring your appetites."

"Thanks, Bobby, you're an angel – a good one!" I told him.

I heard a chuckle as he put the phone down.

I poured the tea, and handed it to Jeremy. "Enjoy your

tea. I'll just slip into something a bit more appropriate," I said. "Excuse me for a moment or ten."

Bobby opened the door to us, looked me up and down, looked Jeremy up and down, then inspected his mouth in the lamp light. He smiled at the small scar on and above his upper lip. "Ah, so I did leave a mark."

"Just so. How are your ribs?"

"You didn't crack them, but not for the want of trying. How is what's-her-name?"

"What's-her-name? I don't know. I heard she was seeing a chap who owns a button factory now. If it's that what's-her-name you mean."

"Then she'll be set up for life, don't you know? I'm always losing buttons, my own and other people's. Come on into the lift, then. Leggy's waiting for you both."

So it was a truce.

I sighed deeply.

"Don't know what you're huffing for, Milady. I could have brought this fellow round here at any time." Still touchy then. So not a smart-alec reply.

"I know, Bobby." I said, dropping a kiss on his cheek. "Bobby, I'm so glad you invited us to supper. It was really kind."

He touched his cheek. "Hmm… You engineered it out of me, Milady, so you did! Not that I wouldn't have anyway."

He opened the lift door and escorted us into the flat. "Go down to the front room at the far end of the corridor. Jeremy, be careful of the cat. It's not called Nuts for nothing!"

I greeted Leggy with a hug and a handshake and did the introductions.

The table was set in the far corner, with four places. There were soup bowls, side plates and the usual cutlery, four tumblers, a jug of water and a bottle of whisky.

Bobby came in carrying a steaming cooking pot in

two kettle-holders. "Sit down will youse, while I get the bread."

We settled ourselves at the table while stew was ladled out and Bobby divvied out wedges of bread, and poured us each a finger of whisky.

"So why have you brought this chap to me?" Leggy asked.

"Because he helped me find the second angel, and more to the point, helped me collect it and store it in a safe place."

That shut them up. For a second or two, and then the questions came full and fast. I fielded them as we ate.

I told the bare minimum. I didn't give any names, nor did I mention the break-in. I told them about the actual painting, and how we got it, including the use of Jeremy's flat-mate's van. I said I was working on getting the others, but I felt unhappy about using the same van.

"You must hire one, then, Alice. A different one for each pick up if necessary, whatever you think fit. We don't want anyone getting any ideas."

"You mean the Merediths?" I suggested.

"Possibly," said Leggy, hedging. "There may be others…"

I frowned. "You know there may be others?" I asked.

"I don't know. I intuit. Suddenly the Merediths are back in town and Miss Thorburn with them. And other people have mentioned things to me, at my various clubs."

"I think Lizzie Thorburn is after them," Bobby said, through a mouthful of stew. "I heard part of the deal with her engagement is that she brings with her a certain painting, or preferably, paintings."

"My God, where did you get that from?" Jeremy asked.

Bobby tapped his nose knowingly. "No names, no pack-drill. A reliable source."

I bet, I thought. The lady herself. Well, she'd be looking, wouldn't she? So that was – possibly – what Bobby was doing at 35 The Boltons.

I reached down to my handbag and picked out a notebook and pen, and drew the mailed fist, sword and rising sun motif. I handed it across to Leggy. "Does this mean anything to you?" I asked.

He polished his glasses on his napkin, perched them on his nose and peered through them. "Where did you see this?" he asked.

I took it back.

"My question first, Leggy. Then I'll answer yours." Bobby reached across, "Give us a squint, Milady."

He took it, and pursed his lips. "Oh dear, oh dear, oh dear!" He looked at Leggy. "Are you going to tell her? Or shall I?"

That bad, eh?

I put down my cutlery and looked at them both expectantly.

Leggy coughed, and mopped his mouth. "The Soldiers of the Dawn," he said at last, leaning back in his chair and gazing at the ceiling. "I came into contact with them during the war. They are a semi-religious sect. Like the Masons, only it stops there. They are more active, they are militant, fanatical and extremist and very secretive – unless they want to make a point. Their way is the only way, like the fascists."

He held up his hand to stop my next question, and took a sip of whisky. "I don't know if they are Nazis, or just extreme fundamentalists. We thought we had stamped them out. I haven't seen this symbol since 1945. So where did you see it?"

"It was left in my flat, to be found, on the mantel, after the place had been ransacked. They took my financially worthless collection of jewelry to make it look like a proper burglary, but I don't think they were after that. I think they followed my contact to my place…"

Now I held up my hand to both Leggy and Bobby who were about to bawl me out about making meetings at my home. "I know. I know. But I didn't make the meeting. I simply rang a contact number and the contact extrapolated my address and turned up. I'm sure he wouldn't have wished me ill. Positive. But he gave me a lot of information, and I still have it. Not written down, except in code in a safe place. OK?"

"When did this happen, Alice?" Leggy asked.

"Last night. Lucky for me I was out. I needed a break. When I got home I met the result of these people's visit."

Jeremy said. "Bobby, do you know anything about these Soldiers of the Dawn? You seem to know everyone."

Bobby acknowledged the compliment. "I knew them some years ago. Like Leggy, I thought they'd been smoked out and destroyed. There were a few fellow-travelers who probably got away, but the brains of the organization went the way of all flesh, only a bit faster" Bobby said. "I know we got the big boys. I got them myself. And bullet holes to prove it."

"Then reflect on the small fry, if you would," Jeremy said, pulling out George's notebook. He read the description, and handed it over for Bobby to look at the pictures. "This is the work of Alice's sidekick, a kid who will be an ornament to the Service in the future. He lives in the basement of her house. This chap wanted to wait in Alice's flat, said he was a friend, but George saw him off."

Bobby grinned. "I know the spalpeen. This is his work? He's pretty good. Look here, he says the man's breath smelt of beer and Parma violets. That's some observation!" he cocked his head for a moment. "He couldn't be lying, could he? Embroidering the truth so he'd get a better tip?"

I turned the idea over a few times; a possibility, but upon reflection I discounted it. "No, Bobby. I'd trust George implicitly. He'd lie for me, but not to me. Do you recognize the man?"

Leggy took the book and drew his brows together. "I know the ring," he said. "It was the ring of the head of the order. A sapphire cabochon cut, set in twirly gold setting. If that got passed on, we have a problem."

"But surely it isn't unique? There could be many rings of a similar appearance."

"Pray that it is," muttered Leggy.

"Where did these people meet?" I asked, after a particularly tender piece of scrag end.

"Private houses, good addresses mostly. In town or in the country – small meetings. There were at most thirteen to a Lodge, often fewer, and most were introduced by other members, although all members would not know all other members. Only the hierarchy knew the other cells. That's why it is just possible that we missed one, that we didn't extirpate the nest of vipers."

"Bad news, then," I breathed.

"Does the description mean anything?" Jeremy pressed.

"Let me think on it," Bobby said. "I don't think that this chap did your break-in, though. If he's wearing the head's ring, he'd let a minion do the dirty work. Also, if he were seen off, he would be recognized. No, I think the kiddey who did the job was someone else altogether."

"Do you think he will be back?" I asked. "Only I've just replaced a lot of stuff. I know I can claim on the insurance, but they won't be too pleased if I continue to do so on a regular basis."

Leggy looked thoughtful. "I don't know, Alice," he said at last. "I think it was done to find something that your contact left with you, and having not done so, to warn you off. Whether you choose to be frightened into not doing any more is your choice."

"Come on, Leggy. You know me better than that. Besides, I want to use the rest of the information I've got."

"And I would dearly love to locate all the pictures, my dear."

I sipped the whisky, and reflected that I had the locations of all of the pictures if Lord Finching had been telling the truth. I could get out now. I could hand Leggy the information and let him and Bobby deal with it.

But I'd promised Lord Finching that I would collect and disempower the pictures. And I hadn't mentioned any of that to Leggy.

I was playing my own game.

We were all playing our own games. But sometimes some of them coincided.

"So would I, Leggy," I said. "This is the artist's daughter talking. I'd really like to see the pictures re-united and exhibited to the public. I'd like Greystoke to get his artistic recognition – even posthumously."

I caught Leggy's astonished face.

"Come on, Leggy. It would be brilliant publicity and get the Merediths spitting feathers."

"And up the interest, and thus the price," Jeremy said. "Are you going to try to buy all the pictures? Although Alice is in the way of locating them, they seem to be, very loosely, the property of an occult group. Another one. Not the Soldiers of the Dawn."

Leggy frowned. "Do you have a name for it, or a leader?"

"A leader, yes. He also wants to see the Merediths get their come-uppance, and it is for this reason he has given me the information. They are not his, I am sure, but he is second in command to Thorburn, the chap whose studio you cleared."

"Fine," said Leggy. "Fine. When you've located them all, ask him for a price. I'll do my best to meet it."

"Er... perhaps you misunderstood, sir, or I was not as clear as I should have been," I said. "The price is vengeance on the Merediths, as far as it will go."

Leggy chuckled. "In that case, I think we have an accord." He put down his spoon, refilled all our glasses, and raised his. "A toast. To come-uppance, to retribution!"

21

I drank water after that toast, and was thus able, the following morning to get up bright and early for my swim with Thelma. While we were breakfasting in the café I asked her for a favour.

"Of course, Alice. Simply ask. It shall be done."

I handed her an envelope, in which I had written out all my plans for the weekend and the coming week in my personal code, with a wax seal of Lord Finching's ring and all relevant addresses. "Could you look after this until Monday. If I don't turn up, or ring you, take it straight round to the address on the envelope." It was Leggy's.

Thelma nodded, eyes wide. "OK. But you will be here on Monday. I know you will," she sounded uncertain.

Was there a frisson of excitement in her voice, or jealousy, that while I might be doing something really rather dangerous, her weekend would be spent doing the laundry and cleaning her flat?

"I shall make every effort to get back for our Monday swim. This is insurance, Thelma. I really am grateful to have met you. You're so helpful and so calm."

Her eyebrows raised and she snorted. "That's how much you know!"

"All right, surprise me. How are you going to spend this weekend?"

"I shall be actively involved in sidecar racing. Although I say it myself, I am a damn fine sidecar passenger. And I intend to be here on Monday. Or I'll let you know."

My turn to gawp. I realized I was guilty of doing a Sam Simmons.

"You devil!" I breathed. *"Chapeau!"* (Hats off to you,

dearie!)

"You still want me to hold your insurance?" she asked.

"Even more so now," I said. "Can I come along some time? It sounds fun.."

"Of course, and have a go if you want. The lads would love it," she laughed, shedding years.

Jeremy was waiting outside when I returned home, and he changed all my locks swiftly and professionally. A man of many parts. I provided tea, toast and encouragement, and read to him sporadically from Mr. Thorburn's notebooks on what he called Temple Etiquette.

"So, basically you always move clockwise round the temple, even if it takes longer?" Jeremy asked.

"That's what he says. It's even more formal than a Roman Catholic Mass, lots of repeating and circling and praising all over the place, wafting incense and candles around. " I sighed and thought enviously of Thelma who'd be out in her leathers riding sidecars over a dirt-track. "Still, it's work, and we have opted for it."

"Just so, Milady." He'd taken to calling me that now. I wasn't sure I liked it.

He stood up, took a final draught of tea, then closed the door and locked it. "Bingo! All done. Lady Finching?"

Blandings was a home for voluntary patients of a nervous disposition in need of special care, the Matron told us. She was a well-corseted party close to retirement age, in her blue creaseless uniform with its little white shoulder cape and starched waterfall of a cap.

She ushered us into her private sitting room at the front of the house, and let us know that she would have appreciated a phone call to warn her of our coming. Alarm bells rang in my head.

"However," she went on, "Lord Finching was here yesterday, and he rang to say a Miss Alice Chamberlain would very likely be visiting in the near future. You have identification?"

I always carried my passport, which some thought odd in peace time, but I preferred it with me. It was a hangover from the war. I handed it across.

"And you, sir? I wasn't apprised of your visit."

"I'm Miss Chamberlain's driver, but I should like to meet Lady Finching, if it were possible." He handed over his identity card. "If you need to check on me, I can furnish a phone number. I'm a civil servant. This is a matter of some importance." He made it sound extremely important.

The Matron scrutinized our documents. "I must ask you to be very calm, and very discreet," she said confidentially, handing them back. "The residents here are normal in the main, but have lapses of a nervous nature. They tend to get agitated with strangers. Some may get violent. We do our best to keep them peaceful, tranquil."

We nodded.

I bet you do, I thought.

Pump them full of drugs or run electrical currents through them.

But I didn't let it show on my face.

I said, "Matron, what we have to say to Lady Finching may upset her. I cannot help that. I shall be as gentle as I can, but for the sake of other people and for herself, the questions must be asked."

"I understand. There will be a nurse who will know what to do if things get out of hand. She'll sit in with you and catch up on her knitting probably. I don't think you'll need her, but, and this is strictly off the record, Lady Finching has had very violent episodes. Someone, somewhere along the line, gave her some very nasty substances which cause her to hallucinate. If she sees terrible things coming for her, she'll attack. That is why she is here. For the most part we can keep her stable, and when we can't we can keep her contained. I'll take you to the parlour, and then bring her to you."

I hadn't met officially mad people before.

I wasn't feeling optimistic.

It must have showed in my face.

"Oh, don't worry about a thing," the Matron assured us. "My staff is very experienced and extremely discreet. What passes between you and Lady Finching will remain within these walls, I promise you that." She rose from her chair and beckoned us to follow her.

We sat around a table in a light room with minimal furniture and barred windows. There were chairs for three of us round a table, and a chair in the corner by the door for the nurse. There was a bell-push beside it, I noticed. A frayed carpet on the floor, some net curtains and a pair of tired prints on the wall were the only other adornments. Jeremy and I looked at each other and waited, hardly daring to speak. It felt so clinical, so cold.

I got out our check list, read through it and tried to memorise it.

Then the door opened, and a nurse came in, bringing with her the physical shell of Lady Finching.

I slipped the list into my pocket, and tried not to show the shock I felt.

I had seen pictures of the Lady in the thirties, in my research; I had seen reproductions of Emily's portrait of her. She was a Victorian, in that she had been born while Victoria was on the throne, but only just. So she must have been just short of fifty, the same vintage, give or take a year or two, as my mother. She looked closer to sixty-five, a bad sixty-five, or worse. The woman I had seen in the society papers and other places had been beautiful, tall, haughty, a capable woman who knew her own mind, confident, bossy even. Not a woman you'd cross and expect to get away unscathed.

The creature that came in was grey, thin, withered, and it would appear from the vacant expression in her pallid watery eyes that she'd left her wits somewhere else. She wore her own clothes, but since she had been here she had lost so much weight and height that they hung off her in loose folds. I felt a deep surge of pity, sadness, yes, and even repulsion, too.

I wondered how much help we'd get from this quarter, but I didn't begrudge my time. Poor woman.

How did you get like this?

Who made her like this?

"This is Miss Alice Chamberlain and Mr. Jeremy Arkwright to see you, Lady Finching," said the nurse, guiding her to the chair opposite us.

I stood up and held out my hand. "Lady Finching, your husband asked me to call on you. You may be able to help us. He asked us to ask you on his account to do so."

She looked at my hand, rather puzzled, then took it. "Nice gloves. I used to have nice gloves, beautiful panne velvet ones that went right up my arms... I was a beauty once you know."

I watched, as with supreme effort she called her wits back from wherever they had been hiding.

The change in her demeanour, in her face, was quite marked. I could see the shadow of the imperious society lady settle back over the old shell.

"Miss Chamberlain? Do I know you?"

"We haven't formally been introduced before as far as I know," I said, as we shook hands.

"I knew a Chamberlain once," she said, sitting down. "Tall chap, artist. Lovely man. Very sexy. I might have married him, only he met some frightful French woman."

Jeremy coughed.

"Lord Wethersley?" I suggested. "He's my father. I'm sure he will wish me to give you his best wishes."

"Is that so? So you're the French woman's daughter. I thought there was something not quite right. You don't look properly English. Wrong complexion."

Yes, well, we can't all look like desiccated corpses, correction, desiccated English corpses. I bit the thoughts back behind my teeth.

"Lady Finching, can you tell us anything about the Sacred Temple of the Angels?" I asked as sweetly as I could. Damn the conventions, I could be blunt too.

That shocked her.

Good.

But she recovered swiftly. "You mean the *Templum Sacrum Angelorum,* the TSA? Of course I could, only I should be breaking my most solemn oaths."

"Lady Finching, I have it from a friend, an artist, whom you took to a meeting at Straddling Hall, that you were involved in some sort of ceremonial magical work. Is this so?"

"Of course it isn't. I refuse to talk about it. I know nothing about it."

Jeremy leaned forward. "Lady Finching, how did you come to be in here? Who brought you to this state? I don't mean to cause you harm or distress, please believe me on that. I seek only to put matters right, to ensure that no other beautiful young women are brought down to spend their lives in places like this. You do believe me, don't you?"

God, he could charm the birds out of the trees. He was so solicitous, so earnest, and, dammit, so bloody good-looking.

I was superfluous for this game and I knew it.

Who would an old woman, locked up without entertaining company for years, choose to talk to?

Why would she talk to me, the daughter of her supposed rival in love, when she could talk to a personable young man?

I let him get on with it, surreptitiously dipping into my bag for a notebook and pencil, but covering them with a handkerchief. I dabbed at my nose, then replaced the handkerchief, but kept the notebook out of sight on my lap with my hands. My shorthand training might once more come in useful.

Meantime, Lady Finching was working her myopic eyes over Jeremy, giving him the full treatment.

"Jeffrey Archer?" she said. "I don't think I've heard of you before."

"No, Jeremy Arkwright," he replied softly. "And there is no reason for you to have heard of me, Lady Finching. I'm not on the social circuit yet."

She sniffed. "If I were out of this place, I could sponsor you. Good-looking fellow like you could do very well for yourself. Not married, are you? I could think of several girls who would be suitable for you. Not too fussy, are you? I mean, a wall-eye, a thick waist, they wouldn't be too repellent if they were allied to a reasonable fortune?"

Jeremy smiled at her. "Lady Finching, I'm not here to talk about me, but to talk about you. I find that far more fascinating."

I watched the old woman preen. I wondered how many others he'd buttered up over the years.

"How did you come to be in a place like this?" he prompted gently.

"Oh, that? It was all a mistake." She sighed, and shrugged. "I agreed to come in, of course, but it was all a bit of a mistake. They said if I didn't come in there would be a prison sentence or worse, so of course I agreed."

"Why should that have happened?" The woman sighed again. "You don't happen to have a cigarette?" she asked. "I think it's so much nicer to chat with a cigarette, don't you?"

Jeremy handed out across his silver case, now filled with Passing Clouds. Her eyes widened as she took one. "I've not had these for many a long day. You're most welcome, young man. Ask away!"

He lit her, handed the case to me, but I shook my head, so he took one for himself, and lit it slowly, inhaling, waiting for the woman to speak again.

"It was so long ago," she said at last, savouring the smoke.

She looked at me. "I lied to you, young woman. I was in the Lodge you mentioned. Years ago. I joined it in my early twenties. For a bit of a frolic, actually. It was new and different, and I liked the idea of being different from the rest of the girls. I was introduced to it by my future husband. He was very into it, a natural psychic, and I thought, well, if I'm going to marry him – and I was, because he was enormously rich and really a very sweet man – I might as well share some of his interests. I had every intention of being a good wife, don't you see?"

She drew heavily on her cigarette. "In the early days I hadn't the vaguest idea what was going on. I just went along with it. We met once a month, at Straddling. It was quite a commitment. The Magus and High Priestess were very thorough people, though, and I eventually got the hang of it all. We decided to live close by. I liked the area, and my husband was keen to be close to the lodge itself. Yes, it was good. They were good times." Her eyes lost their focus, a smile played around her mouth as she remembered.

Then the expression changed.

"We had a couple of new members turn up. People came and went on and off, but these two were different. Twins. And these two were very powerful occultists. You should have heard their inner experiences. They were wonderful. They made our efforts appear so feeble. But more than that, they were building developers. They had contacts in the building trade, knew the right people, and suddenly we had a state-of-the-art house exactly where we wanted it. They brought a lot of new energy into the lodge, did Percy and Archie." She drew once more on the cigarette, looking at something high up in the corner of the room. "They brought in things that would help you reach higher states of consciousness, too. Oh, believe me, they worked. That interesting little white powder worked only too well."

"What was it?" Jeremy asked.

"White powder? Morphine. And Cocaine, too. Don't ask me where they got it, although I do know they had contacts in Hong Kong, and others in Central America – building contracts and such. But they always had some, or could get some. That's why they threw such wonderful parties. It was still the Jazz Age, or the tail end of it. I was around thirty now, and had two children, and the wonderful new house. The girls were a delight, but my husband was off on government business all over the world – I've no idea what he was involved in, but he traveled a great deal. I didn't travel with him. I am not a good traveler. I get sick on the top deck of a tram – not that I ever used such things except in an emergency!

"I made the perfect home at Finchings, but I was bored, particularly when the girls went off to school. Oh, so bored. So when Percy and Archie came to visit, which they often did, before lodge, or just for the fun of it, I often indulged in the white dragon. It really enhanced the magical work, I can assure you."

She looked confidentially at Jeremy. "Truly amazing experiences. Wonderful visions, ecstatic realizations, delights and joys beyond anything I have ever known in this or any other worlds."

She stubbed out her cigarette. "I would not have missed it. No, I would not have missed it. It was wonderful."

Her face was a glowing beacon of joy. "I have seen the gods and been at one with them. I have seen and been with the fount of all light. No matter what happened later, no-one can take that away from me," she exclaimed vehemently.

"What happened, Lady Finching?" Jeremy asked quietly

at last. "Just the broadest outline if it is too painful. I don't wish to cause you undue distress." He pushed the cigarette case towards her and relit her. And we waited.

And waited.

And waited. While she smoked the whole cigarette.

I glanced at the nurse in the corner who was placidly knitting.

She made the slightest shaking movement of her head. I did a similar tiny nod, and settled down to wait some more.

Suddenly Lady Finching stretched herself, drawing her sagging frame upwards, and her eyes focused on both of us. "You really want to help others? I'm past help, let's be honest. But if you really want to stop those bastards, then I'll tell you."

She sank back a little, and looked over our heads, at something that we couldn't see, even if we'd turned, then she nodded at whatever it was, and looked at us again. "By doing this I am breaking my Lodge Oath. I am inviting the Powers I served, the greatest of angels, to cast me down into the Pit. But I should prefer to be in the Pit than in this place."

Her voice was low and bitter. "The highs I got from the white powders were the highs of ecstasy, pure spiritual experiences greater than human mind can comprehend or relate to another. We simply don't have the words. But the lows… oh the lows! I have no fear of Hell. I know it already."

She helped herself to another cigarette, let Jeremy light it for her, and continued. "I know I sound rational. For most part I am. But I must live with the knowledge that I am a time-bomb ticking. I called in bright forces, but I also called in darkness. Things I have seen, you wouldn't even imagine. In the Lodge they were in controlled circumstances, more or less. At first. And you had your protection up. You had your brothers and sisters in the art magical to protect you in times of need. But outside of lodge… Well, let us say some things slipped through. Slip through. And when they do, you react. You have to. You wouldn't be human if you didn't."

I rested my pen, my eyes on the woman.

"If I didn't have enough of the powder… I would see things. Unpleasant things. When they are attacking you, you fight back. When they are attacking your children, you fight back with a vengeance."

She sighed, shivered, reliving an old memory. "One day they attacked my girls. They were in the garden and this creature – I cannot describe it, except to say that it was huge and insect-like, but unlike any insect you have ever seen – this vile monstrosity bore down upon my girls. I took the nearest thing to hand and attacked it. A croquet mallet. And I let rip!"

I felt sick.

She was reliving a personal hell.

"They dragged me off, of course. Their personal maid never regained consciousness. I had killed a dear friend whom my daughters adored in a brutal and unthinkable manner. Luckily for me, she had no family. No-one to take her part. My husband paid off the coroner, the rest of the staff, gave her a proper funeral then sent the girls away to stay with Miss Thorburn in America; she was only too happy to help. We thought it best to get them as far from me as possible for their own sake, while I was encouraged to come here as a voluntary patient."

She looked at me and nodded "Now get this down, please. I know you're writing every word I say; I'm neither stupid nor blind – I want you to know that I came here voluntarily. But I have served my time for killing a good, kindhearted woman in such a vile and vicious manner while the balance of my mind was disturbed. I did it so that our family name would not be dragged through the courts and the mud. I did it so that my girls would not have to endure the shame. I did it so that I would not face the hangman's rope, too, let it be noted. But I have suffered for it every day and every night of my life. It would have been far far better to have faced the hangman."

I scribbled it all down. Every word. When I had finished, I nodded to her, put down the pencil.

She gave a brief nod, a sort of dark smile. "Thank you. If you would care to type it out, for what it's worth, I'll sign it. I don't know whether it would hold up in a court of law, me being here, but it would make me feel that I had made my peace with the world."

I nodded. "I'll certainly do that, Lady Finching. Thank you."

She looked across at the nurse. "Oh, it's all right, Rita. I'm not going to attack anyone here and now. You and the rest of the staff have done your work well. Most of the time here I am peaceable, in control, the perfect patient. I am most grateful to you all. You've done the very best with this bad job, but oh, I miss the outer world. I miss society, I miss my friends. You'd be astonished how few visit. My husband, when he can. And you. Now. Because he asked you to, and because you are on your own crusade. And one friend, she can't be here because she lives abroad, she keeps me in touch. We write, but it's a dreary existence."

She helped herself to another cigarette and inhaled deeply. "Percy and Archie Meredith introduced me to these things. As they introduced many others. Check through the members of the lodge for a start and see where they are now. My husband will give you details if you tell him you are working for me. Check through the society pages of the late twenties and see where the people are now. Check out the Meredith company's building accounts both abroad and at home. If you can do that, and get them, then my hell here will not have been in vain."

She sat back, looking at us defiantly.

Jeremy nodded. "Thank you for being so open with us, Lady Finching. We will do as you say and will endeavour to put things right."

I folded my notebook and put it and the pencil away. "Thank you, Lady Finching," I said. "You have been most helpful. We will treat your honesty with the discretion it deserves. You say your daughters knew Miss Thorburn. Did you know she was back in England?"

"What? But they are in Hollywood, my husband told me. What is she doing back here?"

Oops! I'd let myself in to the big one. Well, let's go for broke, eh?

"Er... She's become engaged to Percy Meredith. Her father died recently."

The woman's face screwed up into a tight ball of wrinkles, then relaxed. "Ah, well they'll be after the angels. They won't get them. My husband has hidden them. They're not flying again. But she's got one of them. Her father had it."

"No," I said gently. "Her father ensured that it would pass to another. It's in a safe place at present."

And the old face relaxed even further. "Then I hope it will be met by the others, and that someone who knows what he or she is doing will purify them on all levels. Thorburn should have done it years ago, but he was not willing to. My husband could have done it. But he didn't. Not properly. He only had them cleaned and restored on the physical levels. It needs to be all four worlds, the physical, the astral, the creative and the spiritual worlds. You need a specialist for that. I can't help you there. I think my husband is too in awe of them."

"An outsider, then?" suggested Jeremy. "Someone not in the Lodge?"

"You are very quick on the uptake, young man. I like that. You must come and visit again. With your secretary."

She turned to the nurse. "Rita, I want to go home. It's

been a good visit, but I'm tired now." She allowed the nurse to help her upright, and pass her her cane, then, as she teetered to the door I heard her say to the nurse, who was virtually supporting her, in a stage whisper "I never thought I'd see Roger's daughter taking a job. The family must have gone to the dogs!"

22

We went to the nearest hostelry.

Jeremy set the drinks down in front of us. Mine was a gin and tonic. What secretaries got bought by their bosses if they needed placating! His was a half of the local bitter.

"I did make rather a hash of that," I admitted, taking a good mouthful. I'd forgotten I liked the drink. It went down very well with a Passing Cloud.

He grinned. "You didn't stand a chance, the poor woman's starved of masculine company of any sort. Can you imagine how awful it must be living in there, even without the knowledge that you are a murderer and not in control of yourself?"

I could. And I too was not sure that death wasn't preferable.

We'd had a chat with the Matron before we left to confirm Lady Finching's background. We were told she was stable for long periods, but then something would set her off and she'd have to be sedated, placed in a safe place for her own protection. I could feel the ice cold needles, the padded cell while the horrors were visiting their old friend. Not a nice place to be at all.

And, added the Matron, she missed her daughters dreadfully. Her husband she could take or leave, but she often brooded on her two daughters. They never wrote, never kept in touch, although a friend kept her up-to-date on their actions, from abroad.

It must have appeared to her that for some reason one day her whole real life just vanished.

I felt the pain.

But I had a life, and more important at this point, I had

a G & T, good quality tobacco and a pleasant companion to share these things with.

And I had my freedom.

"Did you know she knew your father?" Jeremy said quietly. He too had been silent since we had left Blandings.

I shrugged. "Dad knew everybody when he was young. He never mentioned her, but then she might have had a grand pash on him and never told him. He was a fine-looking man in those days. My mother, although she's biased, said she had to fight off several contenders. Perhaps Lady Finching was one of them. I'll ask them." I took another sip of gin. "It might explain why he's not terribly keen on the Merediths."

"I wasn't to start with, but this sickens me. I know she didn't have to take the stuff, but, equally, they didn't have to provide it and push it on her. I don't like the idea of using it to enhance a religious experience. I don't like the idea of being out of control."

"You think they'll fix the wine for us?" I asked over the rim of the glass.

"I don't know what to expect. What do Magicians get up to? Do they do a Black Mass? Do they ride cock-horse over broomsticks or staffs looking cute in their birthday suit? I have no idea what we are letting ourselves in for. All I ask is that we take every possible care. I'd hate to see you ending up like Lady Finching, Alice. Or me."

I smiled. "Unlikely. We've been warned. I doubt she was. Until it was too late. How many others have gone the same way? But I don't think we'll be cavorting in the buff, certainly not at afternoon tea at Sweetie's. I think it's witches who do that. It always struck me as rather silly, thistles, nettles, brambles and cowpats being major features of the English countryside, and the inclement weather. From what I can make out, magicians, or wizards if you like, are more indoor folk, townies, with a bit of education behind them. If you look at the angels, there's Hebrew script on them and according to the Rev. Simmons, it means more than just the sum of its letters."

I downed the last of my gin and tonic and stabbed out the Passing Cloud. "Also, wizards and magicians appear to wear robes, too, which is just as well. I shouldn't like to be in a roomful of variegated nudes, when someone starts swinging a thurible haphazardly!"

I rang Lord Finching to report back, which pleased him, and was surprised to hear that he had rung earlier to tell me he had put a letter in the post which should arrive Monday morning.

Jeremy had gone off to report to Basil, and to organize transport for the weekend, so I opened a can of Scotch broth for lunch.

Society faces, eh?

Maman would know. She and my Father knew everyone.

Perhaps when we delivered the next consignment of angels – always supposing that we would be allowed to take them away.

I ate the soup slowly, savouring the thick gravy, the smooth barley and the tiny shreds of mutton. Then I typed up my shorthand while I still had the memory of it making a copy for Lady Finching to sign and return. I nipped out to post it on the way to my tea date.

I arrived at 35 The Boltons on time. I was let in by a maid of all work who ushered me to the reception rooms on the first floor. The staircase was carpeted now. There must have been a lot of work done since I had heard Elisabeth clatter downstairs to open up for Bobby. The place smelt of incense, but beneath it was the odour of paint.

The maid announced me. "Miss Alice Chamberlain, Ma'am," she said, her voice cracking slightly.

I thanked her, and walked in.

The room spread the whole length of the house, facing

west through balconied French windows set into a bay, and East, over the garden, and another balcony, but straight this time. There were fires in both fireplaces, for there were dividing doors midway, so that the dining area at the rear could be shut out. As it was, the doors were open, and Elisabeth stood alone, wearing close fitting black velvet from top to toe, which did wonders for her blonde hair and for her figure, finished with a long black chiffon scarf embroidered with silver and black beads, and a wristful of silver bracelets that tinkled as she moved.

"Alice, darling," she breathed, coming to greet me, giving me a peck on both cheeks. "So glad you came. You look wonderful. Ah, you've still got the orchid. How quaint."

I smiled brightly. "Thank you for inviting me. You look wonderful yourself, Elisabeth. As to the orchid, well, I had a break in. My jewels got removed."

"How dreadful! You're insured? Of course you are. They took everything?"

I nodded. "Did a lot of damage to the flat too, but it's the sentimental stuff that really hurts."

"Of course. Do sit down, Alice. Look, I've got an idea. Wait just a moment. I'll be back."

She teetered out, and I heard her clomping up to the floor above and her noisy progress across the ceiling. She might be draped like a vampire but she made a lot more noise.

I looked around me.

The room was very Art Nouveau, which wasn't fashionable at all but was a style I rather liked. The mirrored over mantels were of beaten copper with insets of turquoise porcelain, flanked on either side by beaten copper vases filled with peacock feathers. On the wall, beside the front fireplace was copper hook from which hung a silver thurible, loaded with a heady church incense. The smoke crept out in gentle swirls through the pierced lid, perfuming the air. Very arty indeed.

I went to the bow windows at the front and peered out.

A taxi drew up outside, and two noisy glamorous young women got out. I watched them pay the driver off and come up the path. So we were having visitors.

Elisabeth came back in. "I just had this sudden idea. You have no jewels. I have too many. This amethyst pendant, I'd really like you to have it. It's not my colour, and besides, it upsets Percy."

She held out a gold chain with an oval cabochon amethyst set in gold hanging from it. It was perfect.

"It was given to me by an admirer. Percy is very jealous, so I won't get a chance to wear it. I'd be delighted if you would be able to do it justice."

I took the jewel in my hand.

It felt warm and tingling to the touch, compelling.

This jewel provoked a real desire in me. I wanted to wear it.

It wanted to be worn, and by me, make no mistakes there.

It was mine! Or possibly I was its.

I looked into her smiling face. She knew what I was feeling, and enjoying it.

"I'd be delighted, and honoured to do so. Thank you very much, Elisabeth. I'll wear it now."

I slipped it on.

Oh, it felt right. It sat right. I caught sight of myself in the mirror over the fireplace, and I looked stunning with it on.

Behind me, Elisabeth beamed her satisfaction.

I didn't hear the bell ring, I was too busy preening. I felt great in it. "Elisabeth, it will be the start of my new collection. I absolutely love it."

"Then we are both happy, and Percy will be too. Three happy people, with a single action, that can't be bad. Now let's see who has turned up. Your young man, perhaps?"

The maid ushered in the two young women, with squeals and whoops of delight (from the young women, the maid was far more circumspect!), and hugs and kisses all round.

When, finally, the commotion of greetings had died down, Elisabeth turned to me, "Alice, you must forgive me. I had no idea these two were going to turn up. They're my long lost sisters – well, that's what we call each other. We have lived as family on and off all our lives. It's such a joy to see them again."

She separated the two young women.

"This is May and this is June. You may know them by their stage names, Myrna Lauriston and Jacqueline Finching. May and June, this is Alice Chamberlain. She wants to join us in the Work."

I shook hands.

The Finching girls?

What were they doing over here?

I believed Elisabeth; they definitely weren't expected.

"You want to work magic?" asked May in a transatlantic accent. "How did you come to hear of it and come to get here?"

"Percy and I met them – Percy's going to do some work with Alice's brother – well he hopes to, shortly," Elisabeth said. "But what brought you two over here? I thought both of you were all booked up with the studio."

"Archie said we must come. He thinks we ought to see Dad," May told her, flopping into an armchair.

"Why? Is there anything wrong with your father?" Elisabeth asked.

Was there slight panic in the voice? I'd swear I could discern it.

And what pull had Archie got over them that they could afford to throw over a film career?

"No. Not as far as we know. But you know what Archie's like. If it ain't done his way, life ain't worth living," said June. She was the prettier of the two, who, I could see took after her mother, but her voice and speech were slack, unattractive.

"So how long are you staying?" Elisabeth asked. "Are you staying here? You know you're always welcome. I can find room for you."

They both hooted with laughter. "Come off it, Lizzie," May chortled. "Archie's paying for us to have a suite at the Dorchester."

"And your husbands, too? Are they with you?"

Peals more laughter. "Would we come to Europe with our husbands? Really Lizzie! That would be a waste of a trip!" June said. Then added, more sedately, "No, they have to work. This is just a short trip for us. Five days coming, five days here and five days back to New York, champagne all the way."

"It's a publicity thing," explained May. "Lots of photographs of us in nobby places full of toffs, it impresses the socks of Americans who have no history worth speaking of. Archie's squared it with the studio. They like the idea, all good publicity."

"So when are you going to see Lord Finching?" Elisabeth asked. "If it's all publicity, you'll not have time."

There, I had the confirmation.

Excellent.

"Uh-huh," drawled June. "Archie's hiring a private plane. We travel strictly first class. Dad will be part of the deal. His place is so atmospheric."

"And so bloody cold," muttered May, shuddering. "I need a mink coat to go for a pee in the night. Still, the studio will love it. The Yanks just lurve Europe, and Scottish castles are big dollars at the moment!"

"Come on, May, sorry, Myrna. You know it's all Archie's planning. He's up to something, but then, when wasn't he?" June said.

This time I did hear the bell ring.

I hoped it was Jeremy. He needed to hear this.

"Just as long as he doesn't get cross. I hate it when Archie's cross. He can be so cruel."

I heard steps on the stairs, the maid's and light feet in flat shoes. The door opened. "Mr Jeremy Arkwright, Ma'am. I'll fetch the tea now, Ma'am."

He took it well.

Elisabeth greeted him with a handshake while May and June were already elbowing her out of the way.

"Introduce us, please, Lizzie!" May ordered, while June was almost pouncing on him.

"I'm Jacqueline Finching, film star, gorgeous. Who are you? Have you ever thought of Hollywood? You should. I could show you around. You could make a fortune."

She had lost the slackness. It was all predatory feline now. She suited the leopard shoulder-cape she wore over her body-fitting golden beige wool suit.

No girl-next-door, this one.

"Delighted to meet you, Miss Finching. Jeremy Arkwright at your service, here to see Miss Elisabeth Thorburn."

"Do come in, Jeremy. These two reprobates are my long-lost sisters, May and June, alias Myrna Lauriston and Jacqueline Finching. They've turned up quite out of the blue."

"Literally," added May/Myrna. "We came in on the Queen Mary this morning."

The maid brought the tea in.

Elisabeth took control. "May and June, I've invited these people for a purpose. When we've had tea, you can take a little walk around the house, while we do what we need to do, and then, I'll be completely at your disposal. Until Percy comes round around seven. Will that do?"

We lost them when the cake ran out.

They said they would visit her rooms and the new temple.

I pricked up my ears. So they knew about the temple?

Elisabeth noticed my attention. "Of course, girls, go and see what I've done so far, but it's not nearly ready." She turned to me. "I'm having a temple made here. I'm setting up a circle here, as you know. That's what I wanted to talk to you about."

"That's what we're here for," Jeremy said.

"Right," said Elisabeth, as the girls clattered downstairs on high heels. "I love them dearly, but had I known, I would not have put either of you through that! They have become great flirts since they discovered Hollywood, but if you had seen them when they first came over to me, you would be glad of that. But that doesn't concern you. This does." She lifted a leather folder from a mahogany magazine rack.

"Now, you both told me you wanted to learn magic. I need to know why, what you are willing to commit to, how much you already know and where your interests lie. I also need to make a few things clear, and you can think them over, decide if you really do want to get involved. Does that make sense?"

We both nodded.

"Good. Then what I've got here, are sets of questions that I would like you to answer and return to me, if you decide that the Path of High Magic is for you." She opened the folder and handed us each a sheet of paper printed with groups of questions.

I didn't look at mine, but folded it immediately into my handbag. Jeremy, I noticed, folded his and slipped it into an inside pocket.

"Firstly, then, when you come to magic, what you are doing is learning more about yourself and your mind. With mind power you can change things, your life and those of others, in conformation with your will. That is, in fact, all there is to it. But to train the mind, you have to learn its games and how it functions, and that is not easy. Without imagination, you can achieve nothing, without will you can achieve nothing, but if you can harness the two together, you can achieve incredible things. However, and there is always a however, it is not easy, nor is it always pleasant. You will lose friends. You will lose loved ones. And you will feel very alone. You will discover that Magic is addictive. People will think you are strange, and shun you. They may hate you, they will even fear you. You may be threatened for your Art, like many have been before, and probably will be again. Most of humanity is asleep, living behind walls of its own making, believing what they have been taught, never questioning, never waking up to the amazing wonder that is life."

She took a sip of her tea, and put the cup back daintily into its saucer.

Refreshed, she stood up, and took a metal box to the thurible, raised the lid on its long chain, then opened the box from which she took a tiny spoon, and filled it with fragrant resin. She tipped it carefully upon the white charcoal, lowered the lid and spun the thurible gently, breathing in the scent.

"It's a good one," she said softly. "And magic is like incense. You put a little bit around, and get it going, and it permeates far farther than you would ever imagine. I bet you noticed the incense as soon as you came into the house, but I only ever burn it in here, and not that often."

She sat down opposite us again. "Magic is neither good nor bad. It's neutral. The magician who wields it is wielding a power, and even then, he or she may think they are working for good and they aren't, or working for something negative and find that it has turned to good. You, as a novice magicians must be very very rigorous as to your purposes and intents. The wielding is down to you – and you can cause chaos, to yourself as well as to others. You are ultimately responsible for the results of your actions."

"O.K." I said. "So act responsibly at all times. That holds good for daily life too, surely."

"Good. And easier said than done."

"Quite," Jeremy agreed.

"Now, what I am doing, is starting a teaching circle here. Not yet, the temple hasn't been finished, but it will start within the next few months. If you are still interested, I would be delighted if you both would care to come along. Indeed you can come along to our other lodge, before then. It would give you an experience of working as a group."

This was fast! I had read her father's work, and he had checked out his novices and put them on probation for six months, a year sometimes, if he didn't think they were up to it – but that was then, of course. Time had sped up.

She took our nodding acceptance gracefully. "Good. Percy will be pleased. Now, when we meet, we each wear a black hooded robe. This is because we are all part of a team within the Temple. Nothing to distract anyone. Officers wear the emblems and symbols of their position, and the hierophant's word is law, as is the priestess's." She looked at us archly. "Usually they are in accord. If not the temple will disperse. If you cannot take orders from them while in the temple, you need not consider joining. They will not ask you to do things that they would hesitate to do themselves."

She looked at us questioningly.

"No problems, there," I said.

"Fine by me," Jeremy agreed.

"Good. And within the Temple we use other names. These are the names you will use to those around you, but more of that later. We keep the names of our fellows secret. We keep temple practice secret. We keep our robes clean and do not wear them at any time other than when doing magical work. So no fancy-dress parties or swanning around in them."

I bit back a smile.

So she wasn't swanning around in her robe? OK, it didn't have a hood, so it was mufti.

"We keep our Temple life separate from our exterior life, although if you are any sort of magician, you will find the two overlap. And we help our brothers and sisters in Art. Is that clear?"

I nodded.

Jeremy frowned. "That's fine. But who do we worship?"

Elisabeth smiled. "Who or what? The Light, the Word, the Solar Logos, the One... and the God within... you name it. Or whosoever you wish. Do what thou wilt shall be the whole of the Law. Love is the Law, Love under Will."

Enigmatic, too, eh?

Her words were strangely compelling and oh, so familiar.

I felt myself trembling with some sort of odd recognition. Even the room felt sparkling.

"Jeremy, do you need to worship anyone?" she asked.

"Well, I'm not exactly Christian. The war saw to that."

"But you feel there is something more than just the material world? You want to interact with it, to become part of it?" she asked, her eyebrows raising.

I stared at her.

She was describing exactly how I felt. It was uncanny.

I waited with bated breath for his reply.

So did she.

And she knew exactly how we both felt. You could see it in her face.

"Yes," he said at last. "But I make my own decisions and am beholden to none. I fear no bogeymen, and stand firm in my own knowledge of myself."

He said it just right.

"I'll second that," I breathed.

I felt a crackling of energy burst out between all three of us like spurts of white light in the darkness, pulling us together.

Elisabeth smiled. "Welcome home, brother and sister," she said, catching us in her arms. "I knew you were right for this."

I hugged them both, in a desperate sense of oneness and belonging.

It was like rediscovering two old friends whom I never knew I had, or had not seen for centuries, the deepest bittersweet release I had ever felt.

And I was not alone.

We all felt it.

There was a tentative knocking on the door, and giggling.

The mood was broken.

We said our hasty *adieux*, and left Elisabeth to the tender embraces of her long lost sisters.

The fresh air outside brought us down to normality as we walked down the garden path.

"What the hell went on there?" Jeremy asked.

His eyes were wild, and I had never seen him so shaken. "I sort of found myself saying things that echoed throughout time, without knowing what I was saying or doing." He shivered, despite himself, and tried to rationalize. "Do you think it was the incense?"

I shook my head. I couldn't say. I couldn't even speak.

The words wouldn't come out how I wanted them to. I must have looked like a stranded fish.

Finally my voice returned. It sounded to have traveled a very long way. "Can we take a turn around the Boltons?" I croaked. "I need to be walking. There's something safe about walking." Meaning your feet touched the ground and interacted with it.

"Sure," he offered me his arm. I took it. I think I was supporting him as much as he was supporting me.

We started walking, shaky as a pair of convalescents on our first outing, each unwilling to let on to the other how very ropy we felt.

Slowly, slowly we tottered onwards, every step bringing us a bit more down to earth. We passed under the newly bursting leaves of the tall planes, feeling the tousling wind as it blew around us, taking in lungfuls of springtime air.

Gradually I began to feel myself again.

My normal self.

The self I thought was in control. I was glad to be back.

When we were both back in his car and up to conversation I got him up to speed on May and June.

"You think there's more to it than a publicity stunt?" he asked.

His brain was fully functioning again and he looked the Jeremy I knew now. I was glad of that. He ignited the motor.

"Yes. So does Elizabeth, I'm sure of it."

"You think Archie wants them to get the paintings from their father?" he pulled away from the kerb and swung round the oval of The Boltons.

"Don't you?"

He flashed me a smile. "Did they mention their mother?"

I shook my head. "No. I think she no longer exists for them. Understandably, but sadly. Can we pick up some of the pictures this weekend? I think speed is of the essence."

23

The hearse was an inspired choice, if I say it myself.

No-one took any notice of one these days, except possibly to avert their gaze, and you could go anywhere in it. There's always someone dead somewhere along whatever road you go down. More to the point, there was ample space for the paintings, and no-one but no-one would actively choose to search below where the coffin was placed.

I wore a dark jacket of masculine cut, with a white shirt and tie and no make-up; through the car window I could pass as a man. When I got out I would be at once identified as a woman by my skirt, nylons and high heels.

Jeremy had on the undertaker's black suit and tie too, his hair slicked back formally, his face solemn. "I feel like a Freemason!" he grumbled.

"Forgotten your pinny!"

He handed me a black top hat. "We drive in these and people will think we're off on a job." He set his at a rakish angle and winked at me.

"Not if you behave like that," I said. "You're far too dashing and alive for Charon's servant."

I twisted my hair up and stuck the hat on over it so that none was showing at all. I stuck my chin out and inspected my reflection. Although I felt like the Artful Dodger, I'd pass muster – from the waist up. "I suppose we're on overtime, traveling at night?"

"Time and a half for a wealthy client. Widow wants him out of the house so her fancy man can get his feet warm." He flashed me a smile. "You do make a very fetching corpse-carrier," he said. "The skirt rather confuses the gender issue, though."

I eyed him sourly, and got in the passenger seat. "I shall not be a corpse-carrier when I arrive at our destinations. A touch of femininity can achieve a great deal."

We took turns driving and dozing through the night, two hours on, two off with the quilts that we'd brought to protect the paintings wrapped about us. The hearse had no heating; it was incredibly cold. There were some wagons on the road, and a few motorists, but since most goods traveled by rail, and people generally took their entertainment locally on Saturday nights, we had a clear run up the Great North Road.

At an all-night transport stop not far from York, we refueled and Jeremy got out to get us hot tea and a wad.

"I might just as well not have existed," he chuckled, thrusting a steaming mug at me. "All eyes averted. No-one wanted to stand close in case death rubbed off."

"Undertakers are usually unwelcome at the feast," I said, inspecting the interior of the sandwich that lay on the thick pottery plate. It may have contained meat paste, although the predominant flavours were lard, salt and mustard, but it filled a gap and the sweet mahogany tea washed it down wonderfully, filling us with its warmth.

Our first stop was in Scarborough. Or rather, just outside. A long low house on the cliffs, surrounded by rhododendrons. It was early, but not too early, and the house was set away from the road. I combed my hair, sprayed on some cologne, put on a bright lipstick, tied a matching scarf round my neck to counteract the severe black jacket, and slipped on Abraxas.

I got out into the chill air and started down the short drive; the gates were not locked. There were lights on in the downstairs windows. I was glad of that. I didn't go much on the sandy gravel, though. It played Old Nick with my heels.

The housekeeper came to the door. "Aye?" She glared

at me, making me realize that I was hatless and gloveless. Not a good start.

"I've come to see the owner of the property," I began.

"He's not seein' folk. He's poorly."

"I'm sorry to hear that," I said, gently. "Perhaps you could give him a message, then? You see it is urgent, and it comes from the Master."

The cold blue eyes flickered. "Does it indeed? I suppose you know the password?"

"I do. But I will only say it to the owner of the property."

She looked me up and down and sniffed. She could give Angelique a run for her money. If they had international sniffing contests, these two were up there in the finals. "And I suppose you've got the seal?"

I showed her the ring. It was on the index finger of my right hand.

Another sniff. "Aye. You'd best come in. The master will be wanting to see you, though why the Master should choose a mere slip of a girl to do his work, I don't know. Wipe your feet. I've just now polished this hallway."

She turned, waddled in. "Come on then. Shut door. It might be nigh on May Day but it's still chill round here."

I closed the door behind me and followed her into a small study at the back of the house.

"I'll fetch master," she said, shutting me in the room as she left it.

I checked the window. It was open at the top and gave on to a sunken garden behind. For some reason, I wanted a way out – didn't think I'd need it, but you never knew. It might have been a hangover from being in that barred room at Blandings. If push came to shove I could have got through and dropped down and run. I'm sure I could. That sorted, I looked around me. There were glass cases full of books and a desk – there was no chair behind it. In fact there was no chair in the room at all. Just the desk and the bookshelves and an ancient safe. Everything was dusted and polished, but there were no carpets or mats either.

I peered at the titles in the cabinets. Someone with a classical bent here. Lots of Greek and Roman classics in their original languages, and collections from museums, proceedings from meetings in French, German and Italian. A scholar then.

The door opened, and the reason for the lack of chairs was clear. "Fetch this lady a seat, Muriel, there's a dear," he said.

He was a short chap with a halo of fuzzy iron grey hair, and the voice of an angel; melodious, caressing, warm, oh, it was a voice to die for. "I need to know the pass-word, Miss... No, I don't need your name. The pass-word and the seal are sufficient." He closed the door behind him. "You may whisper," he mouthed. "Muriel is very inquisitive and very little gets past her!"

I stepped across to his wheelchair and held out my hand, then I whispered the pass-word in his ear:

Aphrodite.

He examined the ring, smiled and nodded at me, then flicked out his hands and sped expertly across the floor to his favourite position behind the desk. Behind me the door rattled and Muriel brought in a folding chair.

"You'll not be staying long, I hope," she said eyeing me coldly and sniffing. "Only master's got things to do. It doesn't do to upset his routine. And he's poorly. He doesn't need visitors." She wiped her hands on her apron and left the room.

"All of it untrue, but she's a damn fine nurse as well as a cook and house-keeper," said her employer blandly. "Now, you've come for Hanael? Do you have someone to help you lift her? I'm not much use, and although I trust Muriel to shift me around, I don't think she'd take too kindly to shifting Hanael. Doesn't go in for that sort of thing being a chapel person."

I sat down opposite the desk. "I have a friend outside. If you could let me know where the angel is, we could drive up as close as possible. I hope the choice of transport won't discommode Muriel."

"Oh, I shouldn't worry about that. If it didn't discommode her it would be a miracle. But she's a good soul. Now let me take you to where it is, and we'll see what's to be done."

I opened the door for him and he rolled himself along a corridor at the back of the house. He took a key from his dressing gown pocket and turned it in the lock.

"Hanael is in here. Ignore the rest of the stuff, this is my retreat."

The power of incense hit me.

Different from the one that had knocked us for six yesterday, something that made me think of cathedrals and plain-song. He flicked a switch and a tiny lamp came on in the corner of the room, like a jewel, a lantern constructed of different coloured glass that gave out atmosphere but very little light. Against the wall opposite the window stood the painting.

"Hanael," the little man said softly. "I shall be sad to see her go, for she has been a great joy to me. But the Master is right. It's time they were all together again and shown to the world." He looked up at me. "I will have to paint her likeness for myself, shan't I? I can't imagine this place without her." He slipped outside the door, and pointed to another door. "This door will take you to the back of the house. If you have transport, you can get right round here." He took another key. "I'll open it up for your while you get your friend."

We left Scarborough with Hanael wrapped in an old quilt hidden in the back of the hearse. The small scholar belly-laughed at our choice of transport, but Muriel just sniffed as we loaded the painting in the back. As we said goodbye, he kissed his fingers and placed them on my forehead. "May the Gods go with you and keep you safe, sister. When all this is over, I would be glad to speak to you again."

"He knows more than he's telling," Jeremy said as we drove back inland. "What did you make of him?"

"I liked him. I'd like to speak to him again. He felt warm, and that voice – it was so beautiful. Poor soul trapped in that body. He was tiny, like a doll. A deformed doll. And not much chance of forgetting it with the joyful Muriel as his constant companion."

"She sniffed at me," Jeremy chuckled. "She's a great sniffer. And she tutted, too. And humphed. Three out of three. I don't usually rate more than two."

Our next stop was a hundred and twenty miles away, give or take, in the Lake District, over the Pennines across country. We had been averaging over forty miles an hour on the A roads and at night, but what was to follow would lose us that average. Besides, we both needed breakfast if we were to stay reliable, and a toilet. We stopped at Pickering, parked up in the market square and went to the nearest hotel where our needs were met. Then it was back on the road, and over the moors.

God, it was bleak.

I was used to mountains, in that I knew the French Alps, the Massif Central, the Jura and the Vercors, all very different from each other, and all very high. The Pennines were low by continental standards, but that day in grey drizzle they were top of the league in bleakness. I was glad to come down the other side into Kendal.

We stopped here too – comfort stop again – and Jeremy insisted we visit Gawith and Hoggarth, "The Tobacconist!" he said, emphasizing the words with capital letters.

Even in these times of rationing and shortages we were able to restock. They had my favourites, as well as his –

for a price, naturally, and there were so many different pipe tobaccos, rolling tobaccos and snuffs that I came out with papers and a selection of little exciting flavours that would keep me happy for weeks, as well as some seriously good Latakia for Leggy and my father.

Shortly before two and we climbed out of our transport and into the jovial informal atmosphere of the Langdale Inn. Perhaps in this mecca of rock climbing a hearse was a less than sensitive form of transport, but the clientele seemed unperturbed. We stood out from the crowd, but mostly because we didn't have hairy socks and cleated boots or shoes. And of course our accents, although Jeremy had slipped easily into a brogue that was accepted by the locals. I kept my mouth shut. Jeremy ordered drinks and asked for the landlord, getting stares from the rest of the clientele, mostly walkers and tourists, but his speech and manner seemed to fit in.

"That's me; last orders in a couple of minutes, I'll be with thee then," the barman said. He was a big man, rosy of face, wearing a heavy hand-knitted jersey over a checked wool-mix shirt and had hands that made the pint jug he was holding look like a child's tea cup.

I held the ring out for inspection hidden in the curve of my hand.

He nodded. "I'll be with you. Wait for me." He poured us each a half pint of foaming ale and put two slices of pie on a plate for us and shook his head when we tried to offer payment. "I'm surprised you got here so fast. I was expecting sometime next week. OK, Mr. Outhwaite, I can see you're parched, five pints of mild coming up!"

We waited for him in outside. He shooed the last of his clientele out gradually. They made their way across the flat of the valley and gradually disappeared into the hills. A beautiful glaciated valley with a wide sky above and a stream beneath, and the sun flirting between the clouds.

At last the landlord closed up, strode over to his motorcycle combination and told us to follow. He took no prisoners, but then he knew the roads. We skidded round bends in a manner that would have shot the coffin off its stand, but at last we were at the top end of a rutty lane, beside what appeared to be a stone-built farmhouse.

The landlord was waiting for us, pulling off his gauntlets and wiping his nose on a grubby handkerchief. "Pass-word? I should have asked you earlier but not in the bar."

I gave it: Woden.

"Right. The ring's right. You're Miss Alice Chamberlain, right? Good. Just you follow me. If that death cart has a trolley, you can bring it. The ground's not that rough here and yon painting's heavy."

We pushed the trolley after him over the rutty ground to a lean-to shed. He opened the door, and the floor was even lumpier.

Not that rough? You must be joking!

"It's up there," he said, pointing. "In the hayloft. Might be a bit grubby, but it is dry up there."

Yes.

"I'll hand it down to you, Alice," Jeremy said, shinning up the wooden ladder.

There was a scuffling, and a squawking, and a hen flopped over the edge of the loft, half fluttering half falling to the floor.

"Oh, that's Buttercup. She's stupid. She's not laid any eggs up there, has she?" asked mine host.

"If she has, I'm liable to have knelt on them."

"I usually send the wife up after them, but she's at her sister's. I won't give you a hand up there, if you don't mind. I may be in climbing country but I like to keep both feet on the ground. Or on my motorbike."

"Do you want me to come up, Jeremy?" I called as the

straw flew and curses filled the air.

"No thanks. I seem to have got it now. I'm pushing it over the side. Be ready to take its weight and steady it, will you?"

Mine host was more helpful here. Without his aid I doubt I could have held the painting, but together we lowered it gently to the ground. It was carefully wrapped in brown paper and sacking fastened with twine and decorated with straw and feathers. It smelled of barnyard and hens. Jeremy was similarly decorated and spent a few minutes dusting himself off.

"You want to open it? Only if you do, I'm out of here. I'm looking after it as a favour to an old friend, but I don't like the damn thing at all. Glad to see the back of it to tell you the truth," the Cumbrian said, lifting the package bodily onto the trolley while I checked Jeremy's back.

I shook my head. It was the same size and weight as the others and besides, time was getting on. "No, thank you."

He helped us steady it on the trolley as we dragged it down to the hearse and watched as we stowed it on top of the other paintings. Then he shook our hands, wished us good day, and whistled up his dog. As we juddered down his track, I saw him walking up across the fell-side behind his farm, throwing a stick for the old collie. It was three o'clock, and we now had possession of four. That was a good feeling.

We retraced our steps to Kendal then set off towards Lancaster. We were aiming for Southport, and I was driving. The country changed again after Milnthorpe and the further south we went it got flatter. I looked out at the scenery and found myself yawning.

"Can't say I'm that struck on it, either," Jeremy said, taking out a packet of tobacco at random and some papers. "Would a rum butter roll-up make you happier?"

"Indubitably."

"Your wish is my command." He slid the cigarette across his tongue and sealed it. "Shall I light it for you?"

"Please. I suppose it won't fit into my holder?"

"Probably not." He flicked his lighter and drew on the cigarette. "Ooh, that is nice," he said, handing it across. "If you don't like it, pass it straight back."

I took a draw. "You've got to be joking!" It was a delightful taste.

And a good cigarette. I rolled raggy efforts, but this was firm, regular and drew well. "Nice cigarette," I said. "You should roll them for me more often."

"Nothing would give me greater pleasure," he said lightly. "Milady has but to ask."

"Don't Milady me, Jeremy," I said, quietly. "I get it from everybody, but I'm not a Lady, and I have a name."

"OK, Alice. I didn't mean to offend. But you will be a Lady? One day?"

"Possibly. If my brother pegs out before I do, and isn't married and has no kids."

"Ah, you mean the delectable Sylvia is title-hunting? I hadn't put that together. That really does make a difference."

"Hadn't you realized?" I was surprised.

"No, I just thought she was after Guy because he was wealthy and of a good family and local, so she wouldn't have to break with her family when she got married."

I cast him a questioning look. "Eh?"

"Come on, Alice, it's a perfectly good reason. Lots of girls are dead against leaving their family behind. They want to be near them, not miles away with a husband they hardly know," he said.

"Well…" I said. I'd not thought of that. "I suppose so." I inhaled the aromatic smoke. "Angelique says she views life through the cinema and trashy novels," I told him, with a grin. "But Angelique is the hugest snob in the world where our family is concerned."

"Does she indeed? Well then, your brother must have been the perfect catch. She'll be able to call herself a real Lady and have children as members of the Peerage. That makes a whole world of difference. No wonder she has her mind set on him. I did wonder. They don't look right together, something's not right," he said quietly.

I nodded. "Yes; I know it's catty, but there's doesn't seem to be a great deal going on between the ears and the outside doesn't make up for it."

Jeremy guffawed. "Him or her? Sorry, I know he's your brother but …"

"Oh yes. He is indeed. And I suppose I do love him… after a fashion. But my other brother, Gilles... He was the spare, only some Fokker put and end to him. He was everything Guy isn't. He wouldn't have got mixed up with the Nesmith-Browns or anyone like them, although he might have brought home a half-caste blues singer…" I sighed. "Hopefully, he'll be jamming with in that great jazz-band in the sky. He played clarinet. 'And on the liquorice stick, Gilles Chamberlain! Let's hear it for the man!'" and I cheered for my lost brother and the good times we'd shared.

"Yeah!" shouted Jeremy. "One for Gilles, gone but not forgotten.!"

Then he was silent, suddenly, and so was I.

I slowed down as we passed through a village, which was good, as I had to use all my wits avoiding a crowd of riders exiting from a local pub. Luckily the horses had more sense than their owners and kept out of harm's way. A couple of carousing yeomen made at the hearse, but realizing somewhere deep down what the vehicle was, leapt back to safety at the last moment.

"Idiots!" I spat as I swerved. "Not fit to be in charge of horses!"

Jeremy continued rolling cigarettes unperturbed. "Your

brother, Gilles, you miss him a lot?"

"I miss him a lot. And Raoul. I worked with him in France. We were… very close. Very close indeed. I went back to see him – just before you met me. He always said he'd wait for ever for me. Only his time ran out. He was killed last year." I stabbed out the cigarette in the ashtray.

I took my eyes off the road long enough to look at him, capture his attention then turned back to the road, keeping my eyes hard on it while I spoke. "So you see, I'm pretty bad news for guys. The ones I like, who like me, they don't seem to last very long."

I couldn't bear to look at him. "I don't want it to happen again, Jeremy."

There.

It was done.

I'd offered the warning.

He could walk away, metaphorically speaking.

I meant what I said.

I really couldn't bear to have another young man die.

He drew the cigarette silently along his tongue and sealed the fragrant tobacco in the dark brown tube, then lit it and handed it across. "Alice, I won't let it. That was wartime."

"And what do you think this is? If this wasn't dangerous, why are we driving round the country incognito in a hearse?"

He lit his own cigarette. "Because we are eccentric aristocrats with more money than sense?" He coughed. "Sorry, that was in poor taste."

I frowned. "I didn't take offence." I said.

"No, I was thinking of the Finching family. We're doing it for them, I suppose. But they're all a bit mad, one way or another."

"Scratch anyone and you'll find madness of one sort or another lurking beneath the surface. With the rich it comes out quicker because they've got the money to indulge themselves, and years of in-breeding."

He chuckled again. "Not being used to mixing with titles and stuff, I never really thought about it, but you paint an interesting canvas, Alice. I've never been one for pedigree papers, I prefer to meet people and relate to them on merit."

"Me too, so you can call me Alice, eh? But if you are to get into the *haute monde* you need to know about titles and how they work."

"So tell me."

I spent a happy hour or enlightening him on the mechanics of the British peerage, both secular and religious and how things worked in society at the nobby end. At the end of it, I was more convinced than ever that as institutions they stank. I hated hierarchies, yet the whole establishment was based upon it, and, from what I could make out, the magical establishment, that we were getting involved with, was exactly the same.

By the time we reached Southport it was already dark and both of us were flagging.

Jeremy pulled into a petrol station. "I'll just nip in and arrange our accommodation, if that's fine with you. It comes recommended."

"That'd be wonderful," I said, covering a yawn. "I was thinking of finding somewhere after this pick-up, but we'd need somewhere safe for the hearse."

"No problem. Do you have any special preferences when it comes to supper or accommodation?"

"A hot meal would be great but I could sleep on a clothesline, that's about it. Not hard to please at this juncture, not hard at all."

I'd got to that dozy stage where you were awake but you didn't feel quite within the contours of your body. My skin felt stretched and dry, my eyes gritty.

I wanted to get this last pick-up of the day over then go somewhere warm and safe to sleep for ten hours. I was delighted to leave the accommodation to someone else, and leaned back and closed my eyes.

There were occasional lights on the forecourt, but I didn't notice them. It felt so good just to be still, not driving. My body felt like it had been shaking for days, although the hearse was well-sprung. I heard someone snoring as I rested my head backwards. It couldn't be me, could it? It sounded so peaceful. I just rested my eyes and listened to the sound.

Comforting.

The driver's door opened letting in a blast of cold air, and I jerked upright, wide awake. The snoring stopped immediately.

"Didn't mean to wake you, but it's all fixed." He climbed in thrusting a local road map onto my lap. There were big red crayon circles round two places. "We're here. We need to be there."

I rubbed my eyes and peered down at it. "Straight on then," I said. "And ..." I counted, "Seventh road on the right, and we start looking at numbers."

24

It was a large house, of course.

It would be.

And hedged all round by high privets, but it looked run down.

The whole area would have been stunning fifty years ago with big new villas leading down to the sea. Only the sea was beyond the sand dunes and they stretched half a mile or so beyond the end of the road. Our house was fourth from the end, but the dunes were already making takeover moves on the rutty tarmac we had just driven along.

It was pushing eight o'clock now, and I'd had enough for the day. I wanted to be horizontal and unconscious in that order. But I put on my best face and walked up the garden path while Jeremy turned the car to face back the way we had come.

The garden overgrew the path and the blackout blinds were down, but I could hear music, probably from a wireless within. The leaded glass in the front door showed that there was a light in the hallway, but it was muted.

On my finger the Abraxas ring began to throb, and round my neck, I was aware of Elizabeth's jewel growing warm.

I hadn't felt these sensations before, and I didn't like them, but I put it down to fatigue rather than anything of an occult nature. Although I'd had a few cat-naps, I'd not had a lot of sleep in the past thirty-six hours; I knew I would be experiencing strange phenomena.

I glanced back at the garden gate. Jeremy had the back of the hearse opened, and was getting the trolley out, ready to collect.

I rang the bell. It was an old-fashioned metal pull that set off a musical jingling within.

I waited.

Finally I saw a shadow through the coloured leaded glass coming towards me in the passage.

A bolt shot, and the door opened on a chain.

A narrow head peered out. Long nose, pointed head with feathers of sparse grey hair just above the level of the pointed ears, and black sunken eyes beneath unruly white brows. "Yerss?"

"Good evening, sir," I said, and gave him my name, showed the ring. "I come from the Master."

He peered at it, at me, then back at the ring. "Abraxas! You've come for Saturn?" His eyes glittered up at me. "Why should I give him to you?"

"Because you are honour-bound to do so, and I can give you the pass-word," I said slowly.

I was floating with tiredness. I could do without this. But it had been too easy so far.

I took a deep breath and counted to ten in my head, then tried another tack. "Look sir, if I've come at an inconvenient time, I can come back tomorrow morning, but to be honest, I've come a long way, I'm tired and would rather collect your picture for the Master tonight as I'm here," I said quietly.

A female voice came screeching out from somewhere within. "Cyril! Who is it? What do they want?"

He stuck his head back. "Someone wants to take the Master's picture, Madam."

I heard a heavy set of feet coming to the door, and an irate voice. "Get out of the way, fool! I'll deal with this."

Cyril slunk backward out of the way of the on-coming typhoon.

The safety lock was struck away and the door swung wide. Against the gas-lights that lit the passage behind her a vast woman loomed darkly over me.

I am tall, and no bean-pole, but I felt fragile, petite even, in her shadow.

She dominated all she surveyed, her long wavy graying hair a tinselly veil with the light behind it spread around her head and shoulders.

"Well! Explain yourself. I haven't got all night! Come on, girl, stop gaping."

I faltered. Yes, I did.

Me. Who's scared of nothing and no-one.

"I… I've come to collect the painting. The Master sent me. My name is…"

"Alice. Well then girl, stop gaping as though I were the Red Queen. Show me the seal and give me the password." I nearly said 'Yes, your Majesty', but managed to hold it in.

She was as bad as the Red Queen and the Duchess put together. I held out my hand and she tried to take the ring from my finger.

I made a fist and withstood her attempt. "It stays where it is, Madam," I said, levelly. I could feel anger rising but I kept it from showing. "If you cannot see it, I suggest some light."

She humphed, and moved slightly then dragged me into the hallway, holding my hand close to the light.

"Hmm," she sniffed.

Another one.

"It seems in order." Her voice softened, crooning, wheedling. "Now, dear, the pass-word. I've got the picture in my bedroom. You can collect it from there when you've given me the pass-word."

I whispered it: Saturnus.

I had to stand on tip-toe to do so, and she nodded.

"Let me look at you, my dear. I'd like to see who the Master takes into his confidence." She peered into my face, looked me up and down, taking longer than was strictly necessary.

Jeremy was at the door now. "Any problems?" he asked.

He was talking to me, but she took it that it was to her that the question was addressed.

The huge woman stared down her nose at him. "Problems? I don't do problems. They're for lesser mortals." She sniffed again, taking him in. "You're the muscle, eh? Well you can both go and fetch the picture. It's up the stairs, the second room on the left. Off you go!" She shooed us along the passage to the stairs.

I wasn't happy about this.

The little pointy man, Cyril, who had opened the door cowered behind the huge woman . "I could help, Madam Honoria," he suggested.

"There is no way I'd let you in my bedroom," she snapped. "You've done enough damage already today." She turned to us. "Don't just stand there, up you go, the pair of you. I'd trust you where I wouldn't trust this little swine."

We hastened up the stairs. As we turned the corner to the first floor corridor, we shared a glance; Jeremy looked as ill at ease as I felt.

We found the door and he turned the doorknob and thrust the door open, feeling for and finding the light switch at the same moment. Then he strode in, forcing the door backward to trap anyone who might have been behind it. I followed immediately, for there was no living person in there.

It was just a bedroom, issuing smells of old roses and patchouli, and, other more basic scents. It reminded me of a pot pourri of death and made me shudder...

Not the sort you'd expect to find in Ainsdale, but then Madame Honoria was certainly an unusual lady.

Amid the chaos of dusty pink frills and faded satin throws, the grubby swansdown and moth-eaten furs that we could make out through the subdued light of the glass beaded shades, on an easel with its back to the front window stood the angel of Saturn, dropping his influence on what must have been at one time a frivolous boudoir of a room.

Saturn I knew ruled the endings of things, and was very old. This angel, well, he looked ancient, but not kindly beneficent ancient.

Hard and cruel ancient.

We lifted him off the easel. He was heavy.

"Wrap him in the car," Jeremy hissed, not a suggestion, more a command.

I couldn't get out fast enough.

I turned the door handle with some relief. I had half-expected to be locked in this ghastly room forever. I backed out and round so that Jeremy could get through and back down the passage to the stairs. He would be taking the weight of the picture; I would be keeping the thing in balance. At the bottom we laid the picture on the trolley, face up.

Madam Honoria ran her hand lovingly across the angel's unforgiving face. "I hope the Master will keep you safe, my Lord," she said tenderly, then kissed her fingers and planted them on the ancient painted lips. "Not goodbye, but until we meet again."

Yes, of course, I thought!

I helped Jeremy manoeuvre the trolley out of the doorway and turned to thank Madam Honoria and Cyril, and say goodbye.

Jeremy was pushing the trolley out of the gate, when I heard him shout out.

"Hey! Stop that! Get away from there!"

I ran to join him, all tiredness gone, suddenly.

Madam Honoria followed.

She ran like an express train despite her bulk.

Two men, heavy types, in dark suits were breaking into the back of the hearse with jemmies.

"Stop that!" I began to shout, but my throat was grabbed from behind. Madam Honoria had me in a bear-hug with her hand over my mouth and nose.

I fought for breath while she called out in triumph, "I've

got your Queen, Muscles! So be sensible and let my lads do what they need to do."

I could hear the local accent triumphing over the elocution lessons as I fought to get my nose clear of her fingers and free my jaw. Then I bit down hard on the fleshy part of her hand, simultaneously lifting my right leg and stamping down backwards as hard as I could.

I heard a ripping of fabric as her long gown tore, and the satisfactory squeal of pain and rage, then felt her shin and foot against my heel, and heard the bones crunch beneath my foot. I slammed back with both elbows, but they only hit fat. I stamped down again, and I was free. She was down. Squealing, roaring, but I didn't listen, I was too busy catching my own breath and running for the hearse.

Jeremy was using the trolley and the picture as a weapon, and the two men had retreated towards the dunes, but now, from the house came four others. Cyril, screaming like a banshee at me, leapt over his mistress waving his hands wildly in some form of martial art, possibly of his own devising. I spun to meet him, dropped to one knee and shot upward with my fist, connecting as I intended then went for his throat as he keeled over screaming. He wouldn't be getting up in a hurry, but Madam Honoria might.

She wallowed between two helpers along the garden path, clutching her foot and screaming curses at me, invoking Saturn to use his wrath on us both, and on the Master himself. She lashed out a hand at me, but I skipped aside and as the momentum pulled her over, dropped a heavy blow on the back of her head, then ran to the hearse. It silenced her for a moment, and then she was ordering her heavies to recapture her picture and get into the car.

She wanted all the angels, come what may and had realized this was probably her best chance at them. She slapped at the two men trying to assist her and Cyril. "Get the pictures, you fools, they're in the car!"

I was already at the rear door of the hearse, unlocking it. Jeremy had left the trolley to go in close. He had laid one attacker not so much out as into a wimpering curled up heap. Another, valuing his manhood, or perhaps having seen what was attacking him, had his hands out in front of him, edging away at a rate of knots seawards. No wonder the old girl was hurling curses at them.

Jeremy turned to me. "OK?" he asked. He was grinning, rubbing his knuckles, breathing heavily, but looking very pleased with himself.

I nodded and realized I was grinning myself. Together we slid the picture inside the vehicle, threw the trolley in after it, slammed the doors shut. They held, which was a relief.

Madam Honoria's people were coming towards us as we ducked round to the front, one of them grabbed me as I opened the door, spinning me to face him. I nutted him. It hurt but gave me enough leeway to push him away and slam the door behind me as Jeremy rammed the car into gear.

Neighbours were coming out now, drawn by Madam Honoria's din, as well as people erupting from within the house, wearing formal black suits. I hadn't realized she had company. One of the black suits had jumped onto the running board determined to stay with us.

I wound down the window and landed a punch full in his face. I felt the Abraxas ring connect. An interesting bruise, then!

As the black suit fell away a metal badge flashed on his lapel, caught in the light of the street lamp. It was just for a moment, but I knew.

"That was a SOD!" I shouted at Jeremy, winding the window up again.

"I know, Alice, but you were great. I'm very very impressed."

"No. That chap. He was a SOD. He had the badge on his

lapel. Drive faster. There's a motorbike following us."

He swerved round to the right, and then almost immediately took a left, slicing across the main road in front of a bus and a tail of cars. The driver snarled jamming on his brakes across the intersection.

I mouthed a 'sorry!' at him and peered into the wing mirror.

"No bike," I said and we sped down the side streets, dodging from left to right.

I'd no idea where we were. I could see what looked like a main road ahead but it was dark now and the street lights didn't give enough light for me to locate our position on the map in my hands and my head was beginning to ache. Beside me, Jeremy hooted three times and turned the hearse into a workshop doorway.

The wooden gates opened from within and we drove in. The gates slammed shut behind us. Jeremy took his hands from the wheel and let his head flop back with a sigh. "Home!"

I stepped out into the smell of oil and petrol of a car mechanic's workshop, rubbing my forehead, glad to be safe.

Jeremy grasped his friend's hand, pulled him close. "Thanks Frank. I owe you. Meet Miss Alice Chamberlain. Alice, Mr. Frank Fairclough, whom I've known since I was eleven."

He was a big chap, and in the light of the single electric bulb his freckled face almost matched his red-gold hair. He held out a hand like a ham. "Pleased to meet you, Miss Chamberlain. Mam has your room ready. You don't mind the side-car?"

The Faircloughs, Mam, Frank and Elsie, took us in, no questions asked, delighted to see Jeremy whom they called Jem; nothing was too much trouble.

Mam, a kindly managing woman in all senses of the words, ran a boarding house on the front 'for professional people', and was heavily into cleanliness and propriety. She showed me to a single attic bedroom overlooking the gardens and the sea. "Jem can share Frank's room, they've no doubt got lots to talk about," she said as she pointed out the amenities – towels, hot and cold running water in the washbasin, toilet and bathroom one floor down. "I'll put a hottie in for you the while. Supper will be on the table in quarter of an hour. Elsie will bring you down."

I had just enough time for a wash and brush up, to clean the nicotine from my mouth, and to put on a bit of lipstick. I'd taken the tie off, too, and opened the shirt front to reveal Elisabeth's pendant.

Elsie was another red-gold person – her mother wasn't, so I guessed Mr. Fairclough had been – large-boned, even taller than me and about five years younger, an absolute stunner. "Mam says to bring you down, Miss." Her voice was low and warm with the local accent tamed to some extent by, I would guess, some expensive lessons.

"Thank you," I said, slipping my feet back into my shoes. "And call me Alice. That's what my friends call me."

"Thank you, Alice. Are you Jem's girlfriend?" Nothing but direct. She wore no rings, but I heard the warning bells.

"Just a friend," I told her, dropping my own style of speech down a couple of gears as I followed her downstairs.

"He said you work with him. Is that right?"

"At present, yes."

"Then keep an eye on him for me, please, Alice, for us all. He's liable to get into mischief, and I'd not see him hurt. Not for all the world."

Ah, so there it was. She did fancy him. Or fancy herself in love, which was just as dangerous.

"I'll do that, Elsie. As far as I can," I said. And I meant it.

I caught a glimpse of myself in the hall mirror. Despite the repair work I had done I still looked a wreck. Obviously no threat, then.

She took me into the family room at the back of the house, where five places were laid for supper round the well-scrubbed kitchen table. "I didn't put you in the guest dining room, because they've done eating and it's set for breakfast," Mam said,

"And it's so rare we get to see Jem these days. He used to be here all the time. Come on Alice, love, sit down and tuck in."

Jeremy pushed my seat in for me. Mam dished out pease pudding and mashed potatoes for us all and split a black pudding ring between us, "Try some of Elsie's red cabbage, it wins prizes round here," she invited, pointing to a jar of pickles. Then she poured tea. I drank it with relish, even with milk in. It went down so well. It was all wonderful. The soft flavourful food with the sharp crisp red cabbage contrast, the warmth of the people and the room itself, and the not-being-shaken-about. I was oh, so grateful, but I didn't take much part in the conversations that were going on because it was Jeremy they wanted to talk to, after all. I listened, but even that was taxing. I'd faded whereas he'd got his second (or third) wind and was chattering over old times and catching up on the Fairclough's lives in general. He was good at giving very little away about himself. Vague on details, quick to ask questions, and the Faircloughs loved him for it.

So did I. I didn't want these people involved in our escapades. They were too open, too honest. Dammit, they were too nice. I wonder if they knew just how devious their Jem had become, or what work he did. I must ask him.

Another yawn threatened. I put my hand over my mouth.

"Look at Alice, Jem! She's asleep on her feet." That was

Mam. "Come on, Chuck, you get to your bed. There's more tea and biscuits if you need them, but don't feel obliged. A sleep will do you far more good."

I seized the opportunity to say goodnight and joined the hottie

25

I was wakened by Elsie coming in with a tray. She was a bright sight, with a gay frilled pinafore over her Sunday best. She put my tea on the bedside table. "Good morning, Alice. Breakfast in half an hour."

"Thank you Elsie, and Good Morning to you, too." I glanced at my watch.

Half past eight. I'd wanted to be on the road by then. We had two more angels to harvest.

I drank the tea then had a wash. Did some serious repair on my hair and face, then slipped back into my clothes. The soles of my nylons felt unpleasant, but amazingly they hadn't laddered. I polished at my shoes with a handkerchief, refolded the tie into my bag then took the tray downstairs.

Jeremy was waiting outside the guests' sitting room. "Welcome to the world of the living, Alice!"

"I was a bit dead last night," I accepted. "How about you, though?"

"Meeting old friends was as good as a rest for me. And Mam's cooking."

"We need to be going soon," I whispered.

"We actually need to have gone," he said. "The police are hunting a hearse with our number-plate on it. It seems Madam Honoria has made a complaint. Elsie heard it on the radio."

"Eh? That's ridiculous, it's small scale, not national news"

"She likes to listen in on the cops of an evening. We all used to do it as kids, didn't you?"

I shook my head. "At school our listening in was strictly limited – music or an occasional play. "The only time I had access to a radio was in France, and that was a different kettle of fish altogether."

"Quite." He pointed at my pendant. "I thought you said all your jewels had gone."

"Elisabeth gave it to me. Do you like it?"

"Very much. So now you've got two occult trinkets," he nodded at the ring, which I had kept on.

I frowned. "Yes, and they…" I wasn't sure I'd tell him, but at that moment Frank came through the front door, and was slapping Jeremy on the back.

"It's all in hand, Jem. Morning, Alice, tha's looking better nor last night. Now, breakfast, eh, then we'll be off." He led us into the family room.

I looked suspiciously at Jeremy. "We?"

"Ah. Well, yes. Sorry, I didn't want to wake you, but it seemed the best thing. *Fait accompli*, but you'll see. It gets us out of town incognito."

I hugged Mam and Elsie, ("You will look after him for me, won't you, Alice?") and climbed into the cab of the pantechnicon. They'd refused to accept payment, so I had left a ten shilling note under the pillow.

"And come back and see us soon," Mam ordered. "Singly or together, you'll be most welcome."

Jeremy squeezed in beside me, and Frank took the wheel. We set off south. The hearse was in the back with a new set of plates from Frank's workshop.

"You two worked together before?" I asked, looking from one to the other.

Frank grinned. "Not for cash as such. But we got into scrapes together. We came out the other side most times without too much trouble."

"We watch each others' backs," Jeremy said. "Bit like you and me. Take a left here, and head for Knutsford."

"Cheshire, eh?" Frank said. "No trouble."

"You can drop us there, if you want. We'll be out of Lancashire then."

"You're joking!" He glanced at us both. "A day out would do me the world of good, and I'm not at all curious about the cargo. I see nothing, I hear nothing, I know nothing. I say nothing." He did a good imitation of a Hollywood Italian.

"What do you think, Alice?" Jeremy asked. "It's your game. You call the shots."

I looked from one to the other once more.

I liked Frank.

I trusted Jeremy.

Did I trust Frank?

I didn't know. But the hearse might be hunted farther afield than Lancashire, and Sunday was not a good day for hearsing if that were the case. This wheeze was good, and Frank was keen.

"It'll be a long day," I said. "If you're sure you don't mind giving up your weekend, Frank, I'd be delighted to have you drive us."

"Eeh, you're a real lady, Alice!"

"Thank you, Frank, but not true, actually."

Jeremy chuckled, handing me a perfectly rolled cigarette, then passing another across to his friend. "A song might help the miles pass more pleasantly," he suggested.

Frank put the cigarette behind his ear. "I'll sing you one – oh!" he began.

It was a rollicking good journey to our next pick-up, a squire's house outside Ripley in Derbyshire.

Before we reached the door a tiny woman shot out holding her hand high in a Stop gesture. We stopped.

"You need to go round the back," she told us, pointing. "The house is a home for retired gentle-folk. They don't need to see workmen on the Sabbath, nor be disturbed in any way. Round the back please, at once." She wore a matron's uniform, including the waterfall cap and shoulder cape, and was as lean as a whippet.

Frank drove us round and parked in front of a set of stables.

The matron came running out of the back door of the house as I got down from the cab.

"You're Alice, aren't you. Show me the ring. Good. Give me the password!"

I whispered: Sol Invictus.

"Good. You two men, come in here. Alice, you keep yourself clean."

Frank and Jeremy exchanged looks, and they both threw me keys. While they followed the matron into the barn, I opened the back of the lorry, let down the ramp and opened up the back of the hearse.

Almost immediately the two men were coming up the ramp, and stowing the angel, wrapped in a couple of old eiderdowns, on top of Madam Honoria's baleful Saturn.

We locked up and shook hands with the matron. "Thank you. I'm glad he's off. Now if you'll excuse me, my clients' lunch needs supervision. Safe journey to you all, and give the Master my best. Goodbye." She grasped each of our hands swiftly and firmly then sped back into the house.

We all looked at each other.

"What's she on? Can I have some?" Frank asked.

"Are you suggesting that a pillar of the community, a matron in charge of an old folks' home…"

"A retired gentle-folks' home, Alice!"

"Is on some sort of stimulant?" I asked Frank, ignoring Jeremy.

"I'd say she was on something quite interesting," Jeremy said. "Did you see her eyes? They were nearly all iris – no pupil to mention. Even though it's quite bright out here… look at our eyes – not like hers at all."

"Not our problem, though," I said. But I weighed up this piece of information.

Eyes with pinprick pupils?

I'd seen that before recently. Where?

On whom?

We climbed back in the cab and Frank backed us out with great skill. He did a five point turn and we were off.

We stopped at a pub shortly before closing time, since it was the only place open for refreshments, and had a drink and a packet of cheese and biscuits each. Frank turned his nose up at the fare.

"You could have gone home and had your Mam's roast," Jeremy reminded him.

"Aye, well happen she'll save me some. If our Elsie doesn't wolf it down, that is."

We were nearing our final destination now. I asked the landlord if there was a phone. He pointed outside to a public call-box.

I went through the operator and got my Father on the line eventually. "You're not charging me for this call?"

"No, I'm charging Leggy. Jeremy and I will be over this evening. Can we stay the night?"

"You usually do. Your mother will be delighted to see you. Have you got anything for me?"

"Yes. Lots. Maybe the full set by the time we see you. Make room. Oh, and we're bringing a friend. Perhaps he could stay too? He may not want to, but it would be nice for us to offer."

"Hotel Wethersley is always open for you, Milady. Keep safe, and I'll see you soon. I've got Emily and Padraig here. They'll be going back to town tonight. I think there's romance in the air."

"Ding dong!" I said. "See you later Pa. And thanks."

The final place I recognized from Rufus's description.

It had been a school when he visited, and was still was.

Run-down and dispirited, it looked to be on its uppers, as

did the few pale boys in blazers and flannels who wandered around the front forecourt, and made late efforts to get out of our way this grey afternoon.

I slipped out of the cab – which cheered a few of the bored faces considerably - and asked one where I might find the Principal.

He ran off indoors, and brought back an officious-looking balding man, in a black morning suit who introduced himself as The Bursar.

I asked to see the Principal, gave my name and said the Master had sent me.

He looked sneeringly at the transport then at me. "The Principal only sees parents on Sundays, Madam. And by appointment." He turned on his heel.

"Excuse me, but that simply won't do, sir," I said imperiously. "I have a ward, and am looking for a good school for him. My name is Alice Chamberlain. If you would tell the Principal that, I'm sure he will be delighted to see me."

I took out a calling card from my handbag and scribbled on it. "If you would be so kind as to give him this?" I thrust the little scrap of cardboard into his hand. "I'd be very much obliged," I smiled.

I had to force the charm, though. No-one gives me the brush-off. He might be the Bursar, but he wasn't the Principal. I wanted to talk to the Organ Grinder, not his stuck-up, ill-dressed monkey.

He cast a simian eye over the card, pursed his lips but went inside. Then he turned, indicated with his head that I should follow. "You'd better come inside, Miss Chamberlain. Gentlemen, take the lorry round the back, or the boys will be all over it and we don't want any accidents."

To boys or lorry, I wondered.

Three lads were grinning widely. The bursar shooed them away.

Frank started to move the lorry, but Jeremy jumped out.

"I'll go with Alice," he said to his friend.

We followed the bursar inside and he put us in a waiting room.

We waited.

We looked at each other, at the room – there were bars at the windows.

"Remind you of anywhere?" I murmured,

"To keep us in?" Jeremy whispered. "Or to keep Them out?"

"You didn't have a private education? This is par for the course. It all comes back, particularly the smell."

"Boiled cabbage and unwashed young bodies? Nice!"

"No, it's not," I said. This brought the very worst memories of my own school days right back. I'd never send a child of mine to a place like this.

I fiddled with the ring on my finger, and the pendant at my throat.

Jeremy noticed. "Are they trying to tell you something?"

I frowned. "Why do you say that?"

"I heard somewhere that stones are alive, that you can use them for things."

I thought about that. "Last night. At Madam Honoria's. Did you get a feeling something odd was going to happen?" I asked softly.

It was the first time we had been able to talk about it alone.

"Why do you think I locked the hearse? I never felt the need to at the other places. The place gave me the creeps. Why?"

"Both of these were tingling then. I put it down to tiredness."

"And now?"

"I'm not sure. There's something... Not like yesterday,

nothing like yesterday, but a feeling of warmth, a sort of buzzing through them, vibration. I don't understand it."

The bursar came in with an older man, grey, once tall but now stooped wearing an academic gown. "Miss Alice Chamberlain? You have something for me?" His voice was quiet and confiding.

I held out the ring, "And you for me, too."

I whispered the password: Thrice Great Hermes.

"Well, well, well. So the Master really is moving things on at last. You'll follow me? Thank you Bursar, that'll be all. I'll take charge from here on." His voice was gentle but authoritative.

The Bursar didn't look best pleased, but he had that sort of face. As we followed the Head out of the room, I thanked him for his trouble anyway.

The school proper smelt even more of school. Boiled cabbage, old sports gear, grubby children, wood polish, and ... oh, dear, boredom. Dreary, grey all-enveloping terminal boredom. I would have run away.

The Head led us through the back out into what he called the Arts wing. It was a series of Nissen huts off to the left of what had once been stables. They skirted the rugby pitch where boys were playing impromptu and informal games listlessly.

The Head took us into the second of the Nissen Huts and closed the door.

"The picture is behind that cupboard. You'll have to move it, I'm afraid, because I am incapacitated."

We shouldered the cupboard away from its station at the back wall. Behind it, wrapped in a tarpaulin was a large board. We shimmied it out, and unwrapped it to check it was what it purported to be: the angel of Wednesday.

It was.

I sighed.

The Head sighed. "I'm glad it's going. I didn't want it

here. It's just that there was nowhere else, do you see? And now the War is over, we don't need to hide him from the Fascists any more. I do hope he'll be well-looked after."

"He will be brought out into the Light again, sir," I said.

"Good. Tuck him up again. I don't want the boys to see him, you know what they're like… well, perhaps not. But you don't cast your swine before pearls."

We re-wrapped the painting. It was Mercury, but he was better endowed than was usual. Quite outstandingly in fact.

No, you didn't want to put ideas into the children's heads, but from what I'd heard of boys' boarding schools the ideas were already there.

"I'll fetch Frank," Jeremy said, as I finished tying the webbing.

I stood outside the Arts wing with the Head. The Art that took place in that 'studio' I wouldn't have given a fig for. Like everything else that I'd seen of the school, it was drab and lack-lustre.

The Head must have caught something on my face. "I know, my dear. It's rotten, isn't it? It used to be so good here, before the war, but the quality of teachers you get now… and there's not a lot of money about. I can't afford to pay a lot, you see, and all these chaps coming out of the services expect decent wages. Free public education is a wonderful thing, but it's done for me and my kind." He smiled ruefully. "It really was a good school once. There were good teachers and a lot of very bright boys…" his voice tailed off. He was completely disillusioned, poor man, but it didn't make for a good school.

I didn't have anything to say. I touched his arm, gently, then walked towards the two men who were coming down the path with the trolley. "Thank you for giving the angel a place of safety, sir," I said. It was all I could think of.

We loaded up and said our farewells to the Principal then got back in the cab. Frank fired up the engine and sent us down the driveway, hooting at bored boys walking in small groups.

"There's something not right, here," he said. "When I was their age I was awash with energy. They all look like they've been given knock-out drops."

"You're right," I said.

They were wan, only half alive.

"We can ask someone to check the place out," Jeremy said. "But let's get these to their new home."

The big gates were shut. Jeremy slipped out to open them.

He was climbing back into the cab having shut them behind us when a missile shot through the door, narrowly missing his head. It slammed against the dashboard with a crash.

"Holy Shit! Sorry, Alice," he gasped.

I leant down and picked it up.

He was up in the cab now, next to me, slamming the door, and Frank was putting his foot down. "South?"

"Yeah," I said, "as fast as you like!"

I opened my hand round the missile.

It was an old cricket ball, the leather faded and battered, the string tattered.

On it in black ink was a drawing. Of a mailed fist, a sword, and a rising sun.

I peered in the mirror but could see no-one.

But someone in that school knew us by sight now. I didn't like that at all.

I showed it to Jeremy. He raised an eyebrow and pocketed it. "Just a kid being silly," he said. "No harm done."

"Not for the want of trying," Frank murmured. "Odd when most of them looked as though they couldn't spoon up soup out of a saucer."

We were on the Great North Road again now, heading home in fine voice at a very respectable speed for so large a vehicle. Shortly we turned off cross country into the dark clouds sailing in from the west. It was rapidly becoming a Grade "A" grey day outside but within the cab we were noisily bright.

I gave directions, and a few minutes before we reached Wethersley Jeremy said, "Frank, Alice's family is a bit posh. Just thought I'd warn you. They're lovely people, and not at all snooty, though."

"Apologise for me, why don't you, Mr. Arkwright!" I teased. "La, sir, I'm mortified!"

Frank chuckled. "I rather guessed that. OK, Alice, I won't show you up. I'll just drop the cargo and go."

"No, you won't!" I exclaimed. "You'll stay. You need a break. And a decent meal."

"Oh, I could murder a decent meal," he agreed. Then, "Oh, bugger! It's raining. I told Les to fix these wipers, and he never did. I'll have to drive slower. Sorry."

It was pouring and the sky was black when I opened our gates. The water was streaming down my neck, but I didn't care; I was glad to be home.

I closed the gates and clambered back up into the cab, squeezing in next to Jeremy. We did the drive, and I directed them to park outside the stables where my father's art wing was. We left the van and ran across to the back door, where I stumbled straight into the arms of Mrs Mac.

She let us in, handed us towels, and warmed a tea-pot. "All staying? Good. I'll make you some tea, then get Mac to inform Themselves."

She beamed at us. "You, I know, sir, and it's good to see you back again, but you, young man, I don't know." She looked at Frank and then at me, with her eyebrows raised.

"Frank Fairclough, Mrs McMurdy," I said. "Housekeeper, Cook and friend from my childhood. Frank is Jeremy's childhood friend."

"Nice to meet you, Mr Fairclough. You'll have a scone

to be going on with?"

Jeremy and I looked at each other.

Mrs. McMurdy caught us. "I know you two will, but Mr. Fairclough is new here." He was also pleasing to the lady, big strong smiling lad that he was.

We were steaming nicely over mugs of tea and currant scones when my father came into the kitchen. "So we're not good enough for you now, Alice?" he said.

"Nonsense, Pa, we were just drying out."

Jeremy and Frank stood up.

"Sit down, chaps. I take it you took shelter from the storm. And that this is your friend, Jeremy. Nice to meet you, er…"

Frank clasped my father's hand. "Frank Fairclough, sir. Likewise."

"So you drove these two reprobates home? What happened to their car? No. Don't answer that. Have you got the stuff?"

I nodded.

"Yes, sir," Jeremy said.

"Roger, please," said Pa. "No, really, we don't stand on ceremony here. Is it somewhere safe? Only Emily and Padraig are still here. I think they are staying. They saw the two we've got – I had to show them, of course, and Emily did give us provenance. But I don't want them seeing any more."

I frowned. "Is Emily OK?" I asked.

"Oh, yes. She bore up wonderfully, with Padraig's arm round her. But neither of them need to see any more, even if they would like to." He beamed at us all. "So we need to invent a reason for you three being here with your furniture lorry, to keep them happy. Mmm?"

We greeted my mother, Emily and Padraig five minutes later.

I'd been up to stay with a friend and Jeremy had to collect

furniture for his new flat, and since he was in the vicinity of my friend, he'd offered me a lift home. Frank was his friend, helping him with the humping.

What was the furniture?

A very nice bedroom suite. Family stuff, a bit dated, but nicely carved.

"They wanted to throw it away, or put it on the bonfire!" said Frank, scandalized. "Couldn't or wouldn't sell it, for some reason, and it's lovely mahogany. Just because his uncle died in the bed... I mean, a new mattress and it's right as rain!"

My mother nodded. "I'm sure it's of very good quality, if it's mahogany. Absolutely scandalous to think of burning it. I do like modern design, but there's no need to be profligate. I think it's very commendable that you saved the suite. Where are you moving to, Jeremy?"

Oh, damn!

Trust my mother!

"Oh, just off the Fulham Road – South Ken end." Her eyebrows raised. "Indeed? Very near to Alice, then? How nice."

Yes, and what a lie!

"I'd like to keep an eye on her – after the burglary, you understand."

"Of course, dear. A very proper sentiment, too."

I could feel the pair of them sending me up.

Oh, well, why not?

"What burglary was this?" Emily asked.

I shrugged. "Nothing to write home about, rather trivial really," I said. "Last week. I was out at the time, I'm glad to say."

"Took your jewelry, I heard," Padraig said. "Yet you are wearing a stunning amethyst pendant. Do you mind if I look?"

Abraxas was in my pocket, but the pendant was on show.

324

Suddenly I didn't want it touched, not by Padraig, yet I couldn't say why.

He came over and inspected, peering over his glasses at it. "It's very familiar. Where did you get it?"

"My friend gave it to me," I smiled at Jeremy.

He nodded.

"I saw it and thought of her," he said, simply. "Can't have Alice without jewels."

Padraig kept peering and shook his head. "Oh well, perhaps I didn't recognize it. I thought it was one I knew. Worn by someone who called herself a priestess. Not a nice person to know, I can tell you. But obviously I'm wrong. It suits you very well, Alice, my dear." He turned to look at Jeremy strangely, then turned to me. "I'm glad you have someone to look after your interests."

I turned to Emily. "How about you, Emily? Have you someone to look after yours?"

And, bless her, she blushed.

Virgin Spinster, that she was, she had fallen in love with Padraig. Or perhaps she had been in love with him for years, and had only recently received permission to hope.

"I think I have, Alice, thank you," she said pinkly.

Shortly after we'd finished our supper, the thunder really began. There was no way anyone was going anywhere.

"I've taken it you'll all be staying," Mother said. "I'll show you to your rooms, if you like, so that when you wish to retire, you can do so. Alice, you show the young men their room – you two men don't mind sharing, do you?"

"Not at all," they said in unison.

"Then the dark blue room, Alice. They can use the bathroom on the landing, make sure they have everything they need. I'll see to Padraig and Emily."

I led the two men upstairs.

The dark blue room was one of my personal favourites of the guest rooms, being as its name suggested, dark blue, with white woodwork. The curtains were dark blue velvet, the twin beds had matching counterpanes and white-painted head and foot boards, a small table and pair of chairs stood in front of the window, while two light armchairs graced the fireplace. Someone had lit a cheery wood fire to take off the chill, laid out blue and white towels on the beds, and folded back the dressing screen to reveal a pair of fitted wardrobes. The floor was polished boards with dark blue rugs by the beds, brightened by touches of yellow.

Frank looked around him appreciatively.

"I can't promise you a hottie, Frank, but…" I went to a small cupboard, and looked inside. "Ah, yes," I took out a tray on which stood a bottle of whisky, four glasses and an ashtray. "This should do the trick. Do you need anything else?"

"Sure. Where's the toilet? I'm bursting," Frank said.

I directed him to the landing. "First door's a toilet, the next one's the bathroom. Feel free to use both. And if you need anything, like toothbrushes you'll find it in the bathroom cupboard."

I turned to Jeremy. "Thank you for everything you've done this weekend," I said. "I could never have done it alone. I really appreciate it. Everything." I reached out my hand to him, and he took it, pulled me to him.

I didn't resist. There would have been no point. I just sank into him with a sigh and heard and felt the matching one from him. No words, nothing but a feeling of rightness. It felt so good.

I heard the flush of the toilet, and we drifted apart, slowly, so that we were, once more, on either side of the fire-place. I made busy with the whisky and the glasses, as Frank's footsteps crossed the landing.

Jeremy raised he glass, winked and smiled. "Here's looking at you, kid!"

"Just whistle," I replied, raising mine. "You know how

to do that, doncha?"

Frank opened the door. "Are we going …? Oh, any chance of a drink for the driver? And a fag?"

We were cosily ensconced, the three of us, when my father came in.

"She's put them in the pink and the green," he said. "If this bloody rain stops we can slip down and unload and they'll never know."

Frank's open face split into a wide grin. "This is so cloak and dagger! Is it a family trait?"

My father hooted. "So not only have you made the acquaintance of my eldest daughter, but you've studied psychology. Well done, young man, have another whisky. And I'll join you," father said, pouring himself a whisky and downing it in one. "And yes, it is a family failing, we like drama. Artists first, nobs second. Now drink up and come down. It's no fun having guests if they hide themselves away."

"I need to make a phone call, Pa," I said, as I followed him down the stairs, "And I think Frank might need to, too, but be too polite to ask."

"My house is yours, gentlemen," Pa said grandly over his shoulder. "Do whatever you need to, but I'd suggest any calls you need to make be done before Alice makes hers. She can be very verbose."

I gave up and joined Angelique and the Macs and the rest for the Sunday evening dancing session. Eventually I got through to Thelma. "Oh, Alice, thank Heaven you rang. I took flying lessons. Nothing broken, but much bruised, including my pride. So I'll not be up to swimming for a week or so."

I made suitable noises, and told her to hang on to the envelope then went back to the others. Django Reinhardt and Stefan Grapelli were giving it all they had. So was everyone else. I took the arm Jeremy held out to me. We danced.

26

We shifted the angels at six in the morning. The rain had ceased and the whole country was sodden, but inside the hearse and the pantechnicon, the paintings were safe and dry.

With my father supervising, we stowed them in a locked work room off the garage where my father kept the Citroen, and Frank fell in love for the second time this weekend. Or possibly the third. He'd made himself very attractive to both Mrs. McMurdy and Angelique last night, but I think the car eclipsed the ladies for him

After an early breakfast, we left, Frank to return to Southport, his pocket full of fuel coupons, and us to London in the hearse. My mother and Angelique sniffed at our mode of transport, but when I doffed my undertaker's hat their way I got a sparkle out of them. Emily and Padraig were nowhere to be seen, it being far too early for real artists to have risen. The family would say our goodbyes for us and the pictures would never be mentioned. As Padraig's small Morris was parked in the first ex-stable of the block there was no need for him to visit Pa's garage.

Jeremy dropped me off before he went to take back the hearse.

"Straight to work?" I asked, loath to say goodbye.

"Have to, Alice. I'll give you a ring, eh?"

"Please." We held hands, lingeringly, then I let him go.

"I've got the number. Take care, Alice."

I wanted him to kiss me, but he didn't.

Just a quick clasp of the hand and a wink before he drove off.

I unlocked the front door.

There was a pile of correspondence on the shelf. I picked it up and started on the stairs.

The flat seemed cold and empty. I put the kettle on, then the gas fire

Bills, bills and more bills. Estimates since I'd been out of the country. Something more to sort out.

And a heavy sealed envelope from Inverness. I opened it.

It was from Lord Finching.

I read it with disbelief. Then I read it again, and put through a trunk call.

While I waited for it to happen for me, I thought about the implications, and what I was going to say.

Finally my phone rang.

"I'm Caro's great niece," I said down the phone. "I'd like to speak to the Master."

"I'll fetch him for you, sir," the Scottish voice said. "He's been awaiting your call."

I could hear squealing and laughter at the end of the line. May and June must have arrived. Then footsteps, and Lord Finching's voice.

"So glad you called. How's it going? I can't talk for long, got my daughters here with Archie Meredith and the house is full of photographers, dressers, and all those useless types. They're doing something... I'm not master in my own home any more," his voice had a hunted ring to it, and I could see in my mind's eye a creature brought to earth in his own burrow.

But then he rallied. "Excuse me, one moment." I heard him put his hand over the mouthpiece and shout at Mac to close the door. "Sorry about that, I'd forgotten how noisy things can be. They'd wake the dead! Never mind, they'll be gone soon enough. How is it with you?"

"The work is done, sir." I didn't trust the security at Boleskine. "All is safely gathered in, as you might say. By the way, I visited Lady Finching, sir. She said to mention she is of similar mind to yourself on the matter."

I heard a deep satisfied "Aaah. Thank you. I rather hoped she would be. That has set my mind at rest."

"Do your daughters visit her on this trip?" I asked.

"They have no intention of doing so," he said bitterly. "No time is the excuse. Archie Meredith has seen to it that their every moment is occupied in promoting their careers and trying to induce me to hand over something that ... er ... I no longer have. What a pity! Still, he's had my wife, and now appears to have got my daughters. I'll be damned if I'll let him have anything else. Matter of honour, too. Took my oath on it. Don't break oaths. Specially not one made that way. No, he shall not have anything else from me. My man knows what it's all about, so do my bank manager, my doctor and my solicitor; we had a meeting on Saturday morning, so it is all legal and above-board. I am of sound mind. Which I think my daughters are not. So I am leaving things in what I consider a safe place. Do you understand that?"

I understood only too well. And any precautions I might have taken had been blown to hell.

But it was confirmation that Archie was after the pictures and was using the girls as leverage.

"I do, sir." I said. "Then I'll let you get back to your guests. I have some very specific cleaning to arrange. Goodbye to you, sir."

"I knew I could rely on you, just like your great Aunt. Goodbye to you, and I hope we meet again."

I looked at the letter again. And the attachment. I'd been gifted the pictures in his will with the proviso that I take care of them from now on.

I owned the angels if anything happened to Lord Finching.

All I had to do was ring his solicitor who was also his executor, and apprise him of the whereabouts of the paintings, and give proof of my identity, which included handing him the Abraxas ring and giving the various passwords. But in return, I had to get the Merediths and get them at the very least *hors de combat.*

By whatever means was expedient.

It seemed a good deal to me.

I made tea as I thought about the Finchings.

Lord Finching in his strange attire... My father still thought him mad as a hatter, but I didn't. A good old British eccentric, yes; barking, no. Because he had made some poorly-judged choices during his life he was reaping the results, but as a man who had got into occult study for the sake of his soul, and who was in the process of losing everything he held dear I felt he was grasping at a straw: me!

And Lady Finching... another strange one, my mother's contemporary. I'd ask Maman about her, whether she knew her – and my father too – but neither had ever mentioned them as far as I could remember during my youth; this was all before my time, thus very old history.

I felt for Lady Finching so much.

Another life ruined by the Merediths – yes, I know, she didn't have to take the white powder, but to be plied with drugs for religious purposes... that I found reprehensible.

No matter what the resulting ecstasies.

It just wasn't worth it if it led you to where Lady Finching currently was, a murderess, incarcerated until she died for killing a dear friend in front of her beloved children.

It couldn't be, could it?

I hoped she didn't know her daughters were in the country. She didn't need to know they were spurning her for the company of her enemy, the man who had plied and supplied her with white powder.

I thought of her eyes.

And then those of her daughters, when I had seen them

at Elisabeth's.

Lord Finching had known, and I should have guessed sooner.

He'd got them, too, had Archie Meredith, and he was still playing his evil games.

I lit a cigarette and wondered if their mother knew. I hoped not.

And then, by extension, I wondered whether their long-lost sister knew.

What exactly was Elisabeth's part was in this? There was only one way to find out. I stretched out to the phone, but before I could dial it began to ring.

I lifted it.

My sister was screaming down the line. "Alice, come over at once. We have a serious problem. No, I mean it. At once, do you hear? It's bad. I've been trying to ring you all morning and last night. Where have you been? No don't tell me. Just come over. Now!"

I immediately thought of her condition. "Maddy, you're not …"

"No, I'm fine. We just have a problem. A big problem. I can't tell you over the phone. I need you here."

"I'm on my way, Mad," I said.

Hell!

I put on my coat and hat, my shoes and turned off the gas fire. Then I locked up and went downstairs for my bike. At least she wasn't miscarrying. But what it could be that had got her all hot under the collar, I couldn't even guess.

She dragged me into the sitting room, locked the door and poured me coffee with a shaky hand – and that was very unlike her.

She glared at me. "This is strictly between these walls, Alice. Then we must think of what we can do about it." She eyed my hand-bag. "Have you got a cigarette? I really need one."

I tossed the packet to her, and the lighter. "OK. Now tell me in words of one syllable, Maddy. I am a bear of very little brain."

She choked on the smoke. "Bitch!" she coughed.

I sipped my coffee, smiling. It was good coffee, strong and black, and I guessed she had been guzzling it all morning. "Tell me," I encouraged, when she had stopped spluttering.

"Right. You know you and Elisabeth dropped me in it last week? I had to do the decent thing by our brother, and inform his intended of her matrimonial duty?"

I nodded. "Bit of an awful job," I admitted. "Glad I didn't have to."

"Ye-es. Well they came for Sunday lunch."

"Poor you!" I sympathized. "Went through your whole week's meat ration, I bet. And you did the decent thing?"

She nodded. "Bas took Guy down to play snooker after lunch which left Sylvia and me alone together while Enid had her nap." She took a long draw on her cigarette. "I'd got myself into a bit of a state, I suppose. I mean, what do I say to her? You have to let him put his bits into your bits? I know it's crude, but that's all it boils down to, and you wouldn't let anyone you really didn't trust do it, would you? Well, I wouldn't. So I went slowly, and started off about how men and women were different."

"Right," I said. I was grinning; I couldn't help it.

"I'll cut this short if you keep that face on," she smarted.

I passed a hand over my face, smoothing out the grin. "Better?" I asked, but I had to chew the inside of my lip to keep the straight look.

She nodded, and took another drag of the cigarette. "I asked her if she'd ever seen a male – any male – brother would do – naked."

"And?"

"She said, oh yes. Quite a lot, actually. She used to live

near a boy's school and they had to swim naked. She giggled. She said she had been told not to go near the place, but, well – what do you do if you're told not to do something."

"Fair enough. I take it she'd noticed the difference?"

"Oh yes. She said she had. Thought they were funny, particularly when they got stiff and grew. Thought that was great fun."

"Yes?" I said. This was interesting! "Guy might be in for a good time, then!"

"Well, yes. But it gets worse."

"You mean she's not a virgin? That's not a problem, is it? Not these days."

"Speak for yourself. I was a virgin when I married," Maddy said sniffily.

"But only just, I bet!"

Maddy chuckled. "You really are a bitch, aren't you, Al?"

"And no virgin! But back to the problem. That, I take it is not the problem?"

"No. We started to talk about babies and how they got inside you. I asked her how she thought they got there. I mean, eating a baby pill that is specially issued to married women is a bit naïve. But that's what she said."

"What!" I exclaimed. "Where did that idea come from?"

"Don't even ask! So as gently as I could, I said, no. The man had to put it there – through his body inserted into the woman's body. Stop laughing, it was the best I could manage." She took a final draw on the cigarette and stabbed it out harshly.

"And?"

"She laughed."

"Well I would have laughed, too," I said.

"No, you don't understand. She laughed and said, 'No it doesn't. I've been doing that for years with Uncle Archie and Uncle Percy. I've never had a baby.'"

"Holy shit!" I breathed.

"Ah, you've been keeping company with Jeremy, I see! Now do you understand why we have a problem?"

I nodded.

He knew about this.

I remembered bawling him out at some wisecrack he'd made. If he knew, or there were rumours flying at the very least, this was troubling.

"Anything else?" I asked, dreading the answer.

She nodded. "Oh yes. She told me all about them. They've been at it since she was twelve or thirteen – with her parents consent, even their encouragement. And they've both been having her on and off since then."

I groaned.

Poor kid!

All those supposed to have her interests at heart were letting her down. It wasn't just immoral, it was illegal. And sordid, so very very sordid.

I said so.

Maddy's eyebrows raised. "But who would give evidence? It would never get to court. Besides, you've not heard the half of it, Al." She drew on the cigarette angrily. "She sees nothing wrong with it, and really enjoys it, calls it 'being naughty but nice to people'. She loves the attention and their company. It's their secret, i.e. the family's secret, and of course the Merediths. She doesn't love them, just thinks it's normal with close friends of the family, and they give her and her family lots of presents and take them to nice places where they meet more nice people." She stared at me meaningfully.

"Who she can be naughty but nice with?" I suggested.

"I got that impression," Maddy said.

I groaned again. So her eyeing up Jeremy and stroking Basil's lapel when she greeted them was not simple flirting.

And Jeremy had been right.

It was awful.

Maddy continued. "I didn't ask any further. God knows what goes on under Bulgy Algy's roof. No wonder Anthea always looks like she's swallowed a wasp. It might also explain the withdrawn and socially inept brother. Do you think they might have got to him?"

I was sickened at the thought. "Why would any family allow their children to be put into such a situation?" I asked.

"Money," Maddy replied bleakly. "Traditional way of paying off your debts – pass them on to your children."

I laughed blackly. To hear my gentle little sister speak so was horrible. I felt sick. Here was a hell of a problem.

"But what are we going to tell Guy?" Maddy asked.

"Do you think Guy's been there yet? You know?"

"You know! No, I don't. He's so bloody proper, he probably hasn't. But you never know. Do we tell him anything?"

I didn't know. "Did you explain to her that when a girl marries she has to keep herself only to her husband?" I asked. "That Uncle Archie and Uncle Percy would have to go out the window?"

"I think Percy has already gone. He seems to have settled on Elisabeth recently. And what do we tell her?"

"Nothing," I said. "It's none of our business, and she wouldn't thank us."

Besides, I thought, she might just know. Although if she did, how could she bear to let such a man anywhere near her?

I lit a cigarette. "Did Sylvia know that Archie is shepherding the Finching girls this weekend? He put them in a suite at the Dorchester. It wouldn't surprise me if they weren't playing the same sort of tricks."

"I've no idea. I was flabbergasted. She said she had

lots of fun with the twins and Daddy and Mummy were very pleased with her. It seems they weren't at all pleased with Nigel. He was definitely not favourite any more. She became the little princess." She sighed and shook her head. "Al, I was so sickened. Could you imagine Pa and Maman letting us get into tricks like that? It beggars belief."

She poured us both another coffee and continued. "I did ask whether they used contraceptives, but it would appear not," she said, spooning in sugar. "I thought it would be appropriate to ask. I mean, she could have got in the club any time these seven or eight years, but she hasn't. So either she is infertile, or they are."

"For which we give much thanks," I said. "It's more likely her if she's been putting herself about as you say she has. And if that's the case Guy will be unable to continue the line. Well, probably a blessing. Not that we'll know until he's safely wedded and bedded her."

"What? Alice, how can you? That's terrible. We can't let this happen! We can't let Guy marry such a woman. She might have some devilish disease!"

I thought about that, too, and sighed. And I thought about my brother.

Despite all our little ups and downs and the fact that I thought he was a pompous prig, I didn't wish any of this on him. But I couldn't see a way out of it at present, so I played the cynic's card.

"Why not? Maddy, he's chosen to do so."

"You really think so? I think she's chosen him. More to the point, I think she's been told to choose him, by the naughty nunkies. That's what I think." She stared at me with her chin up, challenging me to disagree.

I couldn't.

"If the whole family were in on the assault," I said, "That would make sense. But I don't think Sylvia is attractive enough to get Guy by herself."

"It's a land thing, a money strategy," my sister agreed gloomily. "Put Sylvia on top of the promise of a whole heap of money and Guy will find her very attractive indeed." She sighed. "Put Guy on top of a whole heap of money with his promise of a title, and he immediately becomes very attractive too..."

Then she looked at me, fire in her eyes. "We can't let this go, Al. We can't let these characters into our family. Really we can't. I don't want to have a sister-in-law who has been abused since she was a child, thinking this is the way things are, sitting across the table from me. I don't want any of her family coming near Enid, or dammit, any kids she and Guy might produce, and I don't want her flirting with Bas. I know it's selfish, but it's simply not to be borne."

"So how are we going to stop it?" I asked. "Guy's as keen on the marriage as she and her family and friends are. He's courting her for the money and married status, and he's over twenty-one. Well over. If we started saying he shouldn't marry her, he'd go and do it tomorrow, and if we told him what you've told me, he simply wouldn't believe it! It would be inconceivable to him that anyone could behave like that. Especially his friends. We'd be *personae non grata,* there'd be a big family rift, and he'd be sunk, hook, line and sinker into the Merediths' clutches."

Maddy thought about it. Finally she nodded. "You're right. But we've got to do something. We really have. To let this marriage go ahead would be cruel."

I didn't ask for whom. It wasn't worth the aggravation. I simply nodded. "Yes. We've got to expose the Merediths - sorry, Maddy, no pun intended - for what they are, and I don't just mean this aspect – so that he feels unable to align himself with these important friends of his. I don't know whether it will put him off Sylvia, but what we have to do is bring down the whole sorry edifice." I was thinking aloud now, rather than answering my sister.

I had things to do. I needed to talk to people and to think. "Is Basil in his office today?" I asked.

"You're not going to tell him, Al!"

"No, Maddy, you are. Maddy, you know that Basil's working on the Merediths; this may only be hearsay, but it's all evidence, and from you, it's first hand. Every little bit helps to turn the screw."

"Al, I couldn't!"

"You're going to have to. He won't make you stand up in court, but he won't thank you for keeping it silent. From what I've heard, he may already have an idea that something of the kind is going on. OK?"

"What? How?" she demanded.

I shook my head. "No, I'm not telling you why I think so, except to say I am as shocked as you. However, what's done is done. We must make sure nothing like it happens again. To anyone. The problems are with the perpetrators, not with the victims – and I'm sure Sylvia is not alone in this state, willing or not. There will be others. It stinks."

I looked at Maddy. "For the sake of all other women, girls even, and especially girls, you've got to tell Basil what Sylvia told you. Don't you see? We've got to put an end to it."

She nodded miserably. "I'll tell him tonight."

I shook my head. "No, better sooner than later."

She sighed. "OK Big Sis, I'll meet him for lunch. Get it over with." She was silent for a moment. "And Guy? What about him?"

I shook my head. "Don't know. It's no good me mentioning it to him, as he holds me in very low esteem. Talk it over with Basil. I trust his judgement. He's one of the family now, he can do as he thinks fit. You've done your bit, which we did rather dump on you, but I never thought it would bring all this to light, and I doubt if Elisabeth did."

"No, I'm sure she didn't. She wouldn't have done that

to me, would she?"

"At a guess, I'd say she doesn't know what has gone on in this particular case," I said, slowly. "Although I'm not really sure where she stands on many things..." I went and hugged my little round sister. "I'm sorry what started as a well-meaning action brought this lot out into the open," I began, and then I stopped. "No, I'm not. I'm glad it's out, but I'm sorry you had to be the recipient of it all."

I thought for a moment. "We can't turn back the clock for Sylvia, and from what you've told me, I don't suppose she'd want us too. But with a bit of will, we can make sure that no other kids get the same treatment."

She took my hand in hers. "OK, Al." She sighed a heaver of a sigh, and her shoulders that had been so tense, dropped. "I've been putting myself in her place. I remember how I was at twelve. I was a child, climbing trees and catching my drawers on twigs, not dropping my drawers for dirty old men. To think, we've shared food with them. Hell, Guy even had Maman and Pa give them the full works. I just want to be sick."

I nodded. "Yes. I understand. Totally. And we will get them, one way or another, I promise you. How, I don't yet know, but things are closing in on them."

She gave another sigh. "Thanks, Al. Sooner rather than later, I hope."

She took another cigarette. "You want to have lunch with us? I'll ring Bas and get him to come home."

I shook my head. "I'd be *de trop*. He'd be embarrassed with me there as well. Besides, I've got things to do. You feeling better now?"

She nodded. "Yes, thanks. I couldn't talk it over with Bas straight away, I needed another woman, but I certainly couldn't tell Maman!"

We both fell about laughing at the thought. "I'm here if you need me, Maddy, you know that."

"Yes, but where the hell were you when I needed you last night? Dirty weekend with Jeremy?"

I stood up, hugged her, then went to the door. "I wish! I'll tell you all about it when this is over, Maddy. But it's all connected, believe me. Now I've got to run."

Then another thought struck me. "How did Sylvia take it? I mean, when you spelled things out about it not being normal procedure in most families? Before they went home?"

Maddy frowned. "I thought she disbelieved me. But she looked puzzled. I may have made her think. She went a bit quiet. Then Bas and Guy came up and she suggested Guy take her back home. It was quite late in the afternoon."

"Then you may have made her think, and that might make her hurt. You might get a call from Guy – be prepared."

"Thanks very much. I'll ring Bas at once. Can you see yourself out?"

I telephoned from a phone box at the corner. I told Leggy that the paintings were all gathered together for restoration, but were not for sale.

"I'll get in touch with the restorer then," he said. "Come and report in some time soon."

I promised I would. "I'm working on that other little problem," I said. "I've got some leads."

"Then don't let me stop you. We'll speak later. Good luck."

Yes, I'd need it, I thought, as I dialed the next number.

A plummy voice answered, "London News, Society Editor's Desk." She sounded bored to tears.

"Hello, Bar, it's Alice. Long time no speaky." We had worked in Signals together at one point, but our paths had collided on and off since birth as they did if you were of a similar age, class and locality.

"Alice! I thought you were dead. No-one's seen or heard from you for absolute ages. Where have you been?"

"Nearly dead, convalescing in France, but I'm back, Bar. Can we meet for lunch?"

"Best offer I've had this week, darling, and it's only Monday! Come to my office, there's a dining room just down the Strand."

Her office was halfway up the front of an Edwardian building, and you could see what was left of St. Clement Dane's church from her window. The Luftwaffe had done for that what it had done for so many of our RAF lads. But it would rise again. The lads they'd missed would see to that. And those they'd protected.

"So, Alice," she said, as we settled down at a table in the little brown and white restaurant, "To what do I owe this visit?"

"What do you mean, Bar?" I asked innocently.

"You're up to something. Care to enlighten?"

"I have a young man I want to get on the circuit."

"Sounds promising. What's he like?"

I told her I was doing it as a favour to my brother-in-law, Basil. "His wife would do it, only she's rather pregnant at the moment and not very comfortable with it."

"Basil wants him in, eh? Well, that means he's reasonably personable; Basil's no fool." She looked at the waitress who came for our order. "The usual, please, Betty, and the same for my friend. Thank you." She turned back to me. "And your assessment of the gentleman, Alice?"

"He's a good egg," I said calmly. "I wouldn't endorse someone I didn't trust. And he's quite decorative."

She nodded sagely. "Good enough for me then. And decorative is good. So, when do you want to get him out of wrappers? There are all sorts of things going on." She pulled a handful of invitations from a wallet in her handbag and passed them across. "Go through those and see if there are any you fancy. You're welcome to them, take a few. I'll give you an intro. What's the chap's name."

I told her.

"Sounds a bit workmanlike. Didn't Arkwright invent something. Spinning or something?"

"No relation," I said, quick as a flash. "Comes from different stock completely. Family near Lytham. Big place. Very green. With little flags on it."

"Golfing family, eh? That's alright then. No problems." She poured us each a glass of water.

I took a sip. "What are you up to, Bar? Your office looked abandoned."

"You don't miss much, do you? That bastard Archie Meredith has pinched my best photographer. Doing something with a pair of low-grade Hollywood starlets," she spat.

"The Finching girls?"

She pulled a wry face. "Pair of expensive whores if you ask me. You did not hear that from my lips, but honestly, Alice, they make me heave. Their behaviour is positively common, they act like little tramps. I knew their mother a little – before she went doolally, of course. She would have been mortified."

I raised my eyebrows. "Where did you see them?"

"You mean where didn't I see them? They were at the Café de Paris on Friday night, at Fortnums on Saturday morning – looking rather the worse for wear, it must be said – at a dress show at Harrods on Saturday afternoon, and then at a charity ball at the Dorchester on Saturday evening. They looked good, but they were so slack, Alice. So damned slack. It wasn't what they wore so much as how they wore it. Miss Campbell-Barnes would have had a fit."

I chuckled. Miss Campbell-Barnes was one of our finishing teachers. "You mean the knees were not glued together?" I suggested.

"Hardly! Nor the straps anchored, the make-up set, nor the curls maintained. And the way they talked. You'd never have thought they were well-bred young Englishwomen."

Bar leaned back while Betty brought in our lunch, a dubious piece of grey meat, boiled potatoes and some sorry looking greeny yellow vegetable that may have started life as Spring Greens, all covered in a deep brown gluey gravy. She smiled up at the waitress, "Thank you so much, Betty." Betty refilled our glasses and left. "It's actually not as bad as it looks, Alice," she whispered, picking up her knife and fork.

I did likewise. It wasn't. But it did look very bad indeed.

"So you don't think much of the Misses Finching?" I said, to bring her back on course.

"Indeed I don't. They definitely let the side down!" She put down her cutlery and gave me a great wide smile. "Listen to me, I sound like my mother! A dinosaur at 28! But if you asked me to give them an entry, Alice, I'd have to decline. Even for you, darling."

"I think Archie Meredith is giving them that, Bar. You say you knew their mother."

"A little, but mostly through the magazine. Back issues. She was a fine looking woman, but I heard she went off the rails – about seven years ago, give or take."

"Mind if I have a look at these back issues?" I asked. "Some with Lady Finching in."

"You are up to something!" Bar said triumphantly.

"Something that could be big," I confided. "But I need to get some background research in. You'll be first to know, I promise."

"Deal!" she said with a grin.

I spent a couple of hours working through back numbers of the London News and checking on the year books that Bar kept in her office for reference. By the time Bar was ready to throw me out – she was going to interview a new addition to the London stage: "He's absolutely, gorgeous,

Alice. Italian looks without the grease!" I had a whole sheaf of information on the circle of people around the Finchings, and thus around the Merediths.

She tucked a selection of invitations into my bag as I began to leave. "Go to some of them for me, and do me an impromptu write up," she said. "I can't get to them all."

We said goodbye at the roadside, where she got into the cab. I got into the saddle and headed west.

As I pedaled I went over what I had learned. I needed to talk to Jeremy. No, I really did. I hated ringing people at work, but this was about work, legitimate.

I parked by a phone box outside Chelsea Town Hall and dialed. I got a receptionist, then an extension. A Welsh voice told me it was Mr. Arkwright's phone.

I asked for Mr. Arkwright.

"He's not in the office at the moment, see," said the voice. "I can take a message if you like."

I gave him my name.

"Oh. You should be seein' him any time now."

"Tell him to wait if he rings in," I said. "I'm on my way. Thank you."

27

He was lounging on the porch as I skidded to a halt but stood to attention as I came to meet him.

"I owe you an apology," I said quietly as I let him in. I took my bike out the back to the shed.

"No, you don't," he said, when I returned to the hallway. "I was working on rumour, and I was out of order. So you've heard. Not nice. I came as soon as I could. We need to talk. You don't mind?" He was following me up the stairs on silent feet.

I turned. "No Jeremy. I rang you at the office. I… I …"

He climbed the step below mine so that we were looking each other in the eyes. His were dark blue, I noticed, clear and very compassionate.

I leaned forward.

And we kissed, tentatively.

And then again, tugging and holding each other tightly, making up for lost time.

Finally we parted. Faces big beams, all tension disappeared.

"I've wanted to do that for so long," he said softly.

"Me too. But I couldn't tell you."

He chuckled, "Certainly not! It would be playing into everyone else's hands. And we'd promised ourselves it would never happen."

I took his hand and started up the steps. "I'm glad it did. Come on, I'll make you a restorative brew," I invited.

We drank strong sweet black coffee laced with rum, and smoked Pashas, sitting extremely close on the sofa and devouring each others with our eyes.

Suddenly the world seemed brighter.

"Apart from that," he said at last, "we need to see Elisabeth. I've brought my questionnaire. Do you fancy collaborating on homework?"

"Yes. And we'll drop them in personally?"

He nodded.

"I've got you some social invites to look at, too."

"I'm impressed. Thank you."

"A slight problem. I told my friend that you came from Lytham from a family who had a lot of green acres."

"Alice, you're priceless. I know sweet F A about golf. But I'll learn. Honest, I will."

"It was unfortunately the first thing that came into my mind. She was hinting a spinning connection and disinclined to do the business," I said, laughing. "Bar is a tremendous snob, but actually, quite likeable if you can put that aside."

We sat at the table and got out our homework. "Question one. Why do you want to learn magic?" I asked.

Three quarters of an hour later we were knocking at 35 The Boltons. We handed our envelopes and our cards to the maid and were allowed in to the hallway while she clumped up the stairs. Shortly after we were invited up.

Elisabeth was entertaining Percy.

She wore a bright red wool dress with a very fitting top and a lot of jewelry – the full set, bracelet, earrings, necklace and rings, gold like her hair and sparkling brightly, like her eyes, I thought. Such a look didn't come cheap and it was quite different from when we saw her alone. Percy's taste, I guessed.

I found it very hard to be civil to Percy, knowing what I did about him, but remembering that revenge is a dish best served cold I put on my most charming manners and allowed him to greet me with a hug and a *bise*.

"Darling Alice, how lovely to see you again. And you've filled in our form. How wonderful."

Elisabeth was casting a cursory eye over our homework. It was good. We both knew that. We'd cribbed the answers from her father, making minor alterations in the language style so it didn't look too obvious.

She pursed her lips as she read. "Percy, dear, these two are made for the work. Take a look." She held out our sheets to him.

He waved them away. "No, sweetie, I completely trust your judgement, really I do. If you say they're in, then they're in."

Jeremy and I looked at each other, smiling.

Elisabeth got up and put the papers in the leather folder. "They're in, Percy. This weekend." She looked at us. "You don't have any plans for this weekend, do you?"

"Nothing that can't be put off," I said.

"I'm free. Where do you want us?" Jeremy asked. "And what shall we bring?"

Percy spoke. "Finching Hall, near Framlingham, Suffolk. Come Friday night. You'll meet the rest of us and we'll work on Saturday afternoon, then relax in the evening. We always have very good parties after a ritual, and Beltane, well, that's very special," he winked. "You'll find out. I'm sure it'll be to your taste. Then you can sleep in on Sunday morning and leave after lunch."

He looked at us. "That OK? Good-oh!. And to bring? Whatever you'd bring to a weekend in the country. We have a heated pool, we have tennis courts, and we usually run a little casino. Life's to be lived to the full. We want you to enjoy yourselves. The gods didn't put you here to be miserable. We don't believe in denying ourselves, do we, sweetie?"

"No, darling," said Elisabeth crossing to drop a kiss on his forehead. "You don't need robes yet. We have spares, don't we, Percy?"

"For the moment, yes." He looked at me. "Er, that

jewel?"

"Yes? Elisabeth gave it to me. Mine were all stolen."

"I thought I recognized it. I'm glad you have it. Looks well on you, Alice. You should wear it all the time, as a signature piece." He looked at Elisabeth. "It really didn't suit you, did it sweetie? You're a gold and diamond girl, aren't you? As many as I can get you to accept, and that isn't hard." He brayed at his own joke.

I looked at Jeremy. He inclined his head a fraction.

"Elisabeth, Percy, I'm sorry, we have to go." I said. "We'd love to stay, but we have an appointment at five. You'll excuse us?"

"Of course," said Elisabeth, hugging us. "See you both at the weekend. I'm sure you'll have a good time with us."

"What's she playing at?" Jeremy murmured as we walked back to the Fulham Road. "Last time we were there she was so different. What's she doing getting involved with such a man?"

I shrugged. "We may find out this weekend."

We'd shared my research, and he'd not been idle. Information was coming in from many places that the Merediths' had developed. It all linked to poor materials being used in place of the best quality ones that had been specified. They ran roughshod over planning permission and civil engineers' reports, in fact anything that got in their way, by the judicious use of bribe or blackmail. If their misdemeanours were beginning to show up in Britain, they were particularly noticeable in prestigious building projects in the Commonwealth and Overseas. The country or client paid for the very best – and British made products which were naturally the very best! – and got (often) less than perfect British made products.

Why was I not surprised?

"I need to check with Sam. He's got some stuff for me," he said. "Would you like to come?"

I nodded. "I need to speak with the Rev. Would you like to stay at Wethersley?"

Leggy and Bobby were still there when we arrived with the Rev and Sam.

My mother was glowing. So many people, and so much intrigue. She ordered tea and sandwiches, and we all went into the library, where there was a bright fire and a large table around which we'd all fit, far away from the rest of the world.

"No farther than this room," my father said. It was an order and we all knew it. There were nods and murmurs of assent.

"Right, then, I've got all the pictures here as you know. I'll be cleaning them physically, and my friend, Reverend Simmons here, has offered to do a spiritual cleansing on them – a sort of exorcism service, Reverend?"

The Rev inclined his head then raised it. "It would appear to be a sensible move from what I've heard. I find it clears the air and helps things move on."

No-one demurred.

Indeed, Bobby nodded vigorously even though the Rev was not of his church.

I couldn't have asked for better; the Rev had come up trumps for me. "Thank you, sir," I said. "This is exactly what the current owner asked me to arrange. You must let me have your fee."

The Rev smiled benignly. "No fee, my dear. This is an act of love. It's a privilege."

"Well that's settled then," said Leggy. "Now about the Meredith twins…"

I was at once aware of my pendant. It was growing warm.

And as the meeting progressed, it grew warmer and warmer.

I hate people fiddling with things when I am talking, and didn't want to be guilty of that during others' speeches, but as I listened, the tingling heat increased. I was not imagining it, I swear. It got so warm that I had to beg to be excused for a short while. "Please carry on without me. I'll catch up."

I let the cold tap run in my washbasin and took the pendant off. It was hotter than it should have been just lying on my neck. I let the clear chill water run over it for a while then dried it on a towel and put it in a little black velvet bag that had hitherto contained a powder compact.

I felt a lot happier without the burning jewel, and as I glanced in the mirror I noticed that the skin it had lain against was redder than that around it. I pressed a cold damp sponge on the spot then chose a silk scarf and knotted that round my neck to hide the glow. Very odd.

When I returned Mrs. Mac had dispensed refreshments. A cup of tea had been left for me, and Sam was speaking again.

"... the twins were the cause of their mother's death, not an unusual occurrence, in the closing hours of 1899. Archie was the older by twenty minutes. They were brought up by their grandparents – mother's father, Mr. Meredith, and father's mother, Mrs. Greystoke, at the Meredith home, a large mansion which is no longer extant, and their father, William, who was content with this arrangement being mostly away on business, and his brothers Henry and Arthur; this latter spent most of his time with us at the Vicarage . Mr. and Mrs. Meredith indulged the boys, but were unfortunately killed in a motoring accident when the twins were seven."

"At this point Arthur, Sam's father," the Rev continued, nodding at the younger man, "and William's youngest brother suggested the angel paintings were sold, and William agreed. The middle brother, Henry, didn't. He wanted them kept, but to no avail. William took the paintings down to London where he disappeared, the paintings being bought by his best friends Mr. and Mrs. Thorburn. The twins, at their uncle Henry's request were made wards of court, and placed in the tender care of their grandfather's sister who lived in East Anglia. Here they stayed and went to a minor preparatory school, while they were fed the poison of the paintings by Henry at weekends and at holidays. They learned very quickly how to manipulate people, and used the paintings to give themselves status and power. They were very close with each other, worked as a unit, and were ruthless. In that," said the Rev, "it seems that they took after their uncle Henry.

"When their Great Aunt took them away because of their bad behaviour, and put them in another school, they were heard to threaten to talk with the angels and have her killed. Shortly after, she died, and they were wards of court once more, having found a convenient home with the deputy headmaster of their current school. They stayed there avoiding the Great War, and learning how to make money by various unsavory methods, none of which were actually illegal.

"Their uncle Henry, who was their constant companion, war work permitting, took them around in their holidays and taught them their *métiers de jeunes hommes*, and seemed to get on well with them, until he was killed in Paris, in 1922.

"A crime of passion, it was said," said Reverend Simmons, giving us reason to suspect foul play.

"They seem to be bad news for everyone," Sam commented bitterly.

Rev. Simmons put his hand on Sam's, "It's one way of seeing it," he said softly.

Sam snorted. "Tell me another! Every death was a golden lining for the Meredith boys. They were left the estates of their grand-parents – both of them, although my Grandmother left some to my father and my uncles. They had their father's estate, which was quite something, since he had been running the Meredith enterprises. Then they got their Great Aunt's estate – not to be sneezed at - and finally their uncle Henry's.

"By the age of 23 they were very wealthy young men indeed, and they intended to stay that way, but not necessarily by the sweat of their brows. They saw the need for low-cost housing, but also civic building – town halls, schools, hospitals, that sort of thing. They designed buildings that were very much of the moment, but they kept their costs low. Which meant they flourished." Jeremy looked across at Sam. "For some projects they kept their costs spectacularly low," he said. "They got invoices for the best quality materials, but, wherever they were invisible to the public, used substandard ones, sharing the difference in price with the manufacturer. Which is why the hospital in Bahrain fell down, the university building in Bangalore has cracks from floor to roof, and right here Greystokes estate is developing serious problems – to name but a few. Unfortunately for the clients, the insurance time has just expired. They judge it to a nicety and aren't seen to be greedy."

"I have a whole box-file on them," Sam said, nodding. "I bet you do, too."

"So do we," said Leggy. "But mine is of a personal nature. And I'd ask Roger and Marie-Therese to back me up on this, if they would. We're talking social stuff now. It's time we all laid our cards on the table."

I looked at Leggy and then at my parents. What did they know?

"By 1922," Maman said primly, "I was producing a family. I wasn't on the scene too much. You didn't go into society when you were *enceinte*. Roger still kept up his contacts during the early 1920s. I heard about their parties. I think I went to one later; there was a really good jazz-band. What you now call Dixieland. Brilliant and so new then. And champagne flowed like water. It was very much show for show's sake. There were lots of rowdy red faces and people out of control.

"I suppose because I'd been living quietly for so long, I was quite shocked. I loved the music, and of course I was there with Roger. I would have hated to have not had a protector there. It felt exceedingly ..." she sought for the right word... "Promiscuous. Decadent. *Louche*. That was it. All a bit sordid. There was gambling for heavy stakes and much loose behaviour. I am no prude, but I was horrified to watch as the house was being wrecked by these boisterous, unlovely people."

She looked at my father. "That was where that woman tried to tell me you were once engaged to her, wasn't it? I jolly well told her where she could go. I had a ring, a piece of paper and at least a couple of children to prove you were mine." She seethed, remembering. "What a cheek! She married that queer chap shortly afterwards, the one who used to walk around in full Highland kit and say he was Robin Hood or something-or-other."

"Rob Roy, *Chérie*," Pa corrected gently.

He took Maman's tiny hand in his. "There's never been anyone but you, *Chérie*," he told her, kissing her knuckles one by one. "Only ever you."

I noticed the reactions around the table.

Embarrassment from Sam, from Leggy and Bobby, and smiles of pleasure from Jeremy and the Rev. Two romantics, then.

My father continued. "She – the one you are talking about, *Chérie* – had talked herself in love with me. I never gave her the slightest encouragement, as I told you at the time. But we aren't talking of us, we're talking of the parties.

"I went to a few. They were very arty, if you know what I mean. Bohemian. I liked that. As *Chérie* said, there was always plenty to drink, good music, and anything else you might like to try. If you wanted to lose money, you could, if you wanted to lose your mind, that option was open too. Rooms hazy with *kif,* divans full of sprawling figures, draped rather than clothed, it must be said. But interesting people to talk to, if you wanted to talk, and I'd usually end up talking to people – poets, writers, artists, actors, that sort of thing. My Aunt Caro used to go along regularly, for the discourse, she told me. She used to meet W. B. Yeats there; he was a lovely man, she said. I met Noel Coward a few times, brilliant fun, the waspish old queen! Anyway, that was the good side."

"They sound fun" said Bobby, grinning. "And the bad side?"

"Ah. Nothing exceeds like excess. Everything was excessive. And humans are not creatures who thrive on excess. I watched dependencies being created. Girls who were just out being introduced to drugs and drink, and I'm not talking nicotine and a fruit punch. And to chemmy and blackjack which were *de rigueur* then. The possibility of losing your mind, your reputation, and your fortune were all there.

"However, for some reason the Meredith twins were extremely popular with the *doyennes*. They were, of course, very rich young men, and unmarried and according to the ladies very attractive. Tremendous catches! They made sure they kept that way. I would hazard a guess that they ensured a fair number of young women failed to find husbands, and had fairly short and sad existences. But who was really to blame? The young woman? She needn't have behaved so badly. She wasn't brought up to behave that way..."

He sighed. "That, Alice, is why I wanted to keep you and Maddy from such people. Of course I trust you both to behave well, but I didn't want you to be placed in any sort of temptation. I was extremely cross when Guy brought them over. Since then I've asked a few questions around. It would seem that whatever they're up to, Bulgy Algy is one of their lieutenants. I think Guy was targeted by them, possibly because of his job at the bank. I have no intention of throwing my heir to the wolves. But that is another matter."

"You realize that they are actively looking for those pictures. They see them as theirs?" the Rev said.

My father smiled. "Then I am delighted to give the angels sanctuary," he said. "For as long as they need it."

"There are more hunters than the Merediths," said Leggy, quietly.

This got everyone's heads up.

"Soldiers of the Dawn?" I watched the faces.

My mother looked blank. My father sucked in his cheeks. The Rev raised his eyebrows.

Sam said nothing, but I'm sure a panic crossed his face for a second. Then he said, his voice cracking slightly, "Who are they?"

"Religious extremists, I suppose you would call them," Leggy said quietly.

"Very extreme," muttered Bobby.

"What do they want with them?" Sam asked.

"I should think they would want to destroy them," said the Rev. Simmons. "They are somewhat iconoclastic. And very militant. I thought they had been eliminated."

"So did we, sir," said Bobby. "But it appears not."

"Ugh!" said my father. "How very unpleasant. We'll take particular care of the angels then. I'm not letting some fanatic destroy them."

"That's why they were all over the place," I said. "To keep them separate. Now they are back in danger because they are all in one place." I looked at my father. "You must take great care to keep them safe. You might consider another place for them, once our guests" I nodded to the Rev and Sam, "have seen them all."

"So no-one knows anyone in the SODs?" Leggy asked.

"Madam Honoria and Cyril," said Jeremy. "Not certain, but have suspicions. I checked with the local constabulary this morning. Her name is Honor Bewcastle-Green, born 1890. I don't think she wanted to destroy them, though. She wanted to possess them."

"Honor!" my mother exclaimed. "Huge woman with wild hair? She's joined them? Good Heavens, how some people change. Aunt Caro knew her. Thought a lot of her at one time. They used to ouija board together. Knew there would be another war in 1930. Got it from the spirits. They wanted me to come and do it with them. I told them to go for a walk; the fresh air would do them both more good." She looked around. "How do you know her, Jeremy?"

"She was ... er ... caring for one of the pictures. She had orders from the owner to give it up to us, but she didn't intend to do so without a fight," he said softly. "I'm afraid your daughter put her in hospital. But it was in self-defence and beautifully done. Madam Honoria is a very powerful woman."

Maman looked at me, concerned. "She didn't hurt you, Alice? No. Well jolly good, dear. She was a beast to most people. Always throwing her weight around, and there was a lot of it even then. I never knew what Caro saw in her. So she's a SOD. I can't think of a better appellation."

My mother took a sip of her tea (with lemon, of course) and blotted her mouth with a napkin. Then she lifted her head and addressed the company. "This is all very well, but when is something going to be done about all this?"

Jeremy looked at me questioningly.

I nodded. He could answer. Maman would like that.

"We're all working on it, Lady Wethersley," he said. "Basil, too. At present we are still collating material, but I am at liberty to say that sooner rather than later. And that is all, on the official front." He glanced at Leggy and Bobby, who also inclined their heads. Then at Sam and Rev. Simmons.

"But this is hush-hush and goes no further than this room – until I have clearance to give you a story, Sam."

Reverend Simmons smiled. "Of course, dear boy."

"Sure," agreed Sam. "Not a word." He gave the scout's salute.

Jeremy eyed my parents. Both put fingers over their lips.

"Thank you all. Right, well, I suppose we'd best catch up with the Merediths. In case you haven't been reading the lesser newspapers, Archie is currently swanning around the country promoting a couple of film starlets at the moment. We suspect that he is searching for the paintings, and he will be engaged thus until at least Tuesday evening. Meanwhile his brother is supposedly taking care of the empire. But we saw him less than a couple of hours ago with his fiancée, and I don't think he will be going back to work this evening."

"Miss Elisabeth Thorburn," said Leggy, thoughtfully. "What's her part in all this, Jeremy?"

Sam was sitting forward in his chair, so was the Rev.

Jeremy looked at me.

"Not sure," I said. "Not sure at all where she stands. I would have said she was with them, from our first meeting here, but since then, on further acquaintance, I am not sure at all."

"She's certainly leading old Percy on," said Bobby. "No names, no pack-drill. But there's a price. The engagement and thus the marriage rests upon her providing at least one angel. That I know as a fact."

"And her father knew of this, I am certain," I said. "He got rid of the others, and kept just the one, but in his will, although he left his daughter the house, he made sure that the angel was removed before she came into possession. I think he knew of the engagement, and didn't trust her. He may have been misjudging her, but he was certainly playing safe."

"Indeed," said my father. "Interesting. You've met her several times since, Alice?"

"Yes." I took a sip of tea. "She takes two forms, one, the side she showed here, when Percy is with her, and the other when he is not. Then she is someone completely different."

My mother shrugged. "Many women are like that, darling. It's a survival strategy and the nature of the beast."

Charming!

But not altogether untrue.

"We've been invited to Finchings this coming weekend," I said. "Naturally we accepted."

"It'll be magical?" my father asked.

"Yes, sir," said Jeremy. "But we will be observant."

Leggy chuckled.

Bobby frowned. "I don't like that at all, Milady," he muttered. "You don't know what they might get up to."

"That's true, but that will make us doubly alert and we'll find out," I said.

The Rev. Simmons gazed at me, smiling. "Will you tell me what they do? I'd be extremely interested. Liturgical patterns, don't you see? Fascinating."

Sam looked put out. "Grandfather, how can you?"

"Oh Sam, you can learn from all sorts of people. There's more ways of doing things than you could possibly imagine," he said softly, stroking Sam's hand again. "No need to worry about my immortal soul, dear boy. I shan't be invoking demons from the pulpit."

He smiled at the rest of us. "Could I ask that we adjourn? I would very much like to see the other angels, but I have a meeting with the Parish Council at 8 o'clock."

"Why did you take that pretty pendant off, Alice?" my mother asked, when we were back in the sitting room.

"It was irritating me."

Jeremy frowned. "Again?"

"Yes, why?"

"Do me a favour, Alice. Keep it hidden. Don't wear it."

My mother looked askance. "But you bought it for her, Jeremy," she said.

"I'll buy her another. It doesn't suit, obviously." He smiled wickedly at me, "Gold and diamonds this time, eh sweetie?"

I hooted. "Stop it!"

My mother shook her head. "A young man offers that and you laugh at him! Alice, where are your manners?"

"Private joke, Maman. Jeremy didn't buy the first one. It was Elisabeth who gave it to me."

"Then you should have cleaned it. Before you wore it. Or better still, get Reverend Simmons to do it. You don't know whose neck it's been around or what it's been doing. Really, Alice, I thought you'd know better."

"Er, what are you trying to say to me, Maman?" I asked. "It would have been alright if Jeremy had bought it, but not from Elisabeth?"

My mother drew herself up. "Of course it would have been alright if Jeremy had bought it at a jewellers. It would have been in the window in sunlight, and he would have bought it out of a desire to please, I imagine. That act and the sunlight would have taken out any negative influences. But you had it from Padraig that he thought it had come from a powerful priestess, and we know that Elisabeth is tainted with that brush. Surely you know that stones pick up their owner's emanations?"

My father's eyebrows raised at his wife's vehemence. And possibly her insight. My mother the secret witch, eh? But she was not for turning.

"A good occultist can use a stone as a focus. Look at crystal balls."

"But that's a lot of baloney, end of the pier stuff,

Maman," I argued. "Surely you don't believe that. It's just a bit of applied psychology for silly lonely women done by unscrupulous people, wrapped up in exotic trimmings."

"Don't throw the baby out with the bath water, Alice," my mother replied tartly. "Some people have the knack of using stones and crystals. You can use them to spy with. My old nurse used to do it. On each of us, let me remind you. We all had different stones – our birthday stones. Mine was a little crystal on a chain. The boys had tie pins with theirs – Lucien had a ruby, Marc a topaz – which we wore every day. We were never lost. She always knew where to find us because she called the stones. Ask Angelique. She was there."

Angelique, who was taking coffee, nodded. "That is so. And the boys still have the little tie pins as far as I know. They were very discreet. But effective. Nurse was never at a loss for finding any of the children. I asked her how she did it once, but she wouldn't tell. She said if I couldn't work it out for myself, I didn't deserve to know. But many times she would come looking for them and they'd be on their way back. She said she could see where they were and what they were doing."

"And how did you feel when she called you through your crystal, Maman?" I asked.

Now my mother frowned. "I don't know. It's so long ago."

But Angelique touched her wrist. "Don't you remember, Thérèse? When we were about thirteen – we were supposed to be at your piano lesson, in Nice, but the teacher was not well and the carriage had gone by the time we found out. We went down to the Market in the Old Town and bought ice cream and chatted to some of Marc's school friends."

Maman smiled. "Oh yes. And we were late for the carriage which called at the piano teacher's house an hour later, because we were having so much fun. Yes, I do recall my crystal growing hot and tingling. It might have simply been guilt, though. But it was Nurse who told the coachman where to find us, and she gave us such a telling off, and then when we got home, we got another one from my father. And my mother. And my grandmother, who was extremely put out, since she wanted the carriage to go to her friends in."

All eyes were upon me.

"The crystal grows warm, then tingles?" I said feeling intensely uncomfortable.

My mother nodded.

"Ah!" I hoped it was non-committal.

"We'll move the paintings tonight," my father said, and went to the phone. "Alice and Jeremy, you give me a hand. Go and wrap them up now. Cherie, you and Angelique don't need to know any of this, nor do any of the servants, so I'd be obliged if you would not listen."

Within an hour Pa had called in favours and the paintings had been transported and locked inside a back room next to the brew-house of the local pub, the Wethersley Arms. Larry, the landlord, had no problem finding space, although they took up a fair bit of it. He even helped us carry the things in while his wife took care of the bars. We had a drink with them afterwards; they knew how to make good tipple, did Larry and his lady.

"Er, Larry, I don't suppose you'd mind me working in that room?" my father asked softly as a second pint was being pulled. We were alone at the bar, the shove-ha'penny game having reached a crucial stage in the games room.

"Don't see why not, sir? Will you be wanting it long?"

"I don't know, yet, but I'm quite happy to rent it for as long as it takes. On the QT."

Larry nodded. "Mum's the word, sir. It'll be a privilege to oblige you, sir."

"The thing is," my father explained to us as we settled in

the local taxi, closing the connecting window, thus depriving the driver of any gossip, "I can get there without hitting a road. No-one but your Mother and Larry need know I'm there. I don't even have to enter through the bar."

"That's very good. But we don't actually know how much the others know," I said. "If indeed they know it at all. There might have been a little over-reaction?"

"Better safe than sorry," my father said. "Besides, I wanted to get them out of the house. I'm not happy about them being in the immediate vicinity of my family and friends. And Larry owes me."

"Can you trust him not to talk?" Jeremy asked.

"I think so. I have things on him. Besides, he knows I'm good for a bob or two. He'll keep mum. And the regulars – he'll tell them I wanted to do some work out of Cherie's way. They all think the world of her but wouldn't cross her!"

28

Back at Wethersley there were more visitors. My brother, Guy, and the delightful Sylvia rose to greet us.

"How lovely to see you both," my father said, giving him a hug and her a kiss on the cheek. "It's almost full set. We only need Maddy, Bas and Enid. Alice, Jeremy, come and say hello." He was joviality personified, and sounded genuinely glad to see them both.

I did the decent thing, but found it exceptionally difficult.

Sylvia gave me a brief hug and "Darling... We really didn't expect to see you here, and with your lovely beau."

I tried to discount what Maddy had told me as I kissed the air beside her cheeks. Watching her flutter and press a 'sisterly' kiss on Jeremy without losing my temper was one of the hardest things I'd ever done.

"Well, you're here again," she said, eyeing him up and down. "Lovely to see you. And you, too, Alice. Are you staying long? We must go to the flicks together. They've got "The Maltese Falcon" on again at Amersham. Don't you just love Bogart?"

"Yes, I do. But I'm back in town tomorrow, I'm afraid," I said.

"Sylvia wants to ask you a favour, Roger," said Maman.

"Indeed? Well, my dear, ask away, anything I can possibly do for you I will," Pa invited, sitting down beside Maman on the chesterfield. I took an armchair, and Jeremy sat on the arm. Angelique on the matching armchair, smiled. Guy and Sylvia settled back into the two-seater.

Sylvia held the floor. "For our wedding," she said. "Father wondered if you, being an artist, could provide us with some décor."

"As a present? Of course, I'd be delighted. What had you in mind?" Pa beamed. He liked being involved in things artistic and this would be a labour of love, I could tell.

Sylvia smiled. "We'll be having a huge marquee, as you know. But what we fancied, didn't we, Guy, was a set of angels round it. A blessing of angels would be absolutely marvelous! We could use all the blessings we can get," she laughed awkwardly, with a little snort as a finale. "What we thought was one for each day of the week? Do you think that would be possible?"

"Isn't that a lovely idea, Roger?" Maman said, all keenness for him to go further. "So few young people today have any spiritual motifs at their weddings. Did you think this one up, Sylvia? How clever of you, dear."

My father put on his thinking face, lips pursed and pushed forward. "Angels for each day of the week?" he murmured. "I'll have to do a bit of research. Do you have any idea what they might look like? I wasn't aware that they existed."

"It was my father's idea, actually. He swears they do exist and we just thought it was so very different. Of course, the wedding will be very soon – six weeks now. Do you think you could do it? I mean, it would mean a lot of work for you. I don't want you to be put out, and it is a bit last moment, but Guy said you would be able to do it, didn't you Guy?"

My brother was about to speak, but Sylvia talked over him.

"Of course you did, darling. You always agree with me, and it would be so very very original. I'd be so grateful. Anything you wanted, I'd be happy to pay – whatever the price," she gushed, uncrossing and recrossing her legs so her skirt rose high above her knees for an instant.

Indeed.

Jeremy caught my eye. Was she propositioning my father

in front of his wife? And her prospective husband, his son?

Pa appeared not to notice. "Sylvia, my dear, I need no payment. But I need to have a little think. I'm not sure that it can be done. What exactly were you thinking of, size-wise? Materials to be used? I need a little more to work on."

Now Maman and Angelique were firing questioning glances at each other and at us.

I got up and poured whisky for myself and for Jeremy.

"Anyone else for a drink?"

I took orders and poured – cognac for Maman and Angelique, whisky for Pa and for Guy and cherry brandy for Sylvia – and delivered them. Guy didn't look too happy at all when he took the drink but Sylvia smiled and thanked me with a little nod as she was in full spate.

"I thought life-sized, but quite solid, on board. Because of course we'd keep them afterwards. Couldn't throw them away, could we? Of course, I realize it would take a bit of time for all seven, but you might have something around that you could doctor a bit? I know artists are such clever people. I wouldn't be looking for anything too perfect, just enough to add a bit of atmosphere. Daddy's set his heart on it."

"Has he?" muttered my mother. "He could have thought of it sooner. It will mean Roger working all the hours God sends, and for nothing at all, since he has no intention of charging. How will he ever keep up with the commissions he already has?"

"Oh, I can manage, Cherie. Trust me." He beamed first at his wife, and then at Sylvia. "I have, as it happens, some paintings I can, as you say, doctor a little. They're in my studio. I'll get started on them tomorrow. Promise. OK? You can tell your father the pictures will be ready for him by the day before your wedding. I promise you that and I am a man of my word."

He put his hand up to indicate he hadn't finished. Sylvia subsided back beside my brother while Pa continued. "No need for thanks, Sylvia, it will be my privilege. However, and this is a very necessary however, I need no visits from anyone to see what I'm up to. I must be left in peace to work on them in my studio. Alone."

He peered at each of us in turn, over his glasses, particularly at Maman and Angelique. "I know you will be curious to see them, but if you want them, Sylvia and Guy, you will all have to be patient and trust my artistic integrity." He smiled at his future daughter-in-law. "Is that a deal, my dear?"

Sylvia leapt out of her seat and hugged Pa. She plonked a huge sloppy kiss on his mouth. "Oh, sir, that is absolutely spiffing! I'm so delighted, and it will make us so happy and Daddy will be so pleased. Thank you so very much!"

I downed my whisky in one.

The naughty nunkies were behind it, they must be. Or was it Bulgy Algy working on his own account?

Guy said to the world in general, "When we are married, we'll be living in Cadogan Square, by the way."

"Indeed? How lovely," I said. "Which number?"

"Nineteen. It does need a little work but it's in a stunning position for entertaining. Sylvia found it for us, clever girl. It's just what you wanted, wasn't it, my dear?" he said, patting her hand affectionately. "We'll be doing lots of entertaining, I can tell you. Plus, of course, it's so convenient – central, close enough to the West End, and of course to Maddy and you, dear sister," he raised his glass to me and smiled.

It wasn't a comforting thought. I'd run to London to escape my siblings, well, Guy, anyway.

He looked at our parents questioningly. "Er... You did say you might be able to help setting us up... And of course, all of you would be most welcome guests, any time. You could get back into society, Maman, using our house as a base. We'd love to have you stay."

Yes, I thought cynical as ever, my brother is on the cadge

again. And clever Sylvia has found the little gem. Only it wasn't little. I knew Cadogan Square and the houses did not come cheap, even if they did need a little work on.

"Daddy's promised us five thousand pounds," Sylvia said lightly.

"How very generous of him," said Maman. I caught the look she gave Pa. "I suppose we should seriously think about Mr. Meredith's proposal if we are to consider such a huge sum, Roger."

Pa frowned over his spectacles. "I take it you would like to have yet another *pied à terre* in London, *Chérie*. It's not as though you don't have a place to stay with both of your daughters."

They were playing. I bit back a grin and handed Jeremy my glass. "More whisky," I muttered.

"Yes, Alice's place is not ideal, and Maddy's is far too busy with children and diplomats. We would have a whole suite for you, Maman," Guy pleaded. "You'd be most welcome to stay as long as you wanted at any time."

"Exactly," agreed Sylvia. "Daddy and Mummy think it's a wonderful idea. They love entertaining."

"Thank you, my dears," said my mother to the happy pair. "That's a very kind thought." She frowned at Angelique. "We're going up to town tomorrow, aren't we, Angelique?"

Her confidante nodded. "*B'en sûr, chérie*. We need to have fittings for our wedding outfits," she lied glibly. Angelique was an excellent dressmaker but it would do no harm to hide this from Sylvia and her family.

"Then I'll just have a little look at the house while we're there, you know, to make sure it is really suitable. Oh, the address sounds good, and I know you've set your heart on it, Sylvia, but you know how I hate to put money into anything I've not actually seen? I'm sure it will be stunning, but... well it's my French peasant roots; I'm sure there's Auvergnat in there somewhere." She gave Guy and Sylvia a stunning smile with just enough apology in it.

Angelique hastily applied her handkerchief to her nose and mouth and Pa stuck his pipe in his mouth, clamping his teeth down hard. None of us had ever heard her claim rustic prudence before, or ever practice it. Sylvia looked seriously peeved, her lower lip sticking out rudely.

Maman was not to be stopped. She leaned towards Sylvia confidingly. "Sylvia, do understand, darling. I'm just careful, when it comes to money," she said softly. "It's so hard come by these days. I'll do a little check, then if it feels right, and I'm sure it will, I can have a go at persuading my husband to do more than just consider Mr. Meredith's scheme. Is that a deal?"

Guy put his hand over Sylvia's and held her down, quite firmly.

"Of course you should have a look at it, Maman," he said. "But I think you'll fall in love with it. I'm absolutely certain you will, when you hear the price."

"I'm sure I will too, Guy, but humour me on this, darling. There's a love."

My brother and his fiancée left shortly after, having gained as much of their objectives as they could hope for. We waved them out.

I was glad to see the back of him.

"So they know we've got the angels," Pa said, pouring himself another very large scotch. "Quick work, eh?"

"Such cheek!" murmured Angelique.

"*Autre temps, autre moeurs, chérie,*" my mother said. "We'd better get to bed early if we're to be in town tomorrow. Alice, you'll come with us, clothes-hunting."

"I'd love to. I need some more things. I'm getting back on the circuit."

"About time too, dear. You're working too hard. You need a little fun. Now you must all excuse me. I need to sleep."

My father poked the fire, then regained his seat. Maman had taken Angelique with her, but we stayed.

Pa looked grim. He replaced his pipe in its rack, thoughtfully.

I got out my cigarette case and handed it to him. He looked up, shook his head. "Jeremy, may I have one of yours, my boy. Gauloises don't suit at present."

We sat around the fire, lighting up.

"It's always possible they don't know," I said, playing the devil's advocate.

"Rubbish, Alice, and you know it," Pa said. "It was too soon, and so clumsy."

"So we have a problem," said Jeremy. "It was either Alice's pendant, which I'm not happy about, to be honest, or one of those present this afternoon."

I groaned. "Or anyone else who knows that I'm looking for the stuff," I said. "One could make an educated guess, for Heaven's sake. I'm your daughter, Pa. You are an artist. Where would I take paintings to hide them? They've gone through my flat, and they're not there." I inhaled a lungful of smoke. "I'm sorry to have got you involved, Pa. It was wrong."

"Rubbish, Alice," he said again. "But we got them out in time. That's the main thing. They'll be safe there. And I'm not letting them have them. I'll knock up something cheap and cheerful for them – after all, I'm doing it for nothing. It'll be good enough to fool them," he chuckled.

"Can you do it, Pa? In five and a half weeks? Greystoke took a whole lot longer."

"Greystoke did all the research. All I have to make are copies – not necessarily good ones at that. Mind, I have to clean the others, too. What are we going to do with those?" He smiled. "Bloody Leggy. Another fine mess he's got me into!"

"Roger, I think you should lock the studio," Jeremy said

softly. "Just in case."

My father nodded. "A lot of just in case around these days," he muttered. "Do you two want to come out with me? Just for a breath of fresh air? It'll make you sleep better."

It didn't. It made me fizz like champagne, wanting to throw myself into a certain person's arms and get lost in him for ever. But of course, Pa was there and we had to go indoors, let him lock up, and then get escorted – yes, escorted! – to our own sleeping quarters. We were opposite sides of the house! So, of course I didn't sleep well. I didn't sleep at all. Rather I smouldered and ran my mind through all manner of feverish dreams, so that when the alarm woke me, I'd only just got to sleep and felt like an old dishrag.

We dropped Jeremy off at the Rev's, so that he could spend some time going through Sam's box file. I had decided against asking Rev. Simmons to sort out my jewel, however, but I had no intention of wearing it until I'd done something to it. It lay well-wrapped in my handbag. Then I drove us into Town.

We parked at the southern end of Bond Street, just before it met Piccadilly, and my mother and her best friend dragged me round the few ateliers that had weathered the war and the peace. Designers and directrices were delighted to show us their styles on living models in the hope of winning clients. They all wanted – as did every woman who had seen the pictures – to show variations on The New Look which Dior had put out while I was convalescing in France. But London wasn't Paris. Although life was getting back to normal, the luxury trades – what else was fashion? – were still suffering from rationing and utility. The average person just didn't have the cash, let alone the coupons. Maman did have the cash. And more to the point, she had style and French chic. She would be a great advertisement for any designer; and both they and she knew it. So Maman, Angelique and I watched the clothes that were brought out for us to admire with interest.

"Ah," my mother purred, "How romantic!"

And very pretty.

There were colours, finishes and shapes I'd forgotten existed.

Hopefully there would soon be bright lives to express the New Look.

We visited milliners where gaiety was already back. You can afford to be profligate with expensive materials when creating something relatively small, witty and stunning. Mind, the glorious hats I saw and tried on didn't come cheap. They were top of the range works of art, and were priced accordingly. Maman bought one for Angelique and two for herself, unable to resist, but as I'd no outfit for the wedding, I held back. I kept the styles in mind, since something 'not quite the same you understand, something individual for you, Madam' could be created – but, it was implied that I'd better move fast.

By half past one we were in Maddy's dining room where we enlightened her on Guy's plans.

"Oh Hell!" she groaned. "The last person I want living just across Sloane Street is my brother – well second to last to be honest. His wife is the last."

"Maddy," remonstrated my mother, "such vehemence is unlike you."

"Yes, well I don't like her."

Angelique raised her eyes and looked at my mother.

"Since when has this come about?"

Maddy looked sulky but said nothing.

Maman patted her hand gently. "No more do we," she confided, "but what can't be cured must be endured. I thought you'd be less than pleased, so I'm going to check the place out. I'll suggest to Roger that it's far too expensive and entirely unsuitable."

"Maman, you can't say that. You don't know how much

it is anyway," I said.

"I can say whatever I like. I'm not putting any money Sylvia's way. As it is she'll end up with Wethersley, that's more than enough. Cadogan Square! Give me a place to entertain from and get back into society! I've seen the sort of society she moves in. And that's not the society I choose to move in. One has standards!"

"What do you know, Maman?" Maddy asked, handing the dish of potatoes across to me, mouthing 'what have you told her?'

I shook my head. 'Nothing' I mouthed back.

"Only what everyone else knows, but ignores, or dare not speak out for the scandals that would ensue. Drugs, my dear. And sex. They often go together. And debts – from gambling, blackmail, that sort of thing. There were always rumours where the Merediths are concerned, and as I always say, no smoke without fire."

She looked from Maddy to me, smiling at our startled faces. "I am very concerned for Guy. He may be a pain, but he is my son. I don't want him mixed up with these people. I hadn't realized that the Nesmith-Browns had connections with them when the engagement was first announced. They've only been in the area a comparatively short while." She helped herself to the gravy then continued. "I'm not sure that I approve of the match now, but he's nearly thirty, and Roger and I have always let you make your own lives…" She turned to Maddy. "Do you have your outfit yet? The wedding is in June."

Maddy giggled. "With a bit of luck the baby will be late and I'll not have to go. No. I've not got anything, Maman. If they had chosen to wait a little longer or even taken it a little sooner, then I should be able to have arranged things better, but babies play by their own rules."

"I think you did it on purpose, Maddy," I said.

"If I'd known, I would have done," she acknowledged.

Shortly after lunch I drove them all to view the house.

In a terrace, of goodly proportions, with no 'for sale' sign outside, it looked somewhat less loved than its neighbours. I rang the bell.

No-one answered, of course, even after the second ring, and a long wait.

Maman strode to number 21 and rang.

A butler opened to us immediately.

She gave him her card. "I've been told that number 19 is for sale. Could you tell me whether this is so?"

The butler looked surprised. "Not as far as I know, Madam. It's not actually used, which is a shame, except for storage, and I've heard the roof is in a bad state. Bomb damage, you see. But it's not on the market."

"You couldn't tell me who it belongs to, by any chance?" she smiled sweetly. "My son who is getting married shortly has set his heart on it, for some reason."

"I'll ask for you, Madam. I've only been here six months. Would you care to step within?"

We all trooped in and he took us into a room with hard chairs round the walls just off the hallway. We each took one, trying to avoid each others' eyes.

Eventually the butler returned with the housekeeper.

She oozed housekeeperliness. "Lady Wetherley, Ladies, you want to know about number 19?"

"Yes please, Mrs. ...?" my mother began.

"Howard, Madam, Mrs. Howard. It'll be a pleasure to warn you off, Madam. It belongs to Mr. and Mrs. Nesmith-Brown. They've not been here themselves since the bombing. Some people use it now as a storage facility. Stuff comes in and goes out at all hours, then nothing for a while. I would strongly advise your son to have nothing to do with it, Madam. It will be more trouble than it's worth."

My mother stood up, triumphant, and clasped Mrs. Howard's hand, pressing a ten shilling note into it. "Thank you so much, Mrs. Howard. You have eased my mind totally. Thank you for your time, and your help." She looked at the butler, and another note passed. "And to you, too, sir. We'll trespass on your time no longer. Goodbye."

When we reached the car she was boiling. "Sylvia wants us to buy her family's house for her? I think not!"

Maddy and I were in stitches. It was a really cheeky wheeze. Or it would be if it wasn't happening to us.

The trouble with our family was that we were too damned upright and honest. We were being taken for fools!

"I take it it was Algy's idea?" I suggested. "Or possibly a Meredith one? To get us tied up in the Wethersley Marsham project?"

Maman and Angelique were spitting feathers in French.

I opened the car doors for them and settled them inside. Maddy edged herself into the passenger seat next to me, both of us suppressing giggles.

We listened to the Provençale accents behind us as I started the car. Maman tapped me on the shoulder. "Alice, drop Maddy home for her nap, then take us to your place. I'll phone Roger from there. I'm driving home, Angelique. I go faster than you."

Angelique sniffed. "You're certainly firing on all cylinders now."

"Exactly. It's always down to me. Guy has to know the sort of family he is marrying into, he should think very carefully. They'll steal his eyes while he's asleep then come back for the eyelashes." She tapped me on the shoulder again. "What are you waiting for, Alice. There are things to be done!"

I was glad to be home alone. Maman in that mood was better off with someone who loved her best of all – Pa.

Angelique was no help at all, being as disgusted by what she had learned as Maman. If anything the family honour was even dearer to her than it was to Maman. The hope of having a calming influence in the passenger seat, was, I realized, a vain one.

"Safe journey," I called as I waved them off. I swear Angelique sniffed, her lips pursed in disdain, but she relented for a second, as Maman kangaroo'd the car away, and managed a smile and a regal wave of her gloved hand before leaving me to my own devices.

I sighed, closed the door behind me and did the stairs again, stopping on the one I'd stopped at … about twenty-three hours earlier. And remembered. Yes. It was good. I'd not felt like this for years. Not allowed myself to. But now the genie was out of the bottle. I didn't know how to get it back. I put the kettle on and looked at the Thorburn box. I wanted to read through the whole lot before we went down to Finchings but it was a bit daunting. I went to my handbag for a cigarette, and noticed the little bag with the pendant. I'd have to do something about that. I wasn't convinced that it was a remote viewing device. Come off it, my logical mind told me. There's no such thing. But Maman's story and the rapid appearance of Guy and Sylvia, with their strangely related demands were unsettling. I had thought about ringing Leggy, but in retrospect wanted to keep our actions as secret as possible. I wondered, for about the hundredth time today, what Jeremy was up to. How had it gone with Sam? Did I trust Sam? Possibly. Probably. I certainly trusted the Rev. Simmons. There was a deep well of goodness there. But Sam? And Bobby? I liked Bobby. Yes, I did. I trusted Emily. And Padraig? He knew I was on the hunt. He knew I'd found two of the angels. I thought about Padraig. He was on Emily's side. Wasn't he? But he was a very social person, and liked holding court in hostelries. I would guess that Rufus Grassington already knew two of the pictures had been found. I would guess that Rufus would have told Padraig he had given me information whereby the rest could be found, and they would be drinking together.

The likelihood of anyone remotely interested in the pictures hearing would depend on the choice of bar they were frequenting. It was possible that the leak came that way.

I didn't want to think of my father's old friend as a willing traitor.

Simply put, too many people knew of the angels' existence now, and of my hunting them. Then of course there were the people who relinquished their hold on the paintings to me. It was more than possible someone had been 'got at'.

Everyone had their price – it need not necessarily be money.

I smoked the cigarette, drank the tea I had brewed, put my feet up and got down to Mr. Thorburn's notebooks.

The shrill peal of the telephone woke me up.

It was dark, and I shivered. I staggered to the light switch, pressed it down then sought the phone. "Hello?" I croaked.

"Alice? Can I come over? I miss you."

"Yes. That would be lovely."

I was suddenly awake.

I tidied a few things away, washed my face, did my hair, got the kettle on and took the rubbish down. The little red car drew up as I was climbing the stairs from the basement where the bins lived. And we were together once again. At last.

We drew apart eventually.

I helped fix the hood in place, as the evening was damp, before having the bucket in my hand exchanged for a small wrapped box.

"What's all this?" I asked.

"Find out. A small token of whatever…"

The Trish Trash Polka was once more blaring out of Mr. Stephens's wireless as we passed.

"Who lives on this floor?" Jeremy asked as we reached the first landing.

"No-one. It's empty. Has been since last Christmas. Why?"

"Just wondered."

"It needs some work on. Like sound-proofing the floors. Mr Stephens has rotten taste in music." I closed the door behind him, my face radiating smiles.

He put the bucket behind the curtain below the sink, and we flew together again. I'd missed him, too. But it was right now.

The kettle started to whistle. "I'll get that. You open your present," he said.

It was a necklace. A gold chain with small perfect pearls inserted between every ten links, delicate and delightful.

"Gosh!" I breathed. It was beautiful. Very Coco. Very French. Simple, and classy.

"Is it acceptable?" he asked. He actually sounded worried. "I couldn't run to diamonds."

"It's amazing. I love it. Thank you, thank you so much."

"I wanted you not to be obliged to wear the pendant," he said. "Can I see it on you? You've got such a lovely neck, Alice."

I let him slide the gold chain round under my hair, but as he did so, I took his face between my hands, and pulled him to me and kissed him.

Long. Hard. Deep.

A proper kiss now.

Eventually he got a necklace fastened, but we were quite breathless by the effort.

"Looks wonderful," he assured me. "God, you're beautiful."

"So are you. Do you mind if I have a look. Tea was promised?"

I slipped out of his reach to the new mirror over the mantel. There was no clock there now. That too had gone. I looked very pink, very happy, and the new necklace sat well on my skin. I grinned back at myself, then across at Jeremy who was spooning tea into the warmed pot. "Thank you. It's lovely. But I've nothing for you."

"Being with you is more than enough for me," he said quietly. "Oh God, I sound like some bloody rubbishy film. But take it in the spirit that it is given. Where's your sugar?"

"In the bowl in the cupboard above the sink. It's probably old and lumpy, and I've only got dried milk. I don't take that either."

I took a box of matches from the mantel shelf and lit the gas fire then drew the curtains.

He brought the tea to the sofa, handing me a cup and saucer. "Biscuits in the barrel, if you need them," I offered.

"Not hungry." He sat beside me. "There are things I need to say, Alice. Big things." He was deadly serious.

I felt an ice cold breeze stirring. Dread. Fear.

Time to gird up the loins.

I took a deep breath. Looked back, straight in the eye. I knew how to hide the gremlins. Head up, girl. Nothing can be as bad as your worst fear.

Or can't it?

"OK. I can take it. You're married with a couple of kids. Worse, still, you're engaged to Elsie."

That really was worse case scenario.

He didn't feel married, although he was old enough to be a paterfamilias several times over, and if he had been, Maddy and Basil would have known, but Elsie was something else.

If there was a reciprocation of emotion there, I was lost.

He'd feel honour-bound to keep his promise, I knew that.

He looked at me as though I were speaking in a foreign tongue, screwing up his brow in an effort to understand.

"Elsie," I jogged his memory. "Your friend Frank's

sister. The beautiful girl who pines for you in Southport."

He shook his head. "What are you talking about? She's my like my little sister."

Now I shook my head.

"That's not how she sees herself," I told him.

"No? It's how it is, Alice. I've known her since she was knee high to an ant. She's a lovely girl, but I don't harbour any expectations in that quarter. I couldn't. She's family. Virtually."

I sighed. I wasn't quite sure whether it was relief for my own situation or sadness for Elsie.

"She's in love with you, Jem," I said softly, using her name for him. "Older brother's friends are almost promised to little sisters when they grow up. Didn't you know that?"

He shook his head. "Actually, that's not true. Of course I knew. So I left, left before she could get any ideas. I'd only see them once or twice a year."

I groaned. "Worse thing possible, the glamorous stranger," I muttered.

"But I never – what was it your father said? I never gave her the slightest encouragement."

He caught me shaking my head.

"Wrong again? Oh, shit! I'd hate to hurt her." He looked like a dog that had been scolded by a loving master. I'd never seen that look before.

"I know. You're an old softy inside. Now what did you want to say that was so important? Before I rudely interrupted you?"

"Ah, yes." He pulled his face back to normal, gave a little laugh and said, "I'm afraid I've been extremely unprofessional."

"Pardon?" From what I'd seen of him, he was extremely professional. I was impressed, and it took a lot to impress me. This was looking at him without rose-coloured glasses or the heady champagne emotions I felt. This was pure detachment talking.

"I broke my own rule no. 1. When I was asked to work with you, I wasn't terribly keen, to be honest. I did it out of loyalty to my boss, and because I had an axe to grind – I wanted to get the Merediths. I wanted our relationship to be at best, that of working partners. I was prepared not to like you. I wanted not to like you. I didn't expect you to like me. I intended, I really did, to remain detached." He looked at me with such warmth, I wanted to hug him. "But you danced into my life. I don't want you to dance out again."

"Is that all?" I asked.

"Holy Shit, Alice, is it not enough?"

"It'll do for a start. You can tell me the rest later," I said, Cheshire Cat grin all over my chops. "If it's any consolation, I had exactly the same feelings. I hate people setting me up, as you know. But this time I'm glad they did. I wouldn't have missed these past … what, eleven days? It's been brilliant."

"You mean that? You really do?"

"Of course I do, you silly man!" I looked him in the eye. "If you do dance out again when the job's over, I shall be extremely put out."

He bubbled with happy laughter. "I'll try not to put Milady out. Promise."

He held out his arms to me and I snuggled in. "OK, tell me about your day, and I'll tell you mine."

"Sam came up trumps," he said, opening his cigarette case one handed. I took one for each of us, and wiggled across to light a spill from the gas fire and lit the two, then handed him one.

"Tell me," I said.

And he did.

Sam had been thorough.

On the Greystokes estate alone was enough to incriminate them on unprofessional practices, but Sam had gone further.

He knew the Nesmith-Browns and had decided to go digging in that field too.

There was hear-say, and there was fact.

The fact was that they were deeply indebted to the Merediths. Bulgy Algy never denied it, in fact, he used it as a recommendation – "I owe everything I have to Percy and Archie. They've made me what I am today."

There was a hold over them. Heavy debts on Bulgy Algy's part, generous help from the Merediths was how Sam put it.

The fact was that their fortunes were interlinked. "To the point of the Nesmith-Brown's being installed in a house in Cadogan Square before the war?" I asked.

"Ah," said Jeremy. "That house?"

"The very same, and it was not very clever of Sylvia, was it?"

"No-one ever accused her of being clever. Did you know that Bulgy Algy and Anthea had at one point belonged to the Straddling Hall group?"

"Where did Sam get that from?"

"Eye witnesses to the fire. They were seen there."

"The fire at Straddling?" I frowned.

Lady Finching hadn't mentioned them. Nor had Mr. Thorburn in his writings – well, he hadn't as far as I had got up to. I wondered if I could check with either of the Finchings.

Jeremy nodded. "Do you know what caused it?"

"I got the impression it was a lightning strike. That's the consensus of opinion in reports of it, but the locals hint at dark and devilish deeds. I'll take the keys with us, over the weekend if you want. We could sneak out and have a look, but the fire was years ago."

Jeremy chuckled. "You really don't have any problem breaking into people's property, do you?"

I shrugged. "If the keys are lying about, they're asking

for intruders," I said, conveniently forgetting that I'd broken into the site hut.

"Does that include Elisabeth's place?"

"Eh? No. I was offered the key. I just thought it would make sense to get a copy made. I don't know whether she will have changed the lock, since she's had the place done up."

Jeremy's face creased into a smile. "Do you fancy finding out?"

"When?"

"Now?"

29

We parked in front of a convent on a side road then wandered around the Boltons arm in arm. As usual it was quiet, but Elisabeth's sitting room was lit up.

"Someone's in," Jeremy said.

We were on the same side of the oval now.

"Give it a go?"

A taxi hurtled round the curve, and swung to halt outside number 35. I automatically slowed down.

"That's Percy," Jeremy breathed as a man got out. "That'll keep her occupied upstairs."

A dog flopped out of the cab after him, sniffed around while its master paid the fare, raised his leg at a plane tree.

"No," I breathed. "It's the other one."

I pulled Jeremy towards me and flung my arms round his neck pulling him round in front of me. "It's the mysterious Archie. And from what I understood, he is not a fan of Miss Thorburn."

"Steady on, Alice," Jeremy said, trying to disentangle a bit.

"Stop it, Jeremy. He's seen me in this coat before," I whispered hugging him against me as the cab drew off.

"Oh, that's alright, then," he said, and buried his face in my neck so I could look over his shoulder.

And I did.

Eyes half-closed, and enjoying the attentions being given, I watched Archie Meredith stamp angrily up the path and hammer on the door. I shuddered with pleasure, but kept watching as he pushed the maid aside and slammed the door behind him.

I pulled away slightly. "You can stop now…"

He released me, perhaps a little reluctantly. "Thank you! That was nice. What did you see?"

I told him, adding "Archie looks very cross indeed."

"That'll keep her even more occupied," Jeremy said softly.

We gave the maid time to get upstairs then slipped through the gate to the alley which led to the studio.

Raised voices on the upper floor told their own story. We skittered past the servants' entrance and kitchen window round the to the studio door.

I held out the key.

"Your key, Alice."

I inserted it as quietly as I could into the lock. It fitted. She hadn't changed the lock. I turned it. It creaked, but it turned.

The place was in darkness, but a cloud of incense smoke billowed out, and caught my throat.

I stuffed my gloved hand over my mouth, pinched my nose with the other one. Jeremy silently closed the door, relocked it, and nodded back the way we came.

I was happy with that idea.

When we rounded the corner of the house the kitchen light shone from the now open window, high up the ground floor wall.

Someone behind it was giving vent to previously suppressed fury.

"I don't get spoken to like that, Mr. Archie Meredith. The old master was right. You are a boor. I hope you gets killed. You and your stupid brother. By God and all I hold dear, I curse the pair of you!"

There was a vehemence and a venom in the voice that made my flesh creep.

I shivered.

"Ha!" came the voice again, along with a rattle of crockery, a tinkle of silver. "There. There's your precious tea, Mister Archie. I hope it chokes you!"

She must have picked up the tray and taken it out, for I heard a door close behind her and her muffled footsteps treading the back stairs.

We both ran for the open, but climbed the low garden wall into the adjacent property before retracing our steps.

"They certainly know how to win friends!" Jeremy murmured. "Can I borrow the key?"

I thought we were going back to my place, but he kept driving, turning off down Beauchamp Place. "You want to give the key to Basil?" I guessed.

"When they'll be away, so will we."

That made sense. "You want to hear about my day? There might be something of relevance."

He was up to speed on the Cadogan Square caper by the time we parked outside Basil's.

"How does one get the key for that property?" I wondered aloud.

"I'd have thought you might have found it lying about. You seem to be good at that sort of thing."

I smiled. "I don't think I want to know what's inside the place. But I would like it looked into."

We rang on the door.

It was opened by Basil, who ushered us in. "What's wrong?"

"Nothing," Jeremy told him.

"Good. All Hell's let loose here. Welcome to Bedlam."

Maddy called down the stairs, "Who is it, Bas?" She sounded put out.

I could almost feel the prickles coming off her.

"It's only Alice and Jeremy. Don't panic."

"Family?" I asked.

"Your mother, your brother, your brother's fiancée, his fiancee's brother, his dog, your brother's fiancée's parents, your father. And now you. The full bloody set." He grinned, evilly. "Like I said, welcome to Bedlam. All we need is my old Mum and the Brigadier, my boring doctor brother and his even more worthy wife and their severely plain children – luckily all in the far East as I speak - and we'd think it were Christmas!"

"Look, we were only coming to give you this," Jeremy said, letting Basil see the key. "We'll just disappear." He started to turn.

Basil grabbed him by the collar. "Oh no, you don't. Come and watch the show. I need someone else detached. The rest of them aren't." Then softly. "The key to where?" he asked.

"35A The Boltons, the studio round the back of the house," I said as he pocketed it. "Belongs to Miss Elisabeth Thorburn."

"You are an angel," he whispered. He opened the door for us. "OK, folks. Two more. You two will have a drink? To catch up with the rest of us?" he asked as he shepherded us into the living room. "I'll take your coats. You know everyone I trust?"

The atmosphere in that lovely room was truly awful.

Maman and Anthea Nesmith-Brown glared icicles at each other.

Guy grimaced accusation and disgust at Pa; Bulgy Algy had his arm protectively round his daughter, but she threw it off and leapt up as soon as Jeremy entered the room, and came for a kiss, while his son, Nigel, sat in a corner, pressing himself into the wall, a small Jack Russell at his feet, gazing morosely into an empty glass.

I felt for him. He didn't need to be in this hostility any more than we did.

Maddy fell on us with open arms, then poured us both a large measure of whisky, "How lovely to see you both, do come in," she trilled.

"I'm not family," Jeremy said, hastily making excuses.

"This looks to be a family meeting."

"*Faineant!*" I hissed, grabbing his sleeve.

Basil barred his exit. "The women in this family have a way of being obeyed," he said, shutting the door behind him. "Learn, and obey!"

My mother glared at Basil. "That's rather trite, Basil. We only ask to be listened to. And our ideas discussed in a civilized manner. In case you didn't know we are equal members of society. We do have the vote."

"I stand corrected, Ma'am!" said Basil, doing her a florid bow. "Now I take it the business we were discussing has been resolved. Yes, of course it has. You don't want to bother Alice and Jeremy with it, do you? So let me propose a toast. Everybody's bumpers filled? No? Well let me fill them. Nigel, you look particularly dry. What was your poison?"

"Scotch, sir. And much appreciated." He brought his glass over to the tantalus and watched as the peaty liquid sloshed into the crystal tumbler then turned his slight body so that he enfolded everyone in his gaze, coughed softly, then drew himself up to his full height which was an inch or so more than me. "I'd like to propose a toast too, everyone. By your leave, sir?" he turned to Basil. "Thank you."

He raised his glass and looked pointedly around the room, giving equal value to each of us. "To peace between warring factions."

"Blimey, Guv," I breathed. "You got it bang to rights."

I held my glass high. "I'll gladly drink to that, Nigel," I said and tossed off a mouthful of Basil's expensive firewater.

The others did too, after Maddy, Basil, and Jeremy had followed my example and shamed them into it.

Then Basil proposed his toast. "To whatever needs to be done," he said when he had everyone's attention. "To whatever needs to be done for a balanced outcome."

He smiled at the company assembled around him.

There was a crumbling of defences. They all wanted peace. There was too much at stake.

"And the courage to do it," murmured Jeremy at my elbow.

"I'll drink to that, too," I said softly.

The party broke up pretty soon after. Maddy hung on to us. "Not you two. You're staying. We need to talk," she hissed.

When we finally left, it was well past eleven; I was glad I hadn't been there from the beginning. Pa had tried very hard to calm Maman, but she wouldn't let him. Then Guy came round and she gave him a few home truths. He got shirty, and said she should tell Algy to his face, but Algy was in town with his lady. Sylvia and Nigel knew where they were, and rang them to meet here, insisting on coming along too. Angelique diplomatically stayed at Wethersley, but I imagine she was regaling the McMurdy's with all the goings-on.

"I thought we'd have him out of the bloody marriage," Maddy said. "I thought he'd break it off, but of course Maman was being voluble and Gallic, making a hell of a scene, and you know how Guy hates a scene, so out of spite he dug his heels in with a firm hand."

"What did Algy say about the house?" I asked. "It is his, isn't it? Why would those people lie?"

"He denied everything, said he absolutely never had anything to do with any house in Cadogan Square. Said Sylvia had got it from an estate agent chum, she's been house-hunting for some time it seems. Guy of course hasn't been in the place. He's left it all to her. And Algy said he knew the chap and trusted him. I'll be looking into it tomorrow, by the way," said Basil. "Said if the house really was in a bad state, then he would be taking steps to ensure that his daughter and her husband would not be conned into buying it. He was wonderfully conciliating. It surprised me, to be honest. I thought he was just a bladder of lard. You didn't hear that from me, by the way."

"So Maman brought the family into disrepute," I said as we left. "Ah well, if it's not her it's one of the rest of us, then."

"What have you been up to, Alice?" Basil asked, with a twinkle in his eye.

I kissed him goodnight. "Nothing... yet. But I'm sure I'll think of something."

"You can come in," I said.

He shook his head. "If you ever decide to invite me in, I will arrive without this very memorable little car and with my toothbrush, shaving gear and a fresh shirt."

I smiled. "Might take you up on that sooner than you think. What are we going to do about the pile of invitations?"

"Choose for me. I'll fit in. But not Friday or this weekend. I have appointments then."

"Thursday's best. I'll sort out the least taxing, and let you know tomorrow."

"Meet me for lunch? Westminster tube station, opposite Big Ben. Around one o'clock."

I went for a swim the following morning, to keep the habit going, but it wasn't so much fun without Thelma. I breakfasted at the café at the pool to save spending my coupons and points on basics like bread and butter. It wasn't good, but it filled a gap. I wondered how long rationing would continue. I thought about Thelma and her sweet tooth. I bet Bobby could get sugar. In fact I knew he could. His fruit cake was full of it. He'd never see Leggy go without. I finished the milky coffee then went home, picking up the London Magazine and The Lady on the way.

I wrote a note of encouragement to Thelma and checked out the magazines for who was doing what and where and what they were wearing. Then I drew what I thought I'd need – bearing in mind the current ethos of make-do-and-mend, and the Utility concept of no more than three and a half yards of fabric for a dress. Actually you could get a pretty good dress from that amount, but Dior it was not. His use of fabric was profligate, but oh, God, it looked absolutely fabulous. I had the height and the waist for it. I could look like a queen in his cocktail gowns.

But that wasn't to be. Not yet, anyway.

I spent a long half hour searching through the remains of my own and my Great Aunt's wardrobe, looking for items that could be reused – because Angelique would have sniffed if I hadn't. It was a salutary experience. The burglary had taken care of most of it – I had a sneaking feeling that George had made a fair amount from the rag-and-bone men - and what was left would not have stood a second washing. I made another bag of rags for George.

When I looked at what remained of Great Aunt Caro, there was a sable coat and three very odd hats safe in their boxes.

I gathered my points and my cheque book and went shopping.

Jeremy was waiting at the tube entrance when I struggled through the barrier with my collection of bags at three minutes after one. He greeted me with a kiss, took the shopping and led me round into Whitehall where a dining room was filling up nicely. We joined the queue and were eventually seated at the far end close to the kitchen entrance. We had the dish of the day – there was no choice – boiled mutton and vegetables. I was certainly ready for it.

"Have you decided where we go?"

"Yes. Lady Fortescue's reception tomorrow night. She's a long-time friend of my mother's, although on last night's showing, I doubt that is a plus. But she'll be happy to see me and anyone I bring along. Formal wear, and you can pick me up around seven. It'll be just drinks and canapes I'm afraid. We'll play it by ear, but I think we should be out of there by half past nine. She's a good hostess, so it will be crowded - Arts rather than Finance, but with a sprinkling of the Law and the Services, I should think, as well as the landed gees, so you'll do a lot of smiling and hand-shaking to the great and the good. You'll be required to make a donation to her pet charity – a tenner should suffice. You could claim it off Basil as expenses, possibly," I said. "Will that suit?"

"I'm speechless! Thank you."

The food was delivered to us. We tucked in.

"Keep your thanks until you've come out again," I told him, working my way round a piece of bone. "The weekend will probably introduce you to another group. We need to plan for that, too, although I have a lot less idea what it will be like than tomorrow night's bash."

"Is that why you've been shopping?" he asked.

"In part. I needed some new things anyway. I've been dressing as I did during the war. It's time for a change."

"I always think you look stunning. But I am biased."

"I hope you'll like the new me. There's another reason, too. When I saw Archie, I was 'someone else'. I don't want him to put 'her' and me together."

He grinned. He looked a lot younger when he smiled. In repose his face could be quite grave. "I don't think he will. I think his mind will be on other things."

"Yes? What do you know that I don't?"

"I'll tell you tonight... possibly."

"Hush-hush?" I teased.

"Possibly. But what I meant was, I'll tell you tonight, if you let me see you tonight."

"Fish and chips?"

"You're on!"

At home I took an afternoon off to sort my wardrobe. I'd spent a small fortune and all my points. It felt great, but I'd been lucky to track the stuff down.

I'd also revived my make up. Lady Sarah would be laid to rest. Archie would not connect her to Alice Chamberlain, novice magician. Lady Sarah was Jolly Hockeysticks and traveled with her uncle the Colonel. Alice Chamberlain was sophisticated, cultured, and traveled with her own chosen gentleman companion.

He arrived at half past four, in the little red car.

George was out like a flash.

"I'm going to the chippie later, George," Jeremy told him. "If you want to come, listen for the horn. One long and two short, OK?" He took the stairs two at a time, leaving me behind.

George nodded. "Yessir. Thank you, mister." Then he looked at me. "Bit keen, ain't he?"

"I didn't think he was that keen," I told the boy, and dammit, I got a really dirty laugh back.

"You've not heard the news, then?" Jeremy said, hanging up his hat and coat. "Do you not listen to the news?"

I shook my head. "What's up?"

"Lord Finching has been found dead. In a boat on the loch. We suspect foul play."

"Oh Hell," I groaned. "Yesterday? Does his wife know?"

"That I don't know, Alice. It stinks. He went out to fish, it is said, after seeing his daughters off on a sea-plane. The rest of the entourage, it seems went the scenic route."

"Train? From Inverness? Who took them there? When? Who was there? Most important, where was Archie?"

"Alice, my darling, you ask all the right questions. The Misses Finching were dropped by plane at Southampton to catch the Queen Mary back to the States. Their arrival was beautifully timed. It was leaving at four in the afternoon. They arrived at three, swanned through customs, and were drinking cocktails and waving goodbye at a quarter to four. Archie in his camel coat and homburg hat, was seen with them but got into a limousine, and drove off before the ship left. He was seen to embark, with the luggage, and to give them each a brief hug and disembark quickly."

"How do you know this?" I asked. "More to the point, should you be telling me?"

"Local reporter, an old mate. I rang him up as soon as I heard. On the QT. Look, Alice, it's not hush-hush. I'm interested. And I know you are. He said Archie was in a stinking mood. Nearly pushed him down, and didn't seem at all his usual self."

"You mean the reporter knows Archie?"

"No, Alice. He knows of him, and has been told that he is a pleasant man. Guess who by?"

"A wild stab in the dark – Bulgy Algy?"

"God, Alice, you're bloody psychic!"

"Holy Shit!" I breathed, adding automatically. "Sorry."

Jeremy shook his head. "No, I'll second that. He left Southampton at a quarter to four, in a limousine. About sixty to seventy miles – a couple of hours give or take. He'd be back in London by half past six."

"When we saw him it was much later than that, and he'd got his dog with him."

"Good God!" breathed Jeremy. "I think you might have him there. Alice, you're a genius. He had his dog with him in Scotland. We've got photographs of him with it, but the chap who got into the limo didn't. He's virtually inseparable from the dog. He wouldn't travel without the damned thing. Yet Archie who accompanied the Finching girls to Southampton didn't have his dog. My friend is a dog-lover – his wife has won Crufts best in show – no, not her, oh, you know what I mean."

I chuckled. "Yes. So he would have mentioned the dog were it there?"

I nodded. "I believe so. I'll check with him if you don't mind?"

"Go ahead." I handed him the phone and started making tea while he put the call through. It would take some time to connect. My concern was with the first part of the news.

Lord Finching was dead.

I was now the legal owner of the pictures. I wasn't too happy about that. I went to the loo and freshened up. When I returned Jeremy was putting the phone down.

"We have him, I do believe. My friend says there was no dog anywhere to be seen."

I handed him a cup of tea. "Whereas when we saw Archie last night around nine thirty he did have his dog. But he couldn't have got back from Inverness on the train. It takes for ever. One of the girls at school came from Scotland. She had a hell of a journey – a day and a half. Even with the best will in the world, and by leaving Inverness at the crack of dawn – should there happen to be a train then and all the connections absolutely perfect, he'd be hard pushed to get down to London the same evening, let alone to Southampton and back to London."

"He must have had another plane," Jeremy said. "I really didn't think he wanted the angel pictures that badly," his voice was thoughtful. "It's obsessive."

"They seem to take people that way," I murmured. "Lord Finching wasn't giving them up. He said the house was full of noise when I phoned. No wonder when he thought he'd got shot of them that he went out for a quiet fish on the loch. He wanted a bit of peace, poor man."

"And got rather more than he bargained for – the permanent sort!"

"Yes, and there's another problem," I breathed. "I am now the legal possessor of the pictures."

"Holy Shit!"

"Yes, I suppose angels do. When that gets out I'll be in the firing line."

He was silent for a moment, biting his lower lip. "Then,

Alice, we must see to it that it doesn't get out. Or at least that the will does not go through Probate at the speed of light. I'll do what I can."

But I could do something. I went to the desk to get Lord Finching's letter, then returned and put through a trunk call to his lawyer.

"Archie Meredith doesn't know you're the beneficiary, Alice. I'm sure of that," Jeremy said. "If he did, he'd be down here now, or sending some heavy down. No, Alice, I mean it. I'm not scare-mongering. He's spent a lot of money trying to get hold of those pictures, if the Finching girls' trip is taken into consideration."

I felt sick to the pit of my stomach.

The pictures weren't that important. Not important enough to kill for.

Surely? Not for a sane person.

"What do you know about Archie Meredith?" I asked him.

"We lump him and Percy together because they are twins. Now separate them. He is the older of the two."

"Very reassuring," I muttered. "I will take it that he doesn't know the terms of the Finching will. He will expect the paintings to go first to his wife, and if she is unable to accept them, then to the daughters. From whom he will collect, I've no doubt." We looked at each other, fingers pointing.

"Lady Finching will be in danger," we told each other.

He reached in his pocket for his wallet and flicked through a wedge of business and calling cards. "Blandings," he said withdrawing one. "Ring the Matron."

I identified myself and waited.

Eventually I was put through.

"Ah, Miss Chamberlain. I take it you are concerned about Lady Finching. There's no need, though. She had a bit of a bad turn earlier. We've had to sedate her. She'll be perfectly alright now the drugs have settled her. Nothing to worry about. She's in safe hands here." Matron was brisk and professional.

"I'm sure she is. Does she know about her husband?"

"Know what?" the Matron asked.

"Ah. Then you don't know either?"

"Not unless something has happened since I spoke with him on Monday night. He was perfectly fit then."

"Just a moment, please, Matron," I said, holding my hand over the phone.

I looked wildly at Jeremy. "She hasn't heard that Lord Finching's dead," I whispered.

"That's crazy. It was on the wireless this afternoon. They must have got the local police down to break the news. Never mind, I'll tell her. Move over."

He took the phone. "Hello Matron, Jeremy Arkwright here. I came down with … yes, that's right. I'm afraid I've got some serious news for you. I thought you would have heard, but of course you would have been too busy to listen to the wireless on duty… Of course, I do understand, although I thought the local constabulary would have called on you by now. It's about Lord Finching. Yes… Yes, you guessed right, I'm afraid …Yes, quite… yes… It is rather a poor show, I agree, Matron… Well, I'm sorry, too, to be a bearer of ill-tidings… Yes, I understand. I'm sure you will deal with it most professionally, Matron. Yes… Good Night."

He cradled the receiver.

"Oops! She's not happy. Feels that the emergency services have failed in their job by not informing her immediately the body was found. I think that she's already writing a complaint letter. And Lady Finching naturally doesn't know. Did she tell you why she's been popped full of drugs?"

I shook my head. "I'd like to know what set her off. And

when."

I thought for a while. "Do you think we could legitimately go down and see her? Or is it just nosiness?"

"It's nosiness, of course, Alice. But I think perhaps we could nip down there. Perhaps Friday. Give the old girl a time to get the drugs out of her system. Have you typed up that statement she wanted to sign?"

"Typed up and sent off for her to sign and return, although I'm not sure how it would stand up in law, her being not always compos mentis. I can't ask her to sign it while she's under heavy sedation."

The phone rang.

I picked it up.

It was the office of Lord Finching's lawyer.

A pure Edinburgh accented woman's voice that told me Mr Jardine was already away home. I gave her my number and asked her to get him to ring me in the morning as soon as possible, with regard to Lord Finching.

"Of course, Madam," she said. "Thank you for calling. Goodnight to you."

Jeremy stifled a yawn. "Do you think the chippie's open yet?" he asked.

I glanced at my watch and nodded. "Let's get George!"

30

Thursday was going to be important, I knew, as I dressed that morning. Mr. Jardine rang at nine o'clock, while I was finishing breakfast, but that was fine by me.

"How can I help you, Miss Chamberlain?" he asked, after I had answered a barrage of questions to ascertain I actually was who I purported to be.

I told him.

"I have no intention of letting the Will be read or executed until I have ascertained the truth as to how his lordship met his death," he said grandly. "You may rest assured of that. When that has happened will be soon enough for your secret to be revealed. Er... you do have them?"

"Yes, sir," I said. "Although nowhere in my immediate environment."

"That's good enough for me. Keep them safe. His Lordship was convinced that you were the best person for the job. It's a big responsibility."

"So I'm finding out," I said. "Thank you for reassuring me, sir, and for ringing back. Goodbye, Mr. Jardine."

I cycled to Leggy's immediately after breakfast, to find out what he knew about anything.

"Why should anyone tell me anything, Alice?" he asked, innocently.

"Because you never retired. You just put yourself in mothballs as a disguise," I said, convinced I was right.

"Oh, Alice, I'm a businessman now. A wheeler-dealer. In antiques, bygones and objets d'art. Bobby's out on a call at this moment," he assured me. "Honest injun!"

I snorted. "You're still working. It's a cover."

He sighed, looked at me over his horn rims. "Do we ever

stop doing what we're good at? Now what are you going to tell me? I know you've got something on something – or someone."

I told him about seeing Archie with dog. I told him of our phone call to Blandings. And our visit and the things I had found out as a result of the discussion with Lady Finching.

"Ah!" he said, sucking hard on the pipe, puffing out clouds of blue fragrant smoke.

I continued. "I'm concerned for the safety of Lady Finching. There may be an attempt on her life, so that all things would go to the girls – and thus to Archie. And as I know, the Lady is being sedated at present in a private nursing home."

"Hmm." Leggy pursed his lips. "Do you think the nursing home is pukka?"

"I wondered whether you might be able to find out. I think it is. I hope it is. It felt OK when I went down there, but I don't know. I might just be over-reacting. I'm going to call tomorrow when she should be coming back to normal. I don't know what I might find."

"I'll make some enquiries and let you know. Make sure you take that young man with you, or I'll get Bobby to keep an eye on you. He'd like that."

"They know Jeremy," I said, "but thank you for the thought. And thank you for your help."

"Not at all, my dear. You'd best be off. The little spiv will be back soon. I dread to think what he'll be bringing back for me."

I decided to invest a shilling for the family honour and cycled back to Chelsea Town Hall where I looked at the electoral register. Number 19 Cadogan Square was officially lived in by one Thomas Talbot.

Since it was a fine day, and still comparatively early, I cycled on, right into town, through Victoria, and along Whitehall to the Strand. I tied up my bike outside the Land

Registry buildings, and went in. It would take a bit of time, but I wasn't meeting Thelma until half past one. I came out some time later satisfied. I had the copy I wanted.

I took Thelma to lunch at a Lyons. She was still stiff. "You don't bounce so well over thirty," she said. "And I've never been a light-weight." She tucked into steak and kidney pudding, mash, mushy peas and gravy with a will. "I like this stuff too much."

I collected the envelope I had given her, and told her that the angels were together once more.

"Where are they?" she asked, excitedly. "When can I see them?"

"Not yet. They need some restoration," I told her. "When they're done I'll let you know, but Mum's the word for the moment."

"Are you going to use Rufus Grassington?" she asked.

"Why?"

"Mr. Arnold mentioned him. Said he'd been somewhere and seen Mr Grassington, who was sounding off about angel pictures."

"What?"

"It seems Mr. Grassington thinks they're really important – and he's been telling everyone he's the only person who knows how they work now, who really knows, and that their real owner was scared of their power so he sent them away, all over the country, but it was their time to come together again."

I put down my knife and fork. "And?"

She shrugged. "Mr. Arnold said he knew beer talking when he heard it, but it struck him as odd seeing as you were searching for pictures. He wondered whether they were the same ones."

"Oh dear! Did he say anything? Do you know who else was there?" I asked.

"I think it was at the Chelsea Arts Club, so your guess

is as good as mine. Mr. Arnold went as a guest of … er… quite an important client, so he would have kept a relatively low profile, I think. I'll find out if you want," she offered.

"I'd like that very much," I said thoughtfully. "If other people heard him, he may be in danger."

Or I might, I thought, if he'd mentioned my name.

I cycled home then spent the afternoon with the beauticians, having the full service.

I got home at five thirty, to a wolf whistle from George, so it was money well spent. I went upstairs and packed for the weekend then got my outfit ready for this evening. It was new.

It had to be.

Maman might get away with pre-war Mme Coco's but I wouldn't be doing myself or my protégé any favours trying to do the same. Besides, I was half English, and born in England, so I should fly the Union Jack, not the *Tricoleur* when it came to designers.

What I chose was a very plain dress in heavy midnight blue silk. It had the latest shape, although it was neither as long or as full skirted at M. Dior would have liked, but it did have a deep scooped neckline and tight-fitting three quarter length sleeves, both of which suited me. I felt darkly mysterious in it. Jeremy's necklace enhanced it, so did the extra height I got from my black court shoes. As for a hat – well Aunt Caro had one that would be perfect, a tiny confection in dark blue velvet adorned with a minute delicate veil held on by the eye of a peacock's tail feather. It simply sat on the crown of the head (i.e. was stuck into the hair with an integral comb then pinned on with the appropriate hat-pin) and floated over you like a pretty and insubstantial haze. The veil didn't even get as far as the forehead.

I was preening myself when the bell went. I took Aunt Caro's coat, her best gloves (they were with the hat, bought to be worn together), evening bag – black silk – applied a final misting of Joy, and lipstick, then went. I was really looking forward to the evening.

Lady Fortescue was her usual gracious self. "Barbara said she thought you'd be fetching up here, Alice. She's over there holding court. Dying to meet your friend, by the way. Mr. Arkwright, Jeremy, isn't it? Delighted to make your acquaintance. Any friend of Alice is welcome under my roof. You don't play golf, do you? I knew that was a blinder. Told Barbara so. She's so silly, she believes everything one tells her, and Alice is a bit naughty sometimes. Not that Bar doesn't need a poke occasionally. Go and see her, and she'll point you through to people. Oh, and by the way, you both look stunning. Have a good time, and I hope to speak to you later."

She was sixty, but looked a good ten years younger, due, she always said, to good living.

I slipped my hand through Jeremy's arm and waved at a gaggle of people lining the staircase. "Barbara, darling!"

I heard him smother a laugh.

"Shut up!" I hissed. "I'm doing this for you."

"And I'm truly grateful, but your accent has trilled another two notches up the social scale. You sound like the daughter of a duke at least," he whispered.

"And yours hasn't? Listen to thasel', my Lancashire lad?" I was chuckling now.

Barbara came to greet us, and receive her thanks and kisses, handshake and bow, and then introduced us to those around her.

"This is Tom. He's my photographer. Take a snap of these two, Tom, they at least have a modicum of youth and beauty on their side. Good man. He's only just got back from Scotland doing the publicity on those two slack Finching girls."

"They're movie-stars, Bar, dear," Tom said. "Going to make it big in Hollywood, don't you know? They've already got wealthy husbands over there within the industry."

"Nonsense, Tom!" Bar retorted. "They're a couple of little trollops, no matter how you look at them."

"Can't disagree with that, and I think it's probably safest down a viewfinder. But they have provenance, and their father's a nice chap, despite the rumours that he's barking. Very put upon and put out by the whole business but exceeding generous to we lackeys. Kept a very good cellar with a damn fine collection of single malts. Bottled heaven. Told us to make free of it, but not to let that bastard Meredith or his smelly dog anywhere near them."

There was a flash as he took our photographs. "Good. They'll be in the next issue, I've no doubt."

Barbara chuckled. "Editor, now, Tom? I think not. But we will try to put you in."

"How was it at Boleskine?" I asked. "Apart from icy cold?"

"Oh, the temperature, physical was freezing," Tom chuckled, shooting out the spent flash bulb and writing down who we were on his check-list. "But the emotional temperature was sky-high. There were horrendous arguments. They were all at it – Meredith and Lord F, Meredith and the two girls, the two girls and Lord F, the girls' dressers were at each other's throats, and the dog, that smelly dog, was bloody incontinent. Doubly and frequently! It was fun! But what the hell, Meredith paid well, and the pictures, if I say it myself, are damned good. It's a very atmospheric place. Make a superb film set, but I wouldn't want to live there. Poor old Lord F doesn't now. That was a shock. I've had the cops round shaking my memories out of me."

"So the film-stars have gone home, now?" Jeremy asked. "Back to the States."

"Oh yes. Funny though, I thought Meredith would go with them, in their plane, to gather every last ounce of publicity down at Southampton. He was bossing and ordering all the time, and it would have been no problem for him to have got a photographer out there, but he didn't. Odd that. Nor did he come on the train with us. Can't say I was saddened."

He smiled a crooked smile, that showed a broken front tooth. "It was a long journey and we – the workers – spent most of it drinking and sleeping. We'd worked like dogs those five days, and Meredith's an unpleasant taskmaster, particularly when things aren't going his way. I don't know what he wanted off him, but Lord F wasn't giving it up. Told Meredith he would be the last person he'd give it to. Told him to take his daughters and his stinking dog and go to hell."

He chuckled at the memory. "Not very fatherly, but then the girls weren't exactly daughterly."

Bar chuckled. "That's enough gossip, Tom. I've heard nothing but your Scottish travails since you got back this afternoon. We're working, or have you forgotten?"

A circulating waiter passed, and Tom helped himself to a glass and drank. Then he winced. "God, I hate sherry!"

Bar took his glass immediately and handed him her own empty one. "Mmm. A very nice manzanilla; waste not, want not," she said, and downed the drink swiftly. "It'll see me through the evening. You should develop a palate, Tom."

"I'll stick to brown ale and malt whisky," he muttered. "That way I can mix with all classes – of men."

Bar snorted a laugh as she put the glass on a side table, then slipped an arm round both of us. "Come on, I'll introduce you to people who really matter, not just to gossiping Grub Street boys."

And she did us proud.

By the end of the evening I was certainly back on the scene and Jeremy was hanging on my coat-tails.

We said goodbye to Lady Fortescue. "I think you achieved your end, my dears," she said. "Come and see me in the near future. I'll make sure you get to the right places.

And there'll be no mention of golf."

"Success," I said, slipping my hand through Jeremy's arm as we walked down the steps to the waiting taxi. "You did well. They liked you."

"They liked you, Alice. Quite rightly. I thought your sister had style, but you could teach her."

Praise indeed. "Thank you kindly," I said.

"Where to, Guv?" asked the driver.

"Fancy going out on the town?" Jeremy asked.

I nodded.

"Soho," he said. "I'll tell you where when we get there."

Midnight found us in a little dive in Greek Street where the floor was no larger than a pocket handkerchief and packed. The band was tremendous, so good, in fact that we perched on stools at the bar to listen, mesmerized. The drummer lifted you way above earth. The place rocked with almighty applause when he finished his solo and brought the band back together again, and the clapping continued until the piece finally finished. It was not a 'known' band, just a collection of musicians, but they took us to the stars that night. I waved madly and blew a kiss to the drummer and got a glad eye back as they stepped off the podium. "Buy them a drink, Jeremy, they've earned it!"

"Got them set up already, Alice." He got his cigarette case out. "Isn't that Bobby over there?"

It was, and he was coming over.

"What'll you have, Bobby? The usual?"

Eh? So they were closer than I had suspected, but the barman knew anyway.

He pulled a bottle of Guinness from under the counter and poured it tenderly.

"You're a toff, sir," said Bobby taking a deep draught of the black brew. He wiped his creamy moustache and eyed me up. "And you, Milady, are a picture. I've been hunting for you everywhere. That little lad said you looked like you were going out on the town. I've been in every bloody dive I could think of. What the hell brought you to this place?"

"I might ask you the same," I said archly. "Did you hear the band?"

Jeremy leaned back on the bar, grinning, smoking a Pasha, looking very smug.

Bobby shook his head. "For me, Milady, it was the logical conclusion of my up and down trawl of Soho," he said drily. "I was working, Milady."

He took a pouch of tobacco out of his pocket and started rolling. "Leggy said to tell you that the place you asked about is in serious financial difficulties. The matron is thought to be a good sort, but financial temptation would be hard to resist. He suggests you get down there ASAP and get the lady in question out. Although what you are going to do with her, I haven't the faintest idea. It appears she is unwell at present."

He lit the roll up and drew in the smoke. "I'm only the messenger boy, Milady. And it's too late to go anywhere tonight, apart from to kip."

31

"What do you mean 'Lady Finching is not available'?" Jeremy asked the Matron, his voice low but urgent. It was 8.30 am and we were in her office.

She looked harassed.

"Miss Chamberlain told you we were coming to see her. Even if she is asleep we want to see her."

I was glad he was dealing with this. He radiated righteous indignation and the Matron knew she was cornered.

"So where is she?" he demanded. We weren't playing now.

The Matron was made of stern stuff, I'll give her that. "I'm not at liberty to say, Mr. Arkwright."

We stood silent before her, putting all our effort into our gazes. She was not a small woman, but we could out-face her, looking down at her with iron faces.

We waited.

Eventually she gave in, sighed, sank down into her chair. "I made sure she was settled last night. She was. As well as could be expected. This morning when the staff went in to wake her, her bed was empty. They sounded the alarm, but she is nowhere in the grounds. We have searched everywhere." She sighed. "I'm telling you the truth!" Her voice was high and taut.

She must have realized she was sounding hysterical, for she took a breath and dropped it an octave. "I have no reason to lie. Lady Finching is one of our better residents. Her bills are paid on time, no questions asked. We both knew that this is no way for her to live, but with her history, this is the best she could expect. I never had her down as an absconder. We rubbed along well together, or so I thought. ."

She slumped in her chair. "Until Wednesday morning."

"What happened Wednesday morning?" I asked gently.

"She got a letter. It contained only pictures cut from newspapers."

She delved in a drawer in her desk and brought out a buff envelope and handed it to us. I drew out the contents. A black and white photograph showed May and June with Archie Meredith at the Dorchester. He looked triumphant, sneering almost into the camera while the two girls draped themselves suggestively around him. His dog gazed adoringly up at him. Above it in cut out letters from various headlines was the word 'Beltane'.

I shivered.

"Looks like the man who has everything," Jeremy muttered, disgusted.

"Did you keep the envelope?" I asked.

"No. She had flushed that down the loo. If there was any other communication, she had got rid of that too. By the time I got to her she was crazy, cursing and swearing, threatening all sorts of mayhem. We had to sedate her for her own good."

Yes, and your own peace of mind, I thought, unkindly. And for the greater good, of course. You didn't want to start the rest of the residents off.

"Do you know who these people are?" the Matron asked. "Why would this picture have triggered such a reaction?"

Jeremy said very quietly, "They are her daughters, and that is the man who is responsible for her situation here."

The Matron crumpled. "Oh my Lord! Oh dear, oh dear. Poor woman. Who was the cruel beast who sent her this? If I get my hands on ..." she shook her head.

She was silent for a moment. "Ideally I should inform the police, but I need to speak with the governors first. I was about to do so when you arrived. Meanwhile, if there's anything I can do for you, while you're here. You seem to have her interests at heart, which is more than I can say for the rest of the outside world."

We spoke to the carers. They were contrite. Shocked. Covering themselves. Of course. A job is a job.

We looked at the security. A determined person could get through, despite what the Matron and Lord Finching thought.

And she'd taken a suitcase.

"Time?" Jeremy asked the Matron, when she had finished her phone calls.

She was sitting at her desk looking haggard. Obviously the governors weren't pleased. Her survival was on the line. I felt for her. She was where the buck stopped, here.

She looked up at him. "I was the last person to see her last night – around nine thirty. We keep early hours here. Nurse Tilley looked in through her door around midnight – there are windows in the doors, and said she was there then, but she didn't go in. Since the woman was on medication no-one expected her not to be there. And Nurse Trafford called in on her at 7 this morning. She wasn't there then, and the pillows were stuffed in the bed to simulate a body."

I groaned.

"Matron, this is no reflection upon you or this centre, but could you tell me how the sedation was administered?"

The Matron nodded. "I was wondering when you'd get to that. The first doses are by injections. That's found to be fastest. But yesterday we decided to revert to oral. She hates needles and generally is compliant with taking medication."

She looked me squarely in the eyes. "She could easily have spat the pills out once the nurse had gone to another patient. No-one expected her to not comply. It would have been going against all her patterns."

"Quite," I agreed. "You obviously all did your very best for her."

It looked mucky though.

Lady Finching had had a possible nine hours to get wherever she wanted to go. And the determination of the damned.

"Matron," I asked, remembering. "Did she get my letter? I sent it shortly after we were down last with a document to sign and return."

"I don't remember anything being said... I'll check with the staff for you, and if she did get round to signing it, I'll most certainly let you have it, police permitting," she assured me.

We left her phoning Mr. Jardine.

We could do nothing more there for her. Sympathy was one thing, interference another. This was a job for the police and similar agencies, and we had other things to do.

"Who do you think sent it?" I asked. We were driving back to London.

"Anyone who knew where she was and bore her ill-will. Pity she got rid of the envelope. What's Beltane? Someone's name? A place?"

"It's one of the old Celtic Festivals," I said quietly. "It's what we are going to celebrate this weekend!"

She would know the date, the place and the time.

Who sent her the picture?

Someone with this insider knowledge.

Someone with a malicious mind.

"I don't like this, Jeremy. That picture was enough to turn her." I felt icy, and hugged myself to keep in the chill foreboding that was surrounding me. "She's admitted to us that she committed murder while the balance of her mind was altered. She didn't have to do that."

"Manslaughter," he said. "But you're right. Basil needs to know this." He skidded to a halt by a phone box and went in. I huddled in the passenger seat, fitting a Gauloise into my holder, lighting it.

I wasn't scared.

But the stakes had just got far higher and I was uneasy. I had no idea what to expect from this weekend but I hadn't bargained for the presence of a possible homicidal maniac. Which was a shame, because from what Mr. Thorburn had written about Beltane – the May celebrations of pagan Britain with all their fertility symbolism and the reawakening of the Bride of Earth, it looked as though it might have been a bit more fun that the Christian celebrations that I had been brought up on.

Jeremy poked his head out of the phone box, put his hand over the receiver and looked at me. "Alice, do you want to call it off? Basil is suggesting we might care to pull out…"

"What? No! Of course not," I said. "I just wanted him to know that Lady F has disappeared and that she may be planning to meet up with the Merediths. And if she does, then I think there'll be some fireworks."

He nodded and retreated back in the box, spoke a little longer then hung up. "He's putting out a missing person on her," he told me slamming the car into gear.

"How dare he suggest we pull out!" I exclaimed. "I thought he knew me better than that."

"He probably did it to ensure you chose to continue."

I snorted. Yes, that was tactics, but I hoped Basil didn't think he'd have to use such measures on me. "Do you think she knows of her husband's death yet?"

"It's possible, probable even. I think she'll be making her way to Finchings this weekend. One way or another."

"You mean someone's set her up. She's had help from outside?"

He nodded. "It would make sense."

I thought about it.

There could have been more to the letter than just the picture.

"Someone on the outside, someone from the original group… Someone who bore the Merediths ill-will. Someone who knew Lady Finching's secret," I mused. The Gauloise didn't help me think, but it did calm me. "Any ideas?"

"Don't bite my head off, but what about Leggy? Would he play a game like that? Ends justifies the means sort of thing?"

It wasn't something I wanted to consider, but I knew I had to. Suspect everyone, that was the trick. He had enough enmity for the Merediths to play a card like that, and he used to work in the Special Operations Executive, let's not forget.

"I'd like to say no," I said at last. "But... I honestly don't know. And I don't want to ask him. The water's muddy enough already."

He glanced at his watch. "I've got to go to work, Alice. Will you let Elisabeth know we'll be down at Finchings late this evening?"

The Boltons was in full bloom now.

I parked my bike against a tree, and ran up to the door. The maid answered. Madam wasn't at home. Would she be back before Sunday? Oh yes. She'll be back for lunch. I left a note.

It was such a beautiful day I didn't want to be indoors. I cycled up to Cadogan Square. I wanted to look around on my own.

It wasn't to be.

Maddy was pushing Enid along the pavement in her push-chair. I thought she had a nanny to do that.

I cycled on past her, round the square once more then swept into a mews and parked up. And I watched her. She was good.

The thing about being very pregnant and having a little toddler in a push chair is that you can stop to catch your breath, talk to the child, or strike up conversations with anyone at all of the female gender. She chatted to at least two members of European aristocracy of advanced years, several nursemaids and their charges, assorted housemaids, oh, and various others, including the postman on his second delivery. From the glances that were cast towards number 19, I got the impression that I was seriously outclassed on the gathering of gossip front.

Since she was taking it very slowly I parked my bike by a lamppost and sauntered to the rear of the houses where the garages and service entrances were to be found. Several were open revealing chauffeurs tending their thoroughbred charges, coach-built Daimlers, a Rolls-Bentley. This was rich-man's territory.

I got a whistle from a couple of grease monkeys servicing a piece of top-class engineering.

"Cheers, lads!" I said, with a smile.

"Hey, she speaks! What's a nice girl like you doing down an alley like this?"

"You'd be surprised," I told them.

They were both upright now, the sick motor forgotten.

One, he who spoke, was a snub-nosed cheeky-chappie of around eighteen. The other was probably twice his age, probably related. He grinned and pulled a half-smoked roll up from behind his ear. "Care to enlighten us, then? It's time we took a break from Daisy's innards."

"Yes. I'm trying to find out what goes on in number 19, but strictly on the QT."

"Oh, we are the souls of discretion," said the young one, rolling a cigarette the diameter of a matchstick.

"Indeed? Care for a proper cigarette?" I offered my Gauloises.

"French?"

I nodded.

The older one's eyes gleamed. "Haven't tasted them since the Landings. Cheers, Miss."

I let them light up, and lit my own.

The younger one coughed. "Blimey, Miss, that's strong!" he spluttered.

"So what can you tell me about number 19?" I asked.

"Geezer who lives there ain't a toff. Tommy Talbot, biggest crook I know. And he don't live there all that often. He's East End born and bred. Nasty bit of work."

"He comes and goes," said the younger one. "He has some dodgy friends, too. Why do you want to know?"

"I'm more interested in the house itself," I said. "I heard it was on the market."

"Then you heard wrong. We'd know if there was anything for sale round here, like number 43 what's been made into flats, and no-one's breathed a word about 19. Where would poor Tommy go if he hadn't got that place to bolt into and to use as his warehouse?"

"He uses it as a warehouse? In what way?"

Now they were both eager to dish the dirt.

"I'll tell it, Fred," said the older one. "I seen it all come in. He gets deliveries, see. A big old furniture van comes up and unloads. About once a month, once every six weeks. Then people come and gradually the place empties over a week or two, until the next time."

"What sort of things?" I asked.

"All sorts of stuff. Crates and boxes, sometimes furniture and pictures, and all under the cover of darkness."

"Are you telling me he's fencing stuff?" I asked. "Don't the police know?"

"You tell us, Miss," said the younger one. "I know people have complained, like neighbours, but nothing's been done so far."

"Hell!" I swore.

They grinned.

I took a final draw on my cigarette then ejected it from the holder and crushed it with my shoe.

"If you're going to make a complaint, Miss, you didn't

hear it from us, right?"

"I never heard a thing from you, gents," I said with a wink.

"Nice talking to you, Miss. Come on Fred, back to work, my lad."

I wandered on to the rear entrance of number 19.

It was no different from any of the others in design, but it was less well kept. I got the impression that the inside would parallel it, and also parallel the layout of the garage that Fred and lad were working in – that is to say a deep garage basement that was beneath the working parts of the house, with lifts for people and goods, a sink and electric points. Possibly there would be a service staircase that came down to this level too. I'd got a good look while I smoked my cigarette with my new friends. Number 19 was locked.

I was glad, to be honest, because had it been open I would have gone in.

I gave the door a tentative push but it held firm. I sauntered back past the two mechanics, gave them a wave, and picked up my bike. As I did so Maddy was crossing the road towards me.

She was about to shout, but I put my finger to my lips and nodded to the left. I cycled out of the square and met her at the second corner.

"What the hell are you doing here?" she demanded.

I shrugged. "Nosing. What about you?"

"I'm taking my daughter for a walk. As anyone can see." She glared at me.

"I'll buy you lunch at Lyons," I offered.

"I have lunch ordered at home," she snapped.

"How about a knickerbocker glory then? I'm sure Enid would love a jelly."

"You bitch, Al!" she swore as her daughter caught her name and the magic word and started chanting "Jelly, jelly, jelly!" with eyes full of hope and desire.

Then she bent to Enid. "Yes, your wicked auntie Al will buy you a jelly, sweetheart, and Mummy will make her spend all her pennies on a great big knickerbocker glory."

It was only a few minutes walk, and during that time I told her what the mechanics had told me.

She nodded. "It's all a bit peculiar. Bas said that it was registered as belonging to Bulgy Algy, but someone called Talbot has it on a ten year lease, which will be up in October. And if, as you say, Talbot is a known villain…"

"My sister the sleuth," I chuckled.

"As I was saying before I was so rudely interrupted, sister dear, if he is a known villain, why has nothing been done about him? If various neighbours have complained, and this is a very wealthy neighbourhood, one would expect results. Money talks round here. Normally."

We crossed the King's Road and parked the bike and the push-chair outside Lyons. Luckily we were late enough for the dessert treats to be ready.

"This'll spoil Enid's lunch," Maddy said, spooning red jelly filled with tinned fruit salad into a delighted child.

"What was on the menu for her?"

"Probably something disgusting," Maddy replied with a grin. "It's the staff's day off, so I'm the cook."

"So you lied to me, you evil creature!"

She smirked. "A necessary skill in a diplomat's wife. We could have our lunch here, but in reverse, desserts first? Or we could make a lunch of two desserts."

"Excellent idea!" I agreed.

Later I pushed the bike down Sloane Street and accompanied her home. Enid sat on the saddle supported by her mother for a short way, but it was too high and too wobbly for her to be really comfortable, so we took her into the gardens in Pont Street and let her have a run around while we took the sun. It was a good day, blue sky, warm sun, and spring flowers were at last showing their faces in war-battered London. You couldn't stop nature. Well, you could, but eventually she'd win.

"Does Pa know about no 19?" I asked, meaning had Basil told him about Mr Talbot.

"Yes. I think he'll tell Guy. Our silly brother will have to take a good look at who he's getting into bed with."

"Eh? Pa doesn't know about Sylvia, does he?"

"I don't know. I wasn't privy to the conversation, but I'd say not." She sighed. "Al, it's so awful. I mean, even if he wanted to break it off, he'd look such a cad. If anyone does the breaking off of engagements, it's got to be the girl. Even you know that. Women are allowed to change their minds, men have to stand by their word. It's traditional."

"I know. And it's rubbish!"

"Perhaps, but it's one of the few rights women have." She twisted awkwardly. "Damn this child, it's kicking me." She grabbed my hand and put it on her belly. I felt a movement from within - fascinating. "There, you little rascal, that's your big Auntie Al, and she'll tell you off when you get out for kicking her little sister. So behave."

The kicking continued while she spoke, but then ceased.

"See, the magic touch!" I said, standing up. "I've got to go, Maddy. I'm going to Elisabeth's circle this weekend. Out in the country."

She looked up at me. "Take bloody good care of yourself, then, Al. I don't want you getting hurt."

32

We set off from my place at 6 o'clock. London was crowded, but once we got out the roads were virtually empty between the towns.

This journey into Essex was as different as it could be from the one I'd made two weeks earlier. The weather had improved beyond belief and the countryside had woken into Spring beauty, with cow parsley making a lace edging to the roads, and where there were woodlands, bluebells scenting the air. Above us wild cherry and pear blossom. Traveling in the Morgan with the roof off was glorious, like being on a push-bike, but faster and a lot less strenuous. I loved it. May had come at last with the promise of summer, leaving that awful long cold winter far behind. I hoped it was an omen.

Straddling first.

At the Hall there were chain-link fences everywhere and large lights around the building site, far different from when I last came. Definitely no entry now, with signs everywhere telling us so.

The hall itself loomed darkly. "It looks almost complete," Jeremy said.

"That's what I thought," I agreed. "Do you want to go further?"

A guard dog gave a bark nearby, and another, coming from the house itself, barked an answer.

"No," he said softly. "We are expected elsewhere and time moves on."

There had been no dogs before. Had my visit sparked off these changes?

It was chilly now and getting dark. We strolled back

down the footpath and regained the car, and within five minutes arrived at Finchings.

Percy and Elisabeth greeted us joyfully, and introduced us to Archie, who shifted his spaniel off his lap and rose.

He shook my hand, nodded. "Pleased to make your acquaintance Miss Chamberlain. I've heard so much about you." His words were welcoming but his eyes were not. He stared coldly at me. "I haven't met you before, have I?"

"I'm sure I would have remembered if we had met, Mr. Meredith," I said, with a shy smile.

I wondered just what he had heard about me and from whom. This was a chap who would do his homework. He looked a lot sharper than his twin. "Perhaps you've seen my face in the society papers?" I suggested lightly. "As I saw yours recently. With a couple of film stars?"

"Ah, that's very possible, my dear," he smiled, lips only, and nodded holding my hand still. "The name's Archie. My friends call me Archie, and I'm sure we shall be friends." He raised my hand to his lips and pressed a kiss on it, then allowed me to go. I refrained from snatching away and smiled politely back. I could do cold eyes too. "Thank you, Archie. My name is Alice. And my friend is called Jeremy."

"Pleased to meet you, Jeremy. Now what will you both have?"

We settled on a scotch each, and then were shown to our rooms.

"I thought there would be others," I said to Elisabeth as we walked down a loggia to the guest building.

"Oh, they're all coming tomorrow. I wanted you here tonight so I can take you through the paces and answer any questions early tomorrow morning, before you go into full circle after lunch. I wouldn't ask anyone to go into a ceremony unprepared."

She led us through what I thought was a garden door, but behind it was another range of buildings. Our rooms were in that range, adjoining and sharing the same bathroom which was set between the pair.

"I've put robes in your closets," she said. "For the ritual. But I'll go through all that tomorrow. Just get yourselves comfortable, then come back and join us. You'll find the way back easily enough, I assure you."

I took my suitcase from Jeremy, and went into my room. "See you in a mo'," I said.

I remembered Emily's description of the place.

Ten years on and the place was still luxurious. The rooms were supremely comfortable with fitted furniture in the modern style, simple but extremely rich drapes and fittings, and the bed – well it was huge. But best of all, as I was suddenly very cold, the central heating was on.

I unpacked my case then I went to look at the bathroom; sumptuous - green and grey tiles with a key pattern, a bath large enough for two, with a shower attachment and curtain, a large sink, and in its own cubicle, a toilet and bidet. I was impressed. That really was pushing the boat out in England. Then there were the thick pile grey towels and a plethora of cleansing and beauty products. I was doing a systematic sniff test when Jeremy came into the bathroom for his inspection.

"Impressive, all this just for guests," he commented, stroking one of the towels.

"If you're using this place as a showroom, or a weekend here as a sweetener, this isn't too grand. They must have thought the facilities at Wethersley were prehistoric." I replaced the shampoo on the shelf.

"They didn't stay there," Jeremy said with a grin. "They stayed with Bulgy Algy. Talking of whom, have you ever been to his stately pile?"

"Never been invited. What's your room like?"

"I'll show you mine if you show me yours!"

I chuckled, followed him through the interconnecting

door. The room was identical to my own, but in mirror image.

"Nice," I said.

"No complaints at all," he said, drawing me towards him.

While we embraced, he whispered, "I think we need to be very careful. I wouldn't be surprised if there were scanning devices rigged up. We should give both rooms a good once over."

"*Justement*," I replied, then stopped talking. There were better things to do.

Finding the way back wasn't a problem as such.

We followed the only route open to us, discovering as a result that we were housed in a cul-de-sac. "Rats in a trap," I breathed.

"But rats can learn," Jeremy whispered. "We shall learn. Now let's just play the lovers for them. I think that's what they want."

"So it's just a game?"

"It's work, Alice. Think of it as overtime." He dropped a peck on my cheek. "I do love you, Alice."

"Professional to the last!"

"That's me. And you, too. I've noticed that. It's good. Come on, let's meet the family."

Of course, I had forgotten that.

And families notoriously didn't get on all the time. Well, mine didn't and I don't think we were exceptional.

Voices were being raised.

"It's my house, Elisabeth, and I won't have it!" Archie roared. We could hear him way back in the corridor.

We stopped in our tracks. I slipped my shoes off. They made a hell of a noise on the terrazzo floor. Then we crept forward to listen better.

"You will if you want those paintings back," Elisabeth said. "We all know she went after them."

"Huh," snapped Archie. "What do you know? Only what your little spiv told you. And that's only one. You're on borrowed time, my girl. Those paintings are ours and you know it. If they aren't back here PDQ there'll be Hell to pay. Literally. Oh, yes, Madam, I can call in all sorts of favours, don't you worry!"

Now Percy chimed in, "Archie, we know Alice has them, and so do you. It's just a matter of finding out where she's hidden them. Try to be a little patient. She's a sensible girl. A little pressure in the right direction."

"They aren't at her place, and they aren't at her father's. We've checked both."

I raised my eyebrows – so was it these two who had had my house ransacked? I didn't like the idea of them going round Wethersley.

Jeremy touched my arm, and we shifted along to the end of the corridor. I slipped my noisy shoes back on and linked arms with him. He started to sing. It was a nice voice, and he could hold the tune.

"Heaven, I'm in Heaven," I joined in. Give them enough warning. My heels clattered on the terrazzo as we did an impromptu Fred and Ginger routine.

By the time we entered the drawing room they were all settled and smiles, Elisabeth and Percy on a long sofa, Archie in an armchair by the fire, dog once more on his lap.

"Ah," he greeted us, "you found your way back alright. Good. Come in and get a refresher."

Percy brought me another whisky. "Alice, dear, I see you've acquired some more jewelry."

"Yes, Percy. Jeremy bought this for me. Isn't that sweet? I have to wear it now, don't I?"

"Oh, of course. Of course. And in such good taste, too. Understated but not cheap. I commend you on finding such a generous young man, my dear. I'd hang on to him, if I were you."

"I intend to, Percy," I said, slipping my hand on Jeremy's knee proprietorially. "He's mine for the duration."

"Am I? How delightful to be let into your little secret in public!"

Elisabeth laughed. "You silly man, we're all friends here. And your secret, if indeed it is a secret, is safe with us. *Faites comme vous voudrez.*"

Archie beamed at us. "It's always worked for me. Do thy will, friends. Do all thy will. No if's and but's. You can't make an omelette without breaking eggs, and a soufflé omelette is far superior to a fresh egg gone off. You're here to learn magic. The whole thing is about personal transformation, and you do that by knowing your true will. And acting upon it. That's the hallmark of a good magician."

"And a bad magician?" I asked. "A wicked wizard?"

"Figments of fairy tales," Percy laughed. "No such thing."

"Like witches?" Jeremy asked.

Archie laughed. "Plenty of them about, poor benighted old biddies. And fairies too, but they don't show their faces round here. Sad bunch of losers the lot of them. Dabblers in dung!"

"So what's the difference between the magic of fairy tales and your magic?"

"Good question, Jeremy. You need to know. We don't need dabblers in dung here. Only the best. If you can take it, what we can give you here will stand you in good stead in all aspects of your lives, both of you. But it's not given to the faint-hearted. You have to commit one hundred and twenty per cent. A slip, a single slip, and the powers will work against you. I've seen that happen time and again. You have to be very very focused on what you are doing. But you can have all things – anything in the world - your heart's desire. The difference between the witches, the Christians, virtually any religion and ourselves as ceremonial magicians is knowing that. You are in charge of your own destiny, and can do as You will." He emphasized the You.

"That is the whole of the law. You are a little god, a part of the Creator, and as such you create your very own world down here on earth. You can do exactly as you like. But it takes a very strong and confident person to take that step. Sermon over."

He looked down at his dog, who besottedly looked up at him, and began licking his face adoringly. Both dog and man seemed to delight in the action.

I averted my gaze and thoughts, and considered the argument Archie had put forward. Although in part I agreed, I could see a lot of flaws.

What about natural disasters?

Wars?

What about other people's needs?

If we all rode roughshod over others?

That was what Hitler did and look where it got him. We had free will but only within parameters, but I couldn't openly disagree, for apart from anything else there was a fanatic gleam in his eye.

"You do sermonize, Archie," Percy told his twin. "You'd be a bloody brilliant hell-fire and brimstone preacher if you'd felt the call."

"Yes, brother, but the angels got in first." He had his dog under control now and dabbed at his face with a large check handerchief, then looked over it at us both. "You know about the angels, of course?"

"The Straddling Angels?" I asked.

No point in denying it, so I called them by the name I had met in Mr. Petts's pamphlet.

"The Greystoke Angels," he corrected coldly. "I daresay they are the same ones." He looked icily at Elisabeth. "Her father conned my father out of them."

"He did not, Archie. He bought them fairly and squarely

at auction and you know it."

That was Percy.

Well, I thought, good for Percy.

"That's not what uncle Henry told us," Archie said pettishly.

"And you'd believe everything that old reprobate said. Archie, it's all water under the bridges. The angels got you, that's enough. And now that Elisabeth's father has passed on, they're calling to you again. That's quite understandable. We'll find them for you."

He was placating but firm. Then he looked at me sharply. "Won't we, Alice?"

He turned to Jeremy. "Won't we Jeremy?"

Then he took Elisabeth's hand in his and kissed the knuckles one by one. "You, too, Sweetie. There's always a price. Remember that. We do. Always. Those angels belong to us and with us. We shall not rest until we have them here once more. And if a little blood is spilled... well what's a little blood in the grand scheme of things?"

He looked at Archie, who nodded, then gave us each the full benefit of his icy stare. "Neither Percy nor I have felt any qualms with a little blood, but you might, particularly if it were yours. Understand this, all of you. Those angels are ours and we will have them. And sooner rather than later. Understood? I hope so!"

There was an ominous silence. Then the clock struck eleven.

Percy rose, helping Elisabeth to her feet.

Archie stroked his dog and lifted it gently to the floor. His face relaxed as he touched the animal. "That's it, lights out. Goodnight all," he said, making for the door. "Come on Mr. Crowley, time for a final empty."

Elisabeth came and kissed us goodnight. "Stand firm. It's all under control," she whispered.

"What's that you're whispering to them, Sweetie?"

Percy asked. "Love spells? They don't look as though they need them. Sleep well, young lovers. Don't do anything I wouldn't do, and that leaves you a damn wide range." He ambled over to us and gave me a hug and a sloppy kiss, Jeremy a handshake in farewell. "Come on, Sweetie, let's hit the hay!"

We made our way back to our quarters.

"We're locked in," I muttered. "They know we've got the angels and they're threatening us."

"No, they think they are. Possession is nine tenths of the law, and your father has them safe. They are threatening, but they are negotiating. We give them the angels and they'll teach us the secrets."

"The secret is there is no secret," I spat. "They're just a couple of dirty old men with money and clout. When I think of Sylvia, it makes me sick. How can Elisabeth play up to them?"

"She's got her own game on," Jeremy murmured. "They're threatening her too. Come on, Alice, let's give the rooms a once-over."

We went through both rooms, the bathroom and loo with a fine-tooth comb. They were identical.

We found contraceptives, and what I took as a 'fun kit' of silken whip, velvet handcuffs, and a Zorro mask, guests, for the use of, in the night table drawer. We found a bottle of cherry brandy, glasses, a box of dark-brown hand-rolled cigarettes and matches in the little cupboard below, alongside books with very interesting, if not impossible suggestions that we might care to follow demonstrated by black and white photographs.

What we didn't find was anything remotely like a camera.

Or a spy-hole.

Nor anything that might be attached to some form of recording device.

I carefully replaced the items.

As I tucked the literature back in my bedside cupboard, I looked at Jeremy.

His face was crimson with embarrassment and anger. "I never meant you to see all this sort of stuff, Alice," he said at last.

"It's not a problem. I've come across it before, but it rather takes the magic out, doesn't it? Makes it look so sordid, when while you're actually doing it with someone you really feel is wonderful, it's bloody amazing."

He grinned. "Yes, it does rather cheapen the experience. Tawdry, tawdry, tawdry!"

"And we are not tawdry people," I said.

"Too right! And we are also working. But not on the job, so to speak."

"Certainly not. It would be playing into their hands."

He picked up the bottle of liqueur. "Unsealed. Never trust an unsealed bottle."

He sniffed it, then poured a couple of glasses and tipped them down the sink. "So you and I will look as though we are settling in for a night of passion, I imagine. Try a cigarette. No, don't inhale, just light it and let it burn."

It certainly wasn't any tobacco I'd come across, and smelt like bonfires and burnt oranges. "Stick it outside on the window sill."

The window stuck fast. No matter what I tried it wouldn't budge. "No chance," I said. "We're in here with it."

"Ah well, one won't do much harm. It's quite a pleasant smell, really. A mild relaxant, a bit like a pint of beer drunk fast. Supposed to enhance your love life. So I've heard." He took some others and slipped them into a metal cigarette case in his pocket. "For analysis, before you begin wondering."

"What, all of them?"

He grinned. "Actually, it looks bad having just one cigarette in a case, four or five look legit."

"How many cigarette cases do you have?" I asked.

"As many as I need. This weekend one for Pashas, one for Woodbines, and one for all-comers." He tossed me the gold one with the Pashas. "I've got a bottle of whisky if you fancy another drink."

I lit up. "No, I'm on duty. I'm going to bed. Can I use the bathroom first?"

"Sleep well, my dears?" asked Percy when we came in for breakfast.

I purred. "Mmm, yes, thank you. Haven't had such a good night for ages."

Jeremy yawned, "Excellent night, thank you, Percy."

Archie looked smug. "Accommodation suitable, then?"

"Very comfortable indeed, Archie, thank you," I said. "Really luxurious. Very considerate of you, too, going to all that trouble."

"We don't believe in second best, Alice. You deserve the best." That was Percy.

"Come and have some breakfast, you must be starving," said Elisabeth.

"Plans for today," said Archie, briskly, as we settled at the table with kippers and bread and butter. "Elisabeth will be your guide immediately after breakfast. She will take you to the temple and show you the ropes. Ask all your questions then because once you've left it, it's out of bounds until we enter it this afternoon. Percy and I shall be setting it up, while Elisabeth finalises the arrangements for this evening."

He looked at us both. "There will be a lot of work involved. You will have to make your own amusement, but I'm sure that will be no problem to two young people with initiative."

He leered, snorted, then continued. "There are many people coming this afternoon and even more this evening. It's a traditional time for fun and frolic, May Day. Lunch will be at one, after which we generally take a quiet time, preparatory to the ritual, which will start from the loggia at three o'clock. You will be washed and brushed, wearing robes and nothing else – shoes apart for the ritual and you will not speak to anyone once we are lined up for the procession, not even to each other, is that clear?... Good, and after the ritual you may choose to continue in your robe or get back into mufti. The choice is yours. There will be people in both here. Clear?"

We nodded. "Yes, sir."

"Good. Come on, Crowley, old chap, walkies!"

Elisabeth led us round the house, across a sun terrace and down the steps to a path set around the side of a spacious lawn. "The temple's in the woods," she said. "You are very privileged to be allowed into it without them to keep an eye on you."

"Elisabeth," Jeremy said urgently, "is everything alright?"

"Perfectly in order," she said flatly. "Where is that jewel? Oh, it's yours, and I don't want it back, but …"

"It started to irritate me. I had to take it off. It's safe enough." I looked at her. "I broke the link, didn't I? Just how much do you know? Do they know?"

We were in the woods now.

She sighed. Suddenly she looked really old.

"I'm tired, Alice. I thought I could handle them. I'm not sure I can. I hope I can. I have to believe I can."

Jeremy got out his gold cigarette case.

She took a Pasha gratefully and allowed him to light it. "How did you know there was something wrong?"

He smiled. "The woman I met at the Boltons was strong and determined. She would never allow herself to be treated as Sweetie if there were not some very powerful reason."

"Thank you." She drew in the smoke and as she exhaled,

she grew back to her true self. "They want the angel pictures, as you know. I knew where they went, or rather I knew where the information was. But my father had decided not to trust me. I knew he was ill, but I didn't know he was dying. I was too busy trying to keep May and June on the straight and narrow. It's too late, of course. They were such lovely girls. Corrupted, just like their mother. These men are evil."

"But you are engaged to one of them," I exclaimed. "You are going to marry this man, aren't you?"

She gave a quick smile and a shrug. "Don't worry about me. Let's go to the temple. You'll feel really at home in it, I assure you."

33

It was a perfect Greek cross plan.

When you went in – you left your shoes in a rack in the porch – the altar was in the centre directly under a cupola with a lantern. There was a light burning upon the altar and Elisabeth whispered a name and raised her hand to it. "These people are with me," she said, then turned to us. "Greet the Light, then enter."

She took us round the quarters.

The Magus sat in the East, the Priestess in the West, at the South and North were two more major officers who would complete the bringing in of the elemental powers. "Air, Fire, Water and Earth, starting in the East, traveling sunwise. You will sit among the upholders – which means you will concentrate on feeling the energy of your quarter coming through and bringing it into the temple. And don't think you'll be wasting time. Upholders are as important as the officers. They just don't get the pretty tabard or the glory."

"Once you are in the temple you do not do anything to interrupt the proceedings. If things go wrong – it is possible to set fire to your robe but uncommon – the Ceremonarius will deal with it. That's his job. You will not try to make a break for the door, because you will be stopped by the Guardian, who will have sealed it on the inner and the outer levels. You will do nothing except uphold the energies and focus on the ritual unless your magus, your ceremonarius or your high priestess asks you to do so. OK? Act with the same sort of decorum as you would in a church."

"Fine," I said. "It feels like a church."

"It's based on a templar church. It's a beautiful place to

work. Er... Alice... if you see something strange with the inner eye, do not scream, just observe it. It can only hurt you if you allow it to, so keep it in its place, and tell me afterwards. People do see things sometimes, although not necessarily on their first formal ritual."

She sat us down and taught us breathing techniques to balance us and energise us for magical work. I felt better afterwards but that it was probably as much to do with imagination as the breathing and visualising. Then she taught us about the Archangels of the Quarters. We would be sitting with her in the West, mediating the power of the archangel Gabriel and Cosmic Water, which is Compassion, Love and Emotion ruled by love and compassion, and Inspiration; quite a tall order, I thought, given who would be in the temple with us.

"I will already be in the temple when you come in. Jeremy, you will sit on my left, Alice on my right." She led us to her throne, a copy of St Edward's chair in Westminster Abbey, but without the Stone and a rather more comfortable cushion and hassock, and placed us in the chairs beside her.

"Percy will be opposite me. He will be Magus. Archie is Ceremonarius. You don't need to know the rest. Suffice it to say that there will be a man in the South and a woman in the North. The Guardian sits beside the door, the Seer over there beside Percy. The Messenger reads the working, so sits in the North to take us from the physical temple to the inner one. Just follow it and you'll get there."

"What is the actual purpose of this ritual?" Jeremy asked.

"To celebrate Beltane. It's the time of year when promise is assured. People think May Day is about fertility – but really it's more about the promise of assured fertility. The May Queen was already pregnant – look at the trees and flower, listen to the birds and young animals, they're all on their way. Impregnation and fertilization has already taken place. We are saying thank you for that, and inviting creativity in all its forms to enter and inspire us. It's a very joyous occasion. Very stimulating!"

"We like stimulating!" I said softly.

She chuckled. "In case you are worried, we don't sacrifice virgins on the altar in public rituals. If you want to make that sort of offer to the Creatrix, you can do it in the privacy of your own room. Or nip off into the woods. That's quite traditional by the way, so if you get any desperate longings, feel free. You won't be alone." She was delightfully matter of fact about sexual games.

"Will you be doing that?" I asked.

"Who knows? The Lady will tell me what she wants me to do. I've trusted Her all my life."

"You have a female creator?" I said.

"Makes more sense to me. But she has a consort, a male energy, to balance and supply her needs. That's where the maypole comes in. We'll have one set up on the lawn. It's all great fun. I'm sure you'll have a good time." She ran through a mental checklist as she looked at the altar, counting things off on her fingers, then frowned. "Do you think you could do something for me?"

"Of course."

"Anything."

"Could you go out into the country and find me some hawthorn in flower? It's the only time of year when it's right to bring it indoors, and is lovely in a temple."

"How much do you want?"

"Enough to scent this place and some for the hall? Use your initiative. There used to be a lot of May trees near Straddling Hall. I lived there as a child. My mother always used them as they flowered earlier than many of the others in the hedges. Take a pair of secateurs and thank the tree for its gift."

I was glad to be out of Finchings.

It might have been a very fine house perfect of its type and for its purpose, which was entertaining, but the atmosphere within was unpleasant.

"What do you think she's up to?" I asked.

"She wants us out of the way. But why send us to Straddling Hall? I've seen May blossom in lots of the hedgerows."

We drove through real May Queen weather and he was right. There was creamy hawthorn in flower far closer than Straddling. However, the High Priestess had given us an order, so to Straddling Hall we went. We drove straight up there this time, the way that the construction lorries took. There was no-one around. Often enough men did overtime on Saturdays, but not this day. The site was empty. The lights were off, and there was no sound of either plant or dogs. Just behind the chain-link fence stood a group of hawthorns. The scent was heavy on the breeze, and the flower petals floated like nature's confetti, unlike the blossom we'd passed, these were double and pale pink.

"Clever Elisabeth," I said. "It was a test."

"We've yet to get through the fence," Jeremy said, but that was no problem. Last night it looked locked solid, but now, by light of day, we saw where the watchmen had made a gate to pass through by moving an upright. We shifted it too, and walked through, closing it after us.

"I've got the key, if you're interested," I said. "It's likely to be our best opportunity."

"I'd like to walk over the site, as well. We'd best hasten."

"Dodgy brickwork," he muttered. "Poor footings. These houses are being thrown up."

They'd grown a lot in the short time since I last saw them. If this field of matchboxes was full of homes fit for heroes, I was the Queen of Sheba. "We need to get Sam out here," Jeremy said. "And your father should see it, too. It'll put him right off Wethersley-Marsham."

We turned across the moat and into the courtyard of Straddling Hall. It appeared the same, but the tarpaulin was flapping wildly from the roof of the burnt out range. We ran up the steps to the main door and I went to put the key into the keyhole, when the door fell open before us. I didn't like that. Not at all.

"They're both at Finchings," Jeremy hissed. "They've not had time to get here nor any good reason to be here, not today. There's too much to prepare."

"So who is here?"

"Let's go in and find out."

The door had been oiled. It slid open to the touch. The floor had been swept too, but the smell of dust and cold was still there. The sound of my heels echoed on the tiles like thunder. No way could we be unnoticed, so I decided to grab the bull by the horns.

"Coo-ee!" I called, trying not to think of the French meaning for that sound.

"Anyone at home here?" My voice sounded plummy as it sometimes does when I'm nervous.

From the right side of the entrance hall I heard sounds. Someone was coming to greet us, and in a great hurry, too. Someone large and angry.

"What the hell are you doing here!" he roared.

Then stared.

Then shrunk from being the huge belligerent ogre to my father's friend.

"Milady? Mr. Arkwright?"

I looked him up and down and smiled sweetly.

"I might ask the same of you, Padraig, but I'll answer first. We were sent up here by a friend to find some flowers. For a special purpose, they had to be from Straddling, for some reason. We decided to have a look at the hall out of pure nosiness. The door was open, so we walked in." I looked him firmly in the eyes. "Your turn, Mr. Flynn."

While I spoke Padraig's face had registered a series of emotions, among which were anger, guilt, suspicion and exasperation. It came to rest in bland, for which read devious but hidden.

He shrugged. "Me? Nothing especially odd about me being here. I'm due at the party tonight at Finchings. I thought I'd take a look at the scene of Emily's little contretemps."

We both looked at him disbelieving.

"Come, I'll show you where the satanic forces ripped their way through the roof as a result of their wicked rituals." He grabbed each of us by an arm and almost frog-marched us up the stairs, talking the while.

"I got here about half an hour ago. Like you I found the door open. It seemed quite unlikely but fortuitous, so I thought I'd explore." He whizzed us up another staircase and down the long gallery with the mounted heads. "It's completely empty. It makes no sense, none at all."

"Where's Emily?" I asked.

"Good Heavens, Alice, I wouldn't bring her here. She's safe in Gloucestershire this weekend. It would upset her terribly if she thought I'd come here." He looked at us sheepishly. "You won't tell her, will you? You mustn't tell anyone, in case it gets back, don't you see? She'd think I was prying, but since I'm in the area…" He had let us go now. We were at the door that Scrote had hammered on for admittance.

"Let's go in," Jeremy suggested.

The door was unlocked. I could smell incense on the air. I was getting adept at that, and I recognized that it had been used recently.

"Frankincense," breathed Padraig. "Someone's been working here."

"The person who left the door open, perhaps?" I watched

Padraig's face.

He frowned. "What do you mean?"

"I mean someone had the key, and someone had the opportunity, and the motive. "How about you, Padraig?" I asked.

"Where would I get the key?"

"Someone left the door open for you? Someone who feels guilt about what has happened here and wants to release themselves and what they consider the powers they drew in?"

"And how would I know them? How would I deal with these powers?" he demanded.

Jeremy had walked on ahead and was standing under the big hole in the roof now. He turned. "Mr. Flynn, I may be wrong, but I got the idea you were a Roman Catholic."

"Very observant of you, since most of my countrymen are of that persuasion. But what has that to do with things here?"

"I have it on good authority that the best ceremonial magicians have a grounding in Christian magic of the old school. You'd have that. You also have the best reason of all to want to cleanse this place – your feelings for Emily. Plus your hatred for what happened here. You used emotive words like 'satanic' and 'wicked'. As to how you got the key to the door – well, Mr Flynn, you have a wide and influential circle of friends. I'm sure if you wanted something, you have connections."

Padraig looked down at him. "Very clever, but wrong," he said with a sneer. "This was like this when I got here. I've been wandering around the place. Come."

The pair of them walked together up to the business end of the room. I followed and looked for the spot on the floor that had been blasted by lightning.

Emily's spot.

It was no longer visible.

Over it had been put a blood red cloth on which rested an iron plate about five inches in diameter. A tiny thurible which had held the incense stood on it, and beside it an egg-cup of water, a stone and a feather. But within this microcosm of the world, was a small heap of earth from which projected two humanoid shapes twisted out of wool and pipe-cleaners. They had been savagely attacked with scissors, fire and water before their symbolic burial.

Padraig pointed at this and looked at both of us angrily. "Do you honestly believe I would sully my immortal soul with work like this?"

"Holy shit," breathed Jeremy. "Sorry Alice!"

I felt quite sick.

"No, Padraig," I said at last. "I don't see you doing curses like this."

"Well there's a blessing. But we need to find who does. People could die. It's filthy work."

"Only if you believe it will work," said Jeremy, drawing us both back from whence we had come.

"You think so? Well, each to his own," Padraig commented gruffly. "I hope you're right." He shut the door behind us and looked at his watch. "What about a spot of lunch? There's the local pub or an excellent tea shop in Framlingham?"

"I'm afraid we're already booked, thank you, Padraig," I told him, "but we'll see you at Finchings this evening."

We found our own way out, and fast, cut an assortment of flowering May twigs as directed, which I carefully covered with my silk head scarf, and set off to Finchings.

"I've never seen a curse laid out before," Jeremy said as we sped back. "It made me feel quite queasy. It's got to be Lady Finching, hasn't it?"

"I think there's a good chance. And the recipients…"

"Not a million miles away."

Finchings was bustling when we arrived. We had left

the car in the lane, out of the way of traffic at the entrance of a fallow field. We walked the drive – it was a good length, a quarter of a mile at least, and blocked with the vehicles of caterers, organizers, and sundry others who would supply the wherewithal for the party afterwards. There were people milling everywhere. A marquee was three parts raised on the lawn, lanterns were slung along paths through from the house to the temple, and all through the woods.

Elisabeth was supervising the raising of the maypole in the 'dancing garden'

"Just what I need," she squealed, grabbing the twigs. "We'll give him a scented crown as well."

She wove them onto the nut at the top of the pole, tying them with garden wire and then coloured ribbons. "Help us raise him, you two!"

We joined in with three other chaps and herself to lift the heavy pole (it was a telegraph pole painted in bright colours, its ribbons tied firmly to its sides) and position the base into a purpose-built socket in the centre of a circular lawn. One chap took the weight on a rope and between us we heaved the thing into place, until it settled firmly into its base. Wedges of wood were struck in all around and the rope removed, then the ribbons were all loosened, and floated gaily in the breeze, pastel colours which lifted your heart in the Spring air.

The three workmen were stroking the pole – 'for good luck!' so they said. I understood the symbolism alright, and I'd make my own luck, thank you very much.

I looked for Elisabeth but she was already on her way down to the temple with her bunch of May blossom.

Lunch was laid out in the small dining room we had had breakfast in.

Percy called us in. "Times like this I let Archie get on with things, and Elisabeth, too," he said. "Come and eat. Some people think you need to abstain from everything before a ritual, but you don't. You need a bit of ballast before climbing the inner levels, believe me."

He had loaded his plate with an assortment of goodies from the cold collation laid on the sideboard and was tucking in with a will. "Help yourselves, don't stint. Algy and Anthea will be here this evening, so tuck in while you can."

We did as we were told and sat down at his table.

"So where are these angels?" he asked conversationally. "We know you've got them somewhere. You might as well let us have them since they are ours by right, and they're of no use to you yet. You're both far too young in magic to be able to control them, and they do tend to get out of control and cause problems very easily. They did for my father and my grandfather, and probably my uncle too. He was always mucking about with them. And other people they've come into contact haven't fared too well either."

He looked at us benignly, letting the words sink in.

"We don't want anything to happen to you two, now, do we? Elisabeth wouldn't let me hear the last of it, and that would be a hell of a price to pay."

"Higher than being dead?" I asked.

"Eh? Are you threatening me, young woman?"

"No, Percy, of course not. But I did feel that you were threatening me. Both of us, actually. And I don't take kindly to threats, no matter how beautifully they are veiled. Now I know your brother really doesn't like me. Don't ask me how, it's intuitive. I'm pretty sure he doesn't like Elisabeth – no, hear me out, as I have reasons for saying this – which means he's not that keen on your relationship with her. So where does that leave you? Which way are you swinging? Brother or lover? And how do the angels fit in with all this?"

"The angels belong to us!" snapped Percy. "They came to us through the family. My grandfather painted them, my father sold them, but we should inherit them. Elisabeth's father bought them, but we worked with them. Elisabeth should naturally be allowed a share of them, but they are not hers. They are ours. Our family legacy." He glared at us, daring us to challenge him.

Jeremy looked up from his Gala Pie. "Actually, I'd say by law, if they were anyone's, they'd be Elisabeth's. But her father didn't will them to her. He saw fit to shift them well before he died to what he considered a safe place." He smiled blandly. "But, let's ignore all that for a moment. You're saying they're your family legacy. What if there were another branch of the family? Would that branch have equal rights?"

"Don't be stupid, there is no other branch."

We both looked at him and raised our eyebrows.

"Is there?" he asked at last. "No, can't be. Uncle Henry was a bloody old philanderer but he never spawned any by-blows. None at all. At least, none that survived. We know that for a fact."

"What about young Arthur, your youngest uncle?" I said softly.

"Huh, him? Henry did for him. Turned him into a missionary, and got him eaten by the fuzzy-wuzzies when we were children. He told us himself. When he told us all about the angels."

"Ah!" I said.

"Mmm," said Jeremy. "And you believed everything your Uncle Henry told you. Oh dear!" He forked in a final mouthful of pie, chewed it carefully and swallowed blotting his mouth with a napkin. "Some adults take malicious pleasure telling lies to children. I'm sure you know what I mean." He stood up and turned to leave the table.

"Wait, Jeremy! Are you telling me that my uncle Arthur is still alive?" Percy's voice cracked out.

I stood up too, "Yes, Percy. And more to the point, you have a cousin, who is just as interested in the paintings as you are."

Leaving him to enjoy the rest of his lunch, we sped off to Saxmundham, far enough out of the area to be anonymous, where we put through a series of calls from a phone box. Then, because we still had a half hour to spare, we went to the pub for a bit of Dutch courage before going back to prepare for the ritual.

34

We set off together silently, hand in hand, robed in black with our hoods up, to the meeting point at five to three. Around us, through the other rooms along our corridor similarly attired noiseless figures emerged.

I understood now how Emily found it difficult to tell who was within the black hooded garments. They were the most disguising anonymous clothes I have ever seen, and, with the obligatory silence, ensured anonymity. People raised a hand or nodded in greeting, but the hoods draped down over the faces, concealing often all but the mouth and part of the nose.

We all came together at the meeting point and Archie, his hood thrown back, placed us in order from a list he held. Mr. Crowley sniffed his way up along us all, but didn't move further than a foot from his master. I wondered whether he would go into the temple with us, as Archie placed me in line and hoarsely whispered the password: Ipsissimus.

I thought about that – that very self, that most perfect self (masculine of course!), or the title of the most senior of all ceremonial magicians. I wondered what the password was referring to – or to whom. Was it the masculine aspect of the deity, or the magus? Or even Archie's very self?

I sensed a power struggle between the twins.

Elisabeth as High Priestess had already gone into the temple, but Percy as Magus stood at the rear of the silent queue shrouded in a black hooded cloak while Archie, his dog close to him, took the head, alongside a tall figure with a sword. We processed in silence, two by two along the path we had taken earlier. The sun, which had been shining disappeared behind a cloud the moment we entered the woods. I felt a distinct chill in the air, a frisson not wholly due to the breeze that rustled the new leaves.

Jeremy's hand gave mine a squeeze. I returned it. The reassurance his grasp gave me allayed the eeriness around us. At the door of the temple the Sword-bearer made a series of wide passes. The outer portal was opened. The first two of the black robes had shed their shoes, given the Ceremonarius and the Guardian their passwords and gone through the antechamber into the temple.

Slowly our turn came.

My bare feet shivered on the stone floor, but it was a small price to pay.

Mr. Crowley sat smartly to attention by the door.

I watched Jeremy whisper and be allowed through, and thought how familiar he looked in that black robe. Too familiar by half. How it suited him!

Now it was my turn.

I dragged back my lurid imagination.

"Ipsissimus," I breathed to Archie, whose face had the cruel hardness of an eagle. Without looking at me he inclined his head. The Guardian lowered his sword so that I might pass.

"Those angels are mine. They do my will." Archie's voice seemed to be within my head. "Those who don't ..."

I ignored him, walked beyond him into the serenity of the temple.

A blue light shimmered on the central altar, another red light glowed, hanging over the magus's chair. I raised my hand to them, bowed my head, without thinking of the actions then passed to my own seat beside Elisabeth.

She was sitting erect, a Queen on a throne, still as a statue in the Western Quarter. Her robe was white, Greek inspired, with a cloak of blue lined with gold. On her head was a golden diadem with a horned moon lying on its back at her brow. Her feet were bare but for tiny fragile golden sandals.

Her eyes were closed, but the lids were made up with black and blue lines in the Egyptian manner. She exuded power. She was breathtaking.

All around me the room sparkled and tingled.

More people came in and took their seats until the room was filled and only one place remained. Archie, from his seat by the side of the Magus's throne, signaled for us to be upstanding.

Percy came in.

He had shed his cloak and wore a nemys on his head, striped blue and gold, a long white cotton robe, a gold and blue circular collar and a matching sash and plain leather thong sandals. I'd seen the head-dress and collar in the Egyptian galleries of the British Museum and was glad he had decided not to wear the Egyptian kilt. He had neither the age nor the figure for that. I wanted to snigger, for whereas Elisabeth was every inch the High Priestess in her robes, his did Percy no favours; with his normal clothing he shed power and became a rather undistinguished middle-aged man in fancy dress. But he was the Magus, and would, with his older twin control the ritual.

He took his place in the Eastern Throne, turned to face us, nodded, then lifted his crook and flail, one in each hand, held them out to us, then crossed them over his chest, his chin pointing upward exposing his throat.

I waited.

And waited.

We all waited.

I could sense nervousness around the room. Perhaps this dramatic pause was not normal.

Beside him, Archie hissed something. Percy rose, and addressed us sonorously. "We who see the Creator face unto face salute you at this season of Beltane."

The room breathed a huge collective sigh.

Archie stepped forward, and invited us to invoke.

The ritual was on.

The adoration of the Lord of the Universe, then the purifications, the opening of the gates all gently rolled forward. The rest of those present seemed to know the requisite words and actions, and the whole thing was a graceful slow ballet, with circles of asperging, censing and lighting of candles.

Since I didn't know the words I simply paid deep attention to what was going on, as Elisabeth had told me. I didn't want to let her down, nor Jeremy or myself, either. As we progressed deeper I found myself unable to be detached and think in my normal manner. As each gate opened I felt the inrush of energy flow through to spiral over the altar. I watched and felt. It was all I could do. Air, Fire, Water and …

As she called in the powers of Earth the Northern Officer's hood slipped backwards; I flinched slightly. But why not? Who better to mediate Earth but a mountain of a woman?

With wild grey hair freed from its confines spreading outwards in a great bush, her pale pudgy visage contorted with effort, sat Madam Honoria.

What was she doing here? I hadn't noticed her in the queue, and she would have been noticeable by her limp, if indeed she had been able to walk at all. I couldn't see that broken foot I gave her healing well enough to support the heavy body any distance at all. I peered at her feet, but her vast robe had cascaded over them and beyond across the floor.

Although she, and everyone else, appeared totally focused on the ritual, I suddenly felt very exposed in this position. Jeremy and I were in the front row beside the High Priestess. If we were meant to be seen by all, we could not have been better placed.

I tried to calm myself but peer out from below my hood

at the others around me, but they were all robed and hooded. Perhaps the uniform was my protection. I could make no more of the company than Emily had done at Straddling, years back, and I felt some of her qualms in the pit of my stomach.

Now, beside me, Elisabeth rose, stately and elegant, and glided towards the altar, her hands raised. She invoked the Goddess, in the name of Hathor, Aphrodite, Proserpina and the God or male principle, in whatever form the Goddess chose, to join us at this, Her time of the year, to act out the old rites. I don't remember much of the actual words, but there was a feeling of green, fertile creative energy emanating from her. Percy stepped opposite her and held his hands across the altar from her. He gasped as the energy hit him, and staggered slightly. Elisabeth stood tall, lowered her head in acknowledgement, then regained her seat. And she stayed there, silent and detached for the rest of the ritual.

Percy took a deep breath. "I now declare this temple open at the season of Beltane. May the will of the Goddess and the God and the Creative force be done."

A reply of "So mote it be!" came from the rest of those present.

More incense was wafted, and then came a very long and wordy description that we were supposed to follow with 'our inner eyes'. The person reading it had a speech impediment – not good with her 'r's, so when we got to the Lady Arianrhod and the Druids it all got too much for me, and I drifted off elsewhere. Where, I didn't know. I didn't exactly black out, but I wasn't totally conscious. A sort of waking sleep.

And in the sleep a dream.

I can only call it that.

I was far elsewhere, high above the mountains of the Vercors.

Flying with the raptors, but not a raptor myself.

I knew the terrain from maps and from the ground, but this

was magnificent. I felt to be a being of pure light, everything else being the same, with the sparkle of the day of creation upon it. Slowly I circled down until I was below the tree line, then further still following the sparkling watercourses into alpine meadows.

I was looking for someone, and he was there. He wasn't dead here, my dear friend Raoul. I was so glad to see him, and he me. Waves of emotion, such touchings, such rememberings, such joy. Around us Springtime shared it. On the bank where we'd spread the blanket, mats of violets and windflowers, daisies and celandines; above us wild cherry and plum blossom, pale green leaves, and all around us the songs of birds. To say I felt at one with all life was an understatement. It was, even as I was dreaming it, a mind-expanding experience. And when we came down to the village, I knew I would never see him again. But that didn't matter. I'd said goodbye. In the way I liked best. He had hurt, he said, not being able to tell me to let go, but now, well, life goes on, but differently for we two…

And then, suddenly I was aware of a black shape looming over me.

I came back with a start, panting, disoriented.

The figure in front of me gravely offered a dish upon which tiny squares of coarse bread were piled. I took one and put it in my mouth. It had been sprinkled with salt and was bone dry. I wanted to choke, but stifled the cough.

Now another figure came before me and handed me a chalice. I knew I'd have to drink some, simply to stop the cough, despite my previous intention not to. But after that dream… I took a mouthful. Of pure pleasure. Then handed it back.

I don't know what wine it was, but it was the best I'd tasted in a very long time. It sang to your soul. I floated, now, in a haze of glorious light, totally relaxed and at peace.

Once again I was brought back rudely.

Archie, the Ceremonarius, was giving the notices.

It was just like going to church.

And felt just as inappropriate at this juncture. The last thing I needed was someone to tell me about the next bring-and-buy, but there he was giving us a list of dates for our diaries – which I thought was pretty stupid since none of us had our diaries about our persons – and the information that by Midsummer he would be working the Temple of the Angels, since they were all currently being restored and would be made available by then, or, and he peered towards the West as he said it, They would do their Will.

As if to emphasise this he pointed his crook and flail menacingly.

The swift icy glare of intent and the threatening gesture were for Jeremy and me, but Elisabeth was included too.

The three of us looked back blandly, reflecting the menace. A threat is only a threat if you allow it to be. It happened in an instant; the rest of the congregation appeared oblivious as a flutter of joy ran around the room at the angelic news.

I didn't like the veiled threat inside a magic circle from Archie, nor being out of control mentally amongst all these people, some of whom had their own reasons for wishing me ill. I was the official keeper of the angels and I had no intention of handing them to this bunch.

Now came the closing, basically the opening in reverse. As the energies were unwound and freed I became gradually aware of how chilled I was.

Percy gave a benediction of sorts: "Brothers and Sisters, it is Beltane. Eat, drink and be merry, and do your will, for all pleasures are the gift of the Goddess and the God," closed his book of words with a very suggestive wink then strode to the door.

The Guardian waved his sword again then opened the door. Percy passed through into the outer world.

Archie stood up and directed people out of the room. One

by one we completed the circle that we'd started when we came in, raised our hands in acknowledgement and farewell to the Light and exited.

People crowded together putting their shoes on in the porch. Mr. Crowley whined to get back to his beloved master, getting in everyone's way.

I picked up my slip-ons and moved off up the path barefoot; it made more sense. I brushed my feet off at the first turn, and put my shoes on there. Jeremy, who came out after me, thrust his feet into his brogues and tucked the laces inside so that we could escape as fast as possible.

We were out of the woods before either of us spoke, and then it was only in gasps.

"What do you make of it?" I asked.

"I could murder a fag! Are you going to give them the angels?"

"Why do you ask that?"

"Because I sat there bored by that woman wittering on then suddenly there's an angel standing in front of me, taking me out through a stone arch. I'd really like to know what went into that incense." His face was pale. "And I'd like to know how Madam Honoria fits in."

"With difficulty, I should think," I said cruelly. "Let's get back into mufti. I'm frozen."

My first foray into magic had given me much to think about, but left me icy, sick and disoriented.

I was glad to have my own clothes once more; warm trousers, woolly socks and sensible shoes, plus a pretty Viyella blouse and a lacy knitted cardigan. Jeremy was back in his flannels, warm shirt and tweed jacket.

Elisabeth came towards us, her robe and cloak billowing in the breeze, traditionally last to leave the temple, except for the Ceremonarius, who would be responsible for closing it down. She hugged each of us. "Well done, you two. Get some thing to ground you, to stave off the astral chills. I'll see you later."

We found the friendly face of Beryl Crowe in the Marquee, serving tea. "Sally! So you got in touch with your friend after all!" she said with a smile. "I'm glad. Even if I did warn you off, life's too short to hold grudges, isn't it."

"Yes," I agreed. "Beryl, this is my young man."

Jeremy stuck out a hand, "Jem Arden," he said. "Any friend of Sal's is a friend of mine. Any chance of a cuppa?"

She shook hands. "Nice to meet you, Mr. Arden, and yes, of course there is. And some of that chocolate cake? We keep it under the counter," she winked at me.

"Spoil us, please, Beryl. Sal told me it was the highlight of her trip – and meeting you, of course."

We took our tray piled high with goodies out to the garden. I had been hoping for the reinforcements to be here by now, but there was no sign. However I did see Bulgy Algy and Anthea working their way through a three-tiered tray of cakes at the far end of the terrace, and beside them stood Padraig, in deep conversation.

"Let's get out of here," I whispered, nodding in their direction.

Across to the right where the path snaked down to the temple Cyril was fighting gravity to push a vociferous Madam Honoria in an archaic wheel-chair up to level ground. Her tirade of abuse drew attention, and along with some others, I saw Padraig hurry across to lend his strength to the matter.

To my astonishment, she greeted him fondly, accepting a kiss on both cheeks, before allowing him alone to haul her wheelchair backwards up onto the level path.

Poor Cyril, the constant admirer, didn't stand a chance.

"I didn't know he knew her," Jeremy said softly, pulling out a notebook and pen. "And I didn't notice the wheelchair. I must be slipping."

"Understandable and forgiveable," I told him. "They do seem to be good pals."

We left them to it, and sloped off into the rose garden which led to the heated swimming pool where people were already disporting themselves. I recognized several from the work I had been doing at Bar's office.

In the midst of them, holding court, gleamed Percy, in a tiny knitted bathing costume; he leaped onto the springboard and bounced a couple of times, looking at us. "Come on in, you two, it's the best way of grounding I know – bar one!" He winked and gave us a lecherous chuckle as he did a final bounce, then twisted in mid-air to perform the perfect swallow dive. It was amazing how graceful he was at that moment, a large middle-aged man running to fat in normal life, but in that elegant series of movements I could see the echo of the slender graceful youth he once was and I understood how he and his brother would have appeared to the society hostesses shortly after the Great War: catches indeed.

The other bathers gave him a cheer as his head broke the water into the air, and he took the praise with equal grace. Again he called to us to get our clothes off and join in, but I shook my head.

"We'll try the other sort of grounding," Jeremy told him with a grin. "It sounds more fun." As he turned to kiss me, he whispered, "Anyone you know here?"

"Yes," I said at last. "Let's go."

We were eating chocolate cake and scribbling down names in a summer-house when a slight familiar figure approached breathlessly. "Oh, you're here. Thank goodness for that!"

He plonked down beside us, his small scruffy Jack Russell terrier staying close to his feet. "You don't mind if I stay here with you, for a moment? I'm really scared of what's going to happen."

Jeremy slipped his notebook into his pocket and withdrew a cigarette case.

Nigel shook his head. "I don't, thanks. And I don't smoke anything here. Not saying you are the same as the others, but got to keep a clear head. Er, is that jam tart going begging?"

"It's got your name on it," I told him. "Feel free, we've finished."

He halved it, ate one piece and fed the other to the little dog who wolfed it, like his master, in one. "Thank you." He was shivering, his eyes black holes in the pale thin face. He huddled in his clothes, and he had enough layers on - a Fair Isle pullover and a Harris Tweed jacket over his shirt and tie, and a pair of good quality flannels. He shouldn't have been cold. He reached out a bony hand and took a biscuit, sharing it with his pet. He was some five or more years older than Sylvia, his sister, and looked at this moment five years less.

"What's up, Nigel?" I asked gently.

He shook his head. "I can't tell you," he said looking at us nervously and scattering crumbs. He dusted himself down, picked up the little dog and hugged it close to him, then continued. "If I do, really horrible things will happen to me. But I can tell you this. There's going to be trouble. It's been brewing all week. My sister's gone after Archie, and your brother will follow them." He looked at me intently. "And then there will be big trouble!"

"Why?" I asked.

"Why? Are you stupid? This is Beltane, and Uncle Archie has always promised her she'd be his May Queen, and then he failed to invite her to the celebration."

He looked at our puzzled faces. "She's gone down to beard him in his temple. And if your brother sees what she's up to, there'll be Hell to pay!"

"My brother's here?"

"He followed us down in his car. She traveled with me, because she wanted to make sure I came – to support her. Er... she and Guy have had a bit of a falling out recently.

She wants to go into the magic like you two – she was wild as fire that you were invited to join the circle and Percy said she couldn't until she was 21. Guy told her over his dead body, so she said she was coming down here anyway, and if he really loved her he would let her do what she wanted."

He shivered. "She always gets her own way. The rest of the family's here. We always come. I suppose Guy thought he'd better come as well. She drove like a mad thing, trying to lose him, but he kept up. All the time in the car she was going on about being the Queen of the May, and trying to get here in time. Then when we got here, she was too late for the ritual."

"So what happened then?"

"She went to find Archie. They said he was still in the temple. She told your brother to wait for her up at the Maypole."

35

Guy wasn't by the Maypole, and when we got there the temple door was shut, with my brother slamming at it with his fist, shouting imprecations in French and English and Mr. Crowley leaping up at it excitedly and, it must be said, incontinently.

"Let her go, you filthy beast. *Cochon de merde! Laisse-la. C'est ma fiancée, emmerdeur.* I'll give you a damn good hiding, you blasted perisher!"

His French was much more basic and voyou than his English. I wondered where and from whom he'd learnt that. Maman would be horrified! Angelique could lay about her with her tongue, but Guy's accent was not Provençale at all.

I grabbed him by the shoulders and hissed his name in his ears, "Guy, *arrête! Tais-toi, mon frere!*"

I pulled him backwards away from the door, and Jeremy got his pocket knife into the narrow space and winkled the latch upward so that we could get in. Mr. Crowley bounded before us, whining and barking at the anteroom door.

Guy was beside himself. "He's killing her, she's screaming, listen! Bastard, let her go!"

Now Jeremy grabbed him, from behind around the arms and chest so that he couldn't move.

"Guy, she's not in pain," he said slowly and quietly in his ear. "Those are not cries of pain. Do you understand me?"

"Let me go, damn you! He's killing my fiancée," he shouted, struggling.

Now Nigel and I were trying to hold him back from the door. The three of us made a barrier between him and it, stuck our faces in front of Guy's so that he could not see beyond us.

Nigel said "He's fucking her, you great loon, and she wants it. She's enjoying it. She always makes that noise. Don't you know anything? She does it to please him. He likes it." His voice was bitter, angry, hurt.

It did the trick.

It stopped Guy in his tracks.

"What?"

"You heard. She's been on all day about being his May Queen. This is what it's all about."

Guy's face crumpled with incomprehension. "No. No. Let me see. I think you're all mad. Let me go. I don't believe you! No-one does that"

"You've led a very sheltered life," said Nigel, sadly, letting him go and picking up his small dog. "Don't say I didn't warn you!"

I stood back. "She's your fiancée. Go and save her. If you can."

He turned to Jeremy. "You'll give me a hand, won't you, old chap? You're almost family."

Jeremy nodded, and the two of them slammed through the arched temple door together. Nigel and I poured in immediately behind, Nigel's little dog yapping, and Mr. Crowley barking and widdling alongside.

It wasn't a pretty sight.

She was bent over the altar, her large pink breasts spilling onto the white linen cloth, her thin short frock hitched up so high that the frilly skirt fluttered over her shoulders. Her hair was tousled, and a dreamy, look was on her face, her eyes half closed. Her chubby legs were spread wide, and Archie, his black robe raised, was shafting her with great forcefulness from behind. You had to give it to the man, our entrance didn't affect his stroke for one moment, nor did it affect Sylvia's little screams.

"Sylvia!" Guy's wailing scream changed everything.

She heard alright, and jerked upright with a squeal.

Archie was pushed backward, and probably not in the most gentle manner.

He slammed his hand off her waist and landed a flat slap on her face. "Bitch, don't pull those stunts on me!"

Guy was at him, squaring up prior to punching and doing his Marquess of Queensbury stuff. Jeremy slipped round the other side of the altar (clockwise, like a good occultist!) and administered a kick in the groin and another in the ribs. "There'll be one in the throat if you don't stay there," he snarled at the laid-out gasping heap that was Archie on the floor.

He grabbed Sylvia by the shoulder and tossed her at Guy. "Get yourself dressed, hussy!"

"Leave her alone, can't you see she's been raped?" Guy said defensively, holding her against his chest.

"That was never rape," said Nigel. "She's been playing that game for years." He slapped his sister on the other cheek. "There, a matched pair, you whore. You get a chance for a decent life and you act like this."

He looked at Guy. "She's not worth it, Guy. Chuck her out. Chuck us all out. We're bad news."

He went round to Archie and gave him a vicious kick. "All his fault! Bastard! You should die, but slowly and painfully," he said, spitting. "If I didn't know that, I'd kill you now!"

Guy still looked puzzled.

He looked at Archie, curled whimpering and coughing on the floor, clutching himself.

Then he took Sylvia a little away from him. "He did rape you, didn't he?" he asked her gently, begging her to say 'yes'.

She looked at him with a sneer. "You'd like that, wouldn't you, Mr Honourable? You've no idea, have you? You never even tried to kiss me properly. But Archie did. So did Percy. And their friends. I've had a wonderful time with them. Archie's a far better man than you are. He knows how to make a girl feel wanted, he knows how to appreciate her as a woman. Whereas you, you cold fish…"

She tugged at her ring finger. "You can take this back. I'm going to marry Archie. I'm his May Queen."

She threw the ring on the floor. "I am Queen of the May, amn't I Archie?" She slipped down to her knees where Archie was still huddled moaning softly.

She knelt beside him letting her heavy breasts fall into his face. "Come on baby, suck for Mummy, you'll soon feel better." She grasped his hand and pushed it down between her open thighs.

I don't know how Archie managed it.

He drew on all his strength and threw her off. Then, bent double and limping, he hauled her upright, dragged her to the door and pushed her out of the temple.

"Whore! Slattern! Defiler of sacred spaces! Queen of the May? My wife? What are you talking about?" He sank into the Western throne, catching his breath. Mr. Crowley leaped up and licked his face. Archie licked the dog back, took comfort in his pet, stroking its soft hair.

I looked at my brother. He was swaying gently on his feet. We had to get him out of there.

Jeremy picked up the ring, a large solitaire diamond set between two perfectly paired aquamarines in a twisted setting, and slipped it into Guy's pocket, then we each took one arm, and with Nigel and the Jack Russell bringing up the rear, made our exit from the temple. Immediately Sylvia was back in, throwing herself upon Archie.

Sylvia always got her way. She always had and had no intention of changing now.

I had no love for Archie Meredith, but found myself feeling rather sorry for the chap.

My brother Guy was a dead weight. His face had lost all colour, and his hands were toneless, cold. We dragged him up the path and back to the summerhouse. We dropped Guy on the seat, and Jeremy got out his hip flask. He poured a nip into the top, and handed it to Guy. "Drink it. It'll do you good!" he ordered.

I was chafing his hands. He must have been bad because he let me. Normally Guy wouldn't allow me to touch him except on his terms.

By the time he had tossed back the spirit and started to smoke a Pasha, his colour began to return. He was coming back from somewhere very far away.

"Did that really happen?" he asked.

"Yes," I said quietly.

The other two nodded their heads.

He shook his. "I find it very hard, very difficult, to believe that a well-brought up young woman could behave like that," he said at last.

"Don't blame her," said Nigel. "Just be glad you've been let off your engagement. We are all witnesses to that. She can't be helped. He's ruined her. He's ruined us all." He accepted the capful of spirit that Jeremy offered then looked at the three of us. "They are about to ruin you – if you let them. Be warned."

I smiled at him. "We are, thank you, Nigel."

I looked at my brother. "Do you want me to drive you home, Guy?" I asked. "You don't want to stay here, do you? Not after what's happened."

"I think I'd like that, Al," he said. His voice like a small child's.

I looked at Jeremy, "Permission for compassionate leave, sir?"

"Of course. What about you, Nigel? You're going to be as popular as a snake in a bran tub. Do you want to leave now?"

"Yes please. I've nowhere to go, but I can't stay here any longer."

While I used the phone in the hall, Nigel and Jeremy took Guy to his car, parked right out on the road. He needed to be in his own safe space.

Nigel needed to be away from his family and their friends. His siding with us would count as treachery. I wondered what his life had been like. For perhaps the first time I was seeing Nigel, of whom we all took the mickey, as a real person. He was silent and terrified.

No-one should be brought to that by their family.

I was on my way to join them when a figure I recognized came out of the woods, staggered a little, then fell. And in the distance a dog howled, desolately.

I caught Jeremy's eye – he was coming to meet me and together we ran to the figure which was lying prone, moaning, sobbing.

I turned her over. Her dress was soaked in blood.

Her eyes were wild, pale blue orbs, red-rimmed, full of tears which took her mascara with them down her round red cheeks.

"Sylvia, what's happened?" I demanded. "Who did this to you?" I started to undo the dress to view the wounds that I dreaded to see there.

"Not me," she gasped. "I didn't kill him, Alice. I swear I didn't. He was going to marry me. I was the Queen of the May. I didn't kill him!" She dissolved into crooning sobs.

"Sylvia, you're making no sense. What are you trying to tell me?"

She was sitting up now, tears, snot and black mascara washing over her face. She started doing up her dress. No wounds, just lots of blood.

"Archie's dead. My May King, my husband, is dead. I tried to stop the blood, but…" She sniffed loudly.

I gave her my handkerchief. She wiped her eyes, her nose and finally her mouth. "As you see… I couldn't stop it. He died in my arms."

Jeremy was over with us now.

Was I glad of him!

He slipped off his jacket put it over her shoulders. "Put this on. It will hide the blood and keep you warm."

"You are pretty," she said, gazing into his eyes gratefully. "I bet you're good in the sack."

"I've had my moments," he said drily. "But now is not one of them. Come back to your family. Tell me what happened."

We helped her to her feet. The jacket covered most of the stains, but even with both of us supporting her she didn't travel fast and she was no lightweight.

"What happened, Sylvia?" I asked again, heading towards the house. "What happened to your May King?"

"He's dead. Murdered. An old woman came into the temple while we … were… while we were … talking. Yes, that's what we were doing. He was proposing to me. He wanted me to marry him. He did. I know he did. Only she went and spoiled it all. She slipped behind Archie and cut his throat."

Holy Shit!

Unsaid in a shared swift intake of breath, I could hear us both thinking it.

"What was she wearing?" I asked. "Descriptions as detailed as you can, please Sylvia."

Some thirty yards away her parents were sitting refueling themselves, quite oblivious of their daughter's predicament.

"Black hooded robe – usual thing round here. Only, she took the hood off, so I recognized her as very old. And skinny. Mad grey hair, long and witchy. And she had a ruby ring, a big one on her first finger."

"What was the knife like?" Jeremy asked.

"It wasn't a knife."

"What do you mean? You said she cut his throat?" I asked.

"It was like harvesting tool, a curved blade. A sickle."

We dumped her unceremoniously on her parents. "Take care of your daughter," I told her mother. "She needs you now more than she ever has before."

Beryl was coming past to clear away plates.

"Beryl, there's been an accident," I said. "Can you find somewhere safe indoors for these people. They need to be private. And ring the police and an ambulance, a doctor. It's very urgent!"

Her eyes widened. "Of course. Come this way, sir, madam, miss, we'll have you to rights immediately. I'm trained for this, got my St John's certificates."

What a jewel!

We looked around us. "Have you seen Percy?" Jeremy asked.

"He'll be swimming. He's always in the pool after a ritual." That was Padraig who had sped over. "Why? What's wrong?"

But we were off. We ran through the crowd, looking for black-robed figures, of whom there were many, but heading as fast as we could to the pool area. Padraig was behind us, shouting at us to stop.

Percy bounced up and down on the springboard getting impetus for his exhibition. I watched as I ran towards the pool, slipping on the wet tiles. Once again he executed a beautiful dive, a pike this time. The gaggle of people in the pool kept to the sides during his perfect entry, but again, as he broke the surface, they gave him an accolade. I wondered how many times this ritual had been repeated since I left earlier. He seemed to need and flourish on adulation.

He tossed the water from his face and headed for the steps.

He grasped the two steel hand rails and started to rise when I saw the tiny black shape dart out from the amid the rose parterres.

Jeremy was already speeding towards her, but the floor was wet and slippery, and there were people in the way. Wet people, who had no idea what was going on.

The figure tossed back her hood as Percy hauled himself up out of the water.

She shrieked a single word. "Balance!" and she slashed across his throat.

He tried to protect himself with a hand, but was too late.

I skidded to a halt watching, fascinated as the realization that he was dying and who was responsible for this state of affairs crossed Percy's face. And then with a bubbling hiss his strength left him, and he fell, spurting his life-blood in wide arcs, backward into the pool.

Jeremy was aiming through the horrified, screaming crowd for Lady Finching.

He was too late.

She slashed her robe open, and was leaping, completely naked into the pool, intent on some mad fury of her own while others in bathing costumes or less were clambering out at the far side of the pool. All around the bubbling sinking Percy and the grey naked figure of his nemesis, pink and red clouds billowed as she slashed again and again.

I had to get to her.

I had to stop her from killing anyone else.

Without thinking I dived in. One had to try.

As I surfaced through the pink water, I met her face to face.

We were treading water, me fully clothed and being dragged down, her light as a cork, smiling at me.

"So, Alice, you know what I am doing," she said. "Let me be. My life is over."

"It need not be," I said, knowing it was untrue.

She cackled. "Don't lie to me, Alice. I know you mean well, but don't lie to me. I'm already dead."

Then she leapt upward into the air. "Do what you will,"

she screeched, brandishing her sickle for the last time.

I flung myself backwards to avoid it, but I was safe enough.

Through wings of pink and white water, I watched transfixed as she brought it down on her own throat, causing a a red jet to course upwards and outwards.

I didn't enjoy bringing her back, any more than I enjoyed bringing back Percy, but someone had to bring them home, and I was the only one living left in the pool.

The smell of blood even overtook the chlorine. When Jeremy held his hands out to me, I saw my pretty flowery white blouse was pink. The water was red around me, and I felt sick. He pulled me out and held me close.

"Are you OK?" he asked. I was soaking wet, my clothes heavy and hanging on me and I was soaking him.

"I'm fine, but … excuse me..." I pulled away from him, and deposited my stomach contents as discreetly as I could beneath a rose tree.

36

It was much later when I got to drive back to Wethersley.

Guy and Nigel had thought we'd abandoned them; but they saw the police arrive and had the sense to stay put in the safety of Guy's car. Meanwhile, Jeremy and I changed our clothes yet again, re-packed our cases and gave our statements. He pulled some sort of rank, and we were permitted to depart.

Elisabeth, wide-eyed and pale-faced hugged us before we slipped away.

I knew her part in this afternoon's triple death, and she knew I knew.

Neither of us spoke, except to say goodbye.

I had seen people die before but I had never seen someone take her own life, and the face of Lady Finching behind the spray of her own blood will live with me for a long time.

I understood, oh yes, I understood, but it didn't efface the memory.

Neither Guy nor Nigel had seen what had happened, and I was glad of it.

They had enough to deal with. They sat silent throughout the journey, each locked in his own private Hell, Nigel's little dog between them..

I concentrated on the road.

I didn't want to keep seeing Lady Finching's final smile.

It took me a good three hours to bring us back to Wethersley, the sun almost set. Jeremy had passed me earlier, and was waiting with my parents when we arrived. He'd obviously warned them.

Mother took Guy in her arms and crooned at him, taking

him in. My father welcomed Nigel warmly, insisting he come inside.

I huddled into Jeremy, glad to be back. I had missed his comfortable presence on the silent journey and made up for it now.

"Are you really alright, Alice?" he asked, kissing my forehead as he finally let me go. "You know, you were bloody magnificent. A lesson to us all."

"Don't make me swollen-headed. I just did what had to be done. Like you did earlier."

We walked slowly indoors. "Did you tell them what happened?"

"I did. Gently. I stressed Guy's and Nigel's distress, rather than anything you or I might have felt or experienced. It seemed better that way."

"Couldn't have said it better," I said. "Let them make a fuss of the two of them. We'll get a story out of Nigel, I'm sure. He's been ill-used for years, I should imagine, the poor little scrap."

"Your father will take care of him. Oh, and by the way, he said his barns and his studio have been broken into recently."

I sighed. "Who does he reckon it was?"

He shrugged. "I honestly don't think he cares, but his face brightened when I told him about the engagement being off. So did your mother's. She told everyone, and told them we all had to look suitably sad when Guy turned up, then instructed that a bottle of champagne be cracked open."

Yes, that was Maman.

We joined the others in the snug, where a bright fire burned and a small table was laid. Mrs. Mac brought in bowls of thick pea and vegetable soup and doorsteps of bread for three. I hugged her. She was always there, reassuring and comforting when we most needed her.

I took the soup bowls and our wet clothing down to

the kitchen. "What exactly has happened?" Mrs. Mac demanded.

"Guy's engagement is at an end," I said. "It was ill done on the lady's part, but in front of witnesses, three of whom are here."

"Heavens be praised," she said.

"*Dieu soit béni,*" agreed Angelique, crossing herself. "You will give me all the details in private, please. And what am I to do with all this washing? Oh, and your young man's, too? What can you have been doing?"

"I fell into a swimming pool and he dragged me out. And no details, Angelique, I'm afraid. I can't. It would hurt Guy too much. I was there and it was nasty. Least said, soonest mended. It's past. Let it go."

Angelique sniffed. "That bad, eh?"

"That bad, Angelique. I wouldn't have wished that on him, and as you know, I'm not my brother's greatest supporter."

Mrs. Mac chuckled. "You can say that again. Oh, well, perhaps we don't need to know."

Angelique looked at Mrs. Mac wonderingly. "He always liked to confide in you, Morag. Perhaps, when he's feeling a bit better one of your lemon meringue pies down here in the kitchen…?"

Mrs. Mac bit her lips together. "I'll think about that… Yes, it's worth a try. When I have a bit of spare sugar and can get the lemons... He'll be hurting a bit now though, but as soon as he starts returning to being his own pompous self… Just now we'll be nice to him. He's just a puir wee boy inside."

Angelique sniffed. "His pride is hurt, that's all."

"Perhaps that's all he's got," I said. "If my fiancée behaved like his did, I'd be very shocked and very very hurt."

"And you have a fiancé?" Angelique asked. "You should

introduce me. It's not as though I'm not doing his laundry here."

I shook my head. "No, I don't have one, but I'll rinse the clothes through, no problem. I only brought the stuff down here because it was wet and I didn't want it hanging round in our cases or our rooms."

"You'll do no such thing. I'll not hear of it. Your mother would be most annoyed if I let you touch a young man's laundry, you a single woman!"

"And you, Angelique? Why should you do his washing?"

Angelique beamed, "I'm French, remember, and I have been married, so garments of masculine gender hold no shock for me. Whereas you, well, best wait until you are wed, *n'est-ce pas*? And there'll be no 'anky-panky, washing your smalls in the same water in the same sink"

I chuckled. "Oh, Tant'Ange, you're worse than Maman!"

Angelique's smile became a chuckle. "I try, Alice, I try!"

Sam and the Rev arrived shortly after Leggy and Bobby. My mother did the introductions. Guy knew Leggy, of course, and had met Bobby a couple of times. The others were new to him, and all were new to Nigel.

"We have business to discuss," my father said. "If you choose to join us we must ask you for absolute secrecy."

"Does it have any bearing on what happened this afternoon?" Guy asked.

"It has everything to do with this afternoon after you had left Finchings," Jeremy told him. "But nothing at all to do with what you experienced there. You have my word on that."

"I'd like to join you, if I may," Nigel said, and added quietly, "I'm good at secrecy."

"Then I shall, too," Guy said. "Give me something to take my mind off things."

It certainly did that!

We gave Sam the story he'd been promised.

We gave Leggy the news he'd been looking for.

We gave the Rev the form of the ritual, and with that the information that Elisabeth was every inch a formal High Priestess who didn't cast herself upon the altar, but maintained a dignified presence throughout the proceedings.

We omitted everything about Sylvia's and Archie's Beltane encounter, but left in her witnessing his death subsequent to her decision to end her engagement to Guy.

We went into detail about the death of Percy, and Lady Finching's suicide, and finished on the advent of the police.

"And then," I said to Guy and Nigel, "I drove you home."

Guy looked at me astonished.

I deserved it.

I'll treasure that look for a long long time.

Nigel looked puzzled for a moment. Then he got his tongue into gear.

"Are you telling me that Uncle Archie and Uncle Percy are dead? You saw them both, and they are dead?"

"We saw Percy. We took your sister's word on it that Archie was dead. The amount of blood on her... He wouldn't have survived," Jeremy said. "We had someone call the emergency services but they'd have been too late. So, Nigel, yes. They are both dead."

Nigel nodded, taking it all in. Then he pulled a handkerchief from his pocket, blew his nose loudly, then dabbed his eyes. "Please excuse me. It sounds cruel and heartless, but this is just the best news ever. I'm free. I'm free at last." And he shook with sobs, which gradually changed, as the realization seeped through, to soft laughter.

Leggy stretched his hand across the table and touched

Nigel's. "If it's any consolation, young man, I feel exactly the same. It's wonderful to see you liberated at an age when your life is still before you."

"You, sir? What could they possibly have over you, sir?" Nigel said when he was able to speak once more.

"They put the fear of the devil in me, and ruined my childhood – and were instrumental in nearly killing me. Lady Finching has not died in vain." He raised his glass. "To a noble woman. Lady Finching."

We toasted her in 12 year old single malt. She was worth it, despite being a murderer.

"So what will happen to the angels?" Sam asked. "They've got a lot to answer for. Three more deaths today."

"Don't forget Lord Finching," I said. "It's not the angels' fault. It's people's ideas."

"Exactly," said the Rev. "How are you coming along with the cleaning, Roger?"

Pa beamed. "I'll have them ready by Friday," he said.

"Then I'll come over on Saturday, and we can bring this history to a conclusion," said the Rev. "You are all invited. And any sympathetic guests. I'm really looking forward to it."

While the rest of us made notes in our diaries, my brother looked puzzled. "What angels? You mean you have a set of angels here?"

My mother smiled. "The angels of the days of the week? Oh yes, but not exactly here."

"But …? It was Algy's idea…?"

"No," Nigel told him. "It was Uncle Percy's or Uncle Archie's. I told you. They wanted them. You were just a pawn in the game of getting hold of your father's land and interests and, subsequently, the angels." He looked at the gathered company. "If you want any details that I can give on the way the Merediths work, I will be happy to work with you in any way I can. However, not now. It's been a really long day for me, and Spider needs his final walkie."

The party broke up.

Mother took him aside. "I've put you in the Blue Room with Jeremy tonight. You don't mind, do you? He'll show you where everything is, won't you Jeremy? And, Nigel, you stay as long as you need to. Do you understand?"

I thought he was going to start crying again. His eyes filled up, and he shook his head. "Thank you very much Lady Wethersley. I don't want to be a nuisance... but I really appreciate your kindness." He looked at Jeremy.

"I'll be down soon," he whispered as he got up. "Don't go away."

"Would I dream of disobeying you?"

"It wasn't an order, Alice. It was an optimistic request."

We said good night to our guests; the Rev and Sam got into Leggy's Humber, and went back indoors. Guy said goodnight and went off to bed. My parents and I sat before the fire, sipping single malt in silence.

Jeremy slipped down the stairs to join us. "Nigel's fine," he said. "Thank you for looking after him. I don't think he can go home. I don't know that there will be much of a home left for him, by the time the creditors have done their job."

"Ah," said my father. "Well, he can stay until he decides what to do. We've room enough here. Cherie will enjoy another person to fuss over."

"She's just got Guy back," I said drily.

Maman laughed. "I never lost Guy. He won't tell you so, but he was getting cold feet about the wedding. But a man cannot pull out. I think we should inform the press immediately. Before the opposition has a chance to deny any rumours?"

God, she was good!

"Has Guy given you permission?" I asked.

"Oh, don't you worry about that... Of course he has."

"Then ring Bar. She'll be delighted." Besides, I owed her. I fished in my bag and found my address book. "Do you want me to do the dirty deed?"

My mother smiled. "You know the lady better than me."

Yes, Maman, don't get your hands in the muck.

I went to the phone in the study and sent her a telegram.

```
WETHERSLEY NESMITH BROWN WEDDING IN
JUNE DEFINITELY OFF STOP RING ME
FOR MORE INFORMATION AND ABOUT THE
FINCHING FIASCO STOP LOVE ALICE C
```

I specified that it should be sent to her at the office and at home, in fact wherever she was. I knew she had my numbers, and it would stop others from muscling in.

When I got back to the snug Jeremy was down. "He's getting himself settled," he said. "I forced some of your scotch on him, Roger. He's having it in the bath. I hope you don't mind."

"Bloody good idea," said Pa. "Did you learn anything?"

"Only more filth. He's been sold into abuse for the family's sake, just as Sylvia was. The only difference was that Sylvia was a promiscuous creature and actively enjoyed being the sexual plaything of the Merediths. Nigel was raped at the age of fifteen. He was always a slight person. He didn't stand a chance. Archie was the active one, but Percy also took part. They filled him with terror that if he told he would be killed by the demon angels."

My mother looked sick. "How could they? No wonder he was so scared all the time."

"His parents allowed this to happen?" Pa asked.

"Yes, sir. Er, sorry, Roger."

Pa waved it aside. "They deserve Hell." He wasn't a

believer, but the way he said that sent a shiver down my spine. "Anything I can do to help? Apart from keep Nigel away from them."

Maman said softly, "What will happen to Sylvia? It wasn't her fault."

"No, at first it wasn't," I mused. "But she is twenty years old. She made her decision. We're all better off without her and without Bulgy Algy and Anthea."

Jeremy passed round his cigarette case. My father took one, but Maman asked for a Gauloise. She smoked rarely, but today had been fraught. I fixed one into her cigarette holder; it was long, ebonised wood with a single diamond and a gold rim at the business end. She was class personified. She inhaled as I lit her up, then let the smoke out with a sigh. My shorter plain black holder was pedestrian in comparison. The four of us smoked in companionable silence.

My father downed the last of his whiskey. "Come on, *Chérie*, I'm for my nest."

He kissed me good night, shook hands with Jeremy.

My mother kissed us both. "Have a good night, each," she said, then slipped her hand into Pa's and climbed the stairs.

I pulled out another Gauloise and fitted it into my holder. "A good day's work, Jem," I said.

He smiled. "Can I have one of those?"

"I can deny you nothing," I said, handing him my case.

I watched him very carefully. His reaction would make all the difference.

He flipped the lid and took a cigarette, then closed the case once more, and raised it to his lips. And he kissed it then handed it back. "It belongs to you so it is dear to me." He brought out his lighter, lit us both from one flame.

I was home and dry.

He left my room in the wee small hours on bare feet. I knew it would be a long cold walk to the Blue Room, but he'd do it without a sound, and I doubt if he'd disturb Nigel's sleep. I lay back in my schoolgirl's bed having at last given it a taste of what a woman needed. And I relived it in memory, shortly before I slept.

It was Angelique who brought the Sunday papers to my notice when I came down for breakfast. She rammed in front of me and lapsed into French. "Read this, if you please!" she ordered.

'TRIPLE DEATH AT MAGNATE'S VILLA' ran the headline.

"Don't tell me you and your oh-so-nice-friend didn't have something to do with this!" she demanded, poking a manicured forefinger at the black and white picture.

I made out the pool where two of the deaths took place.

She looked at me accusingly. "It says that Sylvia saw the first murder. Does Guy know? How could he leave her in a situation like that? How could you let him?"

I put my arm around her and moved the newsprint away from my face. "Calm yourself, Angelique," I said gently, in her own tongue. "She had already thrown her engagement ring back at him in a very vicious and very final manner," I said. "He was in a state of shock about a quarter of a mile away. She wouldn't have thanked him for being there. And we left her with her parents. It was all we could do."

She sniffed.

It obviously wasn't what she would have done, but she was marginally placated, for she reverted to English. "Oh, you English are so bloody cold! I don't like the young woman, but she must be in a terrible state, watching someone being killed before her eyes."

I nodded.

Of course, I was used to it and could cope with it as a matter of course, I thought grimly. But she didn't know. She didn't need to know.

She pointed at the pictures of Archie, Percy and Lady

Finching. "This person has been here, yes? How does this affect this family?"

"*Ne t'inquiete pas,* Angelique," Maman told her, coming over. "It sounds cruel, but it suits us very well. These were not nice people. Ask anybody." She was obviously an expert now.

I made a mental note to ask her how Lady Finching's death had affected her sometime.

37

It was a fine day for a drive out of London, and George in his Army Surplus Flying helmet enjoyed every moment of the trip as tail-end Charlie in the Morgan.

We reached Wethersley by mid morning. I introduced George to everyone, even the staff who had been brought in for the afternoon's tea on the lawn. He charmed the lot of them, and I left him with Mrs. Mac and the caterers, helping them in the kitchen. He'd never seen so much food in his life. How and from whence it had come one didn't ask. There must have been some clever pulling in of favours going on, for our family's points had all be used up on Guy's dinner with the Merediths.

Larry had brought the paintings over in a cart the previous evening. Now they were stacked, wrapped from view, back in Pa's studio. We followed him in.

"Blimey, Guv, what 'appened 'ere?" I asked. "You 'ad burglars?"

The studio was immaculate.

It didn't look like a studio.

It had been repainted, bright white, every tool, brush, tube of paint, every scrap of inspirational material, every last grubby 'artistic' item had vanished from sight. The only things left in there were seven easels ranged along the back wall.

My father coughed apologetically. "Your mother got her way again. But she was right. It needed to be done. Oh, don't worry, all the stuff's put away, all my pictures are stowed safely. Except a few bits and pieces I've outgrown. They're at Lowthers."

Jeremy and I stood speechless, looking at the bright

white space, the windows transparent, the ceiling without a trace of a cobweb, the flagstones gleaming from a generous polishing.

"Well, don't just stand there like a pair of boobies," Pa said gruffly. "Give me a hand with these. The Rev will be along in two ticks, and I want it ready for him."

We three undid the angels from their protective cloths, one by one.

They were still big, still impressive, but having been cleaned – and Pa had done a thorough job – and placed in a bright clean environment, some of the darkness seemed to have dissipated. Or perhaps it was never there.

We set them on their easels.

We guessed the order. I knew Friday was Hanael, and that Leggy's angel – I still thought of it as Leggy's – was Tuesday. We were debating the others when Reverend Simmons came in.

After a short greeting he took charge. "That one, all golds and pinks – Sunday. Monday, that lady. Oh, yes, very much a lady, that one. Him, Wednesday, and that one, definitely Saturday. He looks like he's suffered a bit. And lastly... yes, Thursday...."

We put them in order.

I felt the hairs crawling at the back of my neck. Beside me Jeremy stifled a shiver.

"Yes," said the Rev. "They retain it. Now what I have to do is ground it." He turned to my father. "You have done a remarkable job, Lord Wethersley, getting them together and cleaned like this. And thank you so much for providing me with a perfect working space. It's splendid, absolutely splendid."

"I'll tell the co-workers you're delighted," said Pa. "Do you want us to leave you to it?"

"That would be best, I think. At a time like this an audience is unnecessary. If I'm not out and back with you by," he inspected his watch, "let's say noon? Yes, I should be finished by noon. If I'm not with you, come and fetch me." He beamed at us, "No, I'm not expecting anything untoward, I assure you. And a cup of tea after would be most welcome."

So that was that. I wasn't going to see what he did. Which was a pity, because it would have been interesting.

Was I developing a taste for ritual?

But I didn't believe in God *per se*.

But I did believe in good and evil, and I knew that the Rev. Simmons was good to the soles of his boots. I'd like to see how he did things, having spent part of last weekend in a temple of a different sort

Indoors everything was busy. My mother and Angelique were doing flowers, the kitchen was preparing sandwiches, cakes and jellies for an army, and Guy and Nigel were helping set out trestle tables on the terrace at the rear of the house. The sun would hit that, clouds permitting, at two, and continue until sunset. I went with them to spread sheets on the tables, anchoring them with old crockery.

"Who's coming?" asked Guy. "I thought it was only going to be about twelve at the most, us included, but it's like they're preparing for a siege in there."

"Partly my fault," I said. "But also Pa's. You know how he likes a party."

"So how many? And who? They're killing the fatted calf, or at least the fatted pastry."

I smiled. "There are some really important people coming," I said. "And the press will be there."

"What!" Guy looked at me quizzically. "What the Hell is all this about, Alice? What are you up to?"

"Wait and see."

He sniffed and humphed. "Bloody women. Can't understand them," he muttered, stomping off.

They had already started arriving.

Bobby turned up with Thelma looking windblown but exhilarated, both of them. They came inside and peeled off heavy leather coats, helmets, goggles and gauntlets – both of them – and began wiping their noses with gentlemen's handkerchiefs. They had obviously enjoyed the journey down. "We did it from my place in thirty-five minutes," Thelma beamed. "And you know what a pig it is getting through Hammersmith Broadway on a Saturday."

"Ach, it was nothing," said Bobby. "But Thelma, I've got to tell you, riding with you behind was like riding silk. You did all the right things, and without me telling you."

"Well I can drive a motorbike," she said. "I just can't afford to run one."

"You do? Would you like a go of the old girl, and I'll hang on behind?"

"You'd trust me?" She was awed at the offer.

Bobby winked at her. "Well, you know me, I like to live dangerously. It's so much more fun!"

Mr. and Mrs. Arnold Lowther arrived, so did Leggy, in his Humber with Sid Williams, Mrs. Sid and the Gaffer. We were busy introducing people to each other. The Rev, who had finished his spiritual work, his tea and a fairly substantial lunch, came down to meet people. Sam with him, was equally afire with all that had happened in the past week.

My father introduced us to the President of the Royal Academy. He looked like a well-turned out academic, rather than an artist.

"He's an architect," Pa whispered. "They don't get their hands dirty!"

More academicians turned up.

Josiah and his family, all in their little Austin A7, bundled in to bursting – his wife was large to start with and pregnant to boot, his four daughters squashed in the rear seat – exploded onto the lawn, while Padraig arrived with Emily in tow; she wearing a new and very pretty pink dress, all flowers and leaves. It knocked years off her. That and the new haircut. Love must suit her!

Rufus Grassington arrived in a local taxi in full Ariosto fig with the leopard-lady on his arm. "Darling," she said huskily, "What a wonderful place. I can feel the vibes already."

More and more people kept coming. People I'd never met. Maddy and Basil and Enid and the nanny arrived amongst this lot, and then the car that I was looking for joined the queue parked along our carriage way. It belonged to my friend with the mellifluous voice from Scarborough.

I touched Jeremy's arm. "Come, he's arrived. He'll need a hand."

But he didn't.

Muriel was there. "He's driven all the way down in one go," she sniffed. "I hope it'll be worth it. He's not a well man, you know."

We managed to separate him from her, introducing her to Angelique and Mrs. Mac, while taking him to meet Rev. Simmons. And we hit the jackpot there. They knew each other. They had written to each other, had exchanged learned papers.

"So you had the Hanael!" said the Rev, his eyes blazing.

"Yes," expostulated the little scholar, "And do you know Hannah? She had the Lady!"

I hadn't recognized Hannah.

I'd last seen here in curlers, a head scarf, and an overall with gumboots on. Now she was in a country tweed suit, a silk blouse and a very dashing hat, looking a different woman altogether. "So you got them all. I'm so glad. Terrible about the Master, though, wasn't it? But the angels are safe."

"As safe as we can make them," I said.

My wheelchair-bound friend spoke. "Good. You did well." He turned to the Rev. "And you have diffused them? Not completely, I hope."

I watched a shared twinkle pass between them before I moved on.

Bar and Tom arrived with all his equipment, but Elizabeth arrived last of all, wearing black, as became a lady whose fiancé had just passed on. Her long bottle blonde hair had been cut to an inch long, and was now a natural dark brown. She looked every inch a high priestess. I did introductions as far as I could.

My father stood on a chair and waved a crow-scaring wooden rattle. That caught everyone's attention, and shut them up.

He called out the staff, too, because this was an auspicious day, and he said we should all share it.

Then he gave the story. Of an artist, who wanted to leave something of himself, to the local church, a set of pictures. He told the story well, and thankfully, briefly, so that no-one could be bored nor offended. He must have worked it out with the Rev.

He said the pictures had been bought, then used, then lost and now, once more, they had been found and re-united. A set of angels. "And I invite you all to come and see them. They've never been seen by the general public, which was their original intention, so you will be the first to appreciate Mr. Greystoke's work. This way, please. Form an orderly queue, there's good people."

He led us over to his studio, opened the door and went in and raised the blinds.

I brought my wheelchair-bound friend in first, with Hannah by his side.

The room was no longer a studio, but a chapel. I smelt the incense, frankincense with a hint of rose, a waft of holiness in the air, a reminder of what had been done.

They both raised their right hands and bowed their heads as they entered, and I did, too.

The darkness of the paintings had gone.

They were still powerful. Still challenging, but different from before.

They were strong, each of them strong in a different way.

These angels were active creative beings, each with its own sphere of influence.

I worked my way down the row. They should have been in a ring, but that would have been impossible in the space we had available. I was rather glad that they weren't in a circle, because to be surrounded by them... well, I could see why people might have problems with that.

I watched as people went through: Gaffer Williams, supported by his son and his daughter in law, his face running with tears, but not of fear, or any negative emotion, simply joy; Mr. Arnold, amazed because he thought he knew the artist's work; the President of the Royal Academy, shaking his head in disbelief for the same reason. He said to me afterwards, "Are you sure these are by Greystoke?"

"I've got documentation, sir," I said. "I'd be happy to supply it."

Leggy limped through the studio. He came out stiffly, but standing tall. "I can't thank you enough, Alice. I really can't. They've come into their own at last. What are you going to do with them?"

"One of them's yours."

Elisabeth came out. "Yes," she said. "What is going to happen to them?"

"Elisabeth, let me introduce you to a gentleman who knows where your father's papers and books are."

Bobby came through with Thelma. "What's your father done to them? They look almost benign."

"Pa and the Rev," I said. "There's a lot of work gone into them."

Emily came out now, with Padraig.

"How do you feel, Emily? Now you see them again."

"Impressed. And honoured," she said. "I had no idea they were so beautiful. They are beautiful, aren't they, Padraig?"

His face was stern. "Oh yes," he said, off-handedly. "Very beautiful. Very beautiful…" He was watching something in the distance with a puzzled frown.

I followed his gaze.

George was playing air-battles with two of Josiah's daughters and Nigel's little dog, Spider.

Padraig put his hand in his pocket and pulled out a small tin. "Care for a parma violet, anyone?" The skin of his hand was pinkly clean, but beneath his thumbnail ran a black line of printer's ink.

I went across to George as soon as I was able. "George, come with me and keep your head down."

"Why Miss? What have I done?"

"Nothing. There's a couple of people I want you to see. And there's someone I don't want to see you. At least not up close."

"Cor, Miss. Really?" He matched my step, dropping his head so his face wasn't noticeable. We went indoors; I pointed out of the window. "See that Lady in the pink flowery dress? Just there, talking to my mother? Look who's with her."

George looked. " 'At's 'im, Miss. Look at the way he stands. And he's got the same suit on. I noticed him earlier. I went and had a good look, quiet like, from behind the cars. If you have a look on the car he came in, he's got one of them rising sun things on the dashboard. I'll show you if you like. I was going to anyway, but then your Dad started talking and things got all mixed up."

"Come and meet an old friend of mine. He'd very much like to meet you."

I took him across to Leggy who was eating egg and cress

sandwiches.

"You're the young man who did the picture," he said. "I'm delighted to meet you. I've heard so much about you."

"Aw, Miss, you shouldn't 'ave!"

"No, not just Alice. Bobby, my batman, and Jeremy, too, they say you're a very shrewd operator." He held out his hand for a shake.

"Thank you, sir," said George, wide eyed. "I've seen the bloke what come round before Miss Alice's flat was done over. And he's got one of them signs on the dashboard of his car. I 'ad a look."

"Indeed. Well you sit down with me, and I'll get Bobby or one of the others to check that out. You're sure it's him?"

"Positive. But he ain't wearing the ring. I looked."

"He is eating parma violets, though," I said. "And there is black ink under his nails. And there is a problem. He's one of my parents' oldest friends."

"Ah," said Leggy. "Well, let's get Bobby to see that sign in his car."

He called Bobby over. "What sort of car, George?"

"Morris Minor, about two years old, black, JLM 38, about halfway down the drive."

Bobby disappeared for a couple of minutes. When he returned he nodded once. "He's right. I think we should employ this lad, Leggy."

"Is it worth a shilling?" George asked, never one to miss an opportunity to capitalise.

Prices had obviously gone up with the praise.

Leggy reached in his pocket. "Half a dollar do?" he asked flicking a half-crown at him.

George caught it neatly. "You're a real toff, sir, and no mistake."

"Keep away from the chap," Bobby said. "He might just recognize you."

485

"I know. I'm going back to help out in the kitchen. He won't go in there. He's too posh for that. Besides that lady needs a lot of looking after."

I caught up with Jeremy shortly afterwards.

"OK," he said. "What do you want to do about it?"

"Nothing. See what happens."

"It's time to join the others in the library."

Seated around the big table were the President, the Rev. Simmons, Sam, Pa and Maman, Leggy and Elisabeth. There were two seats vacant. We took them.

Mr. Mac was standing behind Maman. Hovering, actually. He could be incredibly nosy when he chose, and he was choosing now.

Maman turned her head. "Mr. McMurdy, we can manage for a moment," she whispered. "Don't doubt we shall be first to call on you when we need you."

"Yes, Milady." The tone was Scottish baronial sepulchral. His pace that of a chief mourner. What a ham!

I looked around me.

All those with any sort of reputable or legitimate interest were gathered about me – Maman excepted, but she was even nosier that Mr. Mac and I couldn't have kept her out.

"The problem remains what will happen to the pictures," I said. "When Lord Finching died I was bequeathed six of them. It will all take some time to go through probate, and perhaps there may be a challenge from his daughters…" I glanced at Elisabeth questioningly.

"I shouldn't think they would want them. They'd like the cash they'd bring, but it would all go to waste." She looked around the company. "I can… er… ensure that they don't want them. I have a certain influence; they listen to me… After all, we don't want them going out of the country, do we?"

"No, no," and "Perish the thought!" came from around the room.

We were all agreed on that.

Elisabeth smiled. "Good. They were my father's. He bought them fair and square, and he used them properly. They were designed as meditation pieces on a large scale. I have not the space for them, nor have I the use for them. I would prefer they went elsewhere, but to a place of safety."

"Sam, your grandfather painted them. What do you think?" I asked.

Sam pulled out a cigarette and lit it. He had given it a lot of thought. "My Grandfather painted them originally for the church. Rev. Simmons's church, St. Michael and All Angels. I think they should go there. But I also think they should be displayed – shown to the art world in general - because they're very different from my grandfather's other work. They show a whole different aspect to his character and his artistic abilities."

"Sir," I said to the President of the Royal Academy, "You've seen the pictures. You've heard what has been said by the two people who have most claim on the pictures. I'm only their guardian, but I am an artist's daughter. I would like to propose a small exhibition under your auspices, of works of a dead academician, after which they could be surrendered to the church for which they were planned. Would you be willing to contemplate that as a suggestion?"

He nodded. "I think I could contemplate that every well. Now you say you only have six of them. Who owns the seventh?"

"I do," said Leggy. "I'll be delighted to donate the picture to this scheme. It's payment enough."

My father looked at Rev. Simmons. "Is that acceptable to you, Reverend?"

"It is. Very much so, thank you. But of course, it all depends on the Bishop."

"Then we are agreed, ladies and gentlemen?" Pa asked. "In principle?"

There were nods and 'ayes' of assent.
I sighed.
A weight fell off my shoulders.
I wanted to laugh.
The angels were finally going home.
Maman waved her hand.
Mr. Mac was over in a shot.
The champagne was duly broached and poured.
It was a moment to savour.
I leaned across to Pa. "I think it might be good if we told Padraig of this," I said.
Leggy heard. "I'll second that, Roger."
"I too," said Jeremy.
"We-ell," Pa said eyeing the President.
"Are these the young people who found them?" the President asked. "The ones who did the spadework?"
"Yes, sir," I said.
"Then how can I refuse? You're talking of Padraig Flynn? Excellent chap. He'll keep mum for us."
It was carried. No reasons were asked, and none given.
"Thank you," I said.
The President got to his feet. "I'll need some supporters when we come to discuss the proposal with our members, and there are a few here. If you don't mind, I'll go and start canvassing now. Splendid meeting, lovely to meet you all." He shook hands with all the men, kissed the women, and was out within half a minute, shouting and waving at Padraig and Emily.

Jeremy and I followed him out, but more slowly, hand in hand. It was over. It felt strange. We wandered past people eating and chatting in the balmy sunshine, catching snippets of conversation as we passed: Muriel congratulating Mrs Mac on her cake, Rufus and Mr Arnold discussing the paintings and how they worked, the President expounding to Padraig, Emily and Josiah the proposed deal... It was all so normal.

And then, of course, it wasn't.

Nigel was waving at us from the corner of the house, beckoning us to follow him, and making 'shush!' movements.

We hurried past the studio where Tom was now making the first official photographs of the angels for some time, with Bar telling him what to do. She caught sight of us in passing. "Wonderful day, Alice. Thank you. Speak with you soon…"

"Of course," I called back.

Nigel was running now, Spider at his heels.

Oh God, I thought, not a repeat of last Saturday!

We ran round the side of the house to the front where all the cars were parked.

He pointed to the far end of the drive.

"My sister's arrived." He panted. "She's got Guy over there. I think she wants him back!"

"What?" I gasped.

"You've got to be joking," Jeremy breathed.

Nigel shook his head. "He's with her, listen!"

Her voice was high, shrill, angry, piercing. "It's traditional. If I don't marry you, I keep the ring."

"No. You threw me and the ring." Guy's voice was deeper but just as angry.

"I want the bloody ring, Guy! You owe me my ring."

"After what you did, I owe you sweet Fanny Adams!" he snapped.

"It's mine, and I want it!"

We hastened to the source of the noise.

Whereas Guy had lost weight this past week – despite Mrs. Mac's best efforts – Sylvia appeared to have gained some, although the monumentally enveloping black coat she was wearing may have had much to do with it. Her anger made her so formidable that Guy looked positively outclassed.

Normally ready to stand up for what he considered his rights, I watched him cower away from her, backing into a tree, although he shouted back just as loudly. "No. No. You threw it back. You don't want me, but you want it. Well, bugger you, Sylvia! You're nothing but a scheming little whore, and a greedy one at that! I'm well rid of you!"

She kept on screaming, "I want it! It's mine and I want it! It's my due, you miser!" Her face was close to his now, her black gloved hand raised threateningly.

He ducked away. "Charming! Then for that you'll get nothing from me, nothing from this family. You're over. Past and forgotten!" He turned on his heel to walk away.

She grabbed at his collar, hauled him back to face her, and leaned over him menacingly.

Her face contorted into a snarl.

We were almost on them now.

She had his face even closer to hers now and was shouting right at him.

"Wrong, Guy! Ring, or you're dead!" She held her hand out. "Ring, or you're dead. I mean it. Archie showed me how. And you'll never know when I'm going to strike, I'm that good."

"I don't have the bloody ring!" Guy shouted, pushing himself free. "And threatening me won't do any good." He ducked a right hook, and dodged away from the tree and ran towards us.

"Need a spot of help?" asked Nigel, catching him, and pushing himself between his sister and my brother. "She can be an evil little cat when she's roused. You've had a very lucky escape, Guy."

Sylvia whipped round, ran our way, rather spoiling the effect by catching her foot in a root.

She recovered almost immediately and spat out her venom in a curse. "Ah, my brother the traitor. You filthy little rat! You're dead, too! I'll have you both. I'll creep up on you when you least expect it, and slit your throats."

Holy shit, I thought, this is Madness.

The eyes confirmed it

I knew I had to haul her back, or at least try.

I walked towards her, putting myself in front of Guy, walking to the left, so that she would focus on me, take her attention from the objects of her wrath. Jeremy caught up with me, and took my hand as we kept her looking at us rather than on Guy and Nigel.

"Sylvia, what are you doing here?" I asked quietly.

"I've come for my ring back. Oh, there's your dishy beau. Hello dishy beau!"

She winked, and waved a silly little hand up at eye-level. "God, you really are dishy. Come here and let me look at you closer, eh?"

He let go of my hand and walked towards her. "Hello, Sylvia. How are you?" His voice was coffee and cream with a dash of brandy, the devil.

She giggled. "Not too bad. I knew you'd be here, so I brought your jacket back."

"That's really kind of you," he said. I knew the smile he'd be using. It worked.

She puckered up. "Mmm. I thought so, too. I had it cleaned, but the blood won't come out. I've been wearing it. To remind me of you, but Mummy said I should give it back. I love it. You were so manly. No-one's ever given me their jacket before when I needed it… But I suppose I'll have to give it back?" She winked as she turned back to the carriage way, and blew him a kiss over her shoulder. "You could escort me to my car."

He didn't move.

"Oh don't be shy," she said and sashayed across to us and slipped her arm round Jeremy's. "I won't hurt you."

"You're not going to let her…" Guy hissed at me.

"Shut up, Guy!" I nodded my head to the right. "Make

your way out of her range the pair of you, and watch."

He accompanied her to her car, with us three following them from a secure distance.

"Tell you what, Sylvia," I heard him say. "You keep the jacket. Just take it and drive off home. Keep the jacket, my jacket, as you know, as a reminder ... of... something that might have happened." He looked over his shoulder at me, regretfully, then shook his head. "Only it's too late now. You were committed and I was free, but now you're free, but I'm already committed..."

She looked at him, fluttered her eyelashes. "You mean that? You mean..."

He nodded. "Oh, in another time, another place, another universe," he said. "It could have been you and me, baby. But in this one? Think of it as a movie, baby ..."

He opened the door for her, helped her in, and closed it. She wound down the window.

"Just take yourself home, safely, Sylvia, and remember this. It would have been great, but it can never be. You don't need to come looking for me nor for anyone round here. This is the past. Spread your wings, doll, and fly into the future, your glorious future, the one you dreamed of as a little girl, sweetheart, with your head held high, It's out their calling to you, you know that" he whispered, and dropped a very sweet, chaste kiss on her forehead. "No regrets, baby. Fare thee well!"

I waited for her reaction.

Dammit, we all did, goggle-eyed.

"Go home, go home, go home," chanted my brother, under his breath.

"And never come back," murmured her brother.

"So mote it be!" I breathed, stamping my foot.

I'd learned something from Mr. Thorburn.

And it worked.

She smiled up at him with a silly besotted look, wiped

her eyes on a frilly little lacy handkerchief, started the car, did a five point turn in the drive, only crunching the gears twice. Then she gave a little wave, slammed her foot down and ate up the space between us and the gates at an unseemly rate.

"You dog!" Guy said in admiration as she finally disappeared.

Jeremy lowered his hand and walked back over to us.

He put his arm round me.

"Phew! Hey, it worked, didn't it? Do you think I laid it on a bit too thick?"

Nigel chuckled. "No, she's always going to the films. It was just like the movies. I'd never have thought of that."

"But you didn't mean it?" Guy asked. "Because if you did, I'd have to call you out for betraying my sister's honour."

"Don't worry about my honour, Guy. I can handle that myself," I told him.

We were walking back to the party now, light-headed and light-hearted.

Whether it would be a permanent change only time would tell, but at this moment, we were sure it would.

"Why didn't you let her have the ring, Guy?" I asked.

"Principle of the thing. She threw it back, she obviously didn't want it. Dammit, I have feelings too. Besides, I haven't got it on me, and I wasn't going to invite her in while I fetched it."

"It might have saved you buying me a new jacket," said Jeremy.

"Cheap at twice the price, tell your tailor to send me his bill," said Guy grandly, slapping Jeremy on the back.

Then he chuckled. "You and my sister seem to be getting on very well these days. I don't suppose I could interest you in an engagement ring? Very good quality, only slightly used?"

Made in the USA
Charleston, SC
16 November 2012